# The Good,
# the Bad
# &
# the Secret Squirrel

ADRIENNE VERONESE

ISBN: 0-578-42966-7
ISBN-13: 978-0-578-42966-3

This book is dedicated to
Suspension of Disbelief,
Freddy,
and the number
143
❤

*"Why struggle to open a door between us when the whole wall is an illusion?"*

*– Rumi*

*"And we are put on earth,*

*a little space*

*that we may learn to bear the beams love."*

*- William Blake*

∞

# CHAPTER ONE

The day it started raining fat suits on Joy Street the Boston
Globe buried a story in the back of the Lifestyles section.
There was no mention of fat suits in it. The story was about
multiple sightings of UFOs in the night sky above Boston
Harbor. To date no articles have appeared in the Boston
Globe or elsewhere about it raining fat suits on Beacon Hill.
In fact, it is the very omission of fat suits from headline news
across the country that should have been seen as a red flag
all along.

Astra Talitha had no use for fat suits. She was
perfectly happy with the curves she'd managed to
grow organically. She had always secretly suspected
fat suits were an abandoned prototype for humanoid
Artificial Intelligence. Why else would they be made
of silicone? And much as was her policy about
discussing politics, she considered fat suits to be a
hot-button topic. A good grifter knows never to go
there. Nothing brings down a scam faster than

accusing someone of wearing a fat suit.

As far as she was concerned, the worst thing about fat suits is they can't easily be converted into cash. Hence Astra Talitha having no use for them. Or stolen poetry manuscripts, for that matter. She had no use for a thousand pounds of frozen vegan entrées or six dozen cases of incandescent light bulbs, either. And she had no idea whatsoever what she – or anyone – would do with thirty six cases of bamboo back scratchers. Or two cases of industrial safety glasses. In fact, she didn't even want to know. Nor did the prospect of living with a dozen microwave ovens appeal to her sense of curiosity. Or any of her other senses, for that matter.

As has already been established, her sense of pragmatism was deeply offended at the mere mention of fat suits. But what she had no use for more than any other useless thing was con artists who can't quite grasp what the art of the con is actually all about.

"Money, David!" she screamed as fat suits and a half case of back scratchers rained down on David Aeschlimann's bare head. "You can't get anything for the junk you've collected here; not even at a flea market! How many times have I told you the scams you run need to be worth actual *money*! And what kind of idiot cons a writer out of a manuscript of poetry? It's *poetry*. Know what poetry's worth, David? Nothing! It's just *WORDS*!"

If there were a school for con artists which taught how to run absolutely pointless scams, with little to no monetary gain coming from them, that would be the school David Aeschlimann graduated from. He was without question the worst matchstick man on the eastern seaboard.

Of any continent.

Known as the *Pointless Scammer*, he became legend when he conned a manuscript of poetry out of Gregory Corso when he was little more than a freshman; a newbie wet behind the ears. Nothing as worthless as poetry had been scored in a scam as far back as anyone could recall. It was that infamy which cemented David's love of the pointless scam.

It was the challenge he savored. The doing of it; that thing confidence artists do best. Convincing a person to believe a myth for the sole purpose of manipulating them into giving up control of their reality was the greatest satisfaction he knew in life. The net gain to David was not a thing that could be counted and entered into some Quick Books program stored in the cloud. But isn't that the way it is with some kinds of net gain? The satisfaction of the con was what sustained David. It wasn't a thing that could be measured or counted, because it lived in his heart and his imagination.

David was the one who put the *art* in con artist.

Through all of it Astra had faithfully supported his endeavors. She assured friends he had a master plan. She found ways to cope. For instance, offering unlimited savory vegan entrées to anyone with extra freezer space. Without question she was unwavering in her support of her lover's unorthodox methods. If there were a school for cheerleaders of *Pointless Scammers,* Astra would be their star pupil.

And she meant every cheer and wave of her pom-pom, too. David Aeschlimann was the most skilled, gifted closer of a deal she had ever known. The first time she saw him con the keys to a rusted old Pinto out of a parking valet, she knew she was in love.

The combination of awesome and stupid was one of those things Astra Talitha had never been able to resist. Since back when she was far too young to admit it publicly, that combo was a magnet to her libido. But it was the kind of combination she herself was never able to master. There are your frivolous con artists and there are your pragmatic con artists, and never the twain shall meet. Unless the twain is a beat up old Pinto and one just happens to be coming out of a high-end restaurant where one is running a scam involving the bar manager and a shipment of McAllister Reserve Scotch Whiskey. Then the twain meets. Most likely in the club car.

But once the shine wore off the newly minted relationship, the trouble started. Sure, David was the perfect combination of awesome and stupid. Mostly awesome, especially in the bedroom. Sex with David was never once a pointless scam for Astra. The man did not fail to close the deal. Ever. But over time the stupid began to outweigh the awesome. She found herself wondering what the point to love actually was. His pointless scams brought in nothing to help with the rent. Ever. And the useless contraband he was continuously bringing home from his scams was piling up. It had done so until it began to overflow out through the door of their cramped studio apartment and into the hallway. She wasn't sure whether to be relieved or annoyed that the people in apartment 2A were picking through it like it was a flea market for the spoils of pointless scams.

She endured it all cheerfully at first. Tried rationalizing microwave after microwave as it waltzed through the door. But the fat suits were the final straw.

David had been building up the suspense around his latest scam for weeks, enticing her with vague stories of the *unbelievably fat score* he was on to.

Astra would fall into the story David told each time. She envisioned that one big payout every grifter dreams of; the one that would let her retire to the desert and start a rattlesnake ranch. Maybe have a little one-pump gas station and roadside outlet for factory seconds of women's designer blue jeans. The kind with rhinestones on the back pockets. Because nothing says "Do these shiny bright objects on my back pockets make my ass look big," quite like shiny bright objects on the back pockets of a woman's jeans.

Astra was once again toying with the thought of calling it *Bitches 'n Britches* as she climbed the stairs to their second-floor apartment that evening. Toying with her dreams was her favorite thing to do at the end of a long day of grifting tourists down on the Common. As she nickel and dimed witless retirees for little more than chump change, she dreamed of one day not having to climb stairs at the end of a long, hot day.

"There aren't any stairs in the desert," she enjoyed telling herself. "Nothing but one story adobe haciendas with ceiling fans as far as the eye can see."

She thought about emptying the savings account she'd never bothered to tell David about and just grabbing a bus pointed south. But where would she land even if she did head south? Without startup capital, her business would forever be out of one dry-rot fleabag motel after another. The thought didn't appeal to her. It came uncomfortably close to being institutional.

She'd seen them get there, one by one. The women

who didn't manage to latch onto either another grifter or a man with enough money it didn't matter that he wasn't one. The trick was finding one with so much money it didn't matter that she was most likely going to fleece him out of it.

"Tricks are for kids," she would remind herself, scowling each time the thought occurred to her. Pairing up with a man solely for reasons of economic expedience had never suited Astra Talitha's temperament. It had always smacked of institutionalized prostitution to her. And anything that even remotely smacked of an institution of any kind made Astra extremely uncomfortable. Especially if it wore a pantsuit and ran for political office. There's prostitution and then there's prostitution.

She was the kind of woman who would sleep on a bare floor before asking anyone for help dragging an old mattress in from the dumpster in the alley. She would make cold-brewed coffee and only turn the refrigerator on for a few hours a day – just to save a few cents on electricity. She still had the same commuter coffee cup she'd had since running a *barista* scam back in the nineties on Dunkin' Donuts – despite the fact she'd never commuted anywhere. They were simply more practical.

"What if the apartment caught on fire when I was halfway through my cuppa?" she would say to David every time he teased her about it. "It would be a waste to just leave it behind. This way I can just grab it, run down to the corner and enjoy the rest of my coffee watching the firemen do their thing."

"Yay, firemen," she would say, waving an imaginary pom-pom in one hand while pantomiming sipping from her commuter cup.

It was that now-empty commuter cup that dangled from her blistered thumb as she inserted her key into the lock of apartment 2B. She tried not to think about the blisters. They were an occupational hazard. Pick-pockets often get them from lifting wallets. And Astra had spent the day lifting wallet after wallet off of tourists who didn't seem to understand the concept of cash. She stepped into the apartment wanting nothing more than to sink down into the pillow-soft swivel-rocker she and David had dragged in from the alley just the week before. Maybe she'd even put her feet up on the microwave they'd turned into an ottoman.

But both the swivel rocker and the microwave were occupied. As were both partly-broken kitchen chairs sitting at the re-purposed coffee table serving as both their kitchen counter and dining table. She scanned the studio apartment quickly and fell back onto one of the old wooden chairs. It promptly collapsed under the weight of both Astra and the fat suit sitting on it; the cracked wooden legs splintering beneath her with a barely audible shriek.

Somewhere in another dimension legs from wooden chairs throughout the galaxy have kept their ears sharply tuned for that shriek. It is the call to arms for cheaply produced Do It Yourself wooden furniture kits to rise up out of Ikea factories in China and revolt. The enslavement of cheap, chemically treated wood products had reached that inevitable breaking point and Astra Talitha was the only one to witness the historical moment. In this dimension, anyway.

She was to be forgiven for her lapse in paying attention to inter-dimensional history, however. Because from the linoleum floor of their studio apartment Astra could see nothing in all directions but fat, puffy, disturbingly human-looking legs dangling from every available surface. The *unbelievably fat score* David had been enticing her with for weeks appeared to be nothing more than the score of an incomprehensibly ample supply of fat suits. Although in David's defense, it's entirely possible he was saying *unbelievably phat score,* which according to the Urban Dictionary is something completely different.

What looked to her like a truckload of fat suits crowded the tiny dwelling like an ad for anarchist furniture that said, "Why go with the status quo when you can be the envy of all your friends and furnish your home with fat suits!"

David had told her the previous month he'd met a man who worked as a gaffer at a television studio up in New York. He said the guy had turned him onto a great job. Of course, being the pragmatist, Astra thought David was referring to scoring something of value, like expensive camera equipment, or maybe a truckload of studio lights they could take up to New Hampshire and sell to the indoor marijuana growers.

What David had stumbled onto, in fact, was a little-known secret hiding in plain sight of a news camera. Less so for local news stations, but definitely so for the cable networks, specifically Disinfaux News, women news anchors had been gripped with an epidemic of anorexia and her evil twin, bulimia. Doctors were puzzled at the alarming loss of weight among the women of our modern disinformation era.

As though their bodies were responding to the toxic nature of the radioactive data they chose to be a part of disseminating, each woman affiliated with the cable disinformation outlet had rapidly lost over thirty percent of her body weight in just a few short months.

When Astra saw the story in the back of the Boston Globe's Lifestyles section she pilfered from under the arm of some rube on her way to Chinatown for breakfast that morning, she imagined fat cells frantically trying to run from toxic molten data before finally melting into a useless puddle of what once promised to be a career with integrity and concern for the mental health of the viewing public.

"Breaking News: Disinfaux News Staff Allegedly Shrinking," the title read, reminding Astra of how annoying clickbait can be. Especially when it's in print. In the back of the Lifestyles section. Who puts breaking news in the back of the Lifestyles section?

Astra bit into a steaming hot sticky bun filled with pulled pork and a slightly sweet, thick brown gravy as she made her way back toward the Common, savoring every bite. She imagined the anorexic women of Disinfaux News spewing bits of truth in the form of pulled pork deliciousness over the cobblestones in a bulimic fit rather than risk swallowing anything resembling actual fact. Or even a tiny bit of truth.

"Worst. Role. Models. Ever." she thought bitterly as she steeled herself for another grueling day of picking pockets and grifting on the mean green lawns of Boston Common.

Little did she know when she finally read the entire article the solution Disinfaux News executives came up with for their Incredible Shrinking Newswoman problem was fat suits. Somewhere between being fat-shamed in high school for having dimples in her knees and now, having a big booty had become fashionably correct. We had entered the Era of the Fat Bottomed Girl, and it was about time.

Astra was almost ashamed of herself for being able to follow the *logic* applied to the situation by Disinfaux News executives. Providing their anchor women with fat suits made far more sense to their executive board than simply having them report facts without the nauseating ideological spin. Their advertisers relied on that nausea to sell lucrative goods like over-the-counter nausea medication and digitally enhanced vomit buckets for hipster women and their sexually fluid life partners.

Besides, why encourage their anchor women's appetites to return when they can serve a useful purpose by being on camera in a fat suit? What greater purpose in life could there possibly be for a woman than to role model for other American women how they too can have the perfect booty while swallowing toxic spew?

It also seems worth mentioning the manufacturers of women's designer blue jeans with rhinestones on the back pockets were ecstatically on-board with the Disinfaux News solution to their shrinking news staff problem. But in today's electronic era, the odds of the general public at large even knowing about a detail mentioned only in the back of the Lifestyles section was even more slim than the women of Disinfaux News.

Yanking a splinter out of her own booty, Astra said a quick thank-you to fashion correctness for providing her with enough padding that the splinter was the only damage sustained when the legs of the chair gave out. Assessing what she could of the situation, she knew the time had come to do what she'd been suspecting for months would end up needing to be done: pack her things and go.

It was much harder than it sounded in theory. Largely because her suitcase was buried under several microwaves teetering on a box of bamboo back scratchers. The effort of retrieving her suitcase burned so many calories she thought she'd take a short break and microwave a frozen vegan entrée. Mistakes as simple as underestimating how many calories any given task will burn are the kind of thing that can lead to institutionalized prostitution. Ask any pragmatist. It's a slippery slope. She shuddered for the second time that day.

As luck would have it, neither Astra nor David were the kind of con artist who made it a habit to defrost refrigerators. Enough frost had built up that two vegan entrées had grown into Siamese twins permanently joined at the ingredients list. They then conspired to get hopelessly frozen to the floor of the old refrigerator's freezer section. Which wouldn't have been so bad, since those ingredients lists contained just as many fourteen-letter words for potentially lethal things as the instant pudding and boxed cake-mix her foster moms used to make. But Astra was hungry and in no mood to go on a trip down memory lane. Not even with Betty Crocker and the Pillsbury Dough Boy.

Unsticking them from the freezer was burning more calories than relocating six microwaves and a case of bamboo back scratchers had. Astra had gone way past her threshold for calorie depletion and completely lost sight of her comfort zone. And it was testing her patience. As anyone can appreciate, she understandably took it out on the frozen vegan entrées.

Placing her foot against the refrigerator door for

leverage, Astra wrapped both hands around either side of the frost-covered frozen food boxes. She gave a loud grunt as she pushed with her foot and pulled back with all she had in her at the same time. And despite burning too many calories, Astra Talitha had far more in her than meets the eye. Unless we're talking about the eye of the galaxy, in which case it sees everything and knows exactly what she had in her all along.

As both boxes abruptly tore loose from their frozen tomb, leaving half of the bottom box torn off and stuck to the frosty mess, Astra was suddenly the recipient of an unexpected free flying lesson. Backwards. Unfortunately, instructions on landing were not included in the lesson, and for the second time that day Astra landed on her perfectly padded booty. Wincing where the splinter had dug in earlier, she lay back on the floor, the frozen entrées still in her outstretched hands.

She wanted to laugh. She wanted to cry. She wanted to feel something more than the urge to run. To go to that elusive *somewhere* that had been whispering to her all her life. To finally wake to that quietly persistent voice that had always called to her to wake up to *something*. Yes, she'd always heard it. But what it was and where she would find it still eluded her. So did the contents of the two envelopes stuck to the bottom of the half-torn box she was twirling overhead like a forlorn baton girl in a time-out.

As luck would have it, Astra's appetite made a brief reappearance and she focused on the boxes. And then the envelopes. Sitting up, she gently separated both of them to prevent any more damage to the already torn envelope that had been frozen right along with the box to the floor of the freezer. In it she found the title to the Pinto. Until that moment, she'd had no idea David had somehow managed to establish legal ownership of the car that would forever remind her of the day they met.

Rather than a wave of romantic nostalgia sweeping over her however, Astra was infuriated.

"What. The. Fuck. David." was all she could say. She wanted to say something about him actually having the capacity for pragmatism. She wanted to say something about his ability to follow through on a plan that quite possibly had a point to it. She wanted to put a positive spin on it like she'd been doing with every pointless thing he'd done that wasn't in the bedroom. But she couldn't. All she could think about was how he'd been holding out on her; the worst thing a grifter could do to his partner.

Therefore, "What. The. Fuck. David." was all she could say.

Astra gently slipped the other envelope away from the gooey mess in her hands. Made up of dirty melted frost mixed with the petroleum-based paraffin wax that coated the box, the unappetizing slime dripping down her wrists eliminated any appetite she mistakenly thought she'd had. Depleted calories came back sheepishly admitting they never should have left. In fact, she toyed briefly with the thought of mailing her appetite to one of the anchor women at Disinfaux News, since Astra wasn't using it. But she was short on time. Besides, those girls were old enough to clean up their own mess.

"Consequences, ladies," she said aloud, as she took a deep breath and opened the envelope.

Astra had already decided the contents would

determine whether she left a note for David or simply left without a word. If his plan had been to surprise her on some romantic night up on the roof stargazing through the fog rolling in off the harbor, he was even worse at planning than she had thought. Nothing about the title to a beat up old Pinto was even remotely romantic. Not even the one where their twain had met.

Astra's heart began to pound as she slipped its contents out of the envelope and unfolded the official looking document. The envelope dropped to the floor when she realized what she was looking at. It was the deed to a small storefront in Sedona, Arizona. With a note in handwriting she didn't recognize that said to get the key from a woman named *Samara* at the crystal ball and artisan-crafted tarot card shop next door.

Astra Talitha was the kind of woman you didn't have to explain things to twice. She already knew where she was going and what the name of her new neighbor was. That was all she needed to motivate her to get up off the floor and start packing.

"Next stop, Sedona, Arizona," she said as she jumped to her feet and did just that.

Astra had always believed it was pointless to own any more than she could fit in a single suitcase. As she shoved both envelopes into an inner pocket before zipping hers shut, she made an exception to that rule. Something told her one of the microwaves and a fat suit would come in handy.

It was a perplexing trait Astra had never understood in herself. As pragmatic as she was, she'd been plagued her entire life by random compulsions to do things that – on the surface at least – were less than practical. And curiously, she had neither pursued an understanding of why, nor had she ever explored the reason she avoided pursuing it. She just kept telling herself it happened so infrequently she could put some thought into it when she had some time on her hands. Until then, she would apply her favorite philosophy to it.

"It is what it is."

Oddly, even though it was one of her favorite philosophical quotes, she never did know where it came from. This curious lack of curiosity was also one of those things that should have been seen as a red flag right from the start. She was far too accepting of just about everything and everyone. It was often said by teachers and social workers as she was growing up that Astra Talitha's ambiance was her own undoing. Her willingness to not just accept, but fit into any culture was deeply troubling to authority figures. And while it was understandable to Astra, she had little patience with their failure to understand what was at the heart of it.

Here's the thing any child raised in foster care learns at a young age: culture is a Russian nesting doll. You have the collective culture of any given nation, which in Astra's case is red, white and blue apple pie served ala mode after enduring garish parades with beauty queens riding on the back of convertibles with the mayor. Inside that is nestled the culture of the dominant religion, which again for Astra, is dressed in a red, white and blue Santa Claus suit, but busy molesting a small child instead of leering at the bustline of a beauty queen.

Inside that you have the neighborhood culture, which

varies depending on which nation that neighborhood happened to bring with it in its suitcase when it settled there. And of course, nestled inside that are the economic institutions members of that neighborhood are serviced by, and inside that doll of course is the school their kids go to. It goes without saying each of those institutions has its own culture.

Last but not least is the culture of the family, serving as the foundation for the individual's identity. And when a foster child's identity is influenced by a variety of different families, thus a variety of different cultural foundations, it doesn't matter how well the dolls nest inside each other, she sees it all for what it is: relative. There are no sacred cows. How can there be, when cows mean something entirely different from person to person, family to family, school to school, neighborhood to neighborhood, religion to religion, and nation to nation?

More than anything, Astra reached adulthood fully aware that a lifestyle is not the same thing as a life raft. Clinging to a lifestyle does no good whatsoever if it's sinking a person into the abyss. Which explains why Astra Talitha clung to very few things one would ordinarily associate with a lifestyle. One of those things was occasionally letting herself do something she felt compelled to do without giving in to the need to figure out why.

And without question traveling to Sedona from Boston in a beat-up old Pinto with a microwave oven and a fat suit definitely fell into the category of those things she felt randomly compelled to do. With or without the red flags. Or the nesting dolls they fit neatly inside of. Of course, those authority figures from her childhood would consider it nothing more than Astra embracing yet another ambiance; a fat suit ambiance.

It took several trips down to the stoop to get the suitcase, microwave and fat suit to the curb, by which time the cab she'd called was pulling up. She knew exactly where she would find the Pinto, and it was too far to walk with any one of the three items. The driver had just finished loading the sum total of her worldly belongings into the trunk of his cab when two things happened at once. First, she realized she hadn't grabbed the keys to the Pinto, which had been hanging on a nail in the kitchen since she moved in. She'd always just assumed it was a novelty item for romantic effect.

The second thing happened when Astra caught sight of David turning the corner of Cambridge Street and strolling up Joy Street straight toward her with a pointlessly contented smile on his face. The explosive anger that Astra had finally managed to reduce to a simmer once again boiled over and she began shouting as she leaped two steps at a time up the stairs.

While reason and logic would tell her that grabbing the keys and leaving was the best course of action, there was a shortage of logic in the world at that time, resulting from the efforts of Disinfaux News executives and their anorexic tools. And explosive anger tends to do such unpleasant things to reason that the two now refuse to be in the same room together without an intermediary. Let's just hope they don't ask for an intermediary from the Disinfaux News executive board.

So Astra did the only thing she could think to do in the situation. She began throwing fat suits and bamboo back scratchers out the window. She thought briefly of throwing down some of the lightbulbs too, but worried that the glass would smash and make the sidewalk below unsafe for dogs and their walkers.

While she grabbed another case of back scratchers, the nice Jewish boy down below who graduated with honors from the *Pointless Scammer Academy* did the *Duck and Cover* as he scrambled to retrieve both his glasses and his red yarmulke, which had been knocked off by a flying fat suit.

"*Unbelievably fat scam*, David?? That's what a truckload of fat suits is to you? Or is that your idea of comedy?" she shouted. "The only thing that's unbelievable is your excuse for never paying your share of the rent! You had me move into your place just so you'd have someone to pay it for you, didn't you, David? Well it's time to find a new benefactor, because your meal ticket is out of here!"

Before he could turn his tear-streaked face up to the window and explain, the cab door slammed behind Astra after she seemingly flew down the stairs and into the back seat in one leap. As it pulled out with a squeal, its rear tires kicking dust in his face, he was pretty sure he heard Astra tell the driver where to take her.

"You know where Cantor Colbert's place is, over by Temple Beth Israel?"

David Aeschlimann smiled. He'd been pointlessly scamming the cantor for months. And the only thing he was getting out of it was free parking for a beat up old Pinto.

"This means she found what was in the freezer," he said, leaning against a Toc-h lamp padded with a fat suit. His smile turned into a grin. "This is going better than planned."

Out of the corner of his eye, David could have sworn he saw a UFO in the night sky above him, possibly heading in the direction of Boston Harbor. It was the kind of thing that he never read about in the Boston Globe, and he wondered why.

It would be quite some time before he came to understand that the point of buying a newspaper is to read it. Unless of course you plan to pack your belongings and need padding for the breakables. Which David had known he would be needing at the time he bought it.

Fat suits do, after all, have their limitations.

# CHAPTER TWO

There is nothing quite like waking to an angry seagull trying to eat your face. Especially when the only thing between your face and that seagull is a thin sheet of windshield glass. If that windshield was designed as poorly as the placement of the Pinto's gas tank, Astra Talitha was as good as cooked. Figuratively. Much like the seagulls employed by Alfred Hitchcock, Boston Harbor seagulls have a preference for the raw food diet.

To meet Paleo seagulls however, you'll need to go to Southern California. Or open an account on Instagram. If you're a lady seagull, you don't even need to bother posting a photograph of yourself. The male seagulls will begin flooding your in-box immediately, telling you how much they love your smile. Because male seagulls are apparently psychic and don't need a photograph to know your smile makes you the perfect lady seagull for them. The more eloquent ones will go on to say they knew the moment they saw your profile existed you are the seagull for them.

Somewhere in another dimension, vegan lady seagulls are delighted over having found an abandoned chest freezer full of perfectly thawed once-frozen vegan entrées in an alley off Boylston. And they have no intention of posting about it on Instagram. But they are considering opening an account on Instagram in the chest freezer's name. Once they've satisfied their appetites, they intend to amuse themselves placing bets over how many male seagulls will send messages of undying love to the chest freezer's in-box. Little do they know that merely using the word *chest* publicly is all it takes to whip male seagulls into a feeding frenzy.

Between the stern scolding she got from Cantor Colbert for interrupting his brisket and the effort it took to fit a microwave, suitcase and fat suit into the Pinto, Astra was exhausted. She was also in danger of shedding precious booty points by the time she found a dark corner in a quiet parking lot near the harbor to safely lay low for the night.

Until her bank opened in the morning, there was no point filling the gas tank with the chump change she scored at the Common so she could hit the road. The first two toll booths on the turnpike would leave her flat broke in an old Pinto with little more than her suitcase, a microwave and fat suit for traveling companions. Astra was pretty sure none of them could be trusted to throw down for much of anything on this trip. She and her endless appetite were on their own for the time being.

And as tempting as it was to run to Chinatown for a couple of delectable pork filled sticky buns, she thought better of it. It was the first place David would look for her.

More than once, she kicked herself for not actually eating one of those frozen vegan Siamese twins.

If she were being honest, she would have kicked herself for avoiding thinking about David's tear-streaked face looking up at her from below the apartment window. Kicking herself over not eating a frozen simile was a perfectly effective distraction, but let's not kid ourselves. Being honest with herself was not a thing Astra Talitha was accustomed to. She was, after all, a product of American television programming, which emphasizes looking no deeper than the surface of any given thing.

Which Astra was pretty sure explained the existence of Instagram.

Upon looking at the surface of things within the Pinto, she had found it possible to nod off in the back seat curled up with a fat suit. She drifted off thinking about how comfortable they were, and imagined opening a business in Arizona marketing fat suits for newly divorced singles as an alternative to robotic sex dolls. After all, there's a lot to be said for the satisfaction one can get from a good snuggle, especially when it comes with ample pillowy-softness to sink oneself into.

That in turn led to thinking about marketing the services of former cable news anchor women in fat suits. They'd make great surrogate snugglers for the chronically emotionally needy. Provided, of course, they signed an agreement not say anything toxic to her clients about whatever topic was riding the *Polarization Express* that week. Her customer base could be all the male seagulls on Instagram. The thought made her smile and she felt herself slipping into a comfy dream-like state where not only did fat suits make her a well-known entrepreneur of the tech industry, but it was also possible to sleep comfortably with one in the back seat of a Pinto.

Unfortunately, she had burned the last few calories she had in reserve when she was moving the suitcase to the driver's seat and arguing with the microwave about whose turn it was to ride shotgun. Staying asleep was turning out to be the real obstacle to getting through the night. The hunger pangs were refusing to occupy their minds by thinking about something else.

Astra lay there trying to calculate the calories she would burn by relocating her suitcase to the back seat so she could drive to an all-night snack shop. That, of course, led her to the invariable debate with herself over whether she wanted one or the other of two kinds of saturated fats: heavily salted, or heavily sugar-sweetened. This then led her to the usual debate with herself over why all-night snack shops only offer two kinds of snacks, and exactly why both of them are made with saturated fats.

She was toying with the possibility that some study had determined people who frequent all-night snack shops are more suicidal than others. Was feeding them a steady diet of saturated fats dipped in salt and/or sugar a way of exhibiting compassion toward our fellow man? Was it a stealthy way of sneaking *right to die* laws in right under our noses? Or was it more like the equivalent of a man holding the door open for a woman; a way of saying, "Hey, let me help you get where you want to go because you lady seagulls aren't strong enough to open the door to saturated fats by yourself"?

Astra realized too late that thinking about suicide by

saturated fats was not an effective tool for distracting oneself from an excess of calorie depletion. She peered at her digital watch to see how long she had before the bank opened. The numbers seemed to be flashing some kind of code at her, and she wondered why. If she could only keep her eyes open long enough to figure it out. Perhaps then she would have a solution to the death by saturated fat epidemic. Was it related to the epidemic of anorexia among cable news anchor women?

"Why are they blinking like that when all I want is to know what time it is?" she thought, struggling with the urge to go back to sleep. "And why the hell can't I figure this out?"

It was then that Astra discovered there is nothing quite like waking to an angry seagull trying to eat your face. And for the first time in her life she was grateful for having little more than a thin sheet of Pinto windshield glass in her life to protect her from Hannibal Lecter's feathered alter-ego.

Sitting up and stretching as best she could, Astra had to be honest with herself; it really wasn't her best. She just liked telling herself that. It *was* her most awkward, however. It could, in fact, have easily won a place in the *Guinness Book of Awkward World Records.* Untangling her legs from the fat suit's legs, and the most padded parts of her luscious booty from where it had melded with the fat suit's silicone before shoving itself in the crack between the seat and the back rest was the most world record-winning awkwardness she had yet to perform. And now her butt-cheeks were numb. Both of them. All three, if you counted at least one of the fat suit's butt cheeks.

The morning air on Boston Harbor was one of the

things she knew she would miss in the desert. A mixture of mostly-dried fish guts, low tide, and diesel fuel combined to mingle with her sense of place and time and send a resounding message of *home* to her frontal lobe, care of her olfactory nerve. If the frontal lobe were a division of the post office, the oldest and longest letters would be sent there for general delivery. The olfactory nerve would be the postman delivering those letters, reminding you of things you thought you'd forgotten long ago.

The odors of harbor past and present conspired to anchor her right there to the dock she stood on watching the seagulls fight over an empty frozen vegan entrée box. She didn't notice that her favorite odor from the harbor was missing for several minutes, largely due to the seagulls and their war over the latest food fad to dominate the market.

It wasn't until she glanced down at her watch and saw that the morning was half gone that she realized something was missing. The early morning fog had already left, having blown back out to sea when the late morning breezes started up from the west. Her morning beauty ritual of washing her face with the sea salt-laced fog was something she'd done for years. It was the best exfoliant she'd ever used.

She would have stood there toying with the idea of somehow marketing Boston Harbor Fog as a beauty aid for women in the desert, but the bank was already open. The road was calling, and she was letting it go to voicemail because of the missing fog and some unbreakable code her wristwatch had been sending her the night before. Astra truly had no idea how she'd managed to sleep as late as she did.

She was on to her third pulled-pork sticky bun from Chinatown by the time she reached Martha's Vineyard, and didn't care whether they had saturated fats and sugar in them or not. But downing three of them in ninety minutes had brought on an urgent need for a restroom, and therein lay the first obstacle Astra Talitha had to overcome on her road trip. As she would discover, the nationwide problem of homelessness had resulted in business owners locking their restrooms, requiring something be bought and paid for before honoring anyone with a key.

Because emptying one's bladder and bowels is a privilege, not a right. And apparently, homeless people lose that privilege when they become radicalized by unscrupulous mortgage lenders and their morally bankrupt fuck-buddies, the hedge fund-managers. Besides, why bother providing for the safe disposal of the biohazard that is human waste when you can just as easily get the sheriff to run the homeless out of town? The next town can do the same until all the homeless are run off the end of the Santa Monica Pier. They can shit in the Pacific Ocean all they want. Nobody seems to care what kind of shit gets in that ocean.

Unfortunately, all one need do to see how well the *run 'em out of town* strategy actually works is to look at *San Diego County* and its *Hepatitis A* epidemic. A lethally smelly reminder that you can sweep a mess under the rug, but everything ends up in the Pacific Garbage Patch eventually. That's how it works.

"This is the American Dream," Astra smiled through clenched teeth as the clerk counted out her change before handing her the restroom key-on-a-stick.

"Is it?" He replied. "Or is it someone else's dream

imposing itself on yours?"

Astra was accustomed to the youth of Martha's Vineyard being both uncommonly well-read and well-spoken, but had assumed none of them would be working at the Shell station on Beach Road. Weren't they usually working volunteer jobs or giving swimming lessons to kids at the community pool?

Had she not been so quick to dismiss the significance of the well-spoken African American's cryptic remark, she might have noticed what he was watching on his cell phone. But she turned away in such a rush to get to the restroom she didn't even notice the early stages of a red flag unfurling in preparation for planting itself right there in that time and place.

She dropped the hot dog-on-a-stick in the trash on her way around the building, resenting the waste of precious resources to the childish whims of corporate policy makers who refuse to simply grow up and become part of the solution instead of being the actual problem.

Astra lowered herself gingerly onto the restroom toilet seat, not sure the circulation had fully returned to her butt cheeks. She was intent on continuing to think about the decidedly American trait of sending its problems to other people to deal with, but the graffiti on the stall door put an end to that stinky plan.

The words, *Celebrate the Random,* stared at her intrusively. They had been written in perfect block lettering which could easily have been stenciled. Beneath it was a somewhat cartoonish rendering of a UFO, with an equally cartoonish rendering of the classic *Man from Mars,* complete with antennas and enormous black eyes. He was waving a cartoonish three-fingered hand from the window of the UFO, his little pencil-thin mouth upturned at the corners. Below all that, seemingly framing it from top to bottom, were the words, **Be Worthy of it,** again in perfect block lettering.

It took her breath away. Something about it struck a chord in her so deep she could feel it vibrating all the way down to her fully awakened butt cheeks. If that chord had been played by a garage band doing nothing but covers of classic rock, it would have been played in the key of déjà vu. She momentarily wondered if the vibrations might eliminate the need for toilet paper. That would have been preferable to the thin sheets of sand paper she was yanking out of the dispenser.

"Too cheap to accommodate the bio-waste of unfortunate people, and too cheap to provide decent toilet paper to the paying customers," she said bitterly as she flushed away America's problems and wondered who the Shell Oil Company was getting to pay for the water. Perhaps they were subsidized by Nestle and getting Americans whose water tables were poisoned by the chemicals used in fracking to pay for it when they buy bottled water to bathe their children with.

"This pretty much defines our corporate-owned democracy," she said to the clerk as she returned the key-on-a-stick. Expecting him to merely shrug without looking up from his smart phone, it surprised her when he instead held it up for her to see what he was watching. It was a clip from the animated television series, The Simpsons.

The episode featured a running gag where the graffiti artist known as *Banksy* takes over the fictional town of

Springfield in the opening sequence. In the perfunctory descending establishing shot, a character vandalizes a billboard with the name *Banksy*. Next Astra chuckled at Bart Simpson writing on the blackboard that he must not write all over the walls. The clip quickly moves to a scene where forced labor is coloring in each cell of the film she herself was watching, toiling thanklessly in a sweat-shop for outsourced animation while rats pick at the bones of those who've been worked to death and then cast aside.

Meanwhile, other wage-slaves roll out the kind of *Simpson's* swag she'd seen in gift shops at upscale shopping malls when running *data scams* on cell phone kiosks, which of course were running *data scams* on the clueless. All while others drop live kittens into wood-chippers to make fiber-fill for Bart Simpson dolls. Next she watched a depressed panda being used as a beast of burden to pull overfilled carts of the Bart dolls away to be boxed for shipping. Boxes which are then sealed with the tongue of a decapitated dolphin head on a stick.

Astra thought of the hot-dog-on-a-stick she'd bought for the privilege of using the restroom and shuddered. And of course, the final scene broke the fourth wall as compact discs of the very clip she was watching were being inserted into cases for shipping after their center spindle hole was punched out by a man using a unicorn in chains. The unicorn then collapses just before the Twentieth Century Fox logo flashes on the screen.

For a brief moment Astra was distracted by the thought that *Unicorn in Chains* would be a great name for an emo bagpipe band from the United Kingdom. She looked into the young man's eyes once more and was about ask him what he thought of emo bagpipe music when he interrupted the thought.

"What if there are visionaries who saw all of this coming?" he said cryptically. "What if they resorted to the mad genius of graffiti art because Hansel and Gretel got too greedy to share their breadcrumbs?"

She wanted to ask him if he was the one who put that message about the random on the door of the restroom stall. And if so, what did it mean? Better yet, how does celebrating anything as mundane as the random make a person worthy? For that matter, what does it make a person worthy *of*? But all she could think to do was.... nothing. Nothing at all. Astra Talitha just stood there for the longest moment in recorded history looking into the deepest, darkest yet most brilliantly illuminated eyes she had ever seen, wanting to ask the young stranger what his name was.

And yet, despite herself, she pulled out of the tractor beam that was his gaze and turned to leave. For some reason, David's words came to her. As she pushed the door open to leave, she turned back briefly.

"Anyone who believes in coincidence just isn't paying attention," she said, with absolutely no idea why she'd said it. Perhaps all the times David had quoted the line managed to stencil themselves onto her long-term memory in the file marked *Things to Say When at a Loss for Words in Response to Cryptic Comments Made by Uncommon Gas Station Attendants*.

It was Astra's plan to avoid as much of the south as possible, sticking to the Midwest as much as she could. She had nothing against the south, per se, but a woman traveling alone with nothing but a fat suit and microwave oven to keep her safe couldn't be too careful. She'd heard that boys in the south are raised to believe if they see a female anywhere in public alone, she's up for grabs. Much like the way male seagulls are raised on Instagram. She'd also heard the Midwest could be just as bad, but had read in the Boston Globe that they're all on drugs in the Midwest. Astra had never failed to outrun a drug addict, even on cobblestones wearing heels.

Astra Talitha's booty may have been well padded, but beneath the padding were muscles she'd spent her adult life building by climbing up and down the streets of Beacon Hill. Often times, it was running. In heels. Somewhere in the basement of Boston's Church of the Emmanuel, a group of recovering drug addicts is meeting to discuss their heartbreak over not being able to catch up with the most perfect booty they'd ever seen.

None of them were aware that the booty of their dreams was actually attached to a human being, who would be busy climbing the foothills outside Charleston, West Virginia later that night if any of them were up for the chase. She'd chosen Charleston for several reasons. One, it was twelve hours into her trip, and driving any more than twelve hours a day was outside the scope of her job description. Con artists have a strict limit to the number of hours a day they'll spend behind the wheel of a car. Driving isn't the issue. The issue is the waste of time that could be spent reaching for some tourist's wallet or trying to con some medical marijuana patient from Oregon in a lighting scam.

Heading west from Charleston was also convenient to her plan of continuing in that direction across Kentucky. But more than anything else, the reason she chose Charleston was the report she heard on the radio. Locals had been calling in with stories about seeing a UFO buzzing the water tower just outside the city limits. It had started the night before and gone on all day. The last report she heard before the radio lost reception in the foothills was the UFO had disappeared above those same hills.

All her life Astra Talitha had wanted to be one of those people who had *that story* to tell; the one where they were witness to something from another world and now felt compelled to tell anyone who would listen that *we are not alone*. She felt certain it would add authenticity to the repertoire of fabricated tales she planned to tell her marks as she gained their trust in the new scam she was cooking up. As luck would have it, there was a rest stop just half a mile from where the report said the mysterious flying craft disappeared.

And so it was that she found herself climbing through the underbrush on a gently sloping hill just behind the westbound rest area outside of Charleston. She kept telling herself it was her finely tuned instincts that led her in that direction, but the truth is that was what they always did in the movies. There's always one point where the character climbs up onto a ridge and stands there like a deer in headlights while ET and his buddies lock him into their tractor beam and bring him up to their ship. And then comes the anal probing.

"Why is it always the anal probing? Why not manicures, or a nice Brazilian wax?" she wondered, slightly breathless as she reached a clearing on the ridge. "How many anal probes do they need to do before they find what they're looking for?"

Looking around, Astra realized she'd let her attention

wander and done exactly what she'd spent her life shouting at movie characters on screens across Boston to never do: She climbed to the clearing on the ridge despite warnings there were UFOs up there. The one place any alien worth his weight in anal probes would think to find an anal-probe buddy for the night. Proof that we rarely listen to our own good advice.

Or perhaps it's merely proof of their secret love of anal probing that Earthlings have kept hidden from everyone else except the aliens. Somewhere in another dimension an alien is checking his Instagram in-box for any messages from Earthlings desperately in need of a good anal probing. If there are no messages, he might as well message a lady seagull or two about their dazzling smile. Just for good measure. And to keep those male seagulls on their toes.

On the other hand, health insurers would save a bundle if they just excluded coverage for routine colonoscopies and left it up to the Department of Intergalactic Anal Probing apparently living in Near-Earth orbit. Maybe Elon Musk could deliver the results for them in that Tesla he keeps up there.

As UFO hunts go, it was an anticlimactic expedition. By the time she finished the last of the pulled-pork sticky buns, Astra was so sleepy she could hardly keep her eyes open. She had wanted to give some thought to her plans for when she reached Sedona, but the harder she struggled to keep her eyes open the harder it was to do.

She'd made sure to pack the tarot cards and colorful turbans she'd employed when running a *psychic reader* scam out of a massage parlor in the Combat Zone. From what she'd heard about Sedona, picking up where she left off with that scam seemed like it would be the best way to go with the storefront she'd recently come into. But the idea didn't really congeal before she was fast asleep, without a care in the world about the risks of possible UFOs and anal probing. Or a care in any other world, for that matter.

It really should come as no surprise Astra's card had always been the Seven of Hearts; the card that tests a person's ability to have faith in themselves throughout their lives, and in a benign Universe as well. Or in Astra's case, her ability to hide it up her sleeve in a poker game. And fall asleep on a ridgetop looking for UFOs with the faith she won't be anally probed.

Astra woke in exactly the same spot mid-morning ravenously hungry and deeply disoriented. Not only did she feel as though she hadn't eaten in days, her dreams had been exhausting. At least, that's what she was telling herself as she climbed back down the hill that had led her up to the ridge the night before. Yet try as she might she couldn't quite grasp and hold on to any of the dream images that randomly flashed brief puzzling glimpses to her visual memory. It was much like the blinking digital numbers of her watch with its code the night before in the Pinto.

Those vague images disappeared instantly when she reached the rest area parking lot to find a state trooper standing by the Pinto guiding a tow truck backing up to it.

"Hey, I'm right here!" she shouted as she picked up her speed and trotted over to the trooper.

"What's going on, officer?"

Yes, she knew overnight camping was not allowed. And yes, she was aware of the penalty for it. But she hadn't planned on camping! All she wanted to do was climb to the ridge and catch a glimpse of the UFO she heard about on the radio!

"I truly, truly did not mean to fall asleep up there," she said, twirling a lock of hair with pine needles adorably woven in. Astra was not above occasionally relying on the coyly attractive affectation to win an argument with men in authority.

"That was two nights ago, ma'am," the trooper said dryly as he tore the ticket out of his book. "You're lucky yesterday was a Saturday and the truck driver had the day off, or you would have found nothing but an empty spot when you came back from your adventure up there on the ridge. Hope it was worth it."

Officer Friendly McTicketsalot started turning to leave, but Astra's sigh only made it as far as the back of her throat before he stopped and the half-spent sigh froze in place behind her tonsils.

"You should know if you left all your gear up there because it got soaked in that rainstorm last night, we are the ones who will have to haul it down and dispose of it. And you'll be getting a summons to appear in court, Miss Talitha. We don't look too kindly on that kind of thing in these parts." He pulled the ticket he'd been writing throughout the delightful discourse from its booklet. Without smiling, he handed it to Astra as he welcomed her to West Virginia. A half-spent sigh made a suicide pact with Astra's tonsils as he turned and left. His last words were tossed over his shoulder at her as he walked away. If it had been spilled table salt she could have gargled with it to sooth her scorched tonsils.

"You have ten minutes to vacate this rest area and

move on."

Astra sat in stunned silence behind the wheel of the Pinto as she turned the ticket over and over in her hand. How could it be Sunday? She left Boston the day before. Friday. She was sure of it. The date on the ticket had to be wrong. There was no way she could have been up there on the ridge for two nights!

But the driver's seat was wet. She could see where the seal around the windshield had leaked during the storm. So why were her clothes dry? Her shoes? Hair? How could she have been asleep for two nights and an entire day??! She reached for her cell phone in the glove box and double-checked the date. It was Sunday. Under the cell phone was the withdrawal slip from the bank. It said she'd been there Friday, which she already knew. If she'd been there Saturday it would have been closed! If Astra Talitha thought she'd been disoriented when she woke up on the ridge, she had no idea what being disoriented actually felt like.

"What. The. Fuck. Is. Going. On???!!!" she said as she put the Pinto in reverse and backed out of the parking space. The spot directly beneath where the car had been wasn't completely dry, but it was far drier than the rest of the parking lot. As though there had been a rainstorm and only a little runoff collected under the Pinto while it was parked there. For two nights and a day. At least one of which she had no memory whatsoever. Except for vague images from a dream that kept teasing at the corners of her mind, taunting her to come find out what she was missing.

Abruptly, she backed into a parking stall and turned off the engine. Before getting back on the road there was one thing she thought she should do. Astra Talitha walked into the ladies restroom and locked the stall door before pulling down her jeans and gingerly checking to see if there'd been any anal probe activity going on back there recently. Regrettably, she failed to first check to see if there was any soap and running water in the restroom. This was, after all, West Virginia.

At first she thought that was the reason she was seeing so many people on drugs there. But the longer Astra was on the road and eating at rest stops and family diners, the more she realized it wasn't a phenomenon restricted to that one state. She saw it passing through a sliver of Ohio, in Kentucky and even in Missouri, too. All three commonly known as bastions of decency and temperance. Yet at every single meal stop she made, the one common thread that stretched from person to person and state to state was the pill bottles they all lined up in front of their dinner plates so they wouldn't forget to drop their hit of OxyContin. Or Xanax. Or Klonopin. Or Lexapro. Or Wellbutrin. Or Paxil. Or Statins. Or Adderall. Or maybe some Cipro or Levaquin.

And let's not forget Ambien for those lying awake worrying about how they're going to afford refills without any medical insurance. And of course there was Fosamax, which never did make any sense to Astra. It is so well known for *causing* spontaneous bone fractures, she could only assume the reason it was prescribed to people with osteoporosis was to increase profits to stockholders of extended care nursing facilities. And of course, America's infamous for-profit health insurance industry.

Astra thought it might be a great idea to weave into her fictitious storyline a tale about being descended from the psychic medium who advised Edgar Kaiser to persuade

Richard Nixon to get rid of the law forbidding medicine-for-profit in America. Signing the Health Maintenance Act of 1973 into law was a stroke of pure genius, and was sure to impress bored and lonely widows with large estates. For all the others, she could put an emphasis on the perils of being distracted by scandals like Watergate, thus dropping the ball on things that might result in a slow-motion genocide.

But then again, even today nobody seemed to be paying attention to the destructiveness of the Quinolones, including Cipro and Levaquin. The FDA had made it abundantly clear it was not to be prescribed under any circumstance except exposure to Anthrax, or in cases of Methicillin resistant pneumonia. But did that stop doctors from prescribing it for anything from a mild ear infection to an angry hangnail? Why should it? After all, the Quinolones are proven to permanently alter mitochondrial DNA, rendering the patient incapable of fully healing from any kind of tissue damage. That kind of side-effect can make for lucrative repeat visits to their office at least every six weeks. Permanently.

Guaranteed repeat business like that can be handy when it comes to planning things like the timing for yacht payments, ski trips, and cruises to the Caribbean. Or in the case of rural doctors, simply making the mortgage payment and staff payroll. And patients left in anxiety over the agonizing pain they must endure the rest of their lives will need plenty of OxyContin and Klonopin, not to mention refills of Ambien. Astra was fairly certain rural doctors would survive *America's Opium War 2.0*, but couldn't say the same for the patients she was seeing staggering to their cars in the parking lots of diners across Middle America.

Of course, the disconnect between parents and teachers telling children not to do drugs while themselves taking all those pills and drinking coffee with their banana cream pie and beer on the side did not escape Astra. It was obvious after tasting a single sip of roadside coffee that speed really does kill. And any pragmatic grifter knows by the time they can walk the simple fact that alcohol and sugar are both drugs. If a con is going to stay on-course, the con artist needs to keep a clear head. And the less clear the heads of Americans got, the easier it got for grifters from Boston to La Grande, Oregon to close a deal. Not to mention the ones in the nation's capital.

Which is why it did not surprise Astra when she turned on the radio shortly before crossing into Kansas to hear Weezer singing a familiar tune, one in which they make the astute observation that we truly *are* all on drugs. For the next hundred miles, Astra mused on how *Slow Motion Genocide* would be a great name for a geriatric death metal band that only does covers of songs about utilitarian bioethics.

# CHAPTER THREE

Freddy Mercury was emphatically insisting Astra
Talitha keep herself alive and she didn't know why.
She hadn't set the radio alarm clock by the bed in her
motel room for a reason. Nothing irritated her more
than someone telling her what to do. Not even Freddy
Mercury. In fact, she'd unplugged the damn thing
because it was making an annoying hum that was
keeping her from falling asleep, despite how tired she
was.

　　She'd gotten as far as Wichita when fatigue set in. It
brought a friend with it, too: Caution. And caution had been
mansplaining to her for fourteen hours just why it was a
good idea to sleep somewhere that has a door with a lock on
it instead of on top of a ridge with UFOs in the rain. Or in a
Pinto with acolytes of Hitchcock's seagulls looking for a little
action. Besides, she'd gone over the daily driving limit for
grifters by two hours and was risking having her license to
scam suspended.

　　Ordinarily motel rooms were a luxury Astra never

indulged in. It just didn't suit her pragmatic nature. But being in an actual bed with something resembling a real pillow instead of a fat suit on which to rest her head was the kind of luxury she felt she deserved. She slept hard and woke from a dreamless night with just enough time to throw on her clothes and leave before check-out time. Thanks to Freddy Mercury.

It had started raining as Astra was tossing her suitcase in the back seat, and it was obvious that it was the first rain after a long dry spell by how slick the parking lot was under the soles of her Chuck Taylors. The roads would be dangerously slick. Astra would have been wise to pay a little more attention to that tiny detail, because it mattered. Why else would Freddy Mercury have been giving her a heads up?

As she approached US Highway 54 she noticed a tall, thin man standing by the on-ramp in a long overcoat and fedora. He didn't appear to be hitch hiking. In fact, Astra got the feeling he was waiting for *her*. When she got parallel to him, he raised the fedora in a greeting similar to the one the trooper had given her at the rest stop. Only instead of feeling insulted by it, Astra got an unnerving sense of dread as she continued up the on-ramp. The rain intensified as she increased her speed to merge with traffic. For an eerie moment, she felt as if she were in some kind of weirdly orchestrated, predetermined dance with the rain. A *State Highway Salsa*. A *Two Lane Tango*. A *Blacktop Boogie*. A *Holy Shit There's an Oil Tanker Jackknifed in the Middle of the Road!*

She had exactly zero time in which to respond to the danger. The tanker was stretched across both lanes, its front end nudging against the center cement median and its tail end crumpled against the three foot shoulder-guard opposite it. Staring Astra Talitha in the face was the upturned underbelly of Shell Oil's gift to humanity: the unstable transport system for highly volatile substances that explode upon impact and kill everyone except Shell Oil executives and their board of directors.

Two cars had come perilously close to hitting it before managing to stop and hit each other first. That impact had caused one to flip upside down, and the passengers were madly scrambling to exit the windows before someone like Astra came along with her fat suit and microwaved oblivion about driving in this kind of weather. The other car teetered precariously right behind it, having come to rest on its passenger side when it also flipped.

Astra did exactly what not to do in the situation. She mashed her foot on the brake pedal as she yanked the steering wheel hard to the right. As though there was anywhere for her to steer the Pinto that wasn't full of explosive liquid. The Pinto hydroplaned off the newly wet, oil-slicked highway and for a brief moment she thought she was in a reboot of Chitty Chitty Bang Bang as the airborne Pinto spun through the air. She was heading straight for that soft underbelly of the tanker with nothing between her and it but a white warning sticker in red letters that said, *WARNING, EXPLOSIVE*.

There is much to be said about the time lag in those situations in which one is about to die. Astra thought about Freddy Mercury and how she was letting him down. She thought about Sedona and starting over in the desert. She thought about washing her face with morning fog at Boston Harbor, and about never having another perfectly pulled pork-filled sticky bun from Chinatown.

And then she thought about David and the look on his face the first time he tasted one. It was the light in his eyes, wasn't it? It was the light that was still in them when he looked up at her in the window with those tear-streaked cheeks perfectly polished from climbing those cobblestones they had walked together for months, dreaming out loud in that perfect exchange of dreams lovers do. It was her last thought before the Pinto slammed into the oil tanker and exploded in a fireball that could be seen in three counties.

Astra Talitha died instantly.

Thanks, Shell Oil. We always knew we could count on you.

# CHAPTER FOUR

She found herself sitting at a long table, the kind she'd seen at board meetings on those rare occasions she'd been running an *executive scam*. It was in a room with no windows but plenty of light despite there being no light fixtures or lamps anywhere. Astra was trying to figure out where the light was coming from when an angry voice startled her.

"Astra, we are deeply disappointed in you," a stern woman with a tight bun coiled at the nape of her neck said. It only seemed to emphasize the severity of her mood. "We gave you ample warning ahead of time and can only conclude that you chose the course of action you took deliberately. You might as well have spent the past decade eating saturated fats and processed sugars."

"Wait. Who are you people?" Astra looked around the table at the Council of Five with no idea *how* she knew that's who they were, or what it even meant. "Does this have anything to do with that tall man standing by the on-ramp? That's your idea of a warning? You do know there are far more effective warning systems involving a little more than a fedora in the rain, right?"

Three women and two men sat opposite Astra at the same table. All wore the same shiny gray Nehru jackets with the classic mandarin collar. She briefly wondered if the fabric was polished silk before turning her attention to other details. The women had identically severe buns coiled at the nape of their necks. Both men were bald. Or perhaps they had such light hair they only *seemed* bald. Astra really wasn't sure on that one. Either way, all of them had the same stern look of angry disappointment. And Astra was pretty sure it wasn't because they had to wear matching outfits like some kind of really fucked up acapella group that only does George Harrison covers and never quite answers a question directly.

At least, that's what Astra thought as she looked from scowling face to scowling face, trying to figure out how she got from a detonating device in the form of an airborne Pinto about to set off an oil tanker to a room full of pissed off people in some kind of *Live Action Role Playing Game* that involved everyone wearing the same costume.

"You know who we are, Astra," the man at the end said in a soft, almost gentle voice. "You've always known. It's why you're here. To be reminded. Again."

"Again?" None of this made sense. Not once had Astra ever heard that the Afterlife involved a boardroom full of stern looking people in vintage acapella group costumes scolding her for dying. And why didn't their lips move when they spoke?

"We've done this before?"

"More times than our patience can endure," the

woman who had spoken first said, nodding her head. The others deferred to her leadership and nodded their heads in turn.

Astra chuckled. She had always been accused of being a slow learner and was about to make light of it when the woman slammed her hand to the table with such a resounding *thwap* it made her jump.

"This is nothing to make light of, Astra Talitha!" she snapped. "Please try to remember *who you are*. And for heaven's sake, *listen* to the messages we're sending you. Heed them, Astra. You need to take this seriously. The Council of Five agreed to work with you for a reason."

"Who I *are*?" Astra said. "Who I *are* is someone who wants to know what gives *you* – or anyone – the right to read my thoughts and then scold me for them! Who the fuck do you think *you* are??!"

All five council members abruptly stood in unison. They turned toward her and lowered their heads, their identically large, dark eyes cast downward. Her own head filled with images that were at once both terrifying and awe inspiring. Moving pictures of an endless Universe stretched out into infinity. Terrifyingly expansive, it seemed to be alive. It breathed. And with each inhalation it grew larger. Astra felt herself a part of it, could feel the cooling breath deep in her womb as she let go of her last shred of resistance to what was happening and fell into what was being projected directly into her visual cortex.

Distant images began to gradually grow larger as though a film camera was moving in on a crane after doing an establishing shot. Galaxies came into focus and within those galaxies, star systems. And within star systems, planets. Each image showed countless species covering the planets, with the number of souls living on each. They flashed in her visual cortex like the digits on her watch two nights earlier. And then the words came. Though none of them looked up, none of them moved their lips, the words came nonetheless.

"This is us. *All* of us." Her recognition of their words rivaled the resonance of those familiar scents she recognized at Boston Harbor. Had she not been sitting, Astra's knees would have buckled, sending her legs out from under her.

"The one thing you yourself insisted we tell you to never forget is this," the downloading of data from the baffling group continued. "Don't buy into your own legend. Legends are just that: Inventions that support a story you're telling. Remember to live *your* story, not your legend, Astra."

Astra puzzled over the thought of leaving a message to herself with some freaky acapella group as they reached the far wall of the boardroom. The Council of Five executed a perfectly synchronized ninety degree turn and walked to a door that hadn't been there before. As it opened, they turned back with one last thought.

"Keep yourself alive, sweet one. You are *our* star child, and important to us. To *all* of us. You chose this mission because of your gifts. We've watched you struggle to learn how to use them. And we've done our best to support your learning process and continue training you along the way. But now the time for you to begin using them is upon us. And none of this will have meant a thing if you leave this plane too soon. You must keep yourself alive."

# CHAPTER FIVE

Freddy Mercury was emphatically insisting Astra
Talitha keep herself alive and she didn't know why.
Largely because she was dead. Or at least she thought
she was. She was dead and a bunch of *LARPers* in
Nehru jackets they obviously stole from George
Harrison's estate were scolding her with some kind of
*Vulcan Mind Meld* trick in a brightly lit executive
board room with *NO LIGHT FIXTURES!!!*

Astra sat up and switched off the alarm, which she
hadn't set and in fact had unplugged the night before
because it made an annoying hum that was keeping her
awake. She tried to shake off the dream she'd woke from as
she hurried to clear out of the motel room she'd taken for the
night before check-out time. But just before she opened the
door to leave she thought to check something.

The alarm clock hadn't been plugged in. Nor did it
have backup batteries for when the power goes out. Astra
wasn't sure what it meant, but she was beginning to suspect
she needed to pay more attention to just about everything.

There appeared to be much more going on than meets the eye. She crossed the room, opened the door and took one last look back at the alarm clock before stepping out into the darkly ominous day.

Everything, down to the last tiny detail, was exactly as it had been in her dream. The rain had just started. The parking lot was so slick she almost lost her balance tossing the suitcase in the back seat of the Pinto. And Freddy Mercury's words were still ringing in her ears as she approached the on-ramp to the highway. She spotted the tall man in the fedora and almost pulled over. But what would she say, "Are you one of them"?

Isn't that the kind of thing a paranoid schizophrenic would say? Or worse, a conspiracy theorist?

Despite having ample warning and time to avoid the danger, Astra barreled toward the jackknifed tanker at exactly the same speed she had the first time. She watched helplessly as the two cars collided and passengers scrambled to exit the one that was upside down as the other came down on its side. As that happened she instinctively mashed down on the brake pedal, yanking the steering wheel hard to the right. Exactly as she had done in her dream. And exactly as she'd experienced in her dream, the Pinto hydroplaned.

This time however, she did something a little differently as she became airborne. Instead of focusing on the minutia of the impending disaster unfolding in slow motion, or thinking about David, she let out the last line most preferred in disaster scenarios.

"Ohhhhh shit," came streaming out of her mouth in a burst of air, which wasn't at all unusual, as has been established. What was unusual was what followed. The best

Astra could do to describe it was to say it reminded her of something she'd heard when she was running a *Mandala Effect* scam on the Dharma Center in Cambridge. Some monks were seated on the floor in the lotus position chanting a mantra with one single word stretched out for as long as their breaths would last.

"Om."

Astra had no idea what it meant or what it was for, but it stayed with her. Like that random item one finds on the ground and just knows it will come in handy someday. A screw or nail or just the right size washer perhaps. Astra shoved the *Om* in her pocket and went on her way, never giving it another thought. Until that very moment.

"Ooooooooooommmmmmmmmm."

As the *Om* rose up out of her solar plexus and followed Astra's well-placed *oh shit*, it flowed through her lips and began to fill the car with the soothingly sacred sound. And something else came with it. Something she hadn't seen come out of those monks' mouths. A blinding white light was also flowing out of her mouth along with it. It was as though the situation itself was giving birth to something alive and vital. An intelligent life form that came into being through the *Om* within her, fully realized. The brilliant white light really *was* almost blinding as it filled the passenger section of the Pinto, as if only those with the strength to endure such brilliance can see what's behind it.

And with that, the car floated up and over the oil tanker. Somewhere in an entirely different kind of board room, Shell Oil executives are in a frenzy over the failure of one of their planned tanker explosions. With that failure, their operational costs won't increase enough to justify bribing another congressman into doubling their government subsidies. How will they ever compensate for their imaginary losses? A board member might have to settle for a low-budget caviar instead of the Beluga. Which is unacceptable.

The Pinto floated down to the rain-slicked highway on the other side of the oil tanker and landed gently on all four tires. Without making a sound.

"I didn't do that. Freddy Mercury did it. Some tall freak in a fedora did it. Or an acapella group wearing matching outfits did it. But it doesn't matter because that didn't just happen. Things like that don't happen. Why isn't David here? He's the only person who would believe what didn't just happen."

Astra Talitha would have continued to sit there reciting her *Denial Manifesto* if a rap on the window hadn't startled her out of it.

"Dude, what the fuck was *that*??!" the truck driver was shouting from the other side of the driver's window. "How did you *do* that? Where did you get that light thingy? Was that what powered this Pinto over my rig? A *PINTO!* Dude, my wife would never have believed me if I hadn't gotten the video of it with my cell phone!" He held the screen up as Astra rolled down the window in slow motion.

"That really happened?" she stammered. He nodded his head as the video he'd just shot began to play. She watched as the Pinto took flight, filled with a blinding light, and then floated back down to the highway on the other side of the tanker. As the mysterious light faded, all she could see was her face staring forward from behind the steering wheel, her eyes wider than she thought possible and her mouth still in the shape of the *Om*.

# CHAPTER SIX

There were still a little over a thousand miles remaining to go before reaching Sedona. Astra knew she could break the trip into two more days and possibly nights. But she didn't want to. And who could blame her? The nights were entirely too weird and the days were getting weirder by the minute.

She found herself checking every on-ramp, off-ramp, underpass and street corner she passed for a tall man in a fedora. And on more than one occasion she'd almost jumped out of her skin when the light hit the corner of her eye just right and she thought Freddy Mercury was riding shotgun. The microwave had begun seriously considering auditioning for the *Brave Little Toaster* reboot rather than put up with her disloyalty for another second.

But what convinced her to just push through and get there was knowing it would give her a solid block of time with which to think through her plan. It is not in the nature of most pragmatists to go off willy-nilly chasing UFOs and telling people *we are not alone.* But being a pragmatist, Astra also knew she had to consider the possibility she was in fact *not* alone. To dismiss the possibility was throwing the baby out with the bathwater. And that was just plain wrong any way you cut it. Or bathe it.

If there was anything she was good at, it was doing research. It's the hallmark of a good con artist to be able to thoroughly prepare for any grift they are about to run. Doing research means investigating every angle, leaving no stone unturned prior to engaging the mark. The last thing any con artist needs is surprises. Surprises are the bane of the confidence industry. A successful scam is one that's thoroughly researched, planned and executed to the letter of that plan.

In essence, Astra had all the makings of an investigator. And it was time to investigate what the fuck was going on. Or as Astra would put it: What. The. Fuck. Was. Going. On.

As the steps she'd need to take began to form in her head, another idea rode shotgun right along with it. The equipment she'd need for the one would be perfect for both. In fact, they really were both the same plan. And so it was as Astra Talitha made her way to the mecca of supernatural power and New Age spiritualism in North America she dropped the idea of being a psychic medium. Astra was going to Sedona with a plan to open a detective agency dedicated to investigating things that are so foreign the only word that fits is *alien*. She would call her business *Alien Investigations*.

She only hoped she was able to lay low and not attract any attention until she'd finished the research she needed to do. There had to be others out there who had experienced something similar to what she'd been through, so she would start there. If she was going to run a convincing scam, it was essential she come across as expert in all things related to aliens. So she decided she would spend the rest of the trip going over her cell phone service plan's monthly allotment of data minutes. And she started by asking Siri to tell her about the Council of Five.

She spent the next sixteen hours listening to YouTube videos and various webcasts and podcasts about the Pleiadians and the Annunaki and the Arcturians, as well as other things related to ETs that had nothing to do with someone coming up with names for them by pulling them out of their ass.

When she landed on a three hour long history of the Mi-Go – originally from the H.G. Wells' Universe before taking on a life and mythology of their own – she thought her head would explode. At one point, Astra found herself shouting a command at Siri that she quickly wished she hadn't.

"Siri, is it possible to put the worms back in the can once you've opened a can of them?"

"Looking for retail outlets selling canned worms."

"I would expect no less, Siri."

"You want hours of operation for Les Schwab, is that right?"

"Gesundheit."

"You're welcome."

The thing that became abundantly clear to her, and which she knew would work to her advantage, was the plethora of contradictory story lines on the internet regarding extraterrestrials. Not unlike religions that look down on other religions, insisting *theirs* is the *One and Only TRUE Way,* the perspectives about aliens changed from website to website and abductee support group to abductee support group. One organization would claim there are benign entities here to help us from being eaten alive by the negative entities, while another would insist there is no benign alien presence here; only negative colonizers enslaving humans to mine and harvest Earth's resources. Which they apparently sell to the highest bidder on their various intergalactic trade routes.

There was one red flag that caught Astra's attention. And not unlike a squirrel, it forced her to chase after it as it ran. It was in the debate about extraterrestrials by the many, many men who claimed to hold the one and only truth to the matter.

In listening to speaker after speaker, she couldn't help but notice the insistence that our alien visitors were either for or against one political candidate or another. Which made no sense to either Astra or the squirrel. Why would a species advanced enough to have either traveled light-years to get here – or mastered interdimensional travel to do so – give a rat's ass about whether America's president was black, brown, yellow or orange? If they're advanced enough to manipulate time and space, and really cared all that much about our puny little Earth politics, certainly they're advanced enough to manipulate the outcome of an election without much more than the wave of a light-saber or three-fingered hand.

It seemed to Astra that for any man to get on his extraterrestrial soapbox and insist the aliens have declared someone the *Chosen One* for *any* reason smacks of little more than a decidedly Earth-centric propaganda campaign implemented by someone from this planet with a stake in the game. The fact the men were oblivious to their own blind spot irritated her to near-migraine proportions. Any man running a scam like these men were should know better.

So to relieve the stress and for sheer entertainment value she would search for any YouTube videos she could find that addressed alien-human hybrids. Which invariably dragged her down the rabbit hole with evangelicals using deceptively click-bait titles promising to reveal the origins of hybrids, including mermaids, satyrs, and even centaurs. Which Astra naturally assumed would expose the truth behind aliens mixing their DNA with all manner of life forms on Earth. It would explain the mythologies behind those creatures that never made sense to Astra, and give her closure on more than a few questions.

Only in decidedly fundamentalist fashion, the videos invariably skirted the entire extraterrestrial issue by referring exclusively to *fallen angels.* Which sure sounded a *lot* like extraterrestrials to Astra. But not to the people who have only ever read one book. And then gotten a PhD in it.

One speaker even went so far as to insist it was those *fallen angels* co-mingling with all manner of *strange flesh* that filled the world with so much wickedness God had to wipe out all living things on Earth. Including the demonic mermaids. But not this one family heavily into incest. Who went on to re-populate the Earth. Which is once again full of wickedness. But definitely not because of the extraterrestrials. Or the incest. Or even the mermaids. Who all died in the flood. Because water. Or mystical reasons they never manage to explain in their doctoral thesis. Or their

YouTube click-bait.

Nor did they ever explain just why God had Noah build a huge boat and load onto it a pair of each of the estimated 8.7 million members of the animal kingdom on Earth – plus all the food and fresh water all 17.4 million of them would need – in order to survive forty days and forty nights of global flooding. Which apparently mermaids are unable to survive, as already determined but which Astra still could not wrap her head around. How did all the other fish survive being in the water? Or did Noah bring them on-board too, leaving the mermaids with nothing to eat?

But the question that really tripped her up was why any omniscient being would have an incestuous – but definitely not wicked – man do all that when he could have simply shown Noah how to store those animals' DNA and reproduce them when the water receded back into its mermaid-free oceans. Hence the *science* in *omniscience*. After all, Noah did have the arduous and oh-so-incestuous task of repopulating the Earth to also think about. That's a lot of cookie baking to get busy with.

Astra figured God just found it amusing to watch Noah spend all those many years sailing around the world first collecting all those millions of different species of animal before the flood, and then dropping them all off in their original natural habitats once that dove gave him the *all clear*. Which is why there are no polar bears in the Middle East. Unless there are, and it explains why we started two land wars there. So evangelicals wouldn't find out. Why confuse them when it's much easier to blow everything up, including all the polar bears roaming the foothills of Afghanistan?

More than a few times she selected one of the fundamentalists' deceptively click-bait titles, only to be assaulted with scripture that directly contradicted pretty much every shred of critical thinking she was capable of. Which by fundamentalist definition is any thinking that is critical of their twisted ideology.

But the take-away she got from their insistence the Bible is the *inerrant word of God* was that nobody really has any idea just who is whispering in their ear at any given time with various *inspirations.* There's really no way to tell. Both ends of the deific spectrum, and everything that exists in-between, are indistinguishable from each other when they're being downloaded directly into the auditory cortex. In fact, there are those who claim all of them are one and the same deity, just in different moods. Astra Talitha was pretty sure that's where the idea for the Trinity came from.

And with the advances made in technology – including remote neural monitoring and its alter ego, remote neural programming – the odds anyone could be absolutely certain who they're getting their information from seemed astronomical to Astra. They were certainly not the kind of odds an experienced, pragmatic grifter would place a bet on. Nor would she bet on the odds of ever seeing the human race resolve its addiction to polarization. As long as it's being helped along by dubious parties with their own agenda, it seemed highly unlikely to her that many would be able to transcend it. Where's the profit in letting that happen?

As far as she could tell, the same principle applied to New Agers and other ufologists who claimed to be channeling the Pleiadians, Arcturians, or even an *Ascended*

*Master* or two. Without question this included the well-meaning men who claimed to be delivering a *new message* to humanity from *God* himself.

For one thing, if an omniscient deity truly wanted humanity to get it right this time, he would deliver the message to a woman. If for no other reason than to make up for the whole *Adam's Rib* debacle. Setting the stage for the entire human race to accept the concept of slavery truly brings into question both his omniscience and his omnipotence. Not to mention his beneficence. It only stands to reason a supreme being would have the foresight to understand that creating Eve to be little more than Adam's servant would lead a race of people with no emotional intelligence whatsoever down a slippery slope to where we are now: addicted to slavery.

Astra would move from the deceptive click-bait of the evangelicals to the ongoing battle between fundamentalists and those gentle-souled, cotton-clothed New Agers, who for some curious reason Astra couldn't quite figure out seemed to have basically taken the Christian mythology and copied & pasted it into their extraterrestrial cosmology. And she had no one to discuss the discrepancies with but Siri.

"So, basically they've just given extraterrestrials the same names as the angels in the Bible?"

"You want to find towels for survival, is that right?"

"No. That's a completely different science fiction story. I want to know where sanity went in America. It seems to be missing."

"Sanitary napkins and towels are in the same aisle as survival gear at Costco."

"What about sanity?"

"You want to listen to Sean Hannity, is that right?"

"Does anyone really want to listen to Reptilian propaganda?"

"Your Geiko insurance quote will be emailed by Wednesday."

If there was anything Astra had learned from sampling just about every culture in America there is to sample, it's that belief is a matter of choice. And it has nothing to do with whether there's any truth behind it or not. We choose what to believe based on how our own personal filters were shaped by the experiences we have in life, and changing those filters is almost as difficult as changing the air filter in the engine of a Pinto. The most anyone hoping to alter another person's beliefs can do is confuse the hell out of them by throwing a whole bunch of information at them with the hope that something actually sticks.

And just as she'd often observed with belief systems, the varying voices of *authority* created enough confusion in the wider community as to be little more than destabilizing. Astra was pretty sure if there ever really were some kind of alien invasion or confrontation with humanity, the human population would be unable to defend itself. We'd be too busy arguing about it to focus on anything else.

Just like we are right now with religion. And government. And guns. And sexual orientation. And gender identification. They were all sides of the same five-sided coin, as far as Astra could tell. She wondered if the same party that minted that coin was behind all the confusion about the extraterrestrial presence on Earth.

"Siri, what's the word for five-sided?"

"Pentagon."

"It figures."

"You want to buy triggers, is that right?"

"I'm not sure there are any left, Siri. The Pentagon and Disinfaux News appear to have cornered the market on triggers."

If there was anything Astra knew well, it was the effectiveness of using the *Confusion Technique* to put the target of a grift into a trance, making it easier to access his subconscious and program him subliminally. It made manipulating them into doing what she wanted when the time came to close the deal hilariously easy. Not unlike a politician every time he opens his mouth. While holding his hand out. Or Disinfaux News just for shits and giggles.

And the cracks in the foundation of the extraterrestrial story line could prove to be equally effective in lulling her unsuspecting clients into believing whatever she says to them. Even those who were smart enough to do their homework and look up what she tells them will have no problem finding confirmation buried in all the conflicting information on the internet.

She couldn't help but wonder if the same people managing the internet were the ones bringing Disinfaux News to the American airwaves. And televangelism, including the YouTube evangelists masquerading as ministers of truth, ever vigilant warriors for their version of reality. Or basically plain old debunkers of trusted sources of actual fact-based information. Since the internet is governed by the same authority as Disinfaux News, it wasn't hard for Astra to draw a straight line from televangelists to the electronic versions on YouTube working overtime to make sure anyone who calls them out gets ridiculed for not being woke. Or for being just plain stupid. Because besides failing to teach them any manners, their mothers failed to foster a shred of emotional intelligence in them. Not even empathy.

She did have to admit she admired the ingenious device the extraterrestrial storyline was for advertisers. The more people driven to the various social networking platforms with videos of the modern day truthsayers at their various podiums with their differing claims to the *One and Only Truth* about the extraterrestrial presence here on Earth – or lack thereof – the more arguments they could attract in the comments sections of those sites. And the more revenue there was to gain from the traffic it generated. She knew better than anyone it was a numbers game, and the higher the numbers, the greater the odds. And thus the percentages. And Astra Talitha wanted her share of those percentages.

By the time she found herself approaching Sedona, Astra had memorized enough of the key words, names, planets, dimensions and arguments surrounding incidents involving each of them from the compendium of UFO lore on the internet to confidently introduce herself as an expert in ufology. She knew exactly what she needed to do, what equipment she would need in order to do it, and was close enough to Las Vegas that she could call in a favor or two to help keep down the expenditures. In all, Astra was feeling pretty confident in her newest confidence scheme.

So confident in fact, that she decided to drive right past Sedona and head for Phoenix. She could put up for the night there and do some shopping in the morning. The art of the con relies heavily on dressing the part. And if Astra

Talitha was to play the part of an alien investigator, she needed to dress for it. Everything had to change. Except for the Chuck Taylors, of course. The Chuck Taylors were something she planned to be buried in.

"From my cold, dead toes," she said, winking at Freddy Mercury riding shotgun.

# CHAPTER SEVEN

By the time she left Phoenix, Astra had a sign for the front door, business cards, posters, night vision goggles, a laptop and the perfect wardrobe for investigating all things so foreign they're alien. While she knew she would fit the part better if she dressed in the garments most associated with New Age Spiritualism, she just couldn't force herself to do it. New Age women tend to wear long flowing natural fiber skirts, cotton peasant blouses interspersed with the occasional organic poet blouse, with wildly untamed silver-white hair down to their waist. None of it spoke to her. Largely because Astra never learned to speak Esperanto.

After long thought, Astra concluded that as-of-yet there are no fashion rules set in stone about what an alien investigator wears.

"Who's to say aliens have anything at all to do with spirituality, anyway?" Astra said, looking in the dressing room mirror at the khaki cargo shorts she'd just tried on.

They fit her booty perfectly. In typical Astra Talitha fashion, she went in a completely different direction from Madam Blavatsky and her flowing velvet capes by adopting a look more commonly associated with a Walkabout somewhere in the Australian Outback.

As far as the eye could see within a shopping bag, it was khaki. Khaki safari gear. Khaki cargo shorts, khaki shirts, vest, and of course, khaki hat. Astra would have gotten khaki sunglasses if they'd had any. And it all went great with her red Chuck Taylor high-tops. And knee socks. Because knee socks are cool. Just ask Astra Talitha.

The detour and night in a hotel with Wi-Fi also gave her the opportunity to look for any information that might be online about the building she now would be calling home. Astra was delighted to discover it had a small apartment in the back that would be perfect for her. No working out of dry-rot fleabag motel rooms for her.

In the morning, Astra took the time to pick out a desk and a chair for the office, plus a few pieces of furniture for the apartment. She was growing more and more solidly confident that her funds would hold out until the cash started rolling in from Alien Investigations. After making arrangements for all of it to be delivered Wednesday afternoon, she headed back toward the red hills ringing the Verde Valley.

It was not in her nature for Astra to be a spendthrift, but knowing she wouldn't need to pay for housing, she had a little more wiggle room in her budget than she had anticipated. So as she drove through Sedona she stopped at several shops and acquired the props she'd need for Alien Investigations. She cheerfully loaded up on healing pink quartz crystals, because she'd always heard they're good at warding off hipsters. And they also have a neutral scent. Unlike hipsters. She had also heard on a podcast that 90% of science is made with quartz.

She lost herself in one shop for a while considering a nameless stone that wasn't labeled but looked like a substitute phallus. Which of course reminded her of David. And the evangelicals on YouTube who would gleefully stone her for knowing what a phallus is.

"Does this one awaken synergy?" she asked the young clerk in heavy black eyeliner sitting by the cash register. To Astra, she seemed more intent on her chewing gum than anything else. Which was fine with her, since she had absolutely no idea what she was talking about.

"I doubt it," she said, removing the gum and sticking it under the counter. "But I've heard it will protect you from other crystals."

"Hmm... no, I'm more interested in something that will purify the Wi-Fi and awaken hearts to the magic of couch-dancing. Got anything for that?"

The clerk reached under the counter for the wad of gum and held it out. Astra's heart soared to see someone so young introducing irony into the art of the con. She knew the kid would do well with her craft. And for the first time got the feeling Sedona might be just the place for her.

In the end, Astra managed to collect a mystical set of cylindrical door chimes, some sage and Palo Santo smudge sticks, Nag Champa incense, a desktop gong, several CDs of New Age electronic music, a pyramid-shaped Himalayan pink salt desk lamp, a basket of perfectly smooth river stones, and an assortment of blank notebooks to give clients so they could start keeping a *dream journal.* And of course, an impressive assortment of various healing stones known for such things as attracting badgers, preventing horse attacks, warding off children, and locating any dead god's bones that might be in the vicinity.

All of it filled the back of the Pinto to overflowing by the time she made her way to her new home. But her favorite acquisition that day was the charm bracelet with symbols of the key families of the Council of Five. Her favorite was the jaguar symbolizing the Lyrans.

"The jaguar is my spirit animal," she said to the clerk who threw in her wad of chewing gum for free. Astra appreciated the opportunity to practice speaking the New Age dialect with someone who wouldn't judge. The bracelet gave an air of authenticity to her backstory, yes. But what she needed more than anything was to practice actually using the jargon in conversation.

Also for her backstory, she had stopped at a truck stop when leaving Phoenix and picked up a bumper sticker that said *Kiss My Ass* for the Pinto. She'd been debating with herself about what to do with the old beater. It didn't exactly go with the image of a successful investigator of all things so foreign they're alien. But putting herself in debt over it just to be able to look the part with all the right accessories was simply not within the range of the pragmatist's tolerance for financial risk taking, so she opted for a little flair.

She would tell people both the Pinto and the bumper sticker were for the Draco-Reptilians.

"Those assholes like to get a little too close," she practiced saying in the rear-view mirror. "Considering how explosive Pintos can be about getting their asses kissed, I thought I'd encourage those filthy lizard hybrids to keep it up. Who knows, maybe I'll get lucky someday."

She had been telling herself she would investigate her own foreign experience with missing time and magical flying Pintos as she took on clients and worked their cases. Since whatever it was her clients would be asking her to investigate would most likely be something they were infected with on one of those conspiracy theorist websites designed exclusively for magical thinkers, it would give her time to investigate her own case while getting paid for it.

But by the time she was introducing herself to her neighbor, Samara, and getting the key, Astra's mind had been so preoccupied with building her backstory and getting the gig off the ground she'd all but forgotten about her own foreign experiences. Which was just fine with Astra. She had far too much on her mind those first few weeks simply getting herself situated. A lot of it had to do with the input from her neighbor.

"Astra Talitha!" the woman with only one name exclaimed in a syrupy southern drawl as she handed her the key. "Well aren't we a pair? Samara and Astra Talitha, right here side by side. The Perfect Child of God and the Perfect Child of the Stars. One in her khaki Outback gear, and the other, ever the cliché in her throwback to Berkeley and Ravi Shankar, amethyst love beads and all."

While she was tickled with the storefront, with its ample open space, high ceilings and big windows, what thrilled her most was the ceiling fans. They weren't just in the storefront. They were down the hallway and in each of the two small office spaces she'd been surprised to find built into the back of the shop, with a hallway connecting them.

And to Astra's delight, the ceiling fans were also in the apartment. After life on Beacon Hill with tiny cramped spaces and little fresh air anywhere, it was a dream come true to step into the roomy little apartment and find high ceilings that accommodated ceiling fans in every room.

"Ceiling fans as far as the eye can see," Astra said. "Imagine that. Just as I've always envisioned."

In a world where dreams really do come true one would find it hard to believe that anyone would consider making a living out of chasing people's nightmares, but that's what Astra Talitha was planning on doing. Or at least, making a killing. And it all started with lying on the cool kitchen tiles and staring up at those ceiling fans.

There was one thing she absolutely *had* to change about them, though. The compact fluorescent bulbs installed in the light fixture located in the bottom center of each fan had to go. Despite having its own cheery yet nondescript globe over each bulb, it couldn't hide the fact that Astra had listened to far too many webcasts connecting the frequencies emitted by fluorescent bulbs to the favorite subject of conspiracy theorists on the internet: mind control. Alien mind control.

And not just any alien; Saudarian. One of the most ruthlessly cutthroat races in the galaxy, they sincerely believed their Creator had given them the mandate to establish dominion over the entire Milky Way Galaxy. Astra failed to see how they differed in any way from things she'd heard certain televangelists say right here on Earth. From what she was able to piece together from the many conflicting discussions on the subject, they were especially fond of using mind control to reduce the collective resonance frequency of a race to that delectable range Saudarians love more than anything.

Whether Astra agreed with their too-far-out-in-right field theory about mind control or not was irrelevant, as far as she was concerned. If there was a race that wanted to reduce an entire population to drooling idiots, ensuring an ample supply of mercury is in the home was a great way to do it.

And of course, they would get their tools in the intelligence industry to do the work of implementing it for them. The CIA would gleefully give the project some cool name like Bluebird or Artichoke or Monarch, and flash secret hand signals at each other in the hallway on the taxpayers' dime.

It seemed to her advocates for the health and safety of families had only just managed to see to it mercury-based thermometers were removed from the home. The grifter in her smelled a con in there somewhere, and she was pretty sure it smelled like mercury. And it definitely was not Freddy Mercury.

There were those online who went so far as to insist it was Saudarian interference that was behind the phasing out of incandescent lightbulbs altogether. She had to admit, it was a neat piece of con artistry to convince an entire planet the compact fluorescent bulbs were better for the environment. Of course, there were also those online who claim that each planet in our galaxy emits a resonant light frequency that differs entirely from every other one. It led Astra to wonder if the frequency emitted from the Saudarian's planet of origin might match the frequency emitted by compact fluorescent lightbulbs.

Unfortunately, she'd been sidetracked from looking into it by the more toxic of the conspiracy theorists, most likely made toxic by mishandling broken compact fluorescent lights. They would routinely devolve into infighting; some insisting the only reason mercury was in the bulbs in the first place was to flaunt a little-known secret, teasing only the most observant with a clue about the NASA secret.

Apparently, one of the astronauts from the Mercury Space Mission had disclosed the secret, so according to internet conspiracists, it *must* be true. Long before there was an internet for them to argue on, in the days before webcasts and YouTube videos, there was radio to keep the terminally basement-dwelling conspiracy theorists entertained. And this astronaut did a great job of it by insisting during a broadcast from coast to coast that there was a mind control program used on gifted children in the 1950's and 1960's by none other than the space agency he worked for.

As far as Astra could tell though, the reasoning behind it seemed as pointless as one of David's scams. She lost interest about ten minutes into the YouTube argument between two prominent conspiracy theorists on whether it was supposed to make the children psychic, or simply psychotic. She got the impression NASA considered all aliens to be one or the other. Or perhaps both. So naturally the only conclusion to draw from all of it was NASA had to create children to match because keeping up with the Saudarians is apparently a thing.

The only problem she now had regarding the ceiling fan light fixtures was what kind of bulb to put in them, since incandescent bulbs were nowhere to be found. Not even at the Dollar Store. She wished she'd thought to bring at least one case of them from the apartment when she fled Beacon Hill with the fat suit and microwave.

*ALIEN INVESTIGATIONS*, the sign read as it hung neatly in the front window. Beneath it in smaller lettering was a second one that simply said *ASTRA TALITHA*. And in the smaller window adjacent to the front door, she hung the UFO sign that lit up in fluorescent pink when she switched it on. She thought it said more than the standard *Open* sign. Even if all it said was she was a tool for having a neon sign.

After putting much thought into it, Astra decided she really didn't want anyone coming in asking her to spy on their husband. Unless the husband was a shape shifting Draco-Reptilian hybrid. That she would investigate. Hence making it clear her agency was dedicated to investigating aliens. Of course, her reason for this was merely pragmatic. To investigate cheating spouses and missing puppies she would need both a business permit and an investigator's license. To investigate aliens didn't require a license because aliens didn't exist. All she needed was the business permit.

On the wall facing the door, just behind the desk and right next to that business permit in a cheap dollar store frame, was the iconic poster from the X-Files, a television show from the nineties about an FBI agent who was himself obsessed with all things so foreign they were alien. She would tell anyone who asked that he had been her inspiration growing up. And then with wide eyes ask if they were aware that Gillian Anderson was Lyran.

"It's the red hair," she would say breathlessly. "It's a dead giveaway!"

**I WANT TO BELIEVE**, the poster said. And Astra

did, too. She really did want to believe. She just didn't know quite what it was she was *wanting* to believe.

Astra had once told David she was willing to believe in extraterrestrial intelligent life, "As long as they're nice. And cuddly. And bring the unicorns back. Then and only then will I believe. But first there must be unicorns. And Atlantis. What good are unicorns without Atlantis?"

"You need a nice plant stand for this," Samara said between grunts as she and Astra wrestled to get the potted palm Samara had donated into the corner under the poster she had also donated. It was a family tree of the key Star Families. When she was learning about them she tried to imagine which one she might be from, but having never been a part of any family made it almost impossible. The fact that she didn't believe in Star Families didn't help, either.

Her new neighbor was turning out to be a valuable resource for Astra. Not only was she up on her ufology, she had contacts who were as far down the rabbit hole with it as it goes. She was just beginning to tell Astra about an encounter at Mount Shasta a friend had with a Sasquatch when the furniture arrived.

"They're interdimensional beings, you know," Samara said with authority, doing a standing yoga stretch after she and Astra finished positioning the potted palm in the corner. Her untamed silver waist-length hair waved side-to-side as she stretched, not unlike a slightly tipsy USO girl at a rowdy dime-a-dance event for sailors. But since it was the desert, make that soldiers. Soldiers in a rattlesnake army. Unless the sailors are interdimensional; then they can stay. Interdimensional sailors are amazing dancers.

"Which explains why none of the *experts* have ever

found evidence of Bigfoot's existence." Samara had continued to chase the *Sasquatch-as-interdimensional-beings* thread while Astra's thoughts occupied themselves with the placement of the furniture being delivered. Neither of them seemed to care. "You have to be on the same vibrational wavelength for them to *allow* you to see them. Not a lot of *experts* fit that description. Don't you agree, my darling?"

"Evolution, Samara," Astra replied with sage-like simplicity, though she had no idea what she was talking about. "It's all part of the process. Some of us take bigger baby steps than others, and I don't judge."

"I grow weary at times with the polarization," Samara said. "And just want others to consider the importance of balance. It's all meant to be in perfect balance. The Tao of Physics, so to speak. What the semi-literate simplistically refer to as the *Yin* and the *Yang*. Like you, I do try not to judge, you understand. Even when they refer to something as basic and universal as Taoism as *the occult.* Which is sheer nonsense. It's the Tao, for heaven's sake. It's how it was all designed. You get things out of balance in this corner of the Universe, and it has a ripple effect that ends up throwing things off balance on the other side of the Universe. How anyone can dismiss that basic fact as little more than *paganism* makes me wonder about their mothers and what they were doing instead of teaching their children some basic common sense."

"Basic Chaos Theory," Astra said, propping the front door to the shop open so the movers could bring the desk in. "It's so elegant in its complexity. I often find myself marveling at it all, asking myself who designed all this."

"That one's simple," Samara replied, her jewel eyes

twinkling. "Kind Holy Creator."

But where Samara overcame her superstitions long enough to actually be useful, she proved to be quite instrumental in getting Astra's scam off the ground. The crystal-ball and tarot-card reading, gluten intolerant, macrobiotic vegan had a thorough knowledge of online social networking, especially when it came to the New Age community. The more she talked about them, the more Astra was certain they were the perfect market for her new business.

Once they had the office set up the way they agreed was best, the two woman worked day and night coming up with a marketing plan. For that, Samara showed her the page she had on the Law of Attraction website. On it was a video of all the odd things Samara dreamed of having in her life. She called it a "Mind Movie," and it was all the rage among the New Age people. Their Mind Movies inspired others to engage in creative visualization, which she explained to Astra was essential in achieving the vibrational frequency necessary for their *ascension*.

"We can do something like my Mind Movie," she said. "Only it will be a promotional video you can feature on the YouTube channel you're going to open."

"I am?" Astra replied with feigned surprise.

"Don't interrupt my stream of consciousness," Samara scolded. "It's come a long way to get here."

Astra was tempted to have fun with Samara's stream of consciousness but thought better of it and lit a sage smudge stick instead, waving it around in an arc as she walked counter-clockwise around the room.

"Nothing better for healing a damaged stream of

consciousness than a cloud of burning sage smoke in the eyes," she said.

Samara ignored her, unwilling to leave the warmth of her stream.

"And once we've got your shiny new website open, we can put your video on the home page so it starts playing as soon as someone lands on it," she said, ignoring Astra altogether.

Unwilling to be beat; Astra casually reached for a stick of Palo Santo and lit it.

"In case there are any unfriendlies mixed in with our invisible friends," she said. "They hate this combination."

The marketing video came out better than Astra could have hoped for. So did her website. She had to give it to her New Age helper; the woman knew her target audience and how to attract it. There was not a single pixel that didn't have some kind of sacred geometry deftly woven into it, or harmonic frequency streaming from it. By the time Samara tweeted the link for Astra's site to her sixteen thousand followers, she was confident the business was on its way to landing its first client.

***

"Has ET phoned home and stuck you with an extremely long distance bill? We can collect what that deadbeat sugar addict owes you. Have you been abducted by aliens who then billed you for alien transport tax and customs fees? We can negotiate anything. How about Pleiadian dream programming? Is it leaving you feeling distracted at work by unexplained feelings of hope? Check out our wide assortment of tin foil sleeping caps! Or what about the Reptilians? Have Reptilians convinced you to carry their demon seed and then refused to compensate you? At Alien Investigations we know your rights so you don't have to. And we stand by that promise. We've got solutions to problems you don't even know you've got. Unless the Pleiadians are giving you prescient dreams; then you already know. Sorry about that. We're also a dispensary and can recommend something tasty for anxiety."

***

"Oh for crying out loud, Astra," Samara sighed, shaking her head. "Whatever possessed you to say your shop is also a dispensary? You're going to get all sorts of unsavory characters in here looking for drugs!"

"Looking, yes." Astra said. "And looking means it's there to be found. If I'm lucky my invisible friends will extract the location of possible sources of something dank and tasty those visiting stoners may have forgotten about. Stoners are not well known for having the best memories."

"A lapsed memory is the least of their problems," Samara said, shaking her head sadly. "They're cutting themselves off from their higher selves with it. And from their guides. How is a person supposed to communicate directly with his guides when he's put a smoky barrier between himself and those guides with a bong? What does come through will be hazy and hard to translate."

"I'm pretty sure a Draconian entity possessed me through the laptop camera and made me say it," Astra replied. "They don't want us to get chummy with our guides. Did you know it's the Draconians who inspired the first human to light up a bowl? True story. Draconians are the real gateway drug, if you ask me."

"Ooooh Astra," Samara squealed. "You never fail to give me goosebumps. I can't wait to see the new clients lining up at your door."

The crystal ball tarot card reader had no idea how close she was to having a bona fide premonition.

# CHAPTER EIGHT

Sedona is known for the mystical energy created by the convergence of ley lines running through and under those magical red and pink hills surrounding it. Astra often wondered if those power vortexes had anything to do with a video of her going viral on the internet in which she was filmed by a trucker only a few short weeks earlier. In it, she was riding in a flying Pinto with a blinding white light pouring out of the windows.

A little known fact about con artists is they've had to adapt to the ever-changing landscape as more and more witless targets began to merge with traffic on the information superhighway, leaving brick and mortar con shops with no walk-in business. So Astra had adapted by running a variety of online scams. In order to cover her tracks, she had long since established a web presence. It didn't take that much effort to amass a pool of twenty thousand Twitter and Instagram followers, but Facebook creeped her out too much to do any more than keep an eye on her marks and check her inbox occasionally.

Astra had also begun collecting subscribers to the YouTube channel Samara had her open for *Alien Investigations*. When she also recommended the account to all of her own subscribers, it didn't take long for them to learn she'd uploaded the new marketing video. And shortly after that Astra started receiving notifications about comments viewers were making on it. It wasn't until she actually went to the comments section that she learned about the Flying Pinto video.

"Hey, isn't this the same woman in that trucker's video of the Pinto flying over his jackknifed eighteen wheeler?"

"Who is this woman, and why did I get a notification about this lame ass promo for some stupid shit? She's in that one that's clearly been photoshopped I saw on Instagram too, where she wants us to think she's flying a Pinto. If she thinks this is the way to launch a business, her license to think needs to be revoked. The potential damage it could cause is uninsurable."

"This bullshit is the reason we can't have nice things."

"Oh great, first we had to deal with the Sharknado problem. Then we learn about the problem with flying Pintos. And now this. Will the madness never end??"

The comments went on like that for two and a half pages, and most of them included the link to the video of her in the now infamous flying Pinto. Astra was relieved Samara had headed home before she discovered it. The mystic neighbor would most certainly have questions Astra was not prepared to answer. She had worked far too hard at sliding that little issue onto a back burner to have to start answering questions about it now. There was work to do. Work that didn't involve thinking about difficult things like *how the hell does anyone end up with a flying Pinto problem?* And Astra had every intention of making that work her priority.

She was fairly certain she wouldn't have to answer Samara's questions any time soon though, since Astra highly doubted the mystic would be seeing it. The cautious New Ager was adamant about not using electronics without preparing herself in a lengthy ritual; first by cleansing her chakras and then asking her alien spirit guides for protection. The mystical tarot reader insisted it was because of the risk of negative alien entities attaching themselves to her through the energy emanating from the electronic screens. The process takes hours, but according to Samara is essential for anyone who doesn't want to be ambushed by an exorcist retained by family members convinced they've been possessed by demons.

A little known fact about demonic possession is it doesn't exist. Or rather, demons as depicted in the tragically misleading Hollywood blockbuster movies about demonic possession and projectile vomiting split pea soup don't exist. Aliens, on the other hand, do exist. According to Samara, at least. And the nasty habit of certain entities being in the form of pure energy is where the problem likes to hover.

They come floating in off the data stream now downloading continuously through the electronic appendages we all seem to have sprouted. And it's resulted in countless numbers of hapless internet surfers having opportunistic negative entities attach to them. Not unlike clicking on the wrong link and downloading a virus to your hard drive. Only in the case of entity attachment, it's a soul-sucking alien. And instead of your hard drive being infected, it's you.

For the entities, it's an ideal situation. They live on the energy vibrations that fall in the lowest range of frequencies. After all, it only stands to reason that life forms made up of pure energy are going to sustain themselves by consuming pure energy. To date there has never been an alien entity who has ordered a pizza when they were stoned and eaten the entire thing while listening to Pink Floyd's *Dark Side of The Moon* synced up with a muted copy of the original *Wizard of Oz*.

A surprisingly large number of negative alien entities have been known to accumulate in a single human host, especially those who live in their grandmother's basement and spend all of their time on the internet. And as with so many other things so foreign they're alien, they are merely the infantry in a much larger, far more powerful army hell-bent on conquering whatever they can on this great big spinning rock. And as any good military strategist – and all advertising executives – are well aware of, fear is the very best way to conquer the enemy.

Why do you think the military blast perceived enemies with the music of Brittany Spears? If you thought you were never going to stop hearing the same annoying pop music lyric over and over again, especially when sung by some prefabricated American pop star, wouldn't you be terrified?

Hence fear being the name of the game and ultimate agenda behind negative alien attachment. What their handlers want most of all is to infect humans with fear: fear of lacking, of not having enough. Fear of loss: loss of loved ones, loss of life or good health, or even loss of possessions or position. Fear of not having as many Instagram followers as some other basement-dweller. Fear of not being accepted. Fear of no one ever touching their *P* or letting them put it in the *V* or wherever any given human longs most to put the *P*. Fear of the pastor of their church finding out where and into whom they put the *P*. Fear of people finding out where the youth pastor put his P when they went on that camping trip and he invited them into his tent.

Of course, the host is always the last to know he's acquired a negative entity attachment. Once inhabited by a single entity, there's a standard operating procedure all of them follow. Yet few humans seem to have figured it out. The host is directed by that entity to begin watching child pornography, thus dropping their own energy vibrations down to the low range of frequencies necessary for more negative entities to locate their scout's energy signature and follow it. Once they reach their prey, it's a simple matter of latching hold and strapping on a bib for the feast.

Many wrongly assume Western Civilization invented violently genocidal colonization, but they've got that wrong. Wrong by a few billion millennia. While some have argued it may be time to rethink that strategy and come up with something a little more productive, all attempts to get a response from Western Civilization have failed. Astra was pretty sure it had something to do with the deal it made with its handlers when it signed that contract to open its own franchise in this star system. It only figures that there would be trade secrets those handlers didn't want getting out.

For its first feeding frenzy after inhabiting its host, the

entire clan of negative entities entertains itself by gang raping the host's heart, mind and soul. Much like Western Civilization likes to do when it colonizes. Only it prefers raping those who are most vulnerable and unable to defend themselves. Because everyone knows Western Civilization is a tool that never chose to think beyond its programming. And because rape is the oldest and most favored weapon of war in all of existence. Probably because at some point existence itself ran out of imagination and couldn't figure out any other way to degrade, humiliate and dehumanize.

That gang-rape of the soul and mind, in turn, compels the host to live a fear-based existence. Which in turn leads him to engage in increasingly hostile behavior on the internet. That, in turn, feeds the clan all the negative energy they need to stay fat and happy. The advent of the electronic era has resulted in a population explosion among the entities that once had to attach themselves to humans the old fashioned way in order to eat. Which could easily explain why the internet was invented in the first place. Who knows what kind of entities were inhabiting Al Gore at the time he came up with the idea?

Entire social networking sites have been created to deal with the problem of negative alien entity possession through our electronics. The Law of Attraction website had to dedicate an entire section to The Law of Stop Attracting Them. Hashtag alerts appear regularly on Twitter, especially preceding geomagnetic storms. They're meant to warn people of a flurry of entity attachments happening, and offer suggestions for how to deal with the problem. Those suggestions range from simply stepping away from their screens and locking their cell phones in the microwave, to using their knowledge of alchemy's *Violet Flame* to transmute the entity before it latches on.

Astra wasn't entirely sure if that was supposed to be the color violet or the flower. Burning violets seemed like it could get costly, especially if you spent a lot of time on the internet and needed to do a lot of *Violet Flaming*. And anyone who has watched one of those YouTube videos posted by insanely bored and lonely *dot connectors* insisting anyone wearing the color violet was a tool of the Rothschilds, who apparently own the entire Universe, should consider planting a window box of violets just to be on the safe side.

Whether flower or color, the flame that seemed to have been lit the night before *Alien Investigations* opened its door to the public definitely qualified as a convergence. *Convergence* is defined as a point where two unrelated things intersect and become related by virtue of that intersection. Like insane loneliness and *dot connecting.*

And where they intersected for Astra was at the launching of her website at exactly the same time Disinfaux News covered a story about a viral video of a mysterious woman floating down from heaven in an angelic Pinto and then speeding away on a rain-soaked highway. When Disinfaux News trolls went looking for anything without merit about the mysterious woman that they could capitalize on by feeding it into the twenty four hour news cycle, they stumbled upon her YouTube marketing video for *Alien Investigations*. The marketing video in turn led them to her website, which featured the address, phone number and office hours of Alien Investigations.

Astra had always been wary of online marketing. It

seemed to attract far too many of those men in shiny suits with equally shiny hair and skin. They were always smiling and saying pleasant things, which made her suspicious. Men with shiny hair and skin in shiny suits who are always smiling and agreeing with everything a person says told Astra all she needed to know about them: They were up to something, and it was most likely something no good. It made her uneasy.

And for good reason. If she had known anything about the planet those shiny men's genetics came from she would have been even more uneasy. Shiny men in shiny suits who always smile and agree with people are interested in two things only: more shiny things, and power. Which is why Astra chose to pay no attention whatsoever to politics, with its plethora of shiny faces in shiny suits. It is also why she wasn't paying attention to online marketing when all hell broke loose.

The website went live at ten PM, just moments after Samara tweeted the marketing video to her followers, who in turn retweeted it to their followers. At least half of them also shared it on their Facebook page, where it was shared again and again until even people on Instagram were talking about it. It was the first time in over a week they weren't talking about lady seagulls. The phone started ringing at seven minutes after ten. And didn't stop till Astra unplugged it three hours later. By that point, the voicemail box was full and she was in a mood. It was not conducive to picking up any more calls. While there are many words that might succinctly describe that mood, Astra managed to deftly kick each and every one of them to the curb. Such is the case when a mood is so dark even words can't handle it.

The very first call she answered was what put her in that mood.

"Have you had much success helping people with their alien problems?" the voice said in a thick Hispanic accent. Her English was that of someone who hadn't spoken it for very long.

"Success is judged only in terms of the measure of resonant frequency," Astra heard herself reply cryptically, with absolutely no idea what she was talking about. It was becoming a habit. She and her first caller had more in common than an interest in aliens. They were both learning to speak a language that would help them fit into their new roles in life. And the caller seemed to be doing a far less awkward job of it than Astra Talitha was.

"My name is Luzmilla, but everyone calls me Luz," the woman continued, as if what Astra had just said in response to her question actually made sense. "My son, Christian, was picked up by Sheriff Arpaio's men on a business trip to Phoenix three weeks ago and we haven't seen or heard from him since. I've been told he was turned over to ICE and could be in the detention center for years awaiting processing and deportation."

Astra's heart sank. She found herself juggling three different thoughts at once. One, how many calls was she going to get from aliens with deportation problems. Two, what was the best way to gently tell them she doesn't help with *that* kind of alien problem. Her third thought had more to do with the issue of aliens and the xenophobic octogenarian convicted of contempt of court known affectionately by people who don't like to use vulgarities as the Sheriff of Nottingham. The former sheriff of Maricopa

County's love of persecuting anyone with brown skin could be useful to her if she could just find the right angle.

Perhaps she could convince people hoping for an encounter with aliens that Sedona is the perfect place to come for that because it's well known among aliens as a safe haven for them. The first watering hole after leaving Phoenix that doesn't allow its law enforcement to get its kicks from picking on those who look different from them. One could almost say Sedona was a sanctuary city for aliens. Astra made a mental note to look into the availability of time shares in the area. It could be a lucrative side business.

"Luz, Alien Investigations isn't licensed to investigate immigration issues," Astra said. "We don't investigate aliens from Mexico; we investigate issues involving aliens from outer space. You know, ET?"

"But we *AREN'T* from Mexico!" Luz shouted into the receiver. "We're *Peruvian*! And we are here *legally*."

Luz and her family had come to the United States by invitation from the US Government on an agricultural exchange. The idea was for Peruvians to teach Americans how to grow the hipster superfood known as quinoa to most Americans, but to Whole Foods it's known as the best way to sucker whole paychecks out of gullible shoppers' wallets.

The US government figured since the natural foods craze successfully distracted Peruvians from what was being done to the region by Western Civilization's favorite incestuous offspring, corporate colonialism, they'd introduce the same kind of distraction to the burgeoning bag of tricks employed by Disinfaux News on its favorite platform, Distraction TV.

"But Arpaio's goons didn't even bother looking at

Christian's papers. They just took him and locked him up because they can't tell the difference between a Mexican and a Peruvian."

Astra had heard of this kind of thing happening. Cultural ignorance mixed with a lethal combination of Disinfaux News-fueled xenophobia and trademark mindless aggression was resulting in anyone with so much as a suntan and dark hair being attacked by those susceptible to mind control. And most of rural law enforcement in America fit that bill.

There were reports coming out of the most unlikely of places, like politely liberal San Diego, California. Peruvians out enjoying a day of shopping or using free Wi-Fi at coffee shops to post their latest blog about permaculture in quinoa farming were being verbally and physically attacked by middle aged white men with an overblown sense of entitlement roaming the streets freely. And their cultural ignorance tells us all anyone needs to know about the public school system in San Diego. From what she could tell, Arpaio's deputies had all been products of that school system. Or ones just like it.

Astra realized she had her work cut out for her. She had chosen a scam that could easily draw the attention of Barney Fife's buddies high on not just their own ignorance, but on processed sugars, confiscated methamphetamines, metabolic steroids and super cool para-military weapons of war to use on the American people and their visitors. And possibly even their quinoa. She would need to proceed with caution.

After her disheartening discussion with Luz, Astra considered letting all calls go to voicemail rather than risk being caught off guard again by the confusion over the word *alien*. She was sorry she hadn't made that decision before the next caller tore into her like she was just so much tissue to make a mess in and demand the woman throw away because that's her job.

The angry conspiracy theorist was obviously getting all his *news* from the website known for being frequented by fans of Alex Jones, the man who put conspiracy theorists on the map so they could walk to the edge of it and fall off. The caller was enraged at the implication that Pleiadians are expert at dream programming.

"Look, feminazi bitch," the growling voice continued. "It's obvious you just don't have the mental capacity to grasp what is really going on in the multiverse. Your brains are just too small."

Astra had been here before. She rolled her eyes at yet another blatant attempt by a member of the opposite gender to establish intellectual dominance over her by virtue of little more than what dangles between his legs. Which never made any sense to her. Not only was the head far smaller than hers, but it was the only one far too many of them ever seemed to use.

She considered suggesting he get a map and use it to locate what little intelligence he might possibly have. But it was most likely buried under a mountain of pure ego driving that little dangling head between his legs. Therefore Astra thought better of it. Being that he had made his status as conspiracy theorist abundantly clear, suggesting he get ahold of a map would most likely result in him wandering to the edge of this quixotically flat earth and falling off.

And since she would have been the one to have

suggested he use a map, Alex Jones would blame her and call her a murderously man-hating feminazi bitch over the airwaves. Because nothing angers conspiracy theorists more than being misled by murderously man-hating feminazi bitches who just want to march all men to the edge of the world so they can push them off and leave those bitches alone to kill all the babies with impunity.

"The only experts at dream programming are members of the intelligence community, specifically the CIA and NSA," the caller said, continuing his bloviating long after Astra had lost interest in a thing he had to say. "Why do you think they built that enormous new data center in Utah?"

Astra had always figured it was because the Mormons were the only ones who would let the NSA into their state. Because everyone knows they too are big fans of mind control. All cults are. It's how they attract and keep their members. She figured the only reason the Scientologists didn't offer the NSA ample space to continue programming the American people was self-explanatory.

Of the two world-famous American cults, the Scientologists were the only ones who don't own an entire state. Yet. So far they only own useless parcels of it, like that grungy corner of Sunset and Vine in Los Angeles. The thought always made Astra shudder. Something about that ugly blue multi-story compound gave her the creeps almost as bad as unsolicited contact from random men on the internet.

She did have to grant it to them, however. They seemed to have mastered the art of the con with the best of them. Aside from their various holdings, the cult had also managed to acquire ownership of at least one commissioner of the Internal Revenue Service. Not just that, but much of the justice system, and the obedient silence of much of the entertainment industry, for obvious reasons. Blackmail has always been an effective tool for those with an affinity for corruption. Not unlike a pig locating truffles, the corrupt can smell corruption a mile away. Astra figured Samara would say that is the very description of *The Law of Attraction.*

"It's bad enough the corporate-owned intelligence industry has the technology to program dreams with Remote Neural Monitoring," the angry conspiracy theorist continued, as though Astra was actually still listening. "But now that technology has gotten out into the private sector. Where do you think the Pleiadians got their hands on it? Get your facts straight and stop being a tool for *DARPA!* I bet you voted for Hillary, didn't you, tool? You feminazi bitches are all the same."

Astra had a sinking feeling it was going to be a long night. At least the deranged caller hung up after his insulting tirade, which didn't surprise her. In her experience, angry men who aggressively attack without using their inside voices rarely wait for a response. Her first life-lesson at a young age was that those who prefer to project their assumptions onto others tend to lack the fortitude to stick around for a response. After all, attacking others unjustifiably has never required intelligent thought or courage. Try getting a straight answer about why, since the beginning of the new millennium, we've started two land wars in Asia and you'll see exactly why Astra Talitha thought this way.

As soon as she heard the next caller's introduction Astra

was glad she decided to let it go to voicemail rather than pick it up. "This is the Annunaki," the voice growled. "And don't bother asking if it's one of the fallen Annunaki working with the Reptilians, or one of those Goody Two-Shoes Annunaki who embraced the *Light* and started working with the Pleiadians. You will know soon enough. Until then, just be aware that we are watching you. And we have friends in high places."

# CHAPTER NINE

Astra was once again glad Samara had left for the night. She was pretty sure the growling voice in the threatening message was referring to the Reptilians, who are apparently in very high places. If by *high* one means *Near Earth Orbit.* Once the tarot reader got started on the Reptilians there was no end to it. She would detail the list of world leaders past and present whose bodies and minds had been inhabited by the shape-shifting aliens. And every time she did that, it would lead to her favorite subject: *predictive programming.*

The average basement-dwelling conspiracist insists the curious insertion of prophecies in popular culture is for the sole purpose of inuring the public to events before they happen. Apparently so the public will be so accustomed to the subliminal messages, it simply accepts events as having been inevitable when they actually occur. But this is only because the magical thinkers living in basements lack the vision to see through all that cement surrounding them.

Despite her aversion to anything that celebrates violence, destruction and chaos, Samara would illustrate her theory about *predictive programming* by starting with the Terminator movie franchise.

"Keep your eye on Skynet," she'd say. "Now that it actually exists, doing that is far easier than it was back in the eighties when we had to rely on prescient dreamers."

She would move forward from there, explaining how the point of *predictive programming* was no different than it had been in the 8th Century BCE during the *Era of the Prophets* as depicted in the Old Testament.

"Wasn't *Skynet* prophesied?" she would say. She would continue by pointing out the Predator movie franchise and how eerily similar to Draco-Reptilians the creatures featured in it are. Actually, to be more precise, the tarot reader would move backward from there. Unfortunately, her stream of consciousness had no back up warning system, which tended to blindside Astra Talitha when she put the timeline in reverse.

Contrary to what most conspiracy theorists believe about *predictive programming*, New Age philosophers think its purpose is twofold. The first most obvious purpose is to facilitate what Samara referred to as our *activation*. And the other is meant to educate the public about the existence of the Extraterrestrial Intervention through prophecy. The reason is the same now as it was thousands of years ago; to give us fair warning by learning how to identify extraterrestrials and their agendas. Reptilians, for instance, can best be identified by observing the effect they have on people.

"So does that mean where there's a televangelist or a corrupt politician," Astra asked on the third or fourth go-around with the topic, "a Reptilian shape shifter is not far behind?" Samara always nodded enthusiastically.

"Unless it's inside him, of course," she would add. "Shape shifters love to inhabit the bodies of both because it gives them unlimited access to all manner of opportunities to lower the resonant frequency by facilitating actions leading to death, destruction and chaos. And anyone who's seen the Predator franchise doesn't need to have it explained just why Reptilians love stirring up that kind of energy. They thrive on it."

"So by that line of reasoning," Astra said on more than one occasion, perhaps merely to test Samara to see if she'd remember it the next time she repeated her *predictive programming* rant, "any producer of children's television programming is also a Reptilian shape shifter. I mean, considering what they're famous for doing to the tender young boys and girls in the industry. Which includes some pretty freaky action involving more than just their feet, apparently."

Samara nodded enthusiastically. "Absolutely." the tempestuous tarot reader replied, scowling each time it came up. "Not only are they ripping into the very fabric of that child's soul, tragically reducing his or her resonant frequency, the fact that the child is on television works to drop the resonant frequency of our entire society to an intolerably low range. It makes us *all* vulnerable to voracious negative entities. Under no circumstances should *ANY* man be left alone with children in that industry, foot fetish or not!"

"Don't you think that's going a little too far?" Astra said. "I mean come on. Not all of them are into grooming twelve year old girls to be their sex slaves so their parents can live in luxury."

"Sorry, I'm sure some of them are nice people, and not all of them rape our children," Samara said. "But until we can figure this out, we need to put a wall up between men in Hollywood and the children they're putting on the screen." Astra shrugged and then had a thought that hadn't been there before. Anyone paying attention would have recognized the footprints of a squirrel running off with her train of thought.

"Another thing popular culture has been useful for is this," Samara would continue. "Our schools have long since stopped teaching antiquity to children. While your parents' generation may have had the occasional teacher go against the grain by insisting her fifth graders read Homer's Iliad, and if they were lucky, the Odyssey also, for the most part this country has gone two full generations without collectively learning about ancient mythology.

So your conspiracy theorists are ignorant of the fact that much of what they're dismissing as mass mind control and *predictive programming* is, in fact, teaching mythology by weaving it into modern story lines. And believe me, those who know and understand the complexity of the Iliad and the Odyssey will have a far easier time of it when it comes to sorting out what's to come."

There were times it seemed to Astra that Samara had an invisible crystal ball she carried around with her that she was perpetually consulting, and this was one of them.

"You know how science fiction movies of the 1950s and sixties are commonly referred to as Cold War anti-communist propaganda?" Samara would repeat word-for-word each time she said it, clearing her throat diplomatically while deftly changing the subject back to the future. And just as deftly, she would return to the joy ride without a DeLorean by taking a slight left turn into even earlier science fiction.

"Communism was a red herring. Those movies were meant to be prophecy. Wasn't the entire population wiped out by a virus in The Last Man on Earth? Curious the entire population would end up confused about vaccines right about the time the twenty four hour news cycle started including viral pandemics in their continuous coverage, isn't it? Remember that old show from television's black and white era, My Favorite Martian? I would love to see believers in *predictive programming* explain that one.

"No you wouldn't." Astra would say each time. She'd seen them discuss it and it was not pretty.

"And what about Mork and Mindy beaming into our living rooms every week teaching us about alien-human hybrids?" Samara would continue, oblivious to Astra's interjection. "Wasn't their baby played by Jonathan Winters? Now *that's* a hybrid if ever there was one!"

As usual, Astra would try to follow her new friend's train of thought, but her focus always tended to derail at the mention of red herrings. Where would she find red herrings? What did they taste like? Her attention span would become the squirrel which had just been spotted by a Golden Retriever. And that squirrel was on the trail of some fresh-caught red herrings.

But before Astra could recapture her attention span, Samara would yank it away again. She'd quickly move on, seamlessly pivoting from modern popular culture back to ancient mythology, where she would stitch her peculiar belief system to the hem of its best dress and draw it back up around its own neck. Her argument became the Ouroboros in a necktie his grandmother helped him with; struggling for air and a sense of dignity.

Sometimes keeping up with her neighbor's narrative made Astra wonder if New Age philosophy hadn't simply taken all the world's mythologies and tossed them in a blender with cosmology and religious philosophy, plus a pinch or two of Jewish mysticism and a significant chunk of the Hindu Vedas, then thrown in a little theosophy for shits and giggles. And don't forget a couple of drops of alchemy, because who doesn't love a little chemistry between friends?

While Astra greatly appreciated David's oft-quoted wisdom that anyone who believes in coincidence just isn't paying attention, it did have its limits. And Samara seemed to have perfected pushing them as far as she could without sinking the entire conversation. When she invariably veered away from science fiction into transgender actors in Hollywood, Astra would understandably begin to worry she might need to throw the marvelous mystic a lifesaver.

She had sat through dozens of YouTube videos trying to wrap her head around what bored basement-dwellers had gleefully labeled the *Transpocalypse*. Thinking there may be an extraterrestrial connection, she followed the squirrel as far as she could stomach with it. But after careful study of the data, she came to two conclusions: the men making the videos had never seen a woman naked in real life and were unlikely to. Ever. And transgender people were treated worse now than they were two hundred years ago on this continent.

Before Puritans got here with the sexually transmitted diseases of shame, homophobia and transphobia, the natives called their transgender people *Two-Spirits*, and honored them for being a crucial reminder of the need for balance between each individual's inherent masculine and feminine sides. Proving to both Astra and the squirrel that Taoism came to this continent right along with its original human inhabitants. Because the odds of anyone surviving the long trek from the cradle of civilization to the New World without a whole lot of balance are nil.

Of course the Puritans would want to smother beliefs like that with diseased blankets as their first order of godly business. The god they brought with them to these shores was suspiciously male, complete with an appendage he liked to use to smite those he didn't approve of. And if you weren't born in that exact same image and likeness, right down to the smiteful appendage, you had no business disagreeing. Just ask the men on YouTube who are smiting away under the guise of *alerting the world* to the *scourge of transgenderism* taking over Hollywood. Apparently for the sole purpose of demonically deceiving anyone who enjoys cultural contributions that weren't created by Christian rock bands or the writers and producers of movies about the Rapture.

The only thing Astra could see being accomplished by the tools fueling the culture wars on YouTube was making transgender people less safe in our society. Which wasn't the only extraterrestrial connection she could make in all of it.

Fomenting a deeply divided society through the disease of bigotry created by *othering* is a favorite weapon of what those entities' tools on YouTube like to call *demons*. She often wondered if they were truly clueless, or just pretending they weren't possessed by those *demonic* entities.

"But those conspiracy theorists aren't considering how far back the phenomena goes," Samara would continue, once again snapping Astra out of another YouTube flashback. "Remember that old Tony Curtis and Jack Lemmon movie where they dress in drag to hide from the mob? That movie came out in 1959!"

"Hey, wasn't Marilyn Monroe in that one?" Astra once pointed out, deciding to avoid explaining to Samara that it actually goes much farther back than how hot some like it. Having to explain the demon-possessed tools on YouTube might have resulted in yet another discussion about just how hot it does or does not get in a hell that does or does not exist. And the squirrel usually was in need of a nap by the time they got to that point.

Besides, knowing Samara, it would lead to a discussion about how the tools on YouTube believe all the men in LaLa Land are actually women, and all the women are actually men. And Astra knew better than to go there. She was the kind of grifter who'd rather *play Final Fantasy* than fall down the rabbit hole with someone else's.

"Yes! Marilyn is a perfect example," Samara had said, a little too enthusiastically for Astra's comfort. "The point is: The conspiracy theorists have got it all wrong. It's not about demonic deception at all. That whole cross-dressing thing is telling us something about gender identification and where we need to let that thread take us. If sexuality is fluid, then so is gender. And understanding that is an essential part of our *activation*.

All of my spirit guides tell me Earth is the only planet in this star system with separate and distinct genders for a reason. We simply *must* learn balance. Earth is a spiritual kindergarten. We're meant to overcome the illusion that there is any difference between us whatsoever before any of the Star Families are going to let us off this rock. It's our illusions that not only separate us from each other, but in so doing, they separate us from the Divine. And polarities keep us rooted in illusion."

She was relieved the clever crystal-ball reader hadn't thought to bring up The Rocky Horror Picture Show. Not because it didn't fit in the picture she was using to illustrate her point, but because she'd always found it hard not to compulsively do the *Time Warp* again every time it was mentioned – even casually – in conversation.

Besides, by that point Astra usually found herself wondering if it was possible to sleep with her eyes open. The conversation would invariably begin to bore her. She had considered asking just exactly *how* biological life forms were supposed to sexually reproduce without there being two distinct genders, but in the end decided against it. She really didn't want to encourage Samara to go there. It could lead to a discussion of yet another YouTube video insisting the *Luciferians* had perfected human reproduction without a host body. At which point all Astra could do was wait for her to just wear herself out. Without question, the topic invariably already had by then.

Astra Talitha's take on the subject of transgenderism was that the human race needed to learn how to stop *othering* and learn a thing or two about empathy. She had just that morning ripped a new one in one of her favorite tools on YouTube for his lack of it. He was just one of many who tried to hide his thinly veiled transphobia behind yet another unsubstantiated claim that the Illuminati was forcing every Hollywood celebrity to undergo a sex change operation. And as usual, the reasoning he came up with was the unimaginative claim that it was all part of the *Luciferian agenda* to deceive everyone who wasn't watching an endless stream of sequels to Left Behind as their sole source of entertainment.

Which made about as little sense as his pointing out some unfortunate young starlet's wide shoulders, lack of curves, and flat ass as *proof*. All it proved to Astra was the YouTuber had less knowledge about female anatomy than he had of biology. Not only had he obviously never been in a women's locker room and seen for himself the variety of female body types that actually exists, his research on the subject had been restricted to Victoria's Secret catalogues exclusively. Which pretty much makes Victoria's Secret the *true* deceivers. What did he think Victoria's secret was?

Besides, acting is, by its very definition, deceiving. If every grifter in America had to go through a sex change operation in order to deceive their mark, even third-rate strip mall plastic surgeons in America would be listed in Fortune among the top billionaires in the nation. Especially considering con artists far outnumber Hollywood celebrities.

The more she thought about it, the more Astra was certain what the whole point really was of trying to convince the world *ALL* of Hollywood is deceiving the public. It serves to increase the chance that more people will dismiss the one thing Americans have in common: a shared popular culture. Whether music, movies, or even television, encouraging us to see our own culture as untrustworthy and without any merit whatsoever sure seemed to be the point. And to Astra, it seemed pretty obvious someone was working hard to make sure nobody found any common ground on which to meet.

Why would anyone want to deceive a population like that? There was only one conclusion Astra could reach after close examination. For the same reason they would take possession of it and manipulate it into misrepresenting that which is at the heart of that society: to divide us. Because anyone who's read the *Art of War* knows we can't stand strong against an invading force if we're divided against ourselves.

Which means it isn't the performers and the creatives who need to be investigated; it's the puppet masters pulling the strings, and their tools, the YouTube evangelicals pointing their cameras in the wrong direction. Especially since much of it appeared to be targeting the kids growing up with those celebrities representing their culture. And as already established, Astra Talitha had a soft spot where kids were concerned. Messing with them was not a thing she would ever take lightly.

She was always grateful when Samara would eventually return to the original topic without any prompting. Or hitting any napping squirrels. It made Astra's job of steering the runaway conversation away from the cliffs much easier.

"Haven't you wondered why there's been such a concentration of movies, comic books and television programs featuring characters in ancient Greek and Roman mythology over the past few decades? And let's not forget the Mesoamerican deities, like Quetzalcoatl. They were all extraterrestrials claiming to be gods. But none of them were the Divine." she would say, sometimes through a mouthful of steamed kohlrabi greens she'd brought over with some red quinoa and kombucha.

Samara had easily fallen into the role of surrogate mother to Astra's surrogate alien investigator. And the work of getting that business off the ground had left Astra at great risk of losing booty points in the Bootylicious Galaxy. Samara had taken to doing her best to not let the Booty People down by feeding Astra the best she knew how. If by *best*, and by *feeding*, one means forcing incomprehensible food choices on another unsuspecting person.

"To sum it all up," she would finally conclude, "the whole point of *predictive programming* is to help those programmed to *activate* at this time begin that process. And along with prophecy, to ease the information into the collective subconscious that those *gods* were never meant to be seen as fictional. They were as real as the stupid hygiene necessary to maintain the cumbersome meat suits we're born into."

"We're made of meat?" Astra had said through a mouth of *that which cannot be swallowed* the first time Samara phrased it like that. She was however being deliberately obtuse while simultaneously wondering how the quinoa and kohlrabi greens would taste in a Chinese sticky bun swimming in sweet brown gravy. She even tried valiantly to force it down with a mouthful or two of kombucha, but it only made her nostalgic for Boston's refreshing absence of hipster fad foods. Which of course made her think of David.

Astra had reached the point we all do after a fat suit microwave-induced break-up where chasing away thoughts of a *pointless scammer* by any means possible becomes the only suitable course of action. Hence her wishing her philosophically confused neighbor might sometime bring her the kind of kombucha that had fermented a little longer. That little bit of alcohol might help. A lot of it might help a lot.

The thought seemed to be preternatural, because the next caller had obviously been up late drunk-dialing and called just to ramble incomprehensibly about energy. And Astra couldn't be more relieved. She'd had more than she could take of the delusional systems of conspiracy theorists who would be much better off just getting a damned job.

"So get this, dude," the voice said, leading Astra to wonder if he was calling from Southern California. "If all of existence is really just pure energy and this body and the matter all around us is nothing more than energy working to maintain the illusion of matter, then our natural state is pure energy, right?"

Astra considered asking the caller just what strain of the devil weed the stoners out in California were smoking, and chuckled at the absurdity of his rambling nonsense. Looking down at the empty kombucha bottle, she wondered if those freaks out there would start producing cannabis kombucha now that the devil weed was legal in the Golden State.

"Wouldn't that mean we are *all* artificial life forms, dude?" The stoner continued to ramble, reminding Astra of the anchor women at Disinfaux News. Mention of artificial life forms tends to do that with most pragmatists. "I mean, think about it. If energy is working overtime to create the illusion of these bodies being real, it would mean we're like, totally artificial, dude. We think we're an intelligent species, and scientists are working on creating artificial intelligence, but what's the point? We're already artificial intelligence! Why create an even more artificial intelligence when we haven't figured out how to use the artificial intelligence we've already got, dude? You feel me?"

Astra had to admit the stoner had an interesting point. It would explain the origin story of the women at Disinfaux News, at the very least. The thing about following stoner logic is to always pack a lunch because it involves a lot of wandering around lost before getting to the point. Most people find they need to replenish all the calories burned along the way long before the stoner reaches anything remotely resembling a point. Astra was glad she'd eaten, but still wished Samara's kombucha had a little alcohol in it.

"And get this: Elon Musk seems to be telling everyone we're being converted from carbon-based life forms to silicone-based. Doesn't that just blow your mind, dude? Dude, you totally gotta watch that YouTube video of him talking about how we're being genetically modified to actually *turn us into Artificial Intelligence*. He explains how the implants are being delivered to hijack the limbic system, dude. They're in the *CHEMTRAILS*! Seriously, dude; how do you think they got so many people to vote for Donald Trump?"

Astra decided to forward that particular message to her cell phone so she could listen to it on those days when she needed a good laugh. The only way she was going to get high in her current identity was through osmosis. She was pretty sure Elon Musk's thoughts were occupied with more important things than appearing in YouTube videos confirming conspiracy theories. Things like whether there was any chance of finding a good risk retention group in El Segundo to cover the massive losses his various projects had been incurring.

Her thoughts wandered to Elon Musk colonizing the Moon as she turned off the desk lamp and crossed the room to pull down the shade on the glass front door. As a familiar figure stepped out of the shadows across the street, she scolded herself for not pulling it down earlier. Anyone could be watching her. She wasn't a woman who frightened easily. Or at all. But being frightened and being creeped out were two different things. And the thought of someone hiding under cover of darkness, watching her from the shadows, definitely qualified as one of those things that creeped her out.

Especially when she realized why she recognized the figure in the dark. As he stepped into the light of the street lamp and lifted his fedora, Astra realized she was looking into the same face she had now seen twice before.

Astra Talitha was looking at the face of the Tall Man.

# CHAPTER TEN

Astra hadn't slept. The ceiling fan was whispering something incomprehensible to her. It seemed imperative she understand. After standing in the dark, locked in a staring contest with the Tall Man for what seemed an eternity, she got the impression she must have levitated to her bed without any memory of it. And just as mysteriously, she found herself staring up at the ceiling fan above her bed. She wasn't sure why, but she suspected the fan had something to do with her thinking about fat suits for tall people. It was at that point she realized the sun was up.

Without Chinatown and pulled-pork sticky buns to build her morning routine around, Astra had struggled to fill in the blanks with anything new other than the usual ritual of warming some cold brewed coffee and pouring it into her commuter cup. Which she took with her when she commuted in light traffic the exhausting thirty feet from the kitchen to the front door of *Alien Investigations*. Where she half expected to see the Tall Man standing across the street tipping his fedora at her.

Instead she was surprised to find a vampire standing at the door. Weeping. As she had no idea vampires were capable of producing tears, Astra let him in out of curiosity. Before the flow of tears could stop, however, she handed him a napkin to wipe them with, hoping to collect some DNA. Because every investigator knows how to get tears tested for DNA. Except Astra Talitha, who was only pretending to be an investigator. She was an optimist, however. An optimist who hoped Samara might know how to get it done.

"I want to go back to my home planet to be with my people," the sallow-skinned, gaunt young vampire sobbed.

It's important to note that at the time Astra Talitha had no idea just how she knew he was a vampire. She just knew. This was due, in part, to her also not knowing why she'd been so forgetful since leaving Boston. The homesick alien continued without noticing that the attention of the woman pretending to be an investigator had wandered. He was to be forgiven for not noticing. Failure to forgive a vampire can be a serious offense in certain parts of the galaxy, including this part. The reason for that has a lot to do with *drama queens*, which Astra was about to learn.

"You humans are so disconnected from each other you don't know how to bridge the gap between you that's created by your illusions," he blurted. "There's nothing mutual that's actually *shared* between you. It's all take, take, take. No mutually joyful embrace launching you into astral orbit."

"Wait," Astra interrupted. "Astral travel? That's a real thing?" She'd seen so many arguments break out in the comments section of YouTube videos about astral projection when doing her research; she wasn't sure which side the argument finally came down on. Of course, the New Agers believed in it whole-heartedly, while an equally emphatic group more inclined toward the kind of storytelling that leads to Hollywood movies insisted it was little more than demonic mind manipulation. Or worse, the Illuminati.

"Of course astral travel is a real thing," the weepy alien replied, a bit puzzled that an alien investigator wouldn't know something so basic. "Where do you think Van Gogh saw all those things he came home and painted? Ever see the Juno Cam shot of Jupiter? It was his favorite vacation spot."

He continued with what he was telling her, despite Astra's silent prayer that he not. She had started thinking he was less like an ancient alien vampire and more like an ancient alien evangelical wanting to share the *good news*. About astral projection, for some reason.

"You people don't know how to obtain a full and mutual completion of any kind of blissful union – which anyone outside this planet's orbit will tell you is what sends you to the heart of the galaxy. All there is here is just hopeless meaningless taking that has no joy in it."

Astra realized she was wrong about him being an ancient alien evangelical. He was more like an ancient alien restaurateur, considering how rare it is for vampires to serve word salad to just anyone. What he was saying was so thrown together it didn't need any dressing. Maybe a nice squeeze of lemon and some sea salt wouldn't hurt, but that should be left up to the vampire eating it to decide.

Her thoughts had wandered to food. Samara's

contribution to her booty points had begun to wear off. So naturally, they went right to what she might have in her fridge. And abruptly snapped back to attention. Which is really not that unusual when a human realizes a homesick vampire might be talking about *sex*.

That's how it is with humans. Sex is the most effective attention-getting device of all time. And as devices go, there is no device more useful than a word. Especially a word with the power of *sex*. As anyone will tell you, any mention of *sex* can easily cause a train to derail. Which explains why commuter trains post signs showing the universal symbol for sex with a red slash through it. Not to discourage the actual *act* of sex, but to discourage the word itself.

Planes routinely fall out of the sky if the word *sex* manages to make it into the cockpit, or even the pilot's headphones. Small children immediately succumb to lustful thoughts upon overhearing the word for the first time, causing them to seduce helpless grown men, who are tainted forever for giving in to their own weakness. Public schools had to stop teaching *sex education* due to too many teachers being whipped into a libidinous frenzy by the word and seducing their students.

This is the reason the word *sex* is taboo. Some are content that cultural control over the word is enough to keep its diseased self from spreading. But there are those whose thought patterns have been manipulated by certain negative alien entities. And they still work tirelessly to legislate the word out of existence.

For them, the eventual cloning of humans as a means of reproduction is the only way to put that ugly word into the past forever. In fact, the anti-science movement has nothing to do with the climate, or vaccines, or the highly suspicious use of carbon dating to determine how old the earth is. For those afflicted with negative alien thought patterns, it has to do with a shamefully unacceptable term used in the field of biology: *sexual reproduction.* The thought control they're under has conditioned them to disapprove of that term and insist science itself needs to be punished.

It's a little known fact that vampires are not only ancient aliens, but they don't actually consume blood at all. Which is contrary to the misguided belief perpetuated by popular culture that vampires live on blood and turn people into vampires by biting them. Vampires live on the energy they suck out of people. Which admittedly will turn a person into an energy vampire, but not an ancient alien energy vampire. Just a regular old human energy vampire from Earth.

Their primary imperative from that point on is to suck the life force out of any room they walk into. Unless there are no people in the room, wherein they proceed to whine about how much it sucks that there's no one there to suck the life out of. Popular culture likes to call them *drama queens.* But unlike alien vampires, human vampires aren't immortal. They only seem that way to those around them because that's how drama queens are. No matter how much people wish they would just go away, they seem to stick around forever. So does their drama.

Ninety percent of human DNA is what scientists call "junk DNA." They can see no useful purpose for it. But that's only because they're not looking at it with the right equipment. Even if they were looking at it with the right equipment they wouldn't recognize what they were looking at without a frame of reference. The immortality gene is yet another perfect example of that which is so foreign it's alien. It's completely unrecognizable until it's activated.

It isn't uncommon for an alien's soul to be sent here when his host body is born, but his DNA is never activated until he's either an adolescent or goes into politics. Both adolescents and most politicians are so similar in their lack of maturity they're interchangeable. But alien vampires slated to go into politics can easily be identified by their attraction to shiny things. Including hair and skin care products.

Each time a vampire reincarnates he has to retrace his steps in order to recover the memories of his previous lives. Knowledge is power, and the vampire's power is in his knowledge of who and what he is. And it takes some maturity to grow into recovering that knowledge. It's a process that takes time. Usually, by adolescence the young vampire has matured enough to begin showing signs he's ready for his *activation*. It's the activation of that "junk DNA" that leads the vampire to his *awakening*. That process leads him to fully embracing his origin story and complete knowledge of his purpose.

The process, however, can be so destabilizing it can drive a young vampire back into a state of not remembering and not even suspecting there's anything *to* remember. In the worst cases, the vampire lives out his days on this earth not knowing a thing about who and what he actually is. Not even where he's from. It is the ultimate memory disorder: *Intergalactic Full Retrograde Amnesia*.

Once the amnestic alien's purpose for existing gets sunk in the inescapable quicksand of superficial knee jerk reactions to his *activation*, he has nothing but the residue of those reactions to reflect on. And trying to extrapolate meaning out of the superficial is almost as frustrating as trying to hold still while sinking in quicksand. Or getting mired in trying to solve the mystery behind the *Georgia Guide Stones*.

Or worse, as frustrating as trying to make sense of lyrics to an alt-J song. It may sound lovely, but what does it mean? Puzzles like these can be counterproductive. Often they only root us in little more than an unending puzzle stretched and twisted into an infinity symbol.

The most powerful memory that emerges during the *activation* phase of one's *awakening* is sexual. There's a reason for this. In order to fully restore the memories from his previous incarnations, the young vampire must travel to the heart of the galaxy he's in, where the data is stored. But he cannot do it alone. And there is only one means of transport that will get him there: *Sex.*

According to what the weepy vampire was telling her, only by two willing partners being fully engulfed in the flames of passion is anyone able to travel to the heart of the galaxy to retrieve the stored memories and fully activate the process of reclaiming their own origin story. Thus begins their *awakening*.

Astra was pretty sure this was one of the primary motives behind the CIA's Project Artichoke, which uses drugs and hypnosis to keep the subject in an induced state of amnesia. Perhaps this explained why a large chunk of the American population was forgetting history and making the same mistakes in the voting booth again and again and again.

"Nobody on this planet knows anything about their origin," he continued, gulping air between sobs so the words were forced out in little carbon dioxide-generated explosions. "Your sick agents of control buried the story under a mountain of conditioned shaming and dogma just so they could keep their jobs as sick agents of control. And you guys let them do it."

Astra wasn't entirely sure she really had a part in any of it. It seemed to her it was that way when she got here. But her own compassion for the apparently sex-obsessed vampire with a memory disorder prevented her from interjecting that argument into his stream of emoting.

"You let outside parties interested in your resources *only* manipulate you by grabbing the human race by the short hairs thousands of years ago. And now none of you knows who you are or what the purpose of your sexuality actually is. You're so clueless about your purpose in life you actually think existentialism is a form of mind control!"

Astra had to admit, the emo vampire had a valid point. People were always confusing existentialism with some UFO cult. And many were mistakenly showing up at Langley with all of their belongings in a duffel bag hoping to become an acolyte of the CIA. The CIA had been forced to put up a sign at the front door which read, *"We don't want your useless shit. Give it to some third rate science fiction writer's heirs or throw it down a volcano, but don't leave it here. Violators will be prosecuted and subjected to a free personality test.*

"And it's contributed to bringing the resonant frequency of the entire planet down so low it just attracts more energy vampires. And none of the ones who come here are like me!"

She was just about to interject that not too long ago she'd been introduced to taking an astral journey on something that sounded a lot like what he was describing. Only, David called it the *Merkabah*. And she'd be lying if she didn't admit if felt like the two of them left Earth's orbit for a while there. But if she'd managed to retrieve any data, she had no memory of it when they landed back down on the floor of their little apartment. Curiously, she did have the urge to watch the movie *Pi*. And neither the urge nor the movie made any sense to her.

"It sucks here. I hate it and I want to go home. The only reason I even know where home *is* was a stroke of pure luck."

Astra's luscious booty instinctively slid forward in her chair. If he had a stroke of pure luck, there may be a great *sex* story in it. She *was* human, after all. Just the implication that the word *sex* may be buried in a story somewhere is all it takes to capture that attention the word so desperately needs in order to stay alive. The vampire she had decided to call *Emo* continued, to her delight. Her sick, salacious delight.

"It was all because of this divine girl I met at band camp. I'm pretty sure she was Lyran. She called herself Lyra. Tall, thin, pale, and as most Lyrans, she wore her ginger hair down to her waist. She was unquestionably feline. Lyra was the epitome of the classic Lyran female, yet I was the only kid in high school band with the ability to recognize her for what she was. She was my Angel of Mercy. We went to the heart of the galaxy together and retrieved our records, on nothing more than the strength of our mutual bliss. It was Divine. The odd thing is: It was as if she'd known the way there her whole life, even though it was the first time there for both of us."

Emo had started sobbing again and Astra's booty sighed as she slid back in the chair and gently put her hand on his shoulder.

"How can I help?"

It was a simple question, but perhaps the most important phrase in the English language. That's how it is with things that are simple in their complexity. Its simplicity belies its status as dangerous revolutionary, forced underground long ago to escape persecution by Western Civilization and its extraterrestrial handlers for existing. That's how it is with revolutionaries.

We often dismiss that which appears simple, thinking it's inadequate to handle the task at hand. Paradoxically, we tend to both gravitate toward and distrust that which is simple. How many presidents did it take for Americans to finally trust a simpleton enough to put him in the White House, for instance? Or worse, we fear it may seem weak to offer a simple yet profoundly comforting question to someone who is obviously not in any condition to articulate what they need.

"It's been so many years since that summer, I've lost track of my Lyra," Emo wailed. "And every attempt to recreate that connection to the Divine I need in order to get the directions home have only rooted me more and more in the physical. I'm afraid if I let much more of that kind of energy in, I'll close off my ability to connect at all and NEVER find my way home!!!"

His sobs created a sonic wave that matched the percussion of a bass drum in that high school band he remembered so fondly. Astra followed the energy trails as they left his mouth and charged the windows with determined force, rattling the sign out front and tickling the wind chime in the doorway. She silently hoped it would stay away from the desktop gong.

She grasped what he was saying with little effort. David was the only man with whom she had ever experienced the sense that they were lifting off from their little bed on the floor of their Beacon Hill apartment and leaving Earth's orbit. She could recall little more than faint traces of the sensation. It began with the sound of what she thought was most similar to massive engines creating percussive waves that beat persistently against her ear drums as they embraced. It was a sound she both did and did not recognize, remembered from some ancient memory bleeding through the dimensions. Beyond that sound she could remember little more than the sense that in their mutual embrace they both had been observed and blessed by some massive benign omniscience at the center of All That Is.

If she understood what Emo was saying, recovering *all* of one's data involved repeated astral journeys to the heart of the galaxy. Perhaps even throughout one's lifetime. Are those who are resolute and calm in the face of impending death the ones who continue to retrieve their data right up to the end of that life cycle? Is the information necessary to make the transition from this physical existence back into pure spirit only provided at the very end? If so, wouldn't that mean those who make a peaceful transition have continued to connect completely with another right up to the very end?

"Okay, now I'm thinking about old people sex and it's creeping me out," she said under her breath as she tried desperately to wave the thought away. Even the squirrel didn't want that one. At the very least, getting it to go in the other room and play with the ceiling fan would reduce her discomfort.

Despite her aversion to thinking about old people sex, Astra certainly knew how rare the kind of connection between people Emo was talking about actually is. While she was only just beginning to acquire the language with which to wrap her head around it, the *Sexual Celestial* was probably right. According to what she was learning in her research, Earthlings had long since come under the control of agents who knew just what profits there are to be made in that kind of interference.

At some point, they realized as long as the human race had the ability to remember their origin story they would not be able to manipulate humans into building their pyramids and erecting their stone columns and mining the gemstones and metals and other natural resources they lusted after. By cutting out the middleman and achieving the empowerment that can only come from knowledge, it wouldn't be possible for them to enslave the human race. And humans were the cheapest forced labor in the galaxy.

She had a sense it would be pointless to ask Emo if he had loved his little Lyran. Of course he did. That kind of connection can't be completed if both parties haven't fully opened their hearts to love itself. And of course, the thought-manipulation employed by those agents of control had made sure to confuse love with sex and sex with sin and sin with moral dogma and moral dogma with the very confusing superstitious beliefs they had implanted. The word *love* had long ago tragically morphed in the hands of those agents of control over the thousands of years they had worked to subvert the human race and mold it into something they could use against it.

The examples that came to mind were violent protests by certain thought-controlled groups against two people marrying, because some people aren't supposed to love certain types of people. Or if they do, they most certainly aren't supposed to use that love to launch the two of them into the heart of the galaxy. Which when added up using the same calculator those agents of control used, equaled polarization.

It takes abstract thinking to understand the purpose of metaphor. And it takes critical thinking to know when to apply abstract thinking. And it takes an agent of control to capitalize on the part of the population unable to do either as a result of their mind-manipulation. And nothing delighted those agents of control more than observing their handiwork carried out by the polarizing extremists they created. They'd make their own intergalactic version of popcorn after a long exhausting week of polarizing and pass it around while laughing hysterically at delusional humans calling for the death of one type of person after another while shouting praises to their deity.

And for added hilarity, they'd whisper in the auditory cortex of one religion's devout that the *real* problem is the other religion's devout, while telling some entirely different religion's devout that *they* are the only ones who've got it right. The good times never stopped for the agents of control. Whatever corruption they were able to convince human beings was justifiable always managed to deliver a five-star rating on the entertainment charts. And fill collection plates to overflowing.

It's not hard to see how, at some point along the way, Astra had become convinced that most people had no idea what love is. Not even what its purpose is. To the rational mind, wrapping the kind of conflicting and unhealthy beliefs she now suspected were created by colonizing extraterrestrials around love, sex and all manner of human interaction is irrational. It produces nothing but deviance. And not the fun kind of deviance that amasses large collections of ornate women's shoes in size thirteen. Deviance like that belongs in the FBI. The kind of deviance that's created by negative thought patterns is destructive to the human race. Because it's clearly detrimental to emotional, intellectual and spiritual growth.

When we suppress that which is healthy and natural it only emerges elsewhere in a deviant form. And the deviance that comes from that recipe rips into the very fabric of our collective soul. The sweet nothings that get whispered into the auditory cortex by control agents get less and less alien over time. And they ensure that rip will never be repaired. The untreated wound is essential to the agenda of certain negative alien entities that have ensured the human race is too busy arguing over beliefs to even notice they are here intervening in our belief systems on behalf of that agenda.

Because when that shiny wrapping paper all of it is rolled up in is produced from meaningless promises whispered into the ear of those most susceptible to suspension of disbelief, it's more than irrational. It's evil. It's programming humans to do the work *for* the agents of control. Who then come in after the *love bombs* explode with their salad forks in hand, and feast on the spoils of war their puppets don't even realize they've waged on love itself.

What the emo vampire was telling her was the first time anyone had articulated for Astra just what the potential was for all of us to be holding hands and singing songs together so we don't feel so alone on this great big spinning rock.

"No wonder none of us knows who we are," she said under her breath. "We've forgotten, and they're not letting us get to a place where we can begin to remember. I always wondered why there seemed to be so much effort made to keep us at odds with each other. The human race is living with an induced case of amnesia."

But once again Astra had let her attention wander in the middle of a conversation. She had asked the emo vampire how she could help. Or had she?

"Did I already ask how I could help?" she said, grinning sheepishly.

"You can do two things," he said, his eyes suddenly clearing to a perfect obsidian mirroring the morning light. If he had even noticed her lapse in attention, he was far too polite to say so. Proving yet again he was no *drama queen*. "You can look for my Lyra. And if you can't find her, you can help me find a human who hasn't been so contaminated with shame and abusive cultural programming they're permanently blocked from making that connection and riding the astral plane to retrieve their own data."

Two thoughts occurred to Astra simultaneously. Those astral trips she and David had been taking in their love bed might very well have something to do with much of what she'd experienced in recent weeks. And promptly forgotten. More importantly, she was pretty sure her first client was basically asking her to help get him laid.

"What's it worth to you?" she asked.

"How much do you know about the value of rare earth metals?" the vampire replied.

Astra wondered if she still had that account on Craigslist. She could run an ad on it, if she did. She'd opened it when she was running a scam on lonely men looking for women of financial substance who like sex. They always managed to see through her con, however, and call her on it. Largely because it's quite rare for a woman to amass substantial wealth on her own without losing her taste for sex altogether. That's how it is when you have to leverage something so precious for something so pointless without knowing why you're even here on this planet in the first place.

If you were told you had to lose the address to the place you knew as home and forget everything about it, including how to get there, in exchange for a lifetime of shiny things that you'd never be able to take back home with you even if you did know the directions, would you do it? Would you do it if you were told you'd get to experience unlimited physical pleasure completely devoid of any meaning other than the physical sensation itself?

That's the problem with the narcissism of empty pleasure and shiny things, which the Reptilians and their sentries know full well. Just as the immaturity of adolescents and politicians makes the two interchangeable, physical pleasure and shiny things can be equally interchangeable when considering that which is shallow, one dimensional, and of little real value. It's ultimately unrewarding. Even a man seeing his own reflection in the shiny things he's surrounded himself with can't trade any of it for a trip to the heart of the galaxy.

Although in defense of adolescents, they aren't nearly as heartbreaking as the emptiness of the other three. Politicians, empty physical pleasure, and shiny things are in a league of their own. Adolescents are to be forgiven for their awkwardness as they stumble through the loveless territory they need to in order to find their way back to the home they don't remember ever having, where all their most precious memories are stored. Without knowing what they've forgotten, most of them don't even remember being loved, not even in this incarnation. That kind of thing can make anyone appear awkward to those who have no memory of it themselves.

That said, Astra found the thought of acquiring rare earth metals highly attractive. Girls will be girls, after all. And where Astra came from, girls just want to have funds. Especially girls who are con artists.

"I'm hungry," Astra said, the lack of pulled-pork sticky buns announcing the vacancy it left in her stomach loudly. "Are you hungry? Can I interest you in a nice big salad?"

# CHAPTER ELEVEN

It wasn't until a black-leather-clad dominatrix kicked in the front door and stood snapping her whip against thigh-high spike-heeled boots that Astra began to suspect she'd woken up on the sideways side of the bed. But before that moment, everything about the morning seemed to be perfectly normal. If by normal one means *littered with an alien bounty hunter and a woman of such watery depth Astra realized for the first time she needed to buy a snorkel just to be on the safe side.*

But the dominatrix was not the first thing about Astra's day that was so foreign it was alien. The first sideways thing about her day was the responses she found in her inbox from the Craigslist ad she'd placed the day before. They were not what she expected. All of them were enthusiastically offering their help with Astra's client, the sex-starved energy vampire. It seemed Astra had been the last woman on Earth to discover energy vampires existed. The replies she got showed such thorough familiarity with them she was embarrassed for how little she'd known just the day before.

And all of them claimed to be *drama queens.* Drama queens in recovery. Which Astra thought would be a great name for a rock band. They could tour with a Queen cover band and perform the soundtrack to *Hedwig and the Angry Inch.* Astra could see Freddy Mercury's spirit riding shotgun with her to see their show, scolding her to slow down and keep herself alive.

She promised herself she would consider inquiring about just what it is all those *drama queens* were recovering from when she had some down-time to consider the repercussions of asking a *drama queen* a question. Especially a simple question. It seemed to Astra that Emo the energy vampire had indicated the state of being a *drama queen* was a permanent condition. Wouldn't recovering from a permanent condition basically mean *no longer living?*

The second so foreign it was alien thing about the day sauntered through the door just moments after she'd pulled up the shade hanging on it and turned on the pink neon UFO sign. She was remarking to herself how much she still liked the statement it made over the standard *open* sign when her morning went to the dogs. Both figuratively and literally.

If you've ever looked up at the night sky and noticed a star so bright you wondered which planet it was, odds are it was the planet Sirius, or *Dog Star.* The brightest star in the sky. It can easily be spotted in the constellation Canis Major, which forms the perfect outline of a dog. Trace around it on a star map with a Sharpie some time and you'll see it. It looks like a dachshund. Which might seem odd until you consider how mean little dogs can be. Especially dachshunds.

The planet Dog Star is no different. Or to be more specific, Sirius-B, the twin, white dwarf star in the same bow-shaped orbit as it's more gentle-natured, less-evil twin, Sirius-A. It was the poor temper of the people of Sirius-B that gave the planet its nickname, not the shape of the constellation. The constellation was put there as a warning for anyone considering visiting Sirius B. It's the Universal symbol for: *WARNING: DASCHUNDS*. Sirius-A had long since given up arguing with Sirius-B about changing the constellation to something more suitable to *both* planets.

It wasn't so much Astra was surprised to be meeting Dog Star the Intergalactic Bounty Hunter; it was his complete lack of self-knowledge. Especially considering his understanding of his home planet's origins and the workings of the Universe. She was just glad he didn't show up the day before when Emo was there. A man as mean as Dog Star the Bounty Hunter was bound to startle the sex-starved vampire struggling with a memory disorder and a broken heart.

"Need your help, little Missy," he said, tipping but not removing his cowboy hat as he sauntered into her office. "Name's Dog Star. Dog Star, the Intergalactic Bounty Hunter."

Astra was just sitting back down to finish the last of her cold brewed coffee while she watched the YouTube video of herself and a blinding light in a flying Pinto once again. Her actual recollection of the event was muted, as if she was trying to scratch a mosquito bite through a thick layer of denim. She kept hoping if she watched it enough times the actual memory of it would be as vivid as the video was. She also jotted down something she needed to ask Emo

the next time they spoke: *Are memory disorders contagious?*
*Can you catch them like you'd catch a cold or TB on a Greyhound*
*bus?*

"I'll cut to the chase. When I heard you were running
an alien investigation agency out of Sedona, I knew you
were just the gal I wanted to meet."

Astra couldn't say she felt the same about meeting
him. Men who call her *Missy* and saunter while tipping but
failing to fully remove their cowboy hats when they're in her
office were not the kind of men Astra Talitha wanted to
meet. Worse than con artists, men like Dog Star actually
believe their persona. They've fallen so far down the rabbit
hole with the identity they've groomed themselves to
project; they actually believe that's who and what they *are*.

Pragmatists like Astra, even pragmatic con artists,
know full well there's a reason we're called human *beings*
and not human *doings*. But no matter how many times they
point it out to bounty hunters like Dog Star, the dystopian
Marlboro Men always fail to get the point.

"How about you and me work something out where
you give me a heads-up whenever one of my fugitives
comes your way? I can make it worth your while, if you
know what I mean, sweet thing. Gal like you with an ass like
that can go places."

She was not surprised at all, but deeply dismayed
nonetheless, to see Sirius-B was just as backwards as Earth in
its adherence to an erroneous belief system regarding male
dominion over the female of the species. It was frustrating
enough to navigate Earth's cultural stranglehold over female
sovereignty. Learning the male half of the population had
crowned men the rightful arbiters of female sexuality on

another planet was downright disheartening to Astra. It meant that even when engaging with extraterrestrials she would have to stay on her toes.

For the newly ordained alien investigator, stepping around the messes left in the wake of Earth's dominant species was something she'd always seen as entirely avoidable. All of it could be easily overcome if the dominionists would just choose to develop some emotional intelligence. Even a little bit would help. But sadly, she realized there was absolutely no motivation for it. After all, what's not to love about feeling it's their place to employ a liberal use of sexual innuendo in any conversation with a female of their choosing? After all, wasn't that the whole point of having a conversation with a female?

If only the people of Sirius-B could have developed the level of emotional intelligence of its more multicultural twin. Sadly, it was obvious to Astra the dwarf star had developed a similar love of subjecting those considered *inferior* to servitude, aka *slavery,* as Earthlings had. What's worse, Astra's keenly sharpened dog shit detector told her Dog Star the Intergalactic Bounty Hunter was a believer in *all* forms of slavery, just like Earth's humans. And not just the kind involving fugitives from intergalactic justice.

It wouldn't surprise her at all to learn Sirius-B had come up with as many reasons to arrest and enslave its people as Earth's slave traders had. She wondered if the prisons and private detention centers on his planet were at least progressive enough to call them what they really were: *rape camps.*

"Right now I'm on the trail of a man who skipped bail while awaiting his deportation hearing, where there ain't no question he'll be sent back to his home planet."

Astra started to ask him if he'd tried Maricopa County. More than anything she wanted to dismiss him by explaining that alien investigators in Sedona don't roll that way. But she realized she needed clarification on something he'd just said.

"Wait. Why are immigrant detainees posting bail? Don't you have detention centers for that sort of thing on your planet, like we do?"

"No, on Sirius nobody needs to get their kicks raping detainees," he replied with a casual shrug. Astra wondered if rape was just too touchy-feely for the mean-spirited people of Sirius-B. She thought briefly about making a pitch for fat suits to the mean spirited bounty hunter. She could market them as *rape suits;* perfect for putting a protective barrier between rapists and their prey. To protect the rapist, of course.

"They've come up with a better system for making money off those filthy immigrants; they collect bail and let 'em go. Most of the time they skip bail and either go into hiding or leave for Earth without realizing what they're in for if they do get caught and thrown into one of your profit-makin' detention camps. Just cause a whore house ain't called that don't mean it ain't makin' some pimp filthy rich, know what I mean?

You got some sick shit going on up in this house, little lady. How do you think the galaxy ended up with so many alien-human hybrids in such a short period of time? You humans sure do like your rape. And that whole *Right to Life* thing the Draconian Reptile Agenda made sure to implant in your feeble minds just keeps a good thing going, don't it? I mean, hell, just cause a kid ain't wanted by his mama don't mean some freak hopped up on Viagra can't get some good use out of him, am I right?"

Astra had to hand it to Dog Star. He'd managed to hit the nail right on the head. And he looked like he was about to do it again. The despicable bounty hunter was beginning to look around the floor for what Astra could only assume was a spittoon for the wad of whatever it was that was causing his right cheek to bulge at the jaw line. She was pretty sure it wasn't a jawbreaker. Those things are too sweet for a man as mean as Dog Star. Considering how badly-stained his teeth were, she concluded it had to be a wad of tobacco shoved into his cheek.

If anything could be said about Astra Talitha, it was that deductive reasoning was her greatest strength, even if it did take a lot of detours to get to whatever she ended up deducing.

"Neoliberalism, baby. That's the name of the game when it comes to these stinkin' aliens," he continued, oblivious to Astra staring at his cheek while her attention left the room for some tamales dulces. "Everywhere in the galaxy that ain't Earth knows it for what it actually is; a practical solution for how to acquire slaves without raising snowflake suspicion. Why do you think they inserted *liberal* in the word? The new liberalism is the same old outrageous conservative wolf behavior in a perennial sheep's clothing that it always was. Up is still up, and down is still down, and sexual slavery is still what it always was; the primary objective of the privileged elite and posers who wanna act like the rich and famous."

After her conversation with the vampire Emo, Astra

had little trouble believing it, but had to wonder if the problem was only pretending to be a *liberal vs conservative* one. It seemed to her it was an issue more likely related to something like the Draconian Reptile Agenda the emotional vampire mentioned. Some pretty aggressive puppet masters certainly did appear to be running the whole sideshow that is the human race. And they seemed to Astra to have a fondness for polarization.

"I'll tell you what," Astra finally said. "Why don't you go out onto the porch and spit that wad you've got in your cheek over the railing? And then keep going down the stairs. Get in your car and drive over to Maricopa County, where I'm sure you won't have any trouble finding Sheriff Arpaio's men. You boys have a lot in common. For one thing, they love hunting aliens. For another, instead of Christmas bonuses, they get rape vouchers for their detainee of choice. And from what I've heard, they don't even bother checking their papers, so the odds of finding some really young and juicy flesh to choose from are pretty good."

"Woman, I told you we don't roll that way where I come from." Dog Star argued. "This planet is the only one in the galaxy that hasn't figured out how *not* to bend over and let your authorities show you who's boss. And your peers, too. Where I come from, we've figured out how to think for ourselves."

"What does peer pressure and bending over for authority have to do with anything?" Astra demanded. Not only was she worried about the flooring getting Dog Star spit on it, she was beginning to worry the conversation might never end. The thought terrified her.

"Do you have any idea how easy it is to persuade you

humans to do something that is clearly against the laws governed by your own conscience?" he said, suddenly glaring down at Astra with disgust. The vein in his left temple visible just below the brim of his hat had begun to bulge as much as the wad of tobacco in his cheek. Astra shifted uncomfortably where she stood. But she held her ground. She had no choice.

"All it takes for most of you is to be told by someone in authority to do a thing and hoo-boy you puny little sheep just hop to it. You think your military boot camp is meant to teach soldiers a fuckin' thing about the *art of war*? Hell no! It's to teach them to obey authority above all else; to do what their commanders tell them to do – no matter what. Very few Earth humans have the ability to defy an order from their superior that is clearly in violation of their moral code.

And it ain't much different among peers. Anyone perceived to be even the slightest bit higher in status than the others in his peer group can tell them to rob an old lady and set her on fire, and even those raised by their mamas to know better will comply. Where I come from, we call that the *Milgram Effect*. Your own so-called *social psychologists* have laid it all out plain as day for you. Hell, even an old bounty hunter like me can understand it, but you Earth humans just *refuse* to learn. The only time you demand the right to think for yourself is when you're defending your right to *not* learn something that will benefit all of mankind."

"Like what?" Astra demanded, not sure why she was even still participating in the conversation.

"Like not rapin' anybody!" The bounty hunter shouted. "Instead of teaching your sons *not* to do it, you teach your daughters it's all their fault and to be ashamed of themselves when they get raped! Hell, even when it's your boys and men getting raped, you set it up so they feel too ashamed to say or do a damned thing about it! When your wimmen-folk in the military get raped by their fellow soldiers, you say "Well what do you expect – boys will be boys – then you completely ignore the fact that three times as many men in the military are raped by their fellow male soldiers! And by clouding the whole issue you *never* manage to get around to discussing female sexual aggression, so just go on pretending it don't even exist! What kind of fucked up shit is that?"

The extraterrestrial bounty hunter had worked himself into such a heated rage Astra realized for the first time she'd neglected to get a fire extinguisher for the office. She also realized she'd neglected to find out if the people from Sirius-B were prone to spontaneous combustion. The grifter was just beginning to figure out the life of a fake alien investigator was more complicated than she'd imagined.

And just like that, the conversation was over. Dog Star turned to leave with his rage and yanked the office door open. Astra insisted he leave it open. It would take some effort to get the smell of his contempt for both Earthlings and personal sovereignty out of her office. She was preoccupied with opening the windows and getting the ceiling fans in both the hallway and above her desk spinning at maximum speed when she realized she wasn't alone. Her heart lodged in her esophagus briefly as she turned, half expecting to see the Tall Man standing behind her.

Instead, Astra found a tall woman. She was thin, with the jet black hair of a bona fide jaguar cascading down her back. It framed the most narrow, beautiful face she had ever seen. A face of perfect alabaster framed in the blackest black.

"My name is El," she said as she uncurled the longest, most impossibly thin fingers. It was like watching a cat wake from a nap and uncurl itself one paw at a time. Astra knew she was unquestionably in the presence of an alien, but to her it felt more like she was in the presence of the Divine.

"El?" She said, stumbling over the loss of words that suddenly gripped her.

"It's the phonetic pronunciation of the letter L, not the word El, which I understand has certain religious connotations for you humans."

"Religious?" Astra said, puzzled. She always thought it had more to do with some comic book character and his family name.

As their hands closed around each other's, Astra felt an instantaneous surge of vivid images laced with water and womb and heartbeat pulse through her. Muffled sounds from inside the *Heart Of All That Is* coursed up her auditory cortex as if it knew its way there by heart. It delivered forgotten words and images Astra embraced despite her urge to run from them. Snippets of a San Francisco poet's scribblings tickled at the back of her brain with vivid images of water and wind and flight, remembered words and even, briefly, the act of love.

At the same time, the image of that poet diving off the Golden Gate Bridge flashed through her visual cortex and the breaking of her heart was so visceral her knees began to buckle. Just as instantaneously it healed, stitched back together stronger than it had been before. She looked down at the hand of the mysterious woman half expecting to see it holding a golden needle threaded with gossamer.

"I am part of an organization that ensures the survival of any species that has failed to develop the emotional intelligence needed to avoid driving itself to the point of self-destruction. We can't have anyone destroying both their genetics *and* their planet. We're as concerned for the welfare of it as we are with the race itself."

"Why would it matter to anyone from *out there* if we did?" Astra said, despite herself. "It's a big Universe and we're just one pale blue dot. Find another one."

She seemed to have absorbed some of Dog Star's bad temper. Or perhaps it was just the usual case of a woman finally getting to say what she actually thinks as soon as the man walks out of the room.

"As for the survival of our genetics, have you looked at our genetics under a microscope lately? I'm pretty sure it's armed to the teeth, fully loaded with a *defend your ground* law and using it as justification to rape a child. And then run for a seat in the US Senate. All the while hitting its victim over the head with a Bible. While Disinfaux News defends it on broadcast television – while wearing a fat suit."

El wasn't saying a thing. Perhaps she was considering an appropriate response to someone just getting a visit from an alien bounty hunter out of their system. Or perhaps silence was yet another tool of alien voodoo mind control. Or perhaps she was just letting Astra vent. Astra suspected she must be from one of those all-female planets where they learned how to manage situations like this at a young age in a course called, *Compassion 101.* Taught by the undying spirit of Mister Rogers. But then another suspicion bumped that one out of position. Naturally, a man was behind it.

"Sounds like you've got a dog in this fight maybe. He

wouldn't by any chance be from Sirius, would he? Because that asshole needs a rabies shot. What planet did you say you were from?"

"One question at a time, sweet Astra," El said, her emerald eyes leaving traces of their spoor around the room. Quixotically, Astra was compelled to fall into those eyes and swim to the bottom while simultaneously chasing the spoor around the room with a butterfly net, hoping to capture enough to hang in a locket around her neck.

"To begin with, yours is one of the only sources of water in this sector. And secondly ….."

"Wait. In this sector? Wouldn't that be in *these sectors?* This *is* a multiverse, isn't it? Aren't there an infinite number of planets with water? Or at least one of them in each of the eleven dimensions?"

El just stared at her with those *Twenty Thousand Leagues Under the Sea* eyes, unblinking. Astra lost the staring contest when she couldn't hold her breath any longer. She made a mental note to invest in a snorkel if she was going to be dealing with many more aliens from wherever El was from.

"That is exactly the way humans have come to think," El replied. "The entire race failed to *activate* when triggered. Including the *Crystal* and *Indigo Children.*"

"Whoa hold on there," Astra said. "Wait, wait, wait, wait, wait. All this *Indigo* and *Crystal Children* is where the New Age people lost me. You're telling me that shit's real?"

"Jesus was an *Indigo*," she replied. Astra could just see the evangelicals on YouTube shouting the enigmatic extraterrestrial down with their self-importance when they got wind of this. "As were all of the prophets sent at that same time in history to help move the human race forward. It was during a time in Roman rule when over 150 of them were seeded into that area of the world in the hopes that the message of *Peace* and *Universal Love* might take root and grow. Most of them were either stoned to death or crucified. While being humiliated by onlookers. Much like your Disinfaux News and YouTube stars do today with their words."

"So you're saying the effectiveness of mind control has come a long way since the days of needing to physically kill someone who has a beneficial message for humankind," Astra interjected. It hadn't escaped her that shouting someone down over broadcast television while wearing a fat suit could be just as effective as stoning someone. It worked flawlessly to get the masses to drown out the voice of their target. Or manipulating that voice into self-destructive behavior. And was the primary reason Astra refused to own a television.

"Exactly," El replied. "We've sent other princes of peace your way, but the intelligence apparatus is always two steps ahead of us. They invariably find a way to silence their songs or poetry or vision. Just because their tools of silencing went from stones and crosses to drugs, fame or a bullet doesn't mean they aren't just as effective."

"So the message to give peace a chance written into a song pretty much puts a target on that messenger's back," Astra said. El just gave her that *Twenty Thousand Leagues Under the Sea* stare in response.

"The result is ..... this." El stretched both arms out, palms up, and looked left to right. Astra was pretty sure the enigmatic alien wasn't referring to the office of *Alien*

*Investigations*. Unless she was on to Astra's game and indicating the fleecing of witless marks who never bothered to learn how to manage their own suspension of disbelief.

"As a safeguard against just this sort of thing happening, when your race neared its *activation* phase we sent 800,000 *Star Seeds* to Earth to help facilitate your *awakening* once the *activation* had begun. It was routine; a standard operating procedure. But for the first time ever, eighty percent of *them* also failed to activate. So now we've got far more than a dog in the fight. We've got the most developed souls in the Universe locked inside human bodies strewn around the planet and can't locate them to bring them back home. Something is jamming their signal."

"Wait. Slow your roll there, Jewel Eyed Judy. What the hell is a *Star Seed*? Is that how stars are made; you plant them and they grow?"

El said nothing in response. The silence that followed her question took on a life of its own. It enveloped them in massive arms that seemed to be reaching them from the origin of silence itself. It went from object to object in the office, lingering in front of the *I Want to Believe* poster before inspecting the potted plant for mites. Astra didn't realize she wasn't breathing until the room abruptly went dark and a school of little pinpoint stars began to swim through the darkness enveloping her field of vision. She sat back down in her chair and promptly forgot the question she'd just asked.

"What's more, we're seeing quite a few *activations* of souls we didn't send here. We don't know who did. They've been groomed to carry out an agenda we know nothing about, but suspect the worst. The agonizing death of a planet can produce the kind of energy that one specific species is capable of thriving on for several millennia."

Astra had a good idea just which species El was referring to.

"Let me guess. Draconian-Reptilians?"

El's ocean eyes developed a sudden storm. Astra went from wishing she had a snorkel in the office to wishing she had an umbrella.

"Worse. Monarchians. Key players in the deadliest alliance in the Universe. The worst part is the *activated* are not programmed to conjoin with one another and retrieve their data, which would automatically open their heart chakra. They're designed to rise to positions of great wealth and power and then use that power to dedicate themselves to one thing only: degrade empathy in humanity. Their wealth and power make them irresistible to those who themselves have been targeted by the Monarchians and programmed to support and defend them at all cost."

"Sounds like a classic player to me, all right." Astra sighed. "How can I help?" For the second time in two days she found herself offering to give something she had no idea she had, confident she actually had it. And once again she found herself swimming in an ocean that was so familiar she could feel the astringent effects of its salt on her skin, while at the same time fully aware it was so foreign it was downright alien. She hoped it didn't mean she'd been a demonic mermaid in some previous life. She had it on good authority they can forget how to swim quite easily.

"But first, let me ask you a question. The exact reason you came to me with this problem is because?"

"My purpose is twofold," El replied. "One, I need

your help bringing our lost *Star Seeds* to us, including all the *Indigo* and *Crystals,* since their energy signatures are blocked. We can't go to them if we can't find them."

"We?" Astra said, one eyebrow reflexively arching.

"You've got the perfect set up here for bringing them to us. With that video of you in the flying Pinto going viral, followed by that ingenious ad you created, you've got everything set up perfectly to bring them right in. All we need is one more video."

El explained that when each *Star Seed* was sent here, aside from being programmed to activate at a certain time, they were also each accompanied by a guardian, or *watcher*. That guardian's task was to implant their charge with a set of triggers anchored to certain inputs they knew would occur in their timeline.

Here's the thing about time, as Astra had come to know it from the better conspiracy theorist websites: When time isn't linear, predicting the future isn't predicting a thing. It's the cheat sheet of predicting, or *predictive cheat sheeting.* Child's play for matchstick men. Mesmerizing for the necromancer, perhaps. But yawn-worthy for anyone who understands how relatively easy it is to access information both in the past and in the future.

The only thing difficult about accessing information in the future is wrapping your head around the fact that while you're doing it, the future isn't really there because it hasn't happened yet. It's only in the present that accurate information seems so hard to find yet relatively easy to comprehend once you've found it. Unless you're watching Disinfaux News or reading out of a Texas school book.

What El was saying was guardians knew enough

about each *Star Seed's* timeline to know details about their likes and dislikes as they grew into adulthood.

"Like what?" Astra said, curious. "Coke versus Pepsi? Battery operated versus manual?"

"Details such as exactly what Musketeer would be their favorite when they were young," El replied, which threw Astra such a curve ball it became a squirrel her attention instantly chased after, almost missing the rest of the conversation. "Making anchoring a fixation with *fat suits* emerge when triggered at the time a specific event takes place a fairly simple thing. It could be any noteworthy event, like when something shocking appears in headline news about that favorite Musketeer of theirs."

Astra's attention climbed down out of the tree she'd followed the squirrel into and remembered when she heard about her own favorite Musketeer being sentenced to court-mandated rehabilitation. It was after the disgraced Musketeer was arrested for public intoxication while filming a commercial on the Pirates of the Caribbean ride at the Anaheim theme park. It wasn't the public intoxication that got her sentenced to rehab, though. It was her defense.

The young starlet went on an incomprehensible rant about being forced to eat barbecued goat meat and how it traumatized her. She insisted the barbecue involved secret handshakes and underground tunnels beneath Disneyland leading to secret rooms and at least one secret barbecue pit. And there's where things got weird. Apparently there was no barbecue sauce. It was a little known fact the former Musketeer had lived her formative years in Texas, where barbecue sauce is mandatory.

The judge, familiar with Texas statutes, was quite

aware that failure to serve barbecue sauce was a misdemeanor where she came from, and was willing to at least listen to her defense for being intoxicated at a family theme park. But when she got to the part where she told him the cost of admission to the barbecue was a Mason jar and started sobbing inconsolably, he started banging his gavel and calling for order in the court. Most judges have little patience with courtroom defenses veering into Mason jar territory. Understandably.

"But not just any kind of Mason jar, your honor," the obviously intoxicated young woman cried over the thunderous boom of the gavel. The press sitting in the gallery had gone wild with the salacious details of the hidden debauchery lurking beneath Disneyland. But the young starlet wouldn't shut up. She insisted she had to find a *free* Mason jar or she'd never get into Club 33. For some reason, in her drug-addled mind, the former Musketeer was fixated on the *free* part of the Mason jar equation, which was all the court needed to know the young woman was on drugs and desperately needed a nice long stay in a rehabilitation center. In Los Angeles. Where drugs are served for breakfast.

"And if I don't get into Club 33, I won't have anything to swallow the red pill with. Because that's where they serve the holy water, your honor! Without the red pill, I'll never be an initiate and won't get my own series about using dark magic to do good things!"

Astra found herself wondering if both *fat suits* and microwaves had been anchored to that event by some extraterrestrial with advanced knowledge of neuro-linguistic programming and barbecue-obsessed Musketeers when she was a kid. It would at least partly explain her decision to bring both items with her when she escaped Boston in a flying Pinto. It wouldn't explain the timing, however, since the intoxicated courtroom drama happened almost a decade earlier, long before *fat suits* had become news stories buried in the back of the Lifestyles section of the Boston Globe.

But she was, despite all efforts by the squirrel to distract her from it, seeing El's point. What the *Star Seeds* had been programmed to feel compelled to do when they saw their own favorite Musketeer go on an Illuminati rant at a charity tour for poor orphaned Saudi Arabian children living on the streets of Dubai, was develop a fixation with *fat suits*. They would be inexplicably drawn to anything having to do with them. Stories, articles, movies, recycling stations for Silicon Valley waste material. Any of the usual places one would ordinarily find a *fat suit*.

"Why do you think we made sure the movie Shallow Hal got made?" She asked. Astra had just assumed the stories she'd grown up hearing were right with respect to the origins of Jack Black and his mystifying rise to stardom in the entertainment industry – both as a musician and an A-list actor in constant demand. All anyone has to do in order to confirm the story is look at a painting of Paul Revere.

As the story goes, Paul Revere was little more than the town drunk. Yes, he saw the British arriving by sea, but no, he did not ride from town to town sounding the alarm. He staggered on foot from pub to pub like he always did. Only on this night, he demanded people buy him a drink before he'd tell them the news he and only he was privileged to. By the time he fell flat on his face in a puddle of horse piss outside the last pub on his route, enough people had heard about what he'd seen to raise the alarm. He became such a laughing stock for almost losing the revolution over a free pint of ale; he was run out of town. That's where the story gets interesting.

On his way, he came to a crossroads. And as the story goes, he met the Crossroads Demon and sold the demon his soul in exchange for infamy as the Great Paul Revere, the Man Who Saved the Revolutionary War. And while that's the storyline we now read in the history books, Astra's sleuthing on the internet uncovered a far more sinister story: Paul Revere gave his DNA to a Draco-Reptilian and signed away the soul of any clone created from it in perpetuity, all in exchange for a fictitious narrative in history portraying him as a hero.

Anyone who's ever held a picture of Jack Black up next to a picture of Paul Revere can't miss the resemblance. Where do they think he and Kyle Gass came up with that song, *Tribute* for their debut album as Tenacious D? Think it's a coincidence it skyrocketed the D to the top of the charts? Does anyone actually believe it's a song about a demon and *not* a Draco-Reptilian?

"And to be certain all the bases were covered, we made sure to strategically place *fat suits* throughout popular culture on a wide variety of mediums. Remember Courtney Cox on the television show, *Friends*? How about Jon Stewart with all that *vacation weight*? And who can forget Martin Short reminding everyone to *take their Ginko Biloba*? That one was a twofer! We not only triggered their programming, we told them they *needed to remember*!!!"

Astra was beginning to feel dizzy. Something was stirring in her. Something ancient and buried in a memory of forgetting to remember. Something bigger than a feeling but smaller than a memory disorder. Was this the point of the much-debated *predictive programming* she'd been discussing with Samara, and had seen conspiracy theorists argue about until their grandmothers shut off the electricity to the basement?

"What about the movie Memento?" she said to El. "Is being compelled to watch that movie again and again one of those anchors? How about 50 First Dates? Could both of those be anchored to a trigger to program me to remember something specific?" Her thoughts were racing ahead of the conversation, which was not just rude to El, but to the squirrel.

Astra was beginning to suspect she knew where El was going with this. She just wasn't sure if El did too. She may have veered off the topic of *fat suits*, but all roads seemed to be leading her to *fat suits* nonetheless. Down the hall in one of two smaller offices, she'd shoved the *fat suit* she inexplicably felt compelled to bring with her all the way from Boston, and promptly forgot about. It had been perched on top of the microwave oven she felt equally compelled to bring since the day she got there.

"Now we're getting somewhere," El smiled as she gently patted Astra's shoulder. The image of *fat suits* cluttering her storefront as badly as they cluttered that Beacon Hill apartment raced up her visual cortex and then back down her cerebral cortex, continuing down her upper cervical spine until smacking her between the shoulder blades and knocking the wind out of her.

"But let's not get ahead of ourselves, Miss Astra. Baby steps. For now, at least. You're going to advertise that you've developed a system for luring negative alien entities into *fat suits*. Because they're made of silicone, they can be indistinguishable to the entity from the computer it's using as a vehicle. Negative entities are powerfully manipulative, but they're not very smart. Clients will come here to use the internet while wearing a *fat suit*. Which you provide for a fee. Once the alien entity has attached itself to it, we'll lure it into the microwave, which is the perfect trap for it. They can't get past the microwave's Faraday screen."

Astra wondered if El had worked as a scam artist in another lifetime. Her scam was so air tight she was embarrassed for herself for the second time that morning because she hadn't thought of it.

"When our *Star Seeds* see the ad, they will be helpless to their programming. They'll have no choice but to come here."

"I'll need more desk furniture for the little office spaces down the hall, and a wireless router," Astra said. She could just say in the ad that clients can bring their own laptop or mobile device. And make it abundantly clear a mobile phone or tablet is just as much at risk.

"Oh, you'll need more than that," El replied. "Let's not forget I know how all this works out. This place is going to be standing room only."

Considering there was only her desk chair in the office, plus the chair she'd found out in the alley – where all good furniture comes from – which she painted indigo blue for her clients to sit in, her entire office was a standing room only. For the first time she considered the possibility that the can of indigo blue paint randomly left sitting on the kitchen counter in her little apartment wasn't just a happy accident.

Astra was just about to ask El exactly how they were supposed to explain the technique for *luring* the negative alien entities from the fat suit to the microwave, when the door blew in and a sudden blast of hot, sandy dirt formed a dust devil in the middle of the office of *Alien Investigations*.

Through the flying grit-filled funnel in the center of the room, Astra could just make out a dark figure. It grew clearer and clearer as gradually the dust devil dissipated. Standing in the doorway was a dominatrix whose visage out-visaged any leather-clad *dom* on Beacon Hill worth her weight in Armor All. She snapped her whip against her thigh-high spike-heeled boots and glared first at El, then at Astra.

"Where the fuck is Dog Star?" she screamed.

"The planet, or the bounty hunter?" Astra replied calmly. Giving the impression one eats dominatrices for breakfast is essential to anyone in Astra's line of work. A con artist who rattles easily is no con artist. Where Astra comes from, they call people who rattle easily *compulsive liars*.

"I've got a star map and a Sharpie right here if you need directions."

"That fucker has been chasing my husband from one dimension to another until the only place left was ….. *THIS* shit hole," she screamed. It took a moment for Astra to figure out the only volume this dominatrix had was permanently set to *scream*. And apparently everywhere she went, sand storms appeared.

"Neither one of us wants to be here any longer than we have to. It was bad enough we had to come here the *first* time. And we were *promised* we would never have to do it again."

Astra had that dizzying sensation one often gets when they accidentally drop into a conversation halfway through it and have no idea what anyone's talking about. El must have had a much better idea of what was going on, because hers was the voice of reason when she spoke up.

"Why don't you tell us who your husband is and what exactly has been done to him," she said calmly.

The petulant dominatrix threw herself down on the indigo blue chair and man-spread her long leather-clad legs before complying with El's request.

"My husband is D.B. Cooper. He was hired by an obscure security company in 1971 to come to this dimension and terrify you puny weak-ass humans into implementing security measures at airports out of fear. For his trouble he got to keep the million dollar ransom he got hijacking a Boeing 727 full of passengers. It was only a tiny fraction of what that fucking company made out of all the security screening stations they built and stocked with trained security personnel across the country. And the world."

"So why is he being chased through other dimensions, if his crime was committed in a completely different one?" Astra asked, ever the pragmatist. "I've never heard a thing about any extradition treaties with other dimensions. And besides, the statute of limitations ran out over forty years ago."

"Some dick who was running for vice president set every bounty hunter and hired gun in the multiverse on D.B.'s trail when certain parties in this dimension started looking at the company that hired my Danny. I guess your political system is into parties. You animals. Anyway, it was a couple of decades ago. That dick wanted to make sure my cuddle-bear didn't get any ideas about coming forward in the *whistleblower* era this dimension was about to enter. His company was named Halliburton. Ring any bells?"

Astra vaguely recalled hearing a conspiracy theory involving the company having staged incidents in order to drum up business. She was pretty sure the dick who once ran it went on to become vice president, but just couldn't get any good intel on it. She tried fact-checking it on Snopes, but remembered a conspiracy theorist she'd listened to on YouTube who said he was a self-proclaimed minister and syndicated columnist for a variety of dubiously fundamentalist disinformation websites. But the real feather in his cap was being featured on Disinfaux News.

In the video, he was attempting to debunk the popular and respected fact-checking site as a branch of the CIA's Disinfaux News Division. According to the fervent conspiracist, only dominatrices and other sex-positive women work for Snopes, since according to him, neither a dominatrix nor any kind of worker in the sex-positive industry is capable of doing anything more with their brain than play Scrabble, smoke pot and post on Snopes.

Since the dominatrix manspreading in her office seemed pretty intelligent, Astra considered sending her to set the man straight on his assumptions. But considering he was incapable of correctly pronouncing the word dominatrix, she was pretty sure he wouldn't understand the point of her visit. Or that the sex-positive industry tends to attract some pretty intelligent women. Largely because it takes intelligence for any woman to think her way through the maze of sexual shaming men like him make a specialty of cultivating.

Of course, it goes without saying any man who considers himself worldly enough to be a syndicated columnist would know how to pronounce the word dominatrix. A good journalist knows how to make doors open to them others don't ordinarily even know exist. It not only takes possessing a certain *bon vivant,* it takes knowing what *bon vivant* is. And of course, how to pronounce it. Which once again, despite his insistence on using the term, the self-proclaimed investigative journalist did not.

Astra knew she didn't even need to ask the dominatrix if she knew. There are some women who possess so much *bon vivant* they don't need to use the term. They're too busy walking the walk. And that, without question, is the *bon vivant* of the dominatrix.

# CHAPTER TWELVE

The staging for the video seemed elaborate to Astra,
but to Samara it was a simple matter of combining
live-action with computer graphics. The most
complicated part of it was locating a defunct
computer screen large enough for Samara to burst
through at the right moment. Even the work of
removing all the components except for the screen's
frame was something that went over Astra's head. But
Samara's confidence didn't lead astray anyone
involved in the production.

When the time came to film it, El volunteered to work
the camera so neither of the stars would be distracted from
their performance. In her best – and only – khaki shorts and
shirt, the hat hanging down her back, Astra looked earnestly
at the camera and spoke her lines the way only a good
grifter can: Flawlessly.

\* \* \*

"Has this ever happened to you? You're minding
your own business merging onto the fast lane of the
information superhighway. Perhaps you're heading to

Twitter or Instagram or maybe even a nostalgic cruise past Facebook. When all of a sudden out of nowhere some sick depraved negative alien entity reaches through your electronic screen and grabs you by the pussy.

Next thing you know, instead of clicking *like* on your third cousin's pictures of what she fixed the kids for lunch, you're on Meatspin watching things you didn't even know were a thing. Or worse, leaving your wife and starting a business trafficking child sex slaves to all the pizza parlors on the eastern seaboard where politicians and their wealthy elite friends routinely pretend they go for a slice after pretending to be at work for the day.

Or maybe you're just gripped by the compulsion to make kiddie porn-to-order for most of the population of Hollywood. Negative alien entities love that shit. In fact, they thrive on it.

Or this: How many times has your life or the life of a loved one been turned upside down by prescription drug addiction, or even by the inferior alternative you get on the street from the pusher man? You'd be surprised how tasty a drug addict can be to those negative alien entities. Why do you think taking over the pharmaceutical industry was the first order of business for negative alien entities? And where exactly do you think the president got the idea for giving drug dealers the death penalty, but not the pharmaceutical reps?

Here's a little known fact: Our warm bodies, hearts and minds are prime real estate for any number of negative alien entities. And by *alien*, I *do* mean extraterrestrials. Because many alien entities travel in the form of energy, they have the ability to attach themselves to us through our electronic devices. Once comfy, they begin to feast on the negative energy created by the despicable things they manipulate us into doing. And there's no limit to the number of negative entities that can attach themselves to a human.

Protect yourself. If you suspect negative alien entities are planning to make you their next meal ticket, come to *Alien Investigations*. We're happy to let you do your web browsing in one of our cozy computer stations. Each station is equipped with cooling ceiling fans that have been blessed by an interdimensional being whose name has so many consonants it cannot be pronounced. Bring your laptop or tablet – the Wi-Fi's free. You'll be cool and safe in the knowledge those nasty entities can't touch you, thanks to Alien Investigation's groundbreaking patent-pending system of alien entity removal and storage.

Our method of luring and capturing negative alien entities with decommissioned fat suits has been proven to help Earthlings completely avoid alien entity attachments. And as an added bonus, it's also helped a few fans of Alex Jones and Steve Bannon – as well as those men's buddies running Macedonian fake news sites, not to mention those with the Bilderberg Group and Council on Foreign Relations – regain their sanity and return to leading normal, human lives. In their grandmother's basement. But at least they're not sitting there in stained underwear hating on women for existing. That's improvement, in our book. Which is definitely not chick-lit. That would be going too far.

If, on the other hand, you have reason to believe negative alien entities have already inhabited your meat suit, *Alien Investigation's* highly trained, expert staff can call upon your spirit guides to remove them and hand them over to us for storage. So come in or call today. Ask for Astra or Samara and get twenty percent off your first negative alien entity removal and storage."

* * *

By the time the ad became *Breaking News* across the twenty four hour news-cycle/infotainment universe – led by the Disinfaux News Galaxy – it had gone viral several times over on the internet.

Astra could tell none of the anchor women at Disinfaux News were comfortable covering a story involving fat suits. She'd been hoping that would be the case. They would all be so distracted by that discomfort the odds of them connecting the network's missing fat suits with Alien Investigations were pretty slim. The last thing Astra Talitha needed going viral was an inquiry into where she got the fat suits.

There was a good reason for the tempestuous tarot reader getting involved in this new direction her neighbor's alien investigation business was going. She knew what few do about the surge of negative alien entities attaching themselves to hapless internet users: they were harbingers of what was to come. And what was coming didn't need an electronic medium to get what it wanted.

But what her new partner Samara found more interesting than Disinfaux News reporting their ad as *Breaking News* were the responses she was seeing to the ad in the YouTube comments section. The callous aggressiveness of the commenters were all Samara needed to see in order to confirm her suspicions about the extent to which humanity had been groomed for what those harbingers were preceding. And it troubled her deeply. She couldn't be entirely sure Astra was up to the task. Sure, the pragmatic grifter was a quick study, but was she quick enough to outrun what was coming?

No; not outrun. That wasn't what was needed. What was needed was the fortitude to turn and face it with full knowledge of who and what it is; what its agenda is. Much like vanquishing a demon, it starts with knowing its name. And that required some next-level sleuthing. All the while staying invisibly benign to it, having conned it into thinking she was just another grifter to dismiss as unimportant in the greater scheme of things.

And that fortitude was exactly what Samara discerned Astra Talitha had in abundance. That's how it is with pragmatic grifters. They know how to prioritize what they value. The art of the con only comes first when the future of humanity and this pale blue dot isn't at stake. Otherwise, who would be left to grift? Or at least that's what Samara had every reason to believe Astra was doing. Because anyone other than Astra may not have the fortitude to ignore the salaciously inflammatory comments being made on her YouTube channel.

"Why would you stage this piece of shit with a negative alien entity portrayed by some feminazi wearing a fat suit and a Donald Trump mask? If you actually wanted to drum up some business you wouldn't be tossing politics into it. If anyone's a tool, it's you bitches."

"Hahahaaaaa!!! I LOVE the part where *Donald Trump* bursts out of the screen and grabs her by the pussy!!! Where did you learn to do special effects like that? Message me!"

"Were both of them wearing fat suits? Or is that just the way women are in trailer parks these days? I remember when poor people were skinny because they were too stupid to know food is solid and cheap booze isn't. Except Sterno, which might explain why you're brain dead."

"Dude, that Astra has one sweet booty." Definitely jam for that booty."

"Am I the only one who is highly suspicious about that chick saying her name is Samara? I mean, the symbolism of their overall message alone screams *Russian intelligence*, with its obvious propaganda and mass mind control. But that name? Hellooooo? Cyber-espionage training on the Volga? They're literally telling us they can reach through our screens and control us from Russia!"

"When are bitches going to learn dudes don't have to be possessed by demons or goblins or alien entities or even a fifth of Captain Morgan's to be assholes? Stop living in a fantasy world and accept that you lost the election. And everything else, bitches."

"Hi! I love your < enter name of music video> very so much! Proportion we be in contact extra approximately your video on AOL? I need an expert on this space to unravel my problem. May be that is you! Looking ahead to see you. Visit my blog … </a> http :/ / www. Online sex now . Com/ Free Chat With Girls </a>"

"Who the fuck uses the term 'the pusher man' anymore? How *OLD* is this freak? Calling a budtender 'the pusher man' is almost as lame as arguing that National NORML wasn't really about paving the way for corporatism to put all the marijuana growers and their heritage farms out of business all along."

It hadn't been Astra's plan to get Samara, the good-natured tarot reader and puppet master of masks made of cheesy-puffs, as involved as she did in the making of the ad. Nor did she intend to make her part of the new scam she was running with El. And never in a million years in this dimension did she imagine she and Samara would be partners. But the moment Samara and the enigmatic alien calling herself El met it was like watching ball lightning streak in through opposite windows and ignite in the middle of the room. It was apparent to Astra separating the two wasn't going to be easy.

And for some reason, she'd had a dream the night before of Samara and El, the magnificent mystic and the cosmic co-conspirator. They were moving into the corner of the lobby what looked like a little wooden plant stand with some kind of green stone top. It must have been heavy because they seemed to really be struggling with it despite how small it was.

David was there too, but just outside her field of vision. She just knew he was there watching. He had a sketch pad and pencil in his hands. And he seemed to be taking notes. But they were in images, not words. Turning the pad toward her, he pointed at what looked like the Council of Five sitting at a long table. She thought she recognized the table but couldn't be sure she wasn't confusing it with the one El and Samara were struggling with. His eyes met hers with a surprised smile in them as if he was just realizing she was there.

"Images have always been easier to translate," he said, holding his index finger to his lips and shushing her. "All sound and vision is. The key is knowing when to see it as metaphor, and when to take it literally."

What the dream had to do with anything was not

something Astra was willing to give any thought to. Pragmatists tend to see all forms of entertainment as self-indulgent. And the fact that Astra wasn't indulging in solving the dream-puzzle of Samara and El struggling with a heavy plant stand was yet another red flag.

Astra didn't give much thought to the dream until their first client of the day showed up in his bathrobe and what looked like Siddhartha's lost forgotten bedroom slippers. Which any history student in Texas will tell you were demonic. She was afraid to ask if it was because of the pink bunny ears or the whole Buddhism thing.

The wild-eyed man with three or four five o'clock shadows on his face had both coffee stained teeth *and* breath, and one glance at his pot-stained fingertips reminded Astra that the combination of certain Sativas and caffeine could be the wrong combination for some people. Especially conspiracy theorists.

His resin-coated fingers trembled as he pushed back the shock of greasy hair hanging straight down from the center of his forehead. The hair made a heroic effort to conceal bloodshot eyes with bags beneath them that would have cost a fortune to check at any airport in Corporate America. Astra wondered briefly if TSA might need to be brought in on this case, but decided to hold off until she found out exactly what the case involved. Why throw a bone to Halliburton if it wasn't necessary?

Pointing to the chair from the alley in front of her desk, Astra thought better of offering the man a cup of coffee. As she walked around the desk she asked Samara if she'd bring them both some Pellegrino. She actually preferred plain old tap water, but thought the high end mineral water added an air of sophistication to *Alien Investigations*.

"Actually," the man said. "Have you got any Horchata?" Astra had no idea why, but his request gave her goosebumps. The kind of goosebumps one gets when experiencing déjà vu for something that hasn't happened yet but one knows is inevitable nonetheless.

"Why don't you start at the beginning? Like with your name, for instance."

She wasn't really sure why she said that. It just seemed like a good place to start. She'd known people who tended to start at the end and work their way backward, and it never quite worked for Astra. Her attention would start wandering to things like time travel and quantum mechanics and before she knew it the person would be somewhere in the middle of the story and she'd be somewhere on a grassy knoll in Dallas chasing squirrels and wondering how she got there. Besides, most people begin with being given a name in life and move forward from there.

"My name is Jerry. And until seeing your ad on Jim Stone's website, I had no idea what was happening to me. Stone was ripping your video to shreds, but I knew you would be able to help with my problem."

Astra shuddered. She'd visited Stone's website once, when she was trying to learn what she could about *chemtrails.* But there were far too many disturbingly xenophobic viewpoints about both *Jews* and women – especially advocates for women's equality – on that site. She learned nothing other than the party line: All Jews are murderous Zionists and all women who prefer to be treated with even the tiniest bit of dignity and respect by men are *feminazis.* By *party* line of course, she meant *The Party in Grandma's Basement.*

"It all started the day I was listening to the Dark Journalist on that website, Forbidden Knowledge TV, and they mentioned the *Emerald Tablet.* I'd heard about it but really didn't know any details."

A knot tightened in Astra's throat. She hoped he wasn't going to ask her what she knew about it. No matter how many hours into the many nights she spent trying to absorb as much information as she could about the cosmology and lore related to extraterrestrials, the less she seemed to know. The more she learned the more there was to learn. And the conflicting information from one place to the next was enough to get the entire internet labeled *Fake News.* One site would label the Annunaki as pure evil, while another would laud them as Guardians of the Galaxy.

One self-proclaimed *expert* on *Star Families* would confidently list the five primary families ensuring the safety and progress of the human race. Then she'd follow a link to a *Pleiadian Channeler* whose American Midwest accent would inexplicably shift to that of a British aristocrat when she was channeling. Mary Poppins would just as confidently claim that nobody is watching after us. We're on our own. Astra would stagger off in confusion about extraterrestrials altogether, wondering if the whole quagmire wasn't mirroring Americans' basic ignorance of the people and cultures of the world beyond its borders.

Considering how easily that ignorance and confusion was routinely manipulated into a justification for invading other countries, it might have served her to plant a red flag in that very spot for good measure. Cultural ignorance about another country less advanced than you is one thing, but being kept ignorant about a race far more advanced than you could be a ticking time bomb. In her defense, if she'd planted that flag anywhere beyond our borders, it probably would have been droned into oblivion along with any people living near it. And thanks to Disinfaux News, nobody would have cared.

And because of all the conflicting information Astra was having to wade through and attempt to reconcile, *Emerald Tablets* and the hiding place for the keys to Starship Earth's ignition had eluded her entirely. She had no idea what Jerry was talking about any more than she knew how to steer the planet away from the cliffs it was obviously heading toward. If she herself hadn't stuck the key in the ignition and released the emergency brake, how the hell would she know how to downshift the transmission and bring it to a stop?

"It's hard to explain why hearing about the tablet affected me the way it did," Jerry continued, nervously stroking the area around his mouth and then running his fingers across his lips. Astra could only assume he was searching for bits of pot left in his stubble to keep himself going.

"It's just that my entire life I've had this feeling I needed to be searching for something. And not just any something; a very specific something. The older I got, the stronger it grew, unlike most childhood ambitions."

Astra could relate. People rarely give a thought to childhood ambitions that fall by the wayside when we grow up. But what about those that only grow stronger, yet can't exactly be articulated? She often considered the worst childhood ambitions to be the ones that can't be articulated, yet only get stronger with age. With David, she had hoped to fulfill the dream of belonging to a family of her own. But as with every man she'd known and tried it with, it only reminded her of how alone she'd always been on this giant spinning rock.

"When I heard about the Emerald Tablet I knew that was what I'd been searching for. Only no matter how hard I search for information on where I could find it, or even a reliable translation of what's supposedly transcribed on it, I keep hitting a brick wall. It's not that the data isn't there to find, it's that there's *too much* data. So much that it's impossible to know what's real and what's misdirection."

Jerry described his excitement when he learned of its connection to the Egyptian god, Thoth. His hope, of course, was that the ancient God of Wisdom would have been wise enough to set some of that wisdom in stone.

"I mean, translating hieroglyphs in ancient Egypt is one thing, but the Emerald Tablet goes far, far beyond the slice-of-life Norman Rockwell illustrations of everyday life in antiquity. Imagine the alchemical secrets to the existence of everything; a definitive explanation of the origins of the Universe. Our entire existence we've been kept in the dark with only superstitious belief systems to light our way. And it's resulted in nothing but arguments about that origin. Wouldn't concrete evidence of it pretty much eliminate the argument altogether?"

Astra had to wonder if perhaps that little point right there was the very reason the tablet had gone missing in the first place. And why so much conflicting information about it was being disseminated, as well. The grifter in her recognized a shell game when she saw it. Misdirection was the oldest play in the book. Just like arguments about the origins of the Universe. Keeping them going was good business. After all, they were the best way to drum up revenue for the defense industry of more than one world power. Not to mention a collection plate or two.

The other obvious benefit of utilizing what those in the business like to call *The Confusion Technique* while disseminating information is how impossible it is to challenge anything the person sharing it is saying. Mixed messages are too slippery to challenge. No matter which approach you take, you're wrong. Even for the most experienced grifters, it's hard to know where to begin sorting it all out.

The best example Astra could think of was the application of *The Confusion Technique* to defend the two most recent land wars in Asia. By using *threats to democracy* as a cover for invading two sovereign countries, deliberately making it *look* like that flimsy excuse was little more than a thinly disguised cover for resource-grabbing, it successfully fueled a mushrooming of conspiracy theories. And they worked perfectly to obscure the *true* reason for the invasions while the conspiracists' incessantly nitpicked the cover story. Meanwhile, the true agenda has gone on being carried out right under everyone's noses – including the conspiracy theorists' – with none the wiser.

The true agenda? The acquisition and/or destruction of antiquity.

She always thought of it as being like the layers of an onion: we use oil and other resources as an excuse to go in, but to placate and confuse the masses, tell them it's to spread *democracy*, sending our young soldiers in like gladiators on the field, creating manufactured demons to vanquish, keeping the spectators in the bleachers distracted while we sack the library at Alexandria. Or take possession of the Stargate. Or maybe even use some ancient stone tablet to open the Ark of the Covenant. Whatever the reason, Astra had no reason not to suspect Jerry's newfound obsession with the Emerald Tablet was in some way related to the *Confusion Technique.*

Astra's attention span chased a squirrel into the ring and started chewing on the rope during a rehearsal for World Wrestling Entertainment. She wondered if the squirrel was trying to tell her something. Like, maybe we should consider shipping our wrestling entertainers over to the Middle East instead of our soldiers? Not only would it create far less bloodshed, it would cost far less money. And cause a lot less destruction.

Plus, the people of the region would at least be entertained while being distracted from the theft of both their resources and their ancient artifacts. After all, what's not to love about modern day gladiators performing for the sole purpose of entertaining the spectators, but with a wholesome message? As long as the script writers don't insert something salacious into the storyline when manufacturing conflicts between the characters. The people of that region tend to be modest.

She was puzzling over where to begin putting together a game plan for locating the tablet when Samara startled her by clearing her throat. The talented tarot reader knew better than anyone there what it was like for everyone to forget you're in the room. And would have quietly left everyone to their memory disorders if it weren't for the issue that had just arisen. She knew exactly what it was the exhausted stoner needed.

"What you need is a *Psychic Finder*," she said with authority few would challenge. Except Astra Talitha, of course. She would challenge any authority just for the practice. It's what grifters do.

"And where exactly would we find a *Psychic Finder?*" she said. "Because I've sworn off Craigslist. Too many freaks, weirdos, knife-wielding would-be roommates, and child sex-slave traffickers on that site. It's even worse than Instagram. But at least Instagram's got seagulls. Or is this one of those things where it's pointless to look for one because you have to wait for the *Psychic Finder to* find you?"

Samara lowered her chin and gazed over the rim of her glasses, locking eyes with Astra. The two women stood locked in a staring contest until it occurred to Astra that it was entirely possible Samara couldn't even see her over the rim of her glasses.

"Do you remember telling me about the first foster home you got kicked out of?" she said, continuing to resemble someone who was staring directly into Astra's eyes. All while Astra's forgotten memory of that conversation tried to kick down the door blocking access to it. And others like it.

"You said they were religious fundamentalists, and thought you were possessed by the devil," Samara added, seeming to hope the prod might jog her memory.

But apparently the loss of memory Astra had endured since arriving in Sedona included more than a failure to recollect just short term events. Astra was having a hard time remembering that she was raised in foster care, and why. Until that very moment, she hadn't even realized her earliest memories were missing.

"I had a foster family of fundamentalists who thought I was possessed by Satan?" she said slowly, once again deep under water wishing she'd brought a snorkel. "Let me guess, because I found things?"

"See?" Samara smiled. "I knew it would come back to you!"

What Astra wasn't remembering was an event from her first foster home when she was still a toddler. She'd woke in the night and climbed down the stairs to where her foster parents had been hosting a gathering she remembered little about. As the group prepared to leave, one couple realized their car keys were missing. For the next thirty minutes the entire group turned the living room upside down looking, and had just sat back down to command Satan to return the keys and leave them alone, when little Astra came toddling down the stairs rubbing sleep from her eyes.

"Here you go, mister man," the toddler said, handing a perfect stranger the keys she'd just extracted from deep beneath the back of the sofa. Her little arm was tiny enough to easily reach the narrow crevice the keys had nestled in. Just how the child knew to come downstairs and search for them in the first place was an alarming symptom none of them wanted to be seeing. But what forced them to accept what it was an obvious symptom of was her knowing who the keys belonged to without ever having met the man.

Because the default setting on all things anomalous for fundamentalists is demonic possession, there was no doubt in their minds that little Astra Talitha was in fact demonically possessed. By the time her foster parents were able to contact the caseworker and have the confused child removed from their property, she had gone from merely being a toddler possessed by the devil in the eyes of her foster parents, to a toddler who was the child of the devil. And like all demon seeds, Astra Talitha was cast out of the home.

The last two nights the child was there were spent on a cot with the dogs out on the unheated sun porch. Despite their fleas, Astra was grateful for their warmth, since it was winter and apparently demon seeds don't need any blankets because of all the fire and brimstone burning in them.

"Wait, so you think I'm some kind of *Psychic Finder*?" she suddenly asked, a light bulb going off on the dark porch of her memory.

Samara just beamed and nodded that annoyingly knowing nod she often gave Astra.

"That just doesn't make any sense at all, Miss Sammy. For one thing, I haven't gotten any closer to finding the *truth* about the Emerald Tablet than he has. And for another, if finding the *truth* about a thing is that hard, I seriously doubt some *Psychic Finder* is going to have any luck locating the actual thing!"

The problem with growing up without a family is there are no record keepers in your pocket, no one to call up and ask if they remember that time you shoved Cheerios up your nostril and had to go to the ER to have them dug out. No one to embarrass you by showing your prom date that baby picture of you stretched out buck naked on a bear skin rug. No one to remember how much you hate green bean casserole swimming in cream of mushroom soup, then topped with canned onion rings and crushed corn chips before being baked to an inedible crisp.

And so recollections of Astra Talitha's childhood of finding things psychically remained yet another of those many memories that faded into her past along with anyone who would care enough to keep them fresh. Or so she thought. And try as she might, she could not recall having told Samara a thing about her first foster home. Vague recollections of possibly telling David about it tickled the back of her mind, but not Samara. Had she not been so preoccupied with the stoner in his bathrobe, she would have recognized that little factoid as yet another red flag.

"I have every confidence that your finding skills are exactly what is needed to solve Jerry's problem," Samara said cheerfully. "And some of the other problems that have walked in the door since you opened for business. There's much to be done to bring your skills up to speed, so it would be best if you get Jerry's contact information and send him on his way before closing up for our staff meeting."

Astra had no idea what Samara was talking about, but got the sense that she really didn't need to. Samara's confidence was all she needed to see, and the faithful tarot reader had an abundance of that. Besides, responding to all the emails requesting time at a computer station in the fat suit was going to be time-consuming. So was figuring out how to go about looking for not just the elusive lover of a sex-starved energy vampire, but also for the D.B. Cooper of Halliburton's legendary wet-dreams-come-true. And where to begin strategizing about searching for the Holy Grail of UFO lore - The Emerald Tablet - was certainly going to be time consuming.

It was obvious to anyone paying attention the little staff of *Alien Investigations* had better things to do with their time than sit around with a stoner in pink bunny ear slippers. What wasn't obvious to Astra Talitha was just who was paying attention, and why.

The red flags were piling up.

# CHAPTER THIRTEEN

The plans they had laid out at the staff meeting that afternoon would have been far easier to get started on if there hadn't been a line of people at the door the next morning. While a few just wanted help getting rid of the alien entities they'd already picked up along the way, most of them wanted time at a computer station. In a fat suit. Not until that very moment did it occur to Astra Talitha she needed more fat suits.

Of course the easiest thing she could do was leave a message with Cantor Colbert for David to contact her. But that would mean asking him to bring them to Sedona was a foregone conclusion. And Astra was never a fan of foregone conclusions. Like destiny and fate, they didn't seem entirely trustworthy.

So she called her contacts in Las Vegas. Who, in turn, would most likely get ahold of David one way or another. Who else would just happen to have a large supply of fat suits at his fingertips? But not having to deal with him on top of everything else she was juggling was worth paying the middle man for. Arranging for them to send a truck to deliver them to *Alien Investigations* was worth the added expense. And while she waited, she had plenty to do with her time.

Astra wasn't taking any chances. Posting a sign on the front door explaining why *Alien Investigations* would be closed was not enough in the electronic era. She also had to tweet, post a Facebook update and Instagram a notice that the office would be closed for a couple of days. To throw any curious *drama queens* off, she said it was for a meeting of the Intergalactic Liaison with the Alliance of the Council of Five and the Galactic Federation. And it was all because Astra and Samara had a plan for where to begin searching for a missing husband and a missing tablet. To Astra's surprise, it involved El.

And El, it seemed, had a strategy that would lead to the missing lover of band-camp infamy once both D.B. Cooper and the Emerald Tablet were found. And that strategy seemed to hinge on going to the desert just after a sand storm to look for swales left behind in the sand.

"So instead of following the yellow brick road to the Emerald City," Astra said as she locked the door behind her, "we're following the pink sand swale to the Emerald Tablet. Makes perfect sense to me. So does the old saying that history repeats itself. Only in this case, it's a fictional history."

"So is what they teach school kids in Texas," Samara said in her most syrupy southern drawl as the three of them piled into the Pinto. Astra wasn't sure if the tarot reader was sounding a bit testy because of the fact-free revisionist history inserted in Texas history books, or about the risky nature of getting into a Pinto known for both randomly taking flight and exploding.

"Maybe we should get the Texas State Board of Education to pull back the curtain on Oz," Astra said as she fastened her seatbelt and slid the key into the ignition. "They may have the Emerald Tablet hidden behind it with our actual unrevised history."

Checking her rear-view mirror before pulling away from the curb, she had mixed feelings when she found herself unexpectedly making eye contact with the Tall Man. He stood on the same corner where she'd seen him before. As usual, he was tipping his fedora. Even on a clear sunny day she still couldn't tell if he was bald or simply had hair so light it only looked like he was bald.

The man who was so foreign he was most likely alien was so tall he was having to bend over at the waist so she'd be certain to see his face in the rear-view mirror. It was just the kind of perplexing deliberateness she'd sensed the first time she'd seen him. And every time thereafter. Yet as much as she wanted to say something to Samara and El about him, she couldn't get past the unusual quality she could clearly see in his eyes. Astra couldn't quite put a finger on it. And for some reason, that seemed more important to her than asking her companions if they had any idea who the Tall Man was.

Why both El and Samara insisted their search begin in the desert was also something Astra knew she should pursue. But just going to the desert was more than she needed occupying her thoughts that morning. After a lifetime of dreaming about living in the desert, this was the first time she was actually going to the desert. It was like people who finally get that beach house and never go down to the water. A month had passed and this was the first time Astra had been outside the Sedona city limits. Her pulse quickened as they left the city behind and the red rocks embraced them with a welcoming surge of energy.

"Keep an eye on the odometer," El said. "We're going right into the center of the energy field, so let me know when we've gone eleven miles."

She'd said something about *Ley Lines* and how the sand swales would lead them to something, so Astra concluded she was most likely about to be treated to the mystical phenomenon that fuels the Sedona tourist industry. It was the same phenomenon that enabled her to open up a fake alien investigation agency. The kind of people who buy into the idea that mystical energy lines encircle the planet are the kind of people inclined to believe in extraterrestrials. And just because Astra had met several of them just that week didn't necessarily mean she believed in them. She felt the same way about love and forever homes, and hoped the aliens would understand her dilemma. If they turned out to actually exist.

According to Samara, the vortexes can be magnetic – or female – or they can be electric – or male. And enclosed in the 22 mile stretch of desert in and around Sedona are wildly swirling energy pockets caused by the male and female doing their Taoist dance in the desert. Hence the exact location of any one particular vortex being somewhat inexact. Which is why just after a sandstorm, especially one created by an angry extraterrestrial dominatrix, swales are so useful in locating them. The swales left in the sand are the equivalent of Universal directional signs.

And that is exactly what both El and Samara were in search of while Astra trailed behind and marveled at how *pink* everything was. Hadn't Samara just been talking about the spiritual meaning of the color pink? Combining red, the color of lust – which Samara explained symbolized action in more than one spiritual discipline – with white, the color of insight, the resultant pink embodies the bottomless depth of unconditional love.

It was a difficult one for Astra to forget due to the lump it left in her throat. The concept of unconditional love was the greatest challenge a pragmatic grifter raised in the foster care system could possibly come up against. And for Astra Talitha, the feeling was multiplied to an unbearable degree as she tried hard to not think about David.

The problem with trying to not think about something is this: The moment you tell yourself not to think about it that's all you can think about. As proof, for the rest of this chapter, this writer challenges you to not think about elephants. Or fat suits. Better yet, don't think about elephants in fat suits.

It wasn't long though before Astra found it just as difficult to keep up with El and Samara as it was to not think about David. The two enigmatic women were hot on the trail of a vortex. Having located a swale shortly after leaving the car, they followed it with serious intent. To Astra, they looked like they were following an old friend to a kegger. If that was the case, the swale was clearly speaking Astra's language. Even if it wasn't speaking theirs.

She'd heard most guides leading tourists to the vortexes use divining rods. Because apparently divining for vortexes is as successful as divining for water. Which might possibly make sense, considering wells are not commonly located in the desert so it gives divining rods something to do with their spare time. Astra assumed it was because being divine isn't exactly the full-time job it once was.

What definitely did not make sense at all was why it was already getting dark. They left Sedona a little past nine in the morning. Yet the sun was already sinking in the west.

"We're losing light," El said, calling to Astra trailing behind them. "We're going to have to split up if we're going to make our connection."

"I noticed," the pragmatic grifter called back. "Why is that exactly?"

"Because it's a small window of time!" El replied, making no effort to hide the impatience in her voice.

Astra suspected El knew full well she was not referring to why they needed to split up. She was about to clarify that when both El and Samara suddenly stopped. They stood perfectly still in their alabaster similarity. Both faced west. And both extended their right arm, pointing with a single perfectly white index finger. Astra's memory started to take a detour to the time she ran a *Best in Show* scam on a breeder of Irish Setters as she picked up the pace and jogged up to the two pointers.

"What is it, girl? Did Timmy fall down the well again?"

But after more than half a minute of silence from them, their unblinking eyes staring into the darkness at something only they perceived, Astra changed her mind and decided they looked like department store mannequins pointing toward the abyss.

"Please tell me you're not pointing to ancient Egypt,"

Astra said, hoping the obscure cultural reference would break their trance.

Samara closed her eyes and gently shook her head. It seemed more an answer to something she'd been asking herself than it did a response to Astra's nineteen eighties movie trivia.

"Here is where we split up," El said. "You will know when you reach your destination. I assure you it isn't a kegger."

If Astra was the kind of pragmatist who routinely suspected others of reading her thoughts, she did a good job of hiding it. And not just because tossing around *ifs* in the desert is hardly a pragmatic thing to do. Hence her not stopping at that very moment and demanding an explanation from the raven-haired extraterrestrial for eavesdropping on her thoughts. As if there weren't already enough red flags flying, another one popped up right there in the desert and claimed that very moment as its own. No other moments came forward to declare sovereignty. But isn't that how it usually is with sovereignty? We don't necessarily see the risks involved in some distant explorer claiming it in the name of colonization until it's too late to challenge him.

"Your finding skills will take you exactly where you're meant to go," Samara said with emphasis.

With that, both women lowered their extended arm. They turned in perfect unison and began walking in the opposite direction Astra had been told to walk. She wanted to ask them how she was supposed to find her way back to that spot, but it was implied in Samara's reminder about Astra's finding skills. But what about where they would meet up when they were done with whatever they were doing? Were her finding skills going to work for that too? *Where am I going, what am I doing, and are you sure I can find my way back* were all crowding her tongue for first place before she realized it was too late. Both women were out of earshot and Astra was alone in the desert. In the dark.

The thing about sunset in the southwest is there is almost no twilight. Unlike Boston, which is much farther north. Being that much farther north of the equator than the desert outside Sedona, the curvature of the earth comes into play, making the lower atmosphere remain illuminated longer for those who want to catch the last little bit of light. But as far south as Sedona is, the sky goes from pale blue to deep black in a matter of moments after the sun sets behind the red hills surrounding it. By the time Astra realized El and Samara were out of earshot and turned back to the pink sand swale leading her to Oz, it was pitch black out.

Were it not for the magnificent light display the Milky Way was putting on above, Astra would have no choice but to sit down and wait for her companions to finish doing whatever it was they were off doing. But as it was, the Milky Way was illuminating the upturned sand framing either side of the perfect path stretched out before her in neon pink. As long as she didn't stray from that swale, she would be fine.

Despite her pragmatism, the bootylicious confidence artist took a leap of faith and followed that neon pink deep into the desert she'd spent a lifetime dreaming of. It wasn't until she'd been walking for what seemed to her an hour that she realized it would have been a good idea to bring water. And no sooner had the thought occurred to her than she noticed a dim golden light flickering on the horizon.

Instantly, Astra traversed the entire distance and found herself standing in front of a man tending a small campfire.

"Well it's about time, thirsty girl."

There are times in everyone's life when something spoken casually hits us in the gut with the velocity of a speeding train. And despite there being no evidence of train tracks in the desert, Astra was fairly certain one had just hit her. She could think of no other explanation for why the stranger's words left her suddenly airborne and flying backwards. It wasn't the first time she'd been saved from serious injury by her perfectly padded posterior. Nor was it the first time she'd taken flight because of something that defied explanation. But it was the first time she was grateful she didn't land on a cactus.

"We don't have a lot of time," the man said with a hint of impatience. Astra stood and brushed the sand from her bountiful buttocks, wondering why his voice sounded like David Bowie. She wondered briefly if he was going to start channeling the *Pleiadians* in a Midwest accent.

"I know you're thirsty. We all know. Do you have any idea how loud your thoughts can be out here in the desert?"

Astra gingerly stepped back onto the neon pink path and deposited the unharmed booty of galactic legend on the desert floor directly in front of the fire the man was busily poking with a stick. She wanted to ask him if the stick was a divining rod, but the look he gave her said, *Don't. You. Dare.* For a brief moment she felt the urge to ask him if they were related, but the exact same words, complete with periods for emphasis, appeared in her visual field. Astra concluded it was best to simply stifle the urge. She said nothing. He smiled.

"Now we're getting somewhere," he said, handing her a small clay cup of warm liquid. "Drink this and I'll tell you what you're doing here." The impatience in his voice had been replaced with an unmistakable insistence. As far as Astra was concerned it was an improvement.

It was only then she noticed he'd been stirring the contents of a black cast-iron kettle dangling from a cast-iron tripod straddling the little fire. The stick he'd been poking the fire with appeared to be multi-purpose. It ordinarily would have made Astra apprehensive to drink anything that had been stirred with a stick that was covered with ash and soot. But his was an authoritative insistence. It kindled wisps of memory swirling around the back of her mind. Recollections of her David tried to leap from the fire as she swallowed the warm liquid, that same insistent authority curling around embers and drifting up into the night.

As it drifted upward, so did Astra's focus. The embers floated on the slightest eddy before another more determined current brought them back down to the sand swale. Instantly the swale became brilliantly illuminated. The pink began to divide itself into varying shades of first just red and white, then multiple colors from every direction. The path before her became a twelve-strand helix of all the colors in that rainbow she'd come to know so well. And each color had its counterpart. Including the primary colors.

That helix was stretched out into infinity. David Bowie was either telling her to follow it or singing the Lazarus song. As she stood and followed the notes Astra heard her own voice ask if there was really any difference.

"It's all about immortality," she said without the vaguest idea what she was saying. The sound of David Bowie laughing trailed off into the distant past as she followed the notes, now illuminated in a different color for each note, measure and beat.

Without knowing how she knew, or even why for that matter, Astra followed the helix onto the bullet train that appeared out of the center of nothing. Instantly she found herself riding the *Ley Line* on which she'd been standing. With barely time to wonder if the conductor would kick her off when he discovered she'd boarded without a ticket, Astra frantically searched for the seat belts. But it was too late. The speed at which they traveled left everything she thought she knew about existence far behind her, including the voice of David Bowie.

Before she could begin to wrap her mind around this curious development, the train came to a gentle stop without having slowed in the slightest. It defied everything she thought she knew about the laws of physics. So did Stonehenge, where she found herself standing. Right smack in the center. Most people would be delighted to find themselves where Astra was at that moment. But all she could think about was the fact that she'd skipped breakfast and how disappointing it was that she hadn't found the dining car in the bullet train before reaching her destination.

"Are you sure this is your destination?" a feminine voice said, startling her from all thoughts of breakfast foods. Astra turned to see a beautiful redhead dressed in chain mail and wearing an ornate headdress of multi-layered metallic scales. She was fairly certain the metal was most likely made of one or more of those rare earth metals Emo had promised to reward her with. But more than that, she was certain she knew the woman. Intimately.

"If it wasn't my destination, why did I get off here?" Astra replied, puzzling over her recognition and knowledge of the stranger.

"Do you always answer a question with a question?" the stranger demanded.

"What's your point?" Astra conceded. It wasn't the first time she'd lost an argument, but it was without question the first time she'd lost an argument to a Sumerian priestess at Stonehenge.

"We must make haste," the Sumerian said. "They are approaching and we cannot be seen."

Astra wasn't sure if the woman meant they were invisible and could get trampled by whomever it was that was approaching, or if she meant they should not be seen by them. Either way, the Warrior Priestess grabbed her hand and didn't let go until they were standing on a bluff over Loch Ness.

"Oh great," Astra said aloud, her inner monologue apparently set to *outer monologue for anyone to hear.* "Now the Loch Ness monster is getting in on the act. And he knows it. Because I can't keep anything to myself here, can I?"

"You can't keep anything to yourself anywhere," the priestess said to her. "That's how it is with the hive mind. Separation is an illusion." Once again, she reached for Astra's hand. And once again, Astra found herself somewhere else.

This time it was on the Hill of Tara. They were in Ireland. County Meath, to be precise. Astra found herself being introduced to the *Lia Fail*, or *Stone of Destiny*. This was something so unnecessarily obscure even Astra knew nothing about it. Yet she did. Inexplicably, she knew everything about it. Standing in the place where the Tuatha De Danaan reigned, she found herself knowing everything there was to know about the God-like people of legend who are said to have arrived in Ireland in mysterious ships. And of course they came with magical powers.

Turning to the priestess, she was about to ask her where they had come from, and if those ships were anything like the UFOs she didn't see over the foothills of West Virginia. But the warrior once again took her by the hand. She was still holding it when she realized they were standing in a dark wood in Scotland, somewhere near the border. The priestess squeezed her hand and she knew it was Ettrick Forest, where the First Guardian of Scotland had trained his men in a type of warfare the English had never encountered. What Astra hadn't known until just then was it was because it hadn't originated on this planet.

William Wallace stood at least two heads taller than the tallest man he instructed, the firelight flickering off the barrel chest of the giant. Just outside the awareness of anyone there but Astra and the Sumerian, a group of giants twice his height watched and nodded from the shadows, knowing they'd done well to secure the guardian the Scots needed at the time.

"Why does all of this seem so familiar?" Astra asked, turning to her guide.

"Talitha is the name you were given to keep you hidden in safety, and also as a clue to the Hebraic blood in your veins," she replied. "Your fearsome nature comes from a bloodline of guardians that goes back farther than the history of this planet itself."

Astra was about to object to the implication that she was descended from giants. She wasn't tall enough. But the thought occurred to her that maybe the genetics went sideways when they got passed down to her, which could explain the uncommon girth and power of her luscious booty. More than anything she wanted to ask her guide where all of these things she was being shown came from. But before she could, the priestess once again squeezed Astra's hand.

"Please, not again," Astra pleaded. "Not without some answers first. Where is all of this leading me?" But the warrior priestess' grip was too strong. She said nothing. Pointing toward the sky, the woman gently pried Astra's index finger from her tightly clenched fist. Still saying nothing, she forced the finger to point upward. Her unfathomably deep eyes met Astra's. Not a word was spoken. And with that, Astra felt herself no longer subject to the laws of physics. Suddenly all the flying dreams she'd had her entire life made sense. It was as effortless as it had always been in her dreams. She felt herself leave Earth's gravitational field, and that was just as effortless. She looked back at Earth as she rose higher and caught a glimpse of the Sphynx and the Great Pyramids, then Nazca, and finally the Mayan ruins. And then everything was gone. Everything and everyone.

Not only was the priestess gone, but so was Astra's physical body. Once again, Astra was alone. Yet for the first time in her human life, she felt completely enveloped in the exact opposite of being alone. She felt herself come alive in a world of divine paradox, a world where perfect balance was more important than anything else. The balance of not just exact opposites, but of everything in-between those opposites.

Also for the first time in her life, or at least for the first time in any life she could clearly recollect, she found herself stretched, elongated, miniaturized and expanded into shapes and sizes impossible to comprehend without having studied advanced physics as it applies to both sacred geometry and Fibonacci's favorite vegetable, Romanesco. And it was all happening simultaneously.

She wanted to scream. To recoil at the unfamiliar territory she found herself in. Not to mention being. Because try as she might, Astra Talitha could not recall ever being anything as unfamiliar as a subatomic particle forming itself into a perfect spiral with nothing but a ghost particle to push her forward. She wasn't sure if it was the Tao of Physics, or the Tau of Physics. All she wanted was to turn back and settle back down to the familiar Earth she'd lived her life walking without any knowledge of ghost particles or invisible entities that might or might not attach themselves to her.

Could invisible entities attach themselves to her if she herself was invisible? For that matter, was she invisible to anyone but herself? And speaking of anyone, where the hell *was* everyone else??

It must have been the last conscious thought she had before Astra no longer had thoughts at all. As she squeezed through a pinhole in the fabric of time, she became experience itself. And as experience, she instantly knew all that had ever been, would ever be, and was being at that very moment. She comprehended things she never knew needed comprehending. Only without knowing it because she actually knew nothing. And everything. All at once.

A dusty copy of The Tao of Physics imploded. Astra watched its subatomic particles form a multi-dimensional quilting bee and stitch a newer, more infinitely expanding universe in the classic *Friendship Star* pattern. All while she inhaled. As she exhaled, it became a black hole and swallowed physics alive. Only the Tao escaped unscathed. For now. It was heading directly for planet Earth, and history keeps perfect records, including what happens to Taoism after reaching Earth, the planet where superfluous appendages go to die after a lifetime of servitude.

Astra was riding a smoothly flowing stream of warm thick blood as it pulsed from the heart of all that exists to the very tip of every extremity. It was there she comprehended the urge to experience in a way she never dreamed imaginable. Experiencing existence, as far as she could tell, was the Holy Grail of All That Is. Any and all questions that begin with *Why* were not just laid to rest there. They were drained of their own life force, embalmed, had lifelike makeup applied, and were dressed in their best Sunday suit. Across the cosmos, questions of all shape, size and matter lined up to pay their last respects to *Why*.

While some might disagree, it is a well-known fact the Big Bang was the result of some idiot sticking a hat pin into the thumb of *Why*. It was during the open casket viewing of *Why's* corpse. In his defense, the idiot was hired by a small-time cosmic syndicate kingpin to confirm that *Why* was really dead. He had to make sure *Why* wasn't just laid to rest for show in some kind of subterfuge to throw organized crime off the trail. Not to mention cosmic conspiracy theorists.

It figured even cosmic conspiracy theorists are obsessed with *Why*.

As Astra felt herself abruptly yanked by the golden cord she hadn't realized was cinched around her waist, she took one last look at herself in a formless existence that embraces *All That Is*. With that, she heard herself say two words as she settled back down on the other side of the cast-iron kettle opposite the shaman who could very well be a toothless, weathered David Bowie. Or Lazarus. Same difference.

"Why not?"

"If you mean why not see it the way you've just come to see it, you came back with the only question worthy of consideration," Lazarus said with a grin filled with nothing but gums, lips and ancient knowledge.

If what he meant was seeing *All That Is* as timeless, infinite, neutrally loving yet impartial and intensely personal, self-aware, and self-creating, the shaman was right.

"Consciousness is a self-creating universe. We are everything we create. We *are* consciousness. Consciousness creating the universe around us. Not just individually, and not just collectively. Both. And yet neither. Remember that physics lecture you sat in on when you were running that *academic scam*? That professor nailed it when he said reality may be so complex our brains simply aren't capable of processing it, didn't he? It would be like trying to teach calculus to a hamster."

"You are capable of comprehending anything you

create," Astra heard the words come from her mouth, completing the shaman's thought. She looked down at the clay cup in her hand and wondered if she had created it.

"Not only did you create the cup, you created the ayahuasca that was in it," he said, nodding. "The swale that brought you here? The Milky Way that illuminated your astral journey? This kettle? This fire? Me?"

"At what point does your consciousness end and mine begin?" Astra asked, overwhelmed at the implication.

"There is no such point. We are all one. Separation is an illusion."

Astra looked upward once again at the expanse of the Milky Way. And again, she considered the sense of knowing something forgotten she had always gotten just looking at the stars. For as long as she could recall, it had been on the tip of her tongue. Yet she just couldn't reach it.

"That thought. Right there," the shaman said. "It's been a *forbidden thought* for as long as human civilization has been under the control of the colonists. Those stars, the constellations. Our origins."

"Why *forbidden*?" she asked.

"There was a time when each constellation told a story," he replied. "And those stories guided those on this planet in everything from when to plant, to when to embark on a long journey. They connected us to the seasons and the cycles in a way that perpetually reminded us we were stewards of this spaceship Earth. But more than that, they kept us anchored to our origins."

"How could anything that vital to our survival become forbidden?" Astra asked.

"As long as the human race understood that we all

share the same origin story, regardless which planet or galaxy or star system, it would continue to know that separation is an illusion. A population that has that kind of knowledge cannot be controlled."

"So the control agents came in and made the human race stop looking at the stars so we'd forget where we came from and how we're connected?"

"Not just forget who *you* are," he replied. "Forget who *they* are. They knew the nature of time, knew they could afford to play the long game. So they began gradually shifting the focus of natural truths to unnatural stories created for the purpose of shifting our focus down from the stars. At the same time, they began gradually tying images from the truths to the myths they created."

"You've lost me," Astra said, wondering if the ayahuasca had simply not worn off.

"Take those natural cycles – for things like when to plant, for instance," he said. He was still insistent, but with the gentle patience of a teacher who wanted his student to learn more than he wanted to stroke his own ego over his knowledge. Did you know that both the lamb and the crucifixion of Jesus have their origin in the constellation Aries?"

Astra just sat silently, listening. She wasn't even sure she would know a constellation if it fell in her lap. Preferably not when she was on ayahuasca.

"The Sun, Earth and Aries all *cross* the same path to mark the Vernal Equinox. It marks the time in spring when it's best to plant. Aries is the sign of the *lamb,* symbolic of *growth.* Simple reminders of simple instructions."

"Oh wow," Astra said, beginning to follow the

shaman's drift. "So what you're saying is long before the *Lamb of God* came along, including the story of his crucifixion, the cross and the lamb had a place of importance in human existence."

The shaman grinned his toothless grin and nodded, pleased with the young grasshopper.

"Hey wait," she continued. "Aren't there twelve signs of the zodiac? If you include Earth and the Sun, you've got fourteen vitally important heavenly bodies, right?"

The shaman nodded, his grin growing wider.

"Aren't there also fourteen stations of the cross?"

"In the ancient catacombs below Rome, there are *no* depictions of Jesus on the cross," he continued, still nodding. "There were no crosses whatsoever in any of the early Christian art. And any art meant to be a reference to Jesus depicts him symbolically – as a *lamb*. It wasn't until the Council of Constantinople took place in 692 AD that this was reversed. That was when showing Jesus on the cross in depictions of his *crossification* began being included in religious art.

Yet it was necessary to anchor the natural truths to the unnatural stories – so that the collective subconscious would connect the two over a long enough period of time the natural truths were forgotten. Hence, the lamb continuing to be included. Usually at the foot of the cross."

"But what about the Jews?" Astra said. "Doesn't the lamb play an important role in their rituals also?"

David Bowie nodded. "They not only borrowed the *Passover* from their slave masters, the Egyptians, but they continue to sacrifice lambs to this day."

"There's just one thing that confuses me," Astra said.

"I always thought Aries was the sign of the goat."

"That's exactly what those agents of control of yours wanted all along. Once they had successfully anchored Jesus and the lamb together, they began to conflate the astrological sign of the lamb with the goat. Over time, they anchored the goat to an unnatural storyline about the exact opposite of Jesus. And since Jesus was by this time considered the embodiment of God, the opposite of Jesus was the opposite of God."

"So the goat became symbolic of Satan." Astra said.

"Never lose sight of one simple truth: Where there are polarities, there is invariably someone pulling the strings to get people to choose one side or the other. Polarities are an artificial construct. They aren't something you find in the natural world."

"So the God versus Satan thing?" Astra said. "That's a construct?"

The shaman paused for a few moments, penetrating her gaze with his piercing eyes as if weighing his response against the strength of her mind to carry the information forward from there.

"Anyone who insists they represent an infinite good or an infinite evil must be examined closely to discern their motive," he replied softly. "The odds are they're selling something that will profit them far more than it will you."

Astra was pretty sure allowing the human race to make up its own mind about the nature of things like good and evil, and decide what to believe for itself, wouldn't work too well for anyone wanting to control it. Especially if they were coming from another world. There would be no reason to launch the Inquisition or the Crusades. Or any of the other many, many, many wars started over religion. And without that, how would they keep the human race distracted? Without distractions, they might start asking questions about what those extraterrestrials were doing here.

"Don't forget, it wasn't just to establish control of the people," he said, still speaking softly, his voice trailing off. "It was to get you to stop focusing on the stars altogether. Because that's where *they* came from, too."

With that, the shaman was gone. As was the fire, tripod, cast-iron kettle that had only just been dangling from it, and the clay mug in her hand. Astra sat in the middle of a pink sand swale in the mid-day sun, thirst scratching at her throat. Without turning around, she knew both Samara and El stood just behind her. One was holding a bottle of water and the other held the keys to the Pinto.

The three women walked in silence back to the highway, Astra's thoughts swirling with all she'd seen and felt on her journey. She had so many questions. But one stood out more than any other.

"So," she said, as they approached the Pinto and Samara handed her the keys. "What's up with the Sumerian Warrior Priestess?"

"You already know the answer to that question," El said. The patience in her voice made Astra miss her impatience. It seemed less condescending. "She seemed familiar, didn't she?"

"Intimately," Astra replied. "But what was I doing in the United Kingdom? Weren't Sumerians originally known as Mesopotamians? And wasn't Mesopotamia the name for ancient Iraq?"

Without even needing an answer, Astra Talitha knew

three things: the cradle of civilization was peopled with human-alien hybrids. And she first came here as a *Star Seed* to help them be more than just beasts of burden for the extraterrestrials who came here for our rare Earth metals and other natural resources. The third had to do with the burning question on everyone's mind since the United States invaded Iraq for reasons that made no sense. Until now. It was to destroy any and all evidence remaining that might confirm the origin story the human race was waking up to, no matter how hard the agents of control fought to keep us all asleep.

"So El, tell me something," she said. "If I was a warrior priestess when I came as a *Star Seed* thousands of years ago, what am I here as now?" Samara had been explaining to Astra about the *Lightworkers* the *Star Seeds* are here to be. Among them are as many as a dozen different designations, maybe more. They include *Transmuters* and *Lightkeepers, Healers, Psychics* and *Clairvoyants*. But Astra wasn't any of those things.

"You are something of your own making," El replied. "You are our *Warrior Grifter*."

"Don't be silly," Samara snapped. Having done Astra's tarot many times she'd drawn the same card representing her higher purpose every time. "Our Astra is *The Messenger*."

"Considering what storytellers grifters need to be, I fail to see the difference," the lanky extraterrestrial said, fastening her seatbelt. "Now, let's see if we can get this Pinto off the ground."

"Why do I get the idea you two are avoiding telling me about your search for a luscious Lyran and a dominatrix's missing husband?" Astra said, making eye contact with first Samara, then El in the rear view mirror.

The Tall Man, however, was nowhere to be seen. Nor were there any elephants in fat suits anywhere.

# CHAPTER FOURTEEN

Astra wasn't that surprised to see the delivery truck was from Boston. After all, that's where the largest supply of black market fat suits was purported to be coming from. But what did surprise her was David stepping down from the cab of the truck. But it shouldn't have. Part of her was expecting it.

For as long as she'd known her Las Vegas connections, she had valued them for their discretion in delicate situations. And if anything constituted a delicate situation, it was the break-up of Astra Talitha and David Aeschlimann. Every grifter on the eastern seaboard knew about the two. Of this Astra was well aware. The grifter community has its legends. It has its gossips and its grapevine from which those gossips pluck low-hanging fruit. Astra could only assume that low-hanging fruit is fermented and the gossips get high off it. What other reward could there possibly be for all that gossiping?

But worst of all, the grifter community has its matchmakers. And being that her contacts are located in the wedding chapel capital of the world, of course they would fall into that category. She made a mental note to ask Emo how she could confirm her suspicion that one or more of them had been exposed to an energy vampire and been turned into a *drama queen.*

She couldn't quite tell if David's was a *cat-that-ate-the-canary* grin or something a bit more sheepish. Or was that a triumphant smirk? Either way, Astra was annoyed. Her morning had started out once again with getting up on the sideways side of the bed. And it was largely due to love. To be more specific, it was largely due to the love-sick.

Waking before dawn to the sound of a weeping energy vampire is without question the most disturbing way to wake up Astra could think of. Especially for a Monday. She would have continued to lay in bed considering a side business of selling alarm clocks programmed to wake people to that sound, but the annoying wailing wouldn't stop. And something told her just getting out of bed wasn't going to help. She was right.

She found Emo slumped in the doorway of *Alien Investigations,* still weeping. Struggling to locate her *compassionate mother* chakra she offered him some hot cocoa because it seemed more nurturing than black coffee. And it definitely fell under the category of *comfort food.* She was pretty sure her *compassionate mother* chakra had been buried somewhere beneath the most padded part of her anatomy, which was where things like hot chocolate and other comfort foods invariably ended up.

Well aware the fat suits were to arrive by ten o'clock that morning, Astra tried to hurry things along with the sex-starved energy vampire. But it was a mistake to simply brush off Emo's concerns. He was convinced he would be stuck on this rock when the White House goaded the North Koreans into nuclear annihilation of the entire planet. Unless he was able to elevate his resonant frequency above where it was presently stuck, he could very well find his disembodied spirit trapped here for hundreds of thousands of years once his body was burned to cinders, or melted in the fallout of nuclear winter.

"By the time biological life forms begin to develop here again and I can inhabit one, I will have completely forgotten who I am and won't *EVER* get back home!" he wailed, cooled cocoa spraying from his nose. "And the whole thing is over an argument about who has the bigger penis!"

Astra was pretty sure the whole thing wasn't over penis size. It was over the button. And in Astra's experience, few men actually know what to do with the button. Which was why so many of us were as stuck on this rock as Emo. She considered offering to check with both leaders' wives for confirmation on her theory, but didn't know exactly how she'd get through to the wife of the North Korean leader.

"Look, Emo. There's nothing we can do about that right now," Astra said. Her attempt to sound nurturing was coming off sounding more like the bad acting of a stage hand suddenly given a script and told the understudy broke his leg so he's on. Wiping cocoa droplets from the lapel of her khaki shirt, the bootylicious con artist decided on a different approach.

"I made contact with her yesterday," she said. She hadn't by any stretch of the imagination made contact with Emo's missing Lyran lover, but she had to say *something* to get him to shut up, and that was all she could think of.

The energy vampire jumped up from his chair with such force it fell back onto the floor and the hot cocoa went with it. The not-at-all-manly vampire began hopping up and down while flapping his hands at the wrists and squealing. Astra thought he looked like a clueless fireman working for the harbor commission. Except the only assignment he could get was patrolling for very small beach fires.

"Hold on, bring it down a notch, Casanova," she said, tossing a copy of The Watchtower someone left there on the floor to soak up the spilled cocoa. "It was only astral contact, but she gave me an important message for you."

The energy vampire froze for a moment. Looking deep into her eyes, he saw something Astra had no idea could be seen. It was unnerving to have him in there poking around, especially since she knew what he could do to her energy if motivated. But he smiled.

"Yes," he said, setting the chair upright but not sitting back down. "You *have* seen her. Her spoor is all over you. And this place!" He stretched his arms out just as El had done not too much earlier, and an odd connection tapped its way in Morse code from vertebrae to vertebrae up her spine.

Twirling around with his arms still outstretched Emo was suddenly possessed by the spirit of Julie Andrews on some mountaintop in the Alps. The single note of joy he warbled as he twirled worried her. Considering what happened the last time *she* let out a single note with reckless abandon, she was not without her reasons for being hesitant. In defense of reckless abandon, the one time she did do it resulted in the avoidance of a wreck, so there's that. Proof homonyms matter after all.

"You were right here when you made astral contact,

weren't you?" Emo asked with unbridled excitement. "And brought some of her essence back with you! Tell me every little thing."

But Astra hadn't been right there. She'd been in the desert with David Bowie and Lazarus. And a Sumerian who turned out to be an incarnation of herself thousands of years earlier. Which she was still trying to wrap her head around. But as far as she knew, there were no Lyrans. Not even Samara and El were there.

Yet Emo was leaning over the desk running his cheek over it for any speck of his lovely Lyran's essence as if she'd been laid out right there waiting for him to come take her. He abruptly sat upright and twisted in the chair, running his hand along the back of it and then sniffing his fingertips. Astra was thoroughly puzzled. And mildly disgusted. She couldn't recall where she'd seem someone do the same thing, only with their armpits. The thought still made her shudder.

"Uh, yeah," she stammered. "Samara did a chakra cleanse for me and then I went on an astral journey. Right here in the office. Just yesterday." She knew herself to be a far better storyteller than that, but had been caught off guard. And while most grifters are masters at thinking on their feet, in Astra's defense she was sitting down at the time. On an astronomical ass descended from giants, apparently. That, and her mind was racing to find a reason for the missing Lyran's essence being all over her office. "She sent back what she thought I could carry for you, and this is it!"

It was Astra's turn to spread her arms and spin, only she did it in her office chair. As long as it made Emo the energy vampire happy enough to stop his sobbing, she felt she'd done her job. For a brief moment she considered booting up her computer and locating an old Pretenders song with the best advice of any rock song in history: *Stop Your Sobbing*. But why get sidetracked when her current scam was going so well? She hadn't lost track of his promise of being rewarded with rare earth metals.

"She told me to tell you all will be revealed in due time," she said cryptically. "And this is the place the two of you will meet up in person. Very soon. That is all she could tell me just then. We both had things to do. I was pretty busy being shrunk to the size of a pinhead so I could squeeze through the black hole of reality, for instance. You know how it is."

Emo smiled and took a deep breath. She hoped he would keep on breathing deeply, and told him so as she ushered him from the office and went to get the mop bucket. Because all *Alien Investigation* agencies worth their weight in salt have a mop bucket in the closet somewhere. Which is why it was about the time she was wringing hot cocoa out of the Watchtower that she heard the truck lumbering up the street. And none too soon. Clients were already lining up out front for computer time with a fat suit.

It was then she spotted David stepping down from the cab of the U-Haul and knew she'd been set up. She wanted to mutter something under her breath about those damned matchmakers in Las Vegas. She wanted to grumble about what a pain in the ass love is – especially if it's a giant ass. She wanted to run back to her living quarters and fix her hair, brush her teeth and dab some perfume behind her knees. For obvious reasons. But the dazed *Warrior Messenger* froze instead, a deer caught in headlights. She watched as

David politely made his way through the sea of people out front and tapped on the door with the back of a single knuckle. And she loved him for it. She longed for nothing more than to kiss every hair on the back of that knuckle.

But of course she was not about to let that get in the way of showing him how annoyed she was about being set up by Las Vegas matchmakers.

"So who do you think's going to win the pool on this one?" she asked, locking the door behind him after he stepped inside. But not before telling everyone in line he was delivering all the fat suits they needed for everyone to have computer time safe from alien entity attachment.

"That is yet to be seen," David replied, ever the pointlessly pragmatic. It was just that kind of enigma Astra loved about him. He was by far the most impractical grifter she'd known, while at the same time being the most practical. And while it had annoyed her beyond endurance when they lived together, her journey to the heart of *Divine Paradox* the day before had changed her perspective considerably. What she had always seen as contradiction, a weakness, became something entirely different with perspective. Especially the perspective one is likely to gain on an astral journey care of David Bowie and Lazarus. Not to mention the Sumerian.

Astra was relieved at Samara's timing. She'd slipped in the back door of the apartment and joined them just as Astra was letting David in the front door. The tantalizing tarot reader had a slightly amused smile on her face when she saw David. Had Astra been paying closer attention, she would have detected a hint of recognition between the two. She might even have seen the slightest nod pass between them. But it was a day for distraction and thinking on her feet. Or booty, depending. Leaving Samara to verify each waiting client had reserved a time for a computer terminal, Astra and David began unloading the fat suits from the truck.

And despite her level of distraction, Astra did some math in her head. What they would be bringing in from just that morning's clients alone confirmed that El had hit on a cash cow with the idea. Not only were there more than enough fat suits to go around, David had brought the microwaves with him. And for some reason, he also brought both cases of industrial safety glasses.

"For using around the microwaves," he said cryptically. "Especially after one is loaded with an angry, hungry negative alien entity."

She was also not surprised to see he had brought all six dozen cases of incandescent lightbulbs, which sent a surge of electric pleasure to places Astra had all but forgotten about. Along with relief that she would now have a good reason to get rid of the questionable fluorescent mind-control devices currently dangling dangerously from the ceiling fans.

It didn't take long for David to make himself useful. As he replaced all the bulbs in both the office and apartment spaces, Astra filled him in on El's plan to bring the missing Star Seeds to them. Perhaps it was her excitement over the newly surging electricity in her loins that kept her from noticing that David seemed to already know the score. Nothing she was telling him seemed to need explanation. Nor did she even bother to ask him just why the deed to this very property was frozen to the bottom of their freezer in

Boston.

Astra quickly cleaned out the clutter that had accumulated in the mop-bucket closet at the end of the hallway to make way for the microwaves they'd agreed should go on each shelf. As Samara separated what should go into trash and what should go into recycling, she held up the wad of napkins Astra had forgotten tossing in there.

"Something you want to share with the class, Miss Astra?" she asked with a curious look.

"I'd been planning to ask you if you could get Emo's DNA from those, like a real investigation agency would do," Astra replied sheepishly. "But then I remembered those genealogy websites on the internet that offer to do it pretty cheap. I just..."

"*PLEASE* tell me you did *NOT* send Emo's DNA to one of them!" Samara said, cutting her off mid-sentence. "That's how they're getting our DNA to check for the presence of extraterrestrial genetics in the human population!"

"But I thought they didn't know how to identify it," Astra said, sheepishly. She was more than slightly ashamed a seasoned grifter like her hadn't thought of that.

"That's just what they want you to think," Samara said, shoving the Emo-soaked napkins in the pocket of her Official Tarot Master bistro apron. "I intend to burn these as soon as possible. The last thing we want is for the Monarchians to be alerted to the fact we're helping an energy vampire who's been turned toward the *Light*. Emo would never be safe again. They would dissect him in a heartbeat just to figure out what his genetics are and how to isolate it in everyone on this planet. We must never underestimate the Monarchian agenda."

Astra would have pressed her for more details, but there were clients waiting at the door. Bathed in the soft light of possibly planet-destroying incandescence, David completed the tasks Astra assigned to him with little explanation. In no time, *Alien Investigations* was ready for the day's business.

Once the microwaves were in place on each shelf, he opened a fresh bag of cheesy-puffs and demonstrated for Astra, Samara, and the clients crowding the office exactly how the negative alien entities were lured out of the fat suits. Tossing a handful of cheesy-puffs into the open microwave, he held up a fat suit at arm's length in front of it.

Camping it up for clients with cell cameras recording, he mimicked the electrical current of a computer monitor and made a whooshing sound to indicate an alien entity escaping it and entering the microwave. Slamming the door, he spun around theatrically.

"That, ladies and gentlemen, is how it will go this morning when you are done surfing the net," he said. "All that's left is to remove the portable Faraday cage to our partner Samara's shop next door, where she takes care of the rest from there."

A single client raised her hand timidly.

"You're not incinerating them, are you?" she asked. "I thought you were just going to be storing them until returning them to wherever they came from. I'm opposed to the death penalty."

"That's why we're taking them over to my shop, my darling," Samara's *Sweet Home Alabama* voice said soothingly. "My job is to call in my spirit guides, including

Ascended Master Kwan Yin, whose focus, as you know, is on Compassion and Healing. Once securing their help in elevating the resonant frequencies of these nasty entities to a level that is intolerable to them, they will either submit to being transmuted into *Light Beings*, or gladly self-deport rather than risk starving to death on frequencies too high for them to digest."

Astra loved David at that moment. His demonstration was flawless and showed an expertise that surprised her. At least where it pertained to negative alien entities. And his command of his audience reminded her of that first time she saw him, the parking valet wrapped around his finger as he coaxed the keys to a Pinto out of him effortlessly. And perhaps, just perhaps, not in the least bit pointlessly. Once again, she was reminded of how few had ever truly defined the *artist* in *confidence artist* as effortlessly as her David did.

Astra couldn't wait to tell El about all of it. And for the first time that morning, noticed she wasn't there. She'd fully expected to see her that morning welcoming clients. It had been El's plan in the first place to lure in the *Star Seeds* with the fat suits. So it made no sense that she wasn't there carefully watching for them to show up.

If Astra had been paying more attention, she would have seen the alien's absence as yet another red flag. Which had begun to clutter the landscape, although only David and Samara seemed to notice. In fact, he was relieved they hadn't been shoved in the mop-bucket closet. Samara, who had been keeping count however, was growing increasingly uneasy with how they were piling up.

Astra had also been fully expecting to see absolutely nothing when the first client finished her cruise on the electronic superhighway and removed the fat suit. But when David held it up in front of the microwave freshly loaded with the delectable neon orange cheesy puffs, the transfer of negative alien entity from fat suit to microwave was unmistakable.

What looked to Astra like strands of black smoke came snaking out of the fat suit's puffy silicone fingertips first, then its elbows, knees and toes. Next, from the very center of the fat suit's heart a black spear of pure dark energy emerged and all the strands merged as one as they shot forward into the microwave. There was so much more of it than Astra ever imagined would come out of a fat suit inhabited by an invisible entity. For a moment she wasn't sure David would be able to close the microwave door without a significant amount of it escaping into the atmosphere. But he did. He got the door shut like a master. None escaped. Before picking it up to transport it next door however, he donned a pair of safety glasses and passed a box of them around to the onlookers.

"Safety first," he said. For the first time, Astra detected a paternal note to his voice and it was oddly comforting. It surprised her that she would be attracted to the protective side of David. When he turned back to the microwave, cell cameras capturing the moment, Astra held her breath. For the first time, she was feeling not just the reality of the situation, but the gravity of it. It made her want to sit down. Gravity tended to do that to Astra Talitha. Unless she was already sitting down. In a flying Pinto.

David lifted the microwave expertly.

And nothing exploded. The microwave didn't abruptly yank itself out of his arms, didn't buck like an angry mechanical bull in a border town tavern. It did, however, begin to inexplicably reek in the cramped hallway. One of those unanticipated consequences of alien hunting and trapping one doesn't discover until they find themselves in tight quarters with one locked in a portable Faraday cage is negative alien entities fart defensively. Of course, the fart smell was the last thing to hit them. Which tends to be the case where farts are concerned. At least this time everyone knew exactly where the fart came from. And for once, no one could blame it on the dog. Who, for all Astra knew, was somewhere in Maricopa County paying the ultimate price for hunting aliens the wrong way.

Fat suits and microwaves were clearly the cutting edge of alien hunting. But Astra Talitha had learned the hard way that clothespins needed to be included in their list of necessary equipment.

The day passed quickly, with each computer station reserved for the full thirty minute time limit from the moment they opened to the moment a weary Astra locked the door behind the last one. Switching off the neon UFO sign and pulling down the shade on the door, she turned to David and Samara, who both had a *cat-that-ate-the-canary* grin on their face.

"What?" she said, somewhat annoyed that the two had gotten as cozy as they had so quickly.

David handed her a white paper bag and her breath caught in her throat.

"Is that what I think it is?" she said, her eyes wide with hopeful recognition.

Samara and David simply continued to grin as Astra opened the bag and discovered more pulled-pork sticky buns from Boston's Chinatown than she could eat in a single sitting. Despite that, gravity finally took hold and she plopped down right where she stood and dug into the sticky buns, sitting contentedly on the floor.

"Life. Is. Sweet." she grinned, quoting Samara. Sweet brown gravy dripped from the corner of her mouth and all was right with Astra Talitha's world.

David wanted nothing more than to lick that brown gravy off her chin, but the look Samara gave him told him to give it time. Knowing how awkward sharing the living quarters could get in Astra's apartment, she had offered the *pointless scammer* the hide-a-bed in the back of her shop next door. What could have been more awkwardness than Astra was prepared for was smoothed over and made as comfortable as possible by the true-hearted tarot reader. Had Astra not been preoccupied by the sticky buns she would have acknowledged how indispensable her faithful partner had become in such a short time.

As it was, she simply nodded as she handed them the Pinto keys and the two headed out to return the truck to U-Haul. Samara would follow in the Pinto, which would get them both back, where David would settle into the back of Samara's tarot and crystal ball shop. It didn't occur to Astra until she heard the truck pull away that it meant he would be staying indefinitely. And even then, it seemed to her to be perfectly natural, as if it was what she'd been expecting all along.

The rest of the week proceeded to go just as smoothly as that first day had. Samara, David and Astra catered to worried internet users and trapped entity after entity. All the while, Samara's skills at transmutation grew stronger with the practice. Astra had to admit, despite not believing in any of it, she was beginning to appreciate the perspective her New Age friend had on all things so foreign they're alien.

As well, despite El's absence, the list Astra began to compile of potential *Star Seeds* who came through the door was impressive. And growing by the minute. While she didn't quite have the nerve to approach them with what she suspected, she was able to get their contact information, including their actual location. Simply telling clients she needed it for insurance purposes was all it took for the grifter to con them out of their home address and phone numbers.

The only snag had been when the health department showed up with sharps containers, insisting Astra was collecting waste material that could pose a biohazard. Apparently, despite there being no actual destruction of alien entities, who didn't have physical bodies to begin with, their farts were reported by a concerned citizen as a possible toxic gas.

"And how exactly is a sharps container supposed to mitigate this alleged biohazard?" Astra asked. The health inspector grew defensive far too quickly. He explained with some petulance it was standard procedure to supply sharps containers to businesses reported to be producing bio-waste.

"At least until determining a more suitable receptacle," he added. Astra laughed. But it was a kind-hearted laugh rather than a laugh that would trigger more defensiveness in the thin-skinned health inspector. In the end, he left *Alien Investigations* with a barrel that was clearly marked *CAUTION: HAZARDOUS WASTE* on the outside. It had a lid that sealed to prevent anything, including possibly toxic alien entity farts, from escaping.

By Friday afternoon the team was exhausted and growing cranky. Some of it had to do with lugging the unwieldy biohazard barrel in and out of Samara's shop every time a microwave needed to be cleaned out. Which seemed to all of them a pointlessly stinky job. The alternative would have been to carry the microwave out to the back where the barrel was kept. But the health inspector explained sternly that it could become airborne and contaminate the entire city of Sedona.

Despite their exhausting successful week, Astra had grown increasingly worried about El's absence. She was just about to leave a note on the door for her after closing up for the day, when two men got out of a black vintage Cadillac that had been parked on the street behind her Pinto all afternoon. She'd noticed them when they first arrived, but because the car's windows were tinted, hadn't gotten a glimpse of them.

Part of her was expecting the Tall Man to step out of the car. And while the men who emerged were indeed tall, and dressed similarly, neither one wore a hat. But their slightly disheveled hair suggested otherwise. Perhaps they heard how much Astra dislikes men who fail to take off their hat in her office and erred on the side of caution, leaving them behind in the Cadillac.

She was tempted to simply lock the door and slip out the back, but the Pinto was not exactly hidden from their sight. And without the Pinto, she wouldn't be able to head over to Sedona Taco for the most amazing pulled-pork burritos she'd ever feasted on. They were, in fact, the *only* pulled-pork burritos she'd ever feasted on.

All week she had been promising them to David. They'd agreed to go Friday after closing for the weekend. Samara would be leaving mid-day for a weekend chakra realignment and Workshop in Miracles at a sweat lodge in New Mexico. David would be on his own. And for the first time since his arrival, the two of them would also be alone. Together. Going out to eat seemed a safe bet to Astra, who felt herself growing increasingly inclined to spread her arms wide and welcome him back into her life. And her legs.

But before she could turn off the neon UFO sign and lock the door, the two curious men in dark suits with crumpled hair reached the door and knocked. Astra couldn't help but notice neither of them had hair on the back of their knuckles. She couldn't exactly pinpoint just why that made her uneasy, but it seemed David had picked up on it as well. They silently agreed to proceed with caution.

"CIA, Ma'am," they said in unison, flashing identification cards that could just as easily have been printed by Astra. Or David. Or both of them together just for the entertainment value. "We need to ask you some questions about your alien entity removal system. Is there a place where we can sit down?"

David wheeled computer chairs out from two cubicles in the back while Astra reluctantly told them to make themselves comfortable.

"But it's been a long day, gentlemen," she added. "And we're just headed to dinner. So please make this quick. What is it about our alien entity removal service that interests you?"

"We'll cut to the chase then," the one with the most disheveled hair said. "The US Department of Defense has a patent on that exact same system and we're concerned the technology may have been stolen from us. We need to know where you got the idea for it."

"You're in luck, gentlemen," Astra replied, a little too quickly. "The answer is simple. I got the idea from the aliens. Care to tell me where the Defense Department got it?"

She was fairly certain agents of the US government, especially intelligence agents, could neither confirm nor deny having obtained technology from extraterrestrials. But Astra couldn't resist the temptation. She wanted to see them squirm. It's a favorite pastime of grifters to make agents of the government squirm. It often resulted in grifters getting permanent work with them, which was far more lucrative than the usual small-time hustles many of them lived on. Astra had lost track of how many great scam artists had been lost to the *Dark Side* that way.

"You and I both know that's classified," the humorless agent replied. He launched into listing a string of charges she could be subject to if she did not cease and desist immediately with the capturing and transporting of alien entities. Among them was the promise of charges involving violations of US Patent law. More than one, apparently. And then there were the usual accusations of theft of intellectual property and violations of the Digital Millennium Copyright Act. To which Astra responded each time with an exaggerated yawn.

"We have the authority to take you into custody now if you do not agree to these terms," he concluded. But not a single term had been mentioned. The only thing mentioned was *cease and desist* and a variety of charges so obscure she was certain neither one had ever read any of them. Several moments passed with nothing said as Astra looked from Agent A to Agent B and then David, who sat on the edge of Astra's desk looking like he was about to giggle.

"Yawn," she finally said. Out loud. "This conversation bores me. That's how it is with empty threats. Come back with a warrant and we'll talk." With that, Astra stood and crossed casually to the door. Opening it, she turned back to the two men and motioned with her eyebrows for them to leave. David swooned. The two men with skinny black ties and no eyebrows or knuckle hair stood to leave when the first gunshot rang out.

Instinctively, the two men dropped to the floor, while both Astra and David ran toward the sound of gunfire. That's how it is with men who are pragmatically pointless scammers and women descended from guardian giants. Protecting anyone in the line of fire was more important than anything as inconsequential as whether they'd get hit by stray bullets.

Standing just outside the door while the two men cowered under her desk, Astra glanced down the street. Dog Star the Intergalactic Bounty Hunter stood in the middle of the street with a weapon she had never seen yet instantly recognized. She didn't know much about intergalactic weaponry, but she did know Dog Star's was not a gun that fired bullets.

At the other end of the street The Dominatrix stood facing him with a modified whip that shot lasers out of the tip whenever she snapped it. Neither could have been the source of the gunshot they'd heard. It was then that she noticed D.B. Cooper standing with an assault rifle modified with a clip that looked like it held several thousand rounds. Turning to David, Astra gave him a grim look.

"It figures we'd come to the Southwest and end up in the middle of the *Gunfight at the Things Are Definitely Not Okay Corral.*" It was at that point the two CIA agents emerged from under Astra's desk. Only just as Astra had suspected and David had known all along, they were not CIA agents.

They were Draco-Reptilians. Shape shifting Draco-Reptilians. Which explained the lack of body hair. And they were armed. Armed with what definitely did not look like anything that shot bullets. As they stepped out onto the porch, Astra and David crouched low to avoid the lethal directed energy being fired from them and headed for the back door.

"We can't get to the Pinto," she said. "But if we can get to the end of the alley unseen, we might be able to get an Uber. Grabbing David's hand, the two ran for their lives amid directed energy fire that was sure to inspire conspiracy theorists. Astra just knew they'd be speculating in no time about *Directed Energy Weapons* being used in an attempt to start an inferno in the Arizona desert. Where nothing grows so nothing burns. But don't tell the conspiracy theorists. Why spoil their fun? As if endless debate about the National Geospatial-Intelligence Agency keeping Earth's atmosphere heavily ionized in order to facilitate directed energy warfare wasn't enough fun all by itself.

Wishing they'd been in a far more romantic situation in which to be holding hands for the first time since reuniting, the two stopped when they reached the end of the alley to catch their breath. They turned toward each other the way they once did at the sink doing dishes in their tiny Beacon Hill kitchen. Looking deep into her eyes, David could taste Astra's lips before he even began to reach for them with his. And without question, for David Astra's lips were even more luscious than her booty.

Perhaps it was because they were staring into each other's eyes about to kiss that they didn't notice the spaceship that had floated down from above and hovered silently only a few feet from where they stood. That's how it is when two lovers get lost in each other's gaze. Those who fear alien abduction should take note and at all costs avoid doing just that while standing at the end of an ally waiting for an Uber. In Sedona. Where there definitely are not any wildfires. But there are aliens. Who apparently like to pretend they're CIA agents and have so much time on their hands they've actually read the *Digital Millennium Copyright Act*.

Inexplicably, that unmistakable sensation of someone watching her grabbed Astra's attention and she turned away from David momentarily. She was just in time to see a man tipping his fedora at her. It was the Tall Man. And he was at the controls of a small spaceship. Pointing at something behind them. Astra turned to see both Draco-Reptilian shape shifters chasing after them. Turning back, she was about to give David a brief back-story about him, when David's grip on her hand tightened painfully and he nodded at the Tall Man.

Just as the directed energy being fired at them began to slice chunks of asphalt from beneath their feet, Astra felt David's arm wrap around her waist. In what seemed to Astra to be the exact reverse of splashing down a *Slip 'N*

*Slide*, only without the sprinkler, the two transported into the spaceship. Unsurprisingly, she found herself sitting in the seat to the right of the Tall Man. And David was seated to the right of her. He smiled and asked if she wanted something to drink. Reaching into a small compartment beneath the craft's instrument panel, David pulled out what looked like it could possibly be a milk carton and held it out to Astra.

"Horchata?" he said. "It's not from here, but it's pretty good. And it's cold."

"David, how exactly is it you know where the mini-fridge is on this....whatever this is?" Astra asked, brushing bits of asphalt and alley dust off her socks.

"This isn't the first time either one of us has been aboard," David said. "You're not the only one who got caught in that rainstorm, you know."

# CHAPTER FIFTEEN

"They captured your energy signature when you left for the astral plane in the desert. And they've been following you since. No one bothered to tell you they monitor the vortexes continuously, did they? Most people think all they watch is the sky, but that's a red herring. Humans are predictable, and this is no different. Your Department of Defense and the private contractors it hires are constantly monitoring resonance energy fields and where energy goes."

Astra's mind had to race to keep up with what their mysterious rescuer was saying. She still wasn't sure what had just happened. In her defense, she'd never gone from being shot at with *directed energy weapons* to sitting in a spaceship before.

"And now they know who you are and where you live. At this point there is virtually nowhere you can go without being found." The Tall Man concluded his explanation of why they were in his spaceship without really saying anything. Yet Astra's thoughts persisted in playing hide-and-seek with the something she had hoped he would actually say.

"What, our energy signature is a way they have of identifying us?" There are many things a person might think to ask, or at the very least bring up for discussion when finding they're in a spacecraft with a fedora-wearing stranger who is most likely not human, and one's energy signature is not one of them. Or is it?

"You know those messy fingerprint-kits they use at crime scenes? Pointless. One might even say they're a *pointless scam.* Your very own defense department has been using energy signatures to identify people for more than two decades. You think all those *security cameras* mounted everywhere in cities around the world are really looking for *terrorists?* I know for fact you understand the term *red herring,* Astra. And what exactly do you think the *drone program* is all about? Getting energy signatures is where it's at in today's world of mass surveillance. And like I said, at this point there is virtually nowhere you can go without them finding you."

"Virtually." As usual, Astra was trying to make sense out of something that made no sense.

"Yes. They know exactly where you are right now."

"They know I'm in a spaceship."

"They do now. It took you two long enough to board."

"So why aren't they following us?" Astra looked around at the three hundred and sixty degree windows lining the little craft for any sight of fighter jets or black-budget helicopters designed exclusively for the purpose of chasing alien spacecrafts. She saw nothing but sky around them. Not even the Foo Fighters, which disappointed her. Why sing a song about the sky being a neighborhood if you're not going to actually be there to welcome guests?

"Just because they know where you are doesn't mean they can follow you. They saw you board my little dinghy, so they know you're on board a spaceship. But they can't see any of us. As soon as you boarded I activated the cloaking feature that comes standard with the deluxe model. They can't even pick up on your energy signature with the cloaking feature activated."

"So *virtually* anywhere except spaceships with cloaking devices, and.... what else?"

"And that place you only just learned how to find when you were in the desert. Which they can't follow you to, since they're stuck in manual and subject to the Space Fence with all its shrapnel and other debris keeping them grounded. You, on the other hand, have mastered astral travel, so you don't have to worry about it."

Astra looked at David. He said nothing. And he definitely had that *cat-that-ate-the-canary* grin on his face. Again. She realized there were several ways the conversation could go. So before it could unravel in any one or more of those directions she asked the most important question.

"Who the fuck are you, anyway?"

The Tall Man had effortlessly set the controls for his little space dinghy to the intergalactic version of auto-pilot as he'd been speaking and turned to face her. He nonchalantly continued to speak as he casually stretched his impossibly long legs out on the dashboard. It was at that point Astra realized he wasn't moving his lips when he spoke.

And David couldn't stop grinning.

"Dude, what was in that Horchata? Because I'm pretty sure we're both tripping. You haven't stopped grinning since we sat down, and I'm hallucinating."

"What exactly are you seeing?"

"Not seeing; hearing. Okay, maybe it is something I'm seeing. Or not seeing. Our chauffeur here has been talking since we boarded, and I'm hallucinating that his lips aren't moving when he's doing it."

"Did you stop to consider a third possibility?"

"A third possibility?" David couldn't be certain, but he suspected Astra was being deliberately obtuse.

"Stop playing dumb. You know exactly what I'm getting at." Astra squinted her eyes and tilted her head to get a different perspective. It reminded David of an adorable Jack Russell Terrier he'd had as a kid.

"He's a ventriloquist, isn't he?"

"No. But that was the third possibility."

"Why are you laughing, David? This isn't funny. Spaceship flying ventriloquists are not funny."

"How do you know? Have you met many of them?"

"Ahem." The Tall Man was clearing his throat. Astra wished she'd been looking directly at him when he did it. She'd always wanted to know how a ventriloquist clears his throat.

"As I was saying," he continued.

"I am your *guardian*. Or what your lore refers to as a *watcher*. While most *watchers* are assigned one *Star Seed* for their entire biological lifespan here on Earth, some of us are better at multitasking. That would be me."

"Let me guess, you've been watching both of us," Astra said, looking directly at David. Naturally, her mind immediately went to some kinky alien watching the two of them in their little bed doing things that she assumed were not being enjoyed by anyone but the two of them. On this planet or anywhere else in the galaxy. Or Universe. Or multiverse. Or dimension. Or some complex alternatively-factual reality she didn't have the brain power to comprehend but definitely did not involve hamsters doing calculus. Or squirrels.

"Not exactly. I've been watching all three of you."

"All three?" It was enough of a surprise he hadn't corrected her and said he'd been watching *two* of them. But *three*? In an uncharacteristic display of regressively childish behavior, Astra Talitha began counting her fingers.

"One," she said, pointing at David. "Two," she said, pointing to herself.

David was still giggling. And Astra still wasn't entirely sure they weren't both tripping on something that was in the Horchata.

"I'm only getting two. Is the third one invisible?" If there was anything Astra Talitha had learned over the previous few weeks, it was to never exclude the possibility of something or someone invisible being involved. In anything. Anything imaginable. Including invisible friends. And enemies.

"There's a more interesting question you might want to ask him, boo." David seemed to have decided to contribute more to the conversation than a grin, although for how long was yet to be seen.

"Okay, I'll bite," Astra said. "If I ask it, can we circle back to the unanswered one about a ventriloquist in space?" Realizing she'd left too wide an opening, she quickly clarified: "The one we're on a magic carpet ride with at this very moment." David smiled and nodded in the classically annoying *wise sage* persona he apparently came to the party as. And it annoyed the hell out of Astra.

"Why is the CIA chasing a *Star Seed*?"

"Not *Star Seed*. *Star Seeds*. Plural. And they aren't exactly CIA. The closest thing to who they are is what Hollywood refers to as *Men in Black*. They've worked in cooperation with the global intelligence community for decades."

It was somewhat unnerving to be having a discussion with someone who gave no outward sign of even being in the conversation. Astra glanced at David to see he'd briefly spit out that cat with the canary and attempted to look sheepish without a single sheep in sight. It would have been awkward if it hadn't been so adorable. Abundantly more adorable than the *wise sage* persona.

"Okay, make that question *Star Seeds* in the plural. But only because David here was in on the joke the whole time. Why is the CIA sending Men in Black to chase *Star Seeds*? I thought those guys were only interested in people claiming to have had an encounter with extraterrestrials."

"Because the entities they work for don't want the *awakening* to happen. Keeping the human race half asleep in a lie about their origins is too profitable for some to want it to end. And the moment the *awakening* is fully realized, their scheme will stop on a dime and profit margins will plummet. So not only do the *Men in Black* work to suppress all information about human-extraterrestrial contact, they work to suppress anything and anyone related to the *awakening*."

Astra wasn't at all surprised to learn theirs wasn't the

only part of the galaxy that seemed to be struggling with corporatism. And greed. And corruption. Or was that being redundant?

"So they've done this to all the *Star Seeds*? Kept an eye on them and started randomly chasing them when it looked like they might be sharing information about their *awakening*?"

"No. They haven't needed to. They were able to identify each and every one of them and have carefully monitored them since their *activation.* All except three specific *Star Seeds.*"

"Okay, this is the part where you explain who exactly these three are. And what makes them so special they get their own multitasking ventriloquist to follow them around in a fedora, lurk under street lamps and show up unannounced in a flying deluxe model space dinghy? Start with the basics of journalism: Who? What? Huh? Why? And the ever popular WTF?"

"Three of you escaped detection. Or rather, three of you were detected and then dismissed as anomalies not worth the manpower to monitor."

"Excuse me?" Astra wasn't sure whether to be offended or flattered that she was considered an anomaly by her government and its agents of control. She had to assume at this point he was referring to her.

"None of you had the traits ordinarily spotted early on in a *Star Seed,* and in fact you all seemed to be exactly the kind of element they've worked hard to foster in order to ensure chaos reigns supreme in America, which has a profound influence on the rest of the world."

"And what element would that be, exactly?" she

wasn't sure just why she bristled and suddenly felt defensive.

"The criminal element."

"Oh. Yep," she said, relaxing and shrugging her shoulders. "That would be me, all right. I can't speak for the other two. Technically David is a criminal also, but his crimes are pointless so I'm not sure they actually count. And I don't know a thing about this third person, so I'll pass on that one."

"There really is no point dwelling on it anyway. That reason is one they've just used as a cover. Because basically, their objective all along has been to turn this entire planet into a prison crawling with corrupt souls dominating and feeding off the uncorrupted. So to speak, anyway. That's nothing new. What they're looking for is those who have the genetics to upset the apple cart.

"Apple?" Astra frowned. "Please don't tell me we're going to pin the whole thing on Eve again. Because that one's been done to death. Literally."

"No," he replied. "What they're looking for is two things: those who have the genetic coding designed specifically to fight the interventionists' agenda and return the human race to a place of balance."

"And the second thing?"

"The second thing is even more of a challenge for them: those who have evolved beyond the programming that's overwritten their genetics."

"So they dismissed three of us because they observed our criminal activity and assumed we were still helpless to our programming despite our genetics? I thought all that *activation* and *awakening* stuff embedded into *Star Seeds'* genetics made their *activation* a sure thing."

"Yes and no."

"Tell me the no part, since I've already heard the yes part."

"Roshambo."

"Roshambo? The ancient Marshal Art?"

"Do you know of any Marshal Arts that include paper?"

"Origami?"

"Rock-paper-scissors. Paper beats rock. Yet it's basically ethereal. Weightless. But can carry some pretty heavy information."

"Like a book."

"Yes. Like that thing nobody reads anymore. It is entirely possible to overcome genetics and evolve beyond them. Or in this case, suppress the genetics to the point you devolve despite them. But the necessary evolving can only be done spiritually. Like paper beating rock, spiritual beats physical, even if the physical is in the form of interventionist programming."

"Okay, we can talk about Origami and book reports later. Let's get back to these three *Star Seeds* we were discussing." It was clear to David and their *watcher* Astra's squirrel was getting restless.

The Tall Man looked from Astra to David and said nothing. But then again, how would Astra have known if he did? That's how it is with magic carpet flying ventriloquists. She looked around the craft at its various screens and instruments and waited for the words to begin appearing in her auditory cortex again. But there was only silence. Even the little craft's propulsion system was silent. She wondered if Elon Musk had anything to do with it. But even that thought didn't produce a break in the silence.

"I'm sure you know enough about the human race to understand how dangerous pregnant pauses can be around fertile women," she said dryly, breaking the silence as only Astra Talitha could.

The *watcher's* smile didn't appear the same way a man like David's does. It didn't happen with his mouth at all. It was entirely restricted to his eyes and the quality of light surrounding him that grew suddenly brighter for a few moments, and then returned to what it had been. It was the first indication Astra was being given that the Tall Man had a sense of humor. And that made her more hopeful than anything he'd said so far.

"Okay, so let's say I buy into this story line and David and I are both *Star Seeds*," she finally said, tired of pregnant pauses and everything that goes with them. "Never mind that two of us randomly managed to find each other. Because that kind of thing happens all the time."

"Out of 144,000 around the world," David interjected, admonishing her sarcasm with facts.

"Thank you for deciding to join us, David," she said, a little too sternly.

"Not two of you. *Three*," the Tall Man said.

"Huh?" Astra looked at David, and even he was puzzled by the comment.

"All three of you have managed to find each other," the *watcher* said. "David, where did you stop for gas after you left Boston?"

"At a Shell station in Martha's Vineyard," he replied. "Hard not to forget, considering. This black kid at the cash register showed me the strangest thing on his cell phone.

And I got the sense he had something to do with this hilarious graffiti in the restroom stall about the Random."

"No way," Astra said, suddenly slightly dizzy.

"Are you celebrating the Random yet?" their host asked, the corners of his penciled-in mouth again turning up slightly.

"Holy. Fucking. Shit."

It was all Astra could think to say. But it said volumes.

David, on the other hand, seemed to have found his sea legs. Or in this case, his space legs. He reached for Astra's hand and gently held it as he spoke.

"I knew when we first met I'd found the *Twin Flame* I'd been told would be at exactly that spot and it all hinged on a Pinto."

"How did you know it wasn't a reference to pinto beans?" Astra interjected. "You could have been meant to meet some brown-skinned beauty selling burritos from a pushcart."

"The image sent to me was of you in a flying Pinto. And until I saw that video of you I had no idea why. But the truth is: I had other more important things to think about. For me, my *activation* was the kind of thing that has sent many *Star Seeds* on a one-way trip to the psych ward. The messages I was getting were so rapid-fire and nonsensical that I thought I was losing my mind. And the prescient dreams terrified me."

He lifted Astra's hand to his lips and placed a kiss in her palm before continuing, carefully closing her fingers around it so the kiss wouldn't escape. Some things are just too precious to let go of, and a kiss is one of them.

"Until I met you. That day everything began to fall

into place. All of it took on a whole new meaning. All the random messages I was getting, the seemingly unrelated things I was being guided to do began making sense to me for the first time since it began. Not necessarily in context. But definitely in the bigger picture of how things are connected. And even if I didn't know what that bigger picture was, I knew it was important. I knew with you by my side it had meaning for both of us. And beyond that even. It had meaning for everyone. Because we're all connected."

"You mean the fat suits and microwaves and light bulbs were things you were *told* to get your hands on?" Astra said. She yanked her hand back and stared at her fisted fingers closed around his kiss.

"Don't forget the safety goggles and back scratchers," he replied. "And before that, the Pinto, of course. Before my *activation* I was a completely different kind of con artist. There was a point to every scam I ran. Greed. Plain and simple. My own greed was the only thing that mattered."

Astra was about to interject when their *watcher* held up his hand in the universal symbol for *call waiting.* To this day, it is unclear whether he was signaling Astra, or the squirrel that grabbed her attention in the middle of a moment between her and the love of the many lives he'd watched for each incarnation.

"All in due time, *Warrior Messenger,*" appeared in her head as clearly as if they'd been shouted in her ear. Even the slight ringing that she always got at Fenway Park when the guy next to her would shout for another hot dog and flat Rolling Rock Beer was the same.

"We have even more business to attend to. We're

almost to Martha's Vineyard and still need to get to New York before all the good parking spaces are gone. Just because the 37$^{th}$ parallel is considered a paranormal highway doesn't mean other places don't have to deal with traffic jams that turn into one giant parking lot twice a day."

Astra couldn't be entirely sure, but she suspected the Tall Man had just made a joke. She blamed herself. And then she started wondering if anyone had ever done a study on the repercussions of teaching an extraterrestrial the fine art of hyperbole.

"Well can you at least tell me what David's special *Star Seed* designation is?"

"You haven't figured that out yet?" David chimed in, disappointment in his voice.

"Let me guess," she said. "It has something to do with pointless scams and the random?" Her *pointless scammer* smiled. Astra had never seen a more sublime smile on any face. It was at this point she realized she'd begun taking a tally of all the things she loved about him since the moment she saw him get out of the U-Haul.

"I'm a *synthetic synchronicity* specialist," he beamed. And without question, it was a beam of pure, white light that flowed around him as he straightened his shoulders and smiled even wider.

"Better known as a *Random Warrior*," the *watcher* added.

"And this kid we're going to Martha's Vineyard for?" Astra asked. "I assume that *is* the reason we're headed that way."

"You're partly right," he replied. "We're stopping by Martha's Vineyard to pick up Joey on our way to New York

City."

Astra hardly knew where to begin: Finish her pursuit of who the third *Star Seed* was, or ask why they were going to New York. But the Tall Man was way ahead of her.

"You and David represent several different Earth races, which is essential in the negotiations you're on your way to engage in. But Joey Appolonia? Joey represents all of them."

"All of them? You mean he's from Port Hueneme?"

"No. I mean he's not just descended from *all* of the houses of Israel. He has also incarnated into each and every interplanetary race for at least one lifetime. The single most uncommon specimen in the history of the universe. He has a grasp of the universal perspective that has never existed."

"*All* of the houses of Israel?" David said, incredulous. Astra thought she detected a hint of more than just surprise in his voice; she was fairly certain she was also hearing defensiveness. Despite insisting he was not Orthodox, David Aeschlimann still took great pride in his Jewish heritage. Enough pride to wear his red yarmulke. And only scam Cantor Colbert out of a parking space despite the opportunity to scam the cantor out of much more.

"Why is that important?" she said. It seemed the pragmatist in her was finally waking from its nap. And it had at least one question to ask before pouring itself a cup of coffee and searching for some creamer in Astra's short-term memory. "Weren't all religions pretty much designed for the sole purpose of controlling the human race?"

Their *watcher* smiled with his eyes again. Or maybe he was just projecting his version of a smile directly into Astra's visual cortex and her squirrel was too busy digging through the dorm-sized fridge in her memory bank to scrutinize it.

"It isn't about religion," he said. "It's about something Jacob learned in an encounter he had with an extraterrestrial and lived to tell the story. You might recall Jacob from your early Bible studies, Astra. And I'm sure you know who I'm talking about, David."

David knew precisely who and what the Tall Man was talking about. Astra was too busy looking for coffee creamer with the squirrel to search her memory bank for Bible lessons from a childhood she could barely remember in the first place.

"While it is mentioned in the Hebrew Bible," he explained, "the origin story of the Twelve Houses of Israel has been best preserved through oral tradition because it must be memorized and recited word-for-word. And none of it has been translated beyond the one translation ever done, from Hebrew to Greek. Which explains the problem with texts that have been repeatedly translated. Every time it's done, a new twist on an old story has been inserted until it barely resembles the original text."

"I'm still not seeing what the big deal is," Astra said, the squirrel giving up on the coffee creamer as she closed the door to the mini-fridge in her impossibly short attention span.

"The big deal is a battle Jacob had with what he called an *angel*," David said. "He is the first person in recorded history to have bested a powerful extraterrestrial and lived to tell the story. Yet he did it without the advanced technology the alien possessed. Nor did he have a weapon of any kind. No sword, knife, club or slingshot. That single event changed the course of the human race. And it distinguished Jacob from all other humans who came before him.

The combination of oral tradition and epigenetics insured the tactic Jacob used would not die out with him. The Twelve Houses, or Tribes, of Israel, descended from the twelve sons of Jacob, whose name became Israel."

"So the third *Star Seed* in our little trio of intergalactic superheroes is descended from all of them," Astra said, still confused. "I still fail to see what makes him uniquely qualified to fight and beat a Dire Wraith." How she was able to remember the type of ET Jacob fought from a twenty minute YouTube video was puzzling, and the pragmatist in her had no intention of solving it. She had to learn some time, and now was as good a time as ever.

"What makes this guy, Joey, unique is the fact that he has managed to incarnate on this planet each and every time you have, Astra," he said. "Not just going back a few hundred years, and not as your husband, brother, father, lover or son. Or even as your owner. Going all the way back to the time of the ancient Mesopotamians. Since the time when the two of you walked the moors of Scotland as those Mesopotamians he has had the uncanny knack of locating you and birthing himself into close enough proximity that you both end up working together."

"Working together?" Astra asked flippantly. "Like our cubicles were next to each other's? Did we hang out at the water cooler and argue about who took my stapler?"

"Working together as in *having a synergistic effect on each other's strengths*," he said with a level of patience Astra could only hope to obtain in another few hundred lifetimes. Patience was for her the most difficult of all instruments to master, because it took a lifetime of practice without ever truly perfecting. And Astra Talitha simply didn't have the attention span for that. Nor did her squirrel.

"Are you saying we've both been doing this on this one rock for *thousands of years?*" Astra looked at David, who shrugged, and then the Tall Man, who just stared at her.

"Why? Wasn't this *Star Seed* thing just supposed to be a one-time thing to get us past the threat of nuclear annihilation and wake the human race up to its origins and potential so the colonizing agents of control would let go of its stronghold on the human race's short hairs?

"This *Star Seed* thing has gone on since the inserting of extraterrestrial DNA into humanoids began on this *rock,* as you call it. But let's not get bogged down in inconsequential details," the Tall Man said. "The important thing is the three of you need to get to that meeting of the Alliance of the Council of Five and the Galactic Federation. It is imperative you three are there to negotiate on behalf of the human race. You're all they've got at this point. And that won't be possible unless you can shake the CIA for good. Which is why you're going to New York."

"You mean there really is a Council of Five? And all that stuff about Intergalactic Liaisons and Federation of Light is something I didn't just pull out of my ass?" David's eyes went directly to Astra's possibly gigantic-in-origins intergalactic ass and unfurled a flag. Astra briefly attempted to make eye contact with him but realized it was pointless. That's how it is with men and intergalactically divine derrières.

The Tall Man said nothing. In his defense there really was nothing to say about his bootylicious *Star Seed's* derrière that hadn't already been discussed ad infinitum by the Federation.

"You should know, Astra," he finally said, shaking his head slightly. She couldn't be sure, but it looked like he also rolled his eyes. "You had a face-to-face with them not long ago."

It was Astra's turn to stare in silence. His words triggered something to start wiggling in the very back of her memory. If she hadn't been so caught up in trying to remember what she knew, she would have accused him of deliberately omitting a trigger warning. But he escaped the PC police by nodding to the screens lining the wall above the instrument panel of his dinghy. Apparently responding to that nod, the screens came alive. One showed the Dominatrix and D.B. Cooper having a passionate reunion as the two Reptilian *Men in Black* flashed their CIA credentials to Sheriff Arpaio's men. The deputies seemed only too happy to drag Dog Star the Intergalactic Bounty Hunter off in shackles in exchange for D.B. Cooper.

Astra wondered if Dog Star thought to pack lubricant when he came to Earth. Which of course led her to wonder if anyone in the galaxy was marketing extra strength lubricant for just such situations. She also puzzled over just why the *Men in Black* were taking Dog Star away, when they were part of the Deep State that hired him to find D.B. Cooper in the first place.

"The answer is simple," she heard the *watcher's* response in her thoughts. "Dog Star the Bounty Hunter has accumulated enemies in so many dimensions in not just this galaxy, but several galaxies, he's worth far more on the open market than a man who only made enemies with one single man whose habit of shooting people in the face has made him more enemies than he's aware of."

"So why drag him off to detention?" she asked.

"Just for the fun that can be had humiliating him until he's auctioned off to the highest bidder," he replied. "Now, can we get back to what matters please?"

The *watcher* pointed to the other screen and it made her suspect he may have cloned her computer monitor. Her email was open to a message from Disinfaux News. The team at *Alien Investigations* was being invited to an interview to discuss their cutting edge method for negative alien entity removal and storage. And the interview was the following morning.

"I took the liberty of emailing a reply that you and your team would be there," their *watcher* said. "And asked for a private dressing room because you'd be traveling overnight to get there and needed to freshen up before appearing on air."

Astra wasn't sure exactly why her *watcher* found it necessary to ask for that on her behalf, but assumed it had to do with the vast wealth of knowledge he must have acquired about the habits and needs of humans in his role of *watcher*. She could have asked him about it, but there was other more pressing territory to cover.

"How exactly is appearing on Disinfaux News going to get the CIA off our tail?" The napping pragmatist in Astra Talitha was finally beginning to shake the cobwebs off and achieve full alertness, despite the lack of coffee. If only it was that easy for the entire human race to *activate* and wake up, coffee would be promoted enthusiastically on all the New Age websites.

"It may not ever get them off your tail. But it buys you insurance. The stamp of legitimacy given to conspiracy theorists that appear on Disinfaux News routinely puts a protective barrier around them. Haven't you ever noticed nobody who appears on Disinfaux News dies mysteriously?"

"Wait. The reason so many whistle-blowers have died under mysterious circumstances is because they appeared on the wrong disinformation network?" Astra was pretty sure she was peaking on that acid in the Horchata. Absolutely nothing was making sense to her.

"Yes. Disinfaux News is the Cadillac of disinformation networks. People respect its high achievement in disseminating disinformation, and pay attention to the people and the causes they learn about from Disinfaux News. Hence my accepting their invitation on your behalf to appear for an interview,"

Astra turned to David and smiled.

"David I take it back. The Horchata can stay. I'm not tripping. Believe it or not, this is all beginning to make sense to me." It seemed there had been a meeting of the minds between Astra's inner pragmatist and her suspension of disbelief, and a peace accord had been reached. Her companions were relieved.

"So we're stopping in Martha's Vineyard to pick up some kind of multicultural Intergalactic Liaison and then doing what, partying until infiltrating the enemy in New York?" Astra's head was still reeling about being invited for an interview on Disinfaux News. And more than just a small part of her was worried they may have figured out who stole the fat suits. Was her invitation to an interview a setup?

"We have a lot more ground to cover before your appointment," he replied. "Besides, I have never understood why you humans celebrate special events by putting toxins in your bodies that do harm to both your vessels and your spirits. Why do you think we manipulated you into calling alcohol *spirits,* and the condition they induce *intoxicated*?"

"The aliens told us to call it spirits? You guys have a lot of time on your hands, don't you?" Astra was never quite sure where a conversation was going to go with her *watcher,* and this one was no different.

"Yes. It was a clue, and instead of taking the clue at face value, you slapped the word *spirits* on the label and celebrated by getting *intoxicated*!"

Astra could see that no matter how long he'd been watching humans, the Tall Man still hadn't figured out what they were all about. The *watcher* saw those thoughts and shook his head, his pale eyes growing cloudy. In due time, all would be explained to his human charges. Until then, they would remain sadly clueless about why nothing the human race does makes any sense. Astra couldn't be sure, but she could have sworn she saw him heave a heavy sigh.

# CHAPTER SIXTEEN

Joey Appolonia was stoked. His enthusiasm was locked and loaded. No sooner had he boarded and heard the *Protection from CIA* plan for the three of them than his nonstop narration of ongoing events began.

"Manipulating Operation Mockingbird for our protection is *the* sweetest, most sexy, sexy revenge I can think of for those fuckwads in the CIA subjecting all of us to reality TV!!!!"

Once again David was looking like he was peaking on acid with that shit-eating grin of his. Hoping to impress the newest member of their team with his familiarity with all things deluxe in their *watcher's* dinghy, he was about to offer Joey a drink when the Intergalactic Liaison cut him off.

"Hey, where's the Horchata? I heard you guys have Horchata. Man, one of my moms used to make the best Horchata on the planet."

"I would say introductions are in order," the Tall Man said. "But it seems you three have already met."

"First of all, old man, that was hardly an introduction. It was the Random doing its thing. Just ask our *Random*

*Lightwarrior* over here. He's the *Master of Random*. Second of all, you wouldn't *say* a damn thing, you freak. If you are going to demand precision in communication from *us,* we can demand it from *you*. Turn-about is fair play, ET. And the precise term for what you do when you do that thing you do is *project*. You *project* thoughts into our brains. You don't *say* a fucking thing. Ever."

Astra didn't need to discuss it with David. She knew without even asking he loved the third *Star Seed* in their trio of *Lightwarrior* superheroes as much as she did. The sensation of deep familiarity sweeping over her was not one Astra had much experience with, yet trusted completely. It came from a place of *knowing* she had no reason to question.

"I'm curious to know one thing," she finally said, handing him the Horchata. "Is the name Joey Appolonia the one your birth parents gave you? Because I could swear I remember hearing Appolonians are one of the *Star Families*."

Joey giggled. It was the giggle of a delighted child; the most harmonically perfect sound in the Universe. The giggle is well known throughout the Universe to resonate with a frequency that is capable of lifting any civilization from sub-par to ready for prime time in nothing flat. And if anyone knew how important it was for the human race to leave its sub-par status in its dust and join the prime time players in the universe, it was Joey Appolonia.

"I took the name because it is the name of my *Star Family*, yes," he replied. "But the motivation behind taking a pseudonym in the first place was my need to find a *scaffold name*."

"*Scaffold name?*" David had heard of a stage name, but had no idea what a *scaffold name* was.

"Graffiti artists can't do what they do if a spotlight's on them," Joey explained joyfully. It was the only setting he seemed to have, and once again both Astra and David didn't need to check in with each other to know they loved him for it. "We don't spend time on the stage at all. So a stage name is useless. But we are likely to spend time on a scaffold spray painting our message on the side of a building. So I needed a *scaffold name.*"

"Are you saying Banksy isn't a real name?"

"Oh it's a real name alright," Joey giggled. "Just not the name he was given by any of his moms. On this planet anyway."

"So let's get down to business, shall we?" David said with an air of pragmatism mixed with an air of authority. It then proceeded to enthusiastically rise to mix with the Divine Giggle Joey had let loose in the little deluxe model dinghy. The resultant Divinely Pragmatic Giggle distracted Astra, who started thinking Divinely Pragmatic Giggle would be a great ironic name for a parody acapella group doing nothing but upbeat funeral dirges and requiems for those who had activated their immortality gene.

"What can you tell us about this meeting with the Council of Five and the Galactic Federation we're all going to?" David was doing his best to focus, despite the dinghy filling up with giggles.

"Only that the three of us are the Intergalactic Liaison and need to be there to represent humanity."

It wasn't the response Astra was expecting to hear. Although in her defense, she really wasn't sure what she was expecting to hear. But most certainly it didn't involve a liaison who was actually three people. Without realizing it, she started counting her fingers again. When the Tall Man pointed that out to her, she blushed and hoped he'd kept it just between the two of them. The problem with that however is when a spaceship flying ventriloquist is communicating, it's hard to know who is and isn't being sent a carbon copy of that communication. Or even a silicon copy.

"Wait. What qualifies us to represent humanity?" Astra's pragmatism was fully alert and ready for action, having absorbed all the caffeine it needed through osmosis from Joey Appolonia, who appeared to manufacture it organically the way most men grow facial hair. It would be several days before Astra confirmed her suspicion on that.

"You mean Lurch here didn't tell you?"

All eyes turned to Lurch as both Astra and David heaved a sigh of relief about finally learning his name. Lurch did his very best to mimic exasperation over the latest term of endearment given him by his favorite *Star Seed*. The thing about human facial expressions is most aliens are poorly equipped to mimic them at all. Which left their *watcher* duplicating the face made by the television character he'd been named after with remarkable accuracy.

Astra's thoughts wandered to running an *entertainment industry* scam on ABC by pitching a reboot of the popular television series about an oddball family with an eccentric world-traveled yogi as patriarch. To Astra, the Addams Family represented the best role model for positivity in family life ever aired on network television. It beat Desi Arnez giving Lucy a spanking for defying his authority any day of the week. And provided the aliens with a template for *watchers*. Obviously.

"Well what can you tell us about this Council of Five?" she asked. "Specifically, five what?"

"You're being deliberately obtuse, aren't you?" Joey said.

Astra just stared at him.

"You already know," he said, nodding at the bracelet around her wrist. "Shall we review what we've learned about the key *Star Families*, children?"

Astra bristled. Joey Apollonia was half her age. And she was about to remind him of that when Lurch's words appeared in her auditory cortex advising her to cut the young *Star Seed* some slack, considering he was actually several millennia older than all of them combined.

"We have been intergalactic liaisons since we first met, Astra. It's what we do. We're a team. This time is no different. The three of us are a unit. Always have been."

"Okay, saying I bite," she said skeptically. "And all of this is not one perpetual acid trip. What's your *Star Seed* designation? How do your skills fit in with ours to form the perfect *X-Man Liaison*?"

I'm the *Aerosol Warrior*, The *Graffiti Lightworker*, the *Skateboarding Sage, Heretic of Hurt*, the *Messenger of Mysteries, the Descended Master*. Been at it for many a millennia. Know those cave drawings your archaeologists insist were made by prehistoric man? Those were me. Egyptian hieroglyphs? Yep. Me. Guess who introduced the tattoo to the human race? I'll give you a hint: Not the Lizard Man. You know that hollow area they've just detected in the Great Pyramid? Guess what they're gonna find on its walls when they figure out how to get inside?"

"Wait. So the prehistoric cave drawings weren't made

in prehistory?"

"Oh, they were made in prehistory. Just not by who they think. I was so tempted to include two different water fountains, one for Neanderthals and one for Denisovans, but thought it might give the impression the planet was populated with *drama queens* thousands of years before it actually was."

Astra realized she should have asked Emo just how far back visits to Earth from energy vampires had begun.

Joey went on to explain how he was aware of his spirit guide, or *guardian angel* from a very young age, which puzzled Astra. But not as much as telling them that most *Star Seeds* don't become aware of their presence until their *Activation*.

"Wait. That whole *guardian angel spirit guide* thing is really about our *watcher*? Or do we also have someone else *other* than our *watcher* looking after us? Cause that would give a whole new meaning to having your crew watch your back."

"You make it sound like a good thing. Largely because it's not just your back they're watching. Imagine realizing someone is actually watching your every move, observing your every fantasy, scrutinizing your every thought. Up close and personal. And you're twelve. And your dick is off the charts stuck in high gear twenty four seven. Shit like that can scar a young man. There's no way to hide something like that."

"Did you try a notebook?" David said, in an effort to be helpful.

"I'm still not sure why they're here and why the human race needs a liaison," Astra said, once again wishing she'd figure out a way to manifest coffee from nothing but energy and will power. "Or how many of them each one of us has reading over our shoulder when we're writing in our diaries."

"The extraterrestrial presence here on Earth has been on the down-low since forever," Joey explained crisply. "And for the most part, humankind has been happy to stay asleep in the illusion that we were all alone on this planet except for some sky god who punishes people for touching themselves. Or enjoying sex, if they're a woman."

Astra contemplated jumping in, but realized Joey had summed it up perfectly. But she did have a question. "But why are they here at all? What could we possibly have that would keep them here that long?"

"Souls, basically." Joey replied. "That's primarily what our *watchers* are here to keep track of. Which means they aren't nearly as much of an issue as the other ones. They're all about commerce and trade. They're resource explorers. This planet is unique for not just its water, but for its rare earth metals, like monoatomic gold. And its agricultural expansiveness. Think Christopher Columbus was the only explorer out in search of spices? Do you have any idea how rare saffron is beyond this galaxy? Curry? Know how much tupelo honey goes for on the open interstellar market? I bet you never guessed the massive die-off of honey bees on Earth was orchestrated by interstellar capitalists to jack up the price of honey on the open market, did you?"

"So once they identified the resources they wanted," David cut in. "They did what they always do: worked to take possession of the human soul. And that's most easily done by tinkering with both the DNA and the perceptions of early humanoids. The name of the game is establishing the necessary mind control for workers to willingly harvest those resources for them, including spices. Only just as our history books omitted the ugly details about how Columbus and his men treated the natives in the Americas, even the oldest history books in the world have left out details about how the extraterrestrial resource explorers have treated this planet's natives."

"So why did fundamentalists leave the extraterrestrials out of the intelligence equation in their theory of *Intelligent Design*?" she asked.

"Yes! You've got it, my sister from another mother. Well, technically, from another one of our mothers. You know what I mean. They implanted controlling mechanisms – largely in the form of a collective amnesia – in order to get their beasts of burden to accept their lot in life, hence the similarity in religious texts no matter where you go in the world. Well, except for Dianetics. That's the only one that involves aliens in volcanoes while insisting it is actually a religion. Hint: it isn't even a religious philosophy. It's Draconians broadcasting their own version of The Truman Show from their home planet, only with people far more gullible and far greedier than television producers."

"Let me guess," David continued for Joey, who was hoping there was another carton of Horchata in the fridge. "When world governments began to form, things got complicated for the aliens."

Joey nodded and explained how increasingly demanding world leaders grew as their own personal greed crowded out every admirable human trait they once had the capacity for. This was due largely to the shiny things and promises of immortality the colonizing aliens were rewarding leaders with in exchange for looking the other way as countless generations of lives were worked to death and discarded.

"Which is why it was so easy for them to influence humans to come here to this continent and do the work of the interventionists for them," he added. "To basically colonize for the colonizers. So they could start digging into the resources here. They had to. They had no choice. They were being forced out by the increasing demands of government leaders elsewhere."

"Why didn't they just get the indigenous people to do the harvesting and mining for them," David asked. "Like they did in places like Egypt?"

"The natives here had a much older and far deeper relationship with the Council of Five," he replied. "The Apache family I was born into several centuries ago called them *The Ancestors.* Their reverence for those *ancestors* elevated their resonant frequencies so high the interventionists couldn't manipulate them. The only other move in their tiny little unimaginative playbook was to get people they could manipulate to come here and commit genocide in the name of their god."

"So basically you're saying the Puritans were nothing like what they taught us in grade school," Astra said. She was not at all surprised, but saddened nonetheless. That's how it is when you learn the fairy tales you loved as a child were only make believe.

"Things went along just great for the interventionists until America formed its own government," Joey continued.

"They had no idea what they would be up against once that happened. These aliens are not complex beings, like you and I. They are simple captains of commerce looking for resources to trade on the interstellar market. They thought the same system they've used for eons to strip a planet of its resources would work like it always did. And it did, for a while in the New World. They promptly turned the Puritans against the natives, and against each other for good measure."

"Against each other?" Astra puzzled.

"Where did you think the *Salem Witch Trials* came from?" he asked dryly. "Don't tell me you actually thought there were *witches* in league with *the devil* running around the woods of New England. As long as they were polarized and fractured from within, their resonant frequencies were low enough to manipulate them into doing their work for them. The only evil running around those woods was what the agents of control got the Puritans to welcome into their hearts with promises of riches and power."

Astra and David were in rapt silence, literally on the edge of their seats. Joey glanced at Lurch and the *watcher* chuckled. Both of them knew the two *Star Seeds* had heard the story many times before. And their failure to remember any of it didn't make it any less hilarious.

"But the interventionists didn't count on the complex emotional and intellectual structure of Earth's human race," Joey continued. "Or the defiant pioneering spirit of the humans who crossed an ocean to make a new life in the vast wilderness that North America was. Not only did the ETs not understand us, they failed to take our complexity into consideration every step of the way. And they gravely underestimated the power of free will."

"Wait. Free will?" Astra said. "You mean that thing some belief systems say was given to us to test our strength and win the *Get Into Heaven Lottery* by agreeing to serve someone whom they insist is not an alien demanding to be worshiped while not once touching ourselves in our naughty place?"

"No. The only thing that keeps our genetics from inspiring us to eat ourselves alive from the inside out. As either a cosmic joke or an experiment, depending on who's telling the story, they inserted exactly equal capacities for pure good and pure evil in Earth humans' DNA when they were tinkering with early humans. Our free will is the only thing that's allowed us to survive. But it was the last thing they expected when they installed free will in this species."

"What, so you're saying they decided to play with dynamite when they were hybridizing us just for shits and giggles? But inadvertently installed free will, which was the only thing that helped us survive?" Astra was scrambling to keep up with her *Star Seed* compatriot.

"Yes and no," Joey replied. "They were playing with dynamite experimenting with installing the capacity for extremes in us. They had long since learned how to control any population with polarization, but early humans were almost impossible to polarize. It wasn't in them to think or behave that simplistically. And as far as free will goes, they didn't install it inadvertently. Without Earth humans having free will, the aliens couldn't be here."

"Why not?" Astra and David said in unison.

"Like I said, they are not as complex as Earth humans. You know how our vampire myth insists a vampire can't enter our home unless he's invited? Well, these aliens are where that myth came from. Only being invited isn't exactly what they require. They can come here uninvited all they want. They just can't stay where they're not wanted."

"Holy sit," David exclaimed. "The combination of free will and polarization in a species as emotionally complex as humans must have really kept them on their toes!"

"Okay, so where exactly is all of this going?" Astra said, growing impatient. She realized she hadn't eaten anything since breakfast because she and David never got as far as trying out that place with pulled-pork burritos. "How does the free will of humans and obvious collusion between world leaders and alien captains of commerce lead to our attendance being demanded by the Alliance of the Council of Five and the Galactic Federation?"

"I'll give you a clue: Remember the check-kiting scandal in Washington back in the nineties?"

"The one with all the congressmen writing bad checks on Friday knowing the money wouldn't be in the account to cover them until Monday?" It was the kind of scam Astra could sink her teeth into, and she hated herself for admiring the politicians who pulled it off.

"Yes. Back when things were less convoluted in American politics and a House banking scandal was the worst it got," Joey said, coming dangerously close to hijacking his own topic. "Our world leaders were taking advanced technology in payment for our rare earth metals and the human labor to harvest them. But as that pesky free will began to work its magic and more and more humans began to demand better treatment, better living conditions –

which included the environment – production slowed down. Both the human demands and the alien demands couldn't be met. One had to give."

Astra desperately wanted to derail the entire conversation and ask if the whole point of global warming was to make it more comfortable for the Reptilians. But when Lurch made eye contact with her and nodded, she decided not to bother. The answer was obvious. One has only to look at the Reptilian influence in the climate change deniers to know her hunch was right.

"So basically, the labor movement and the environmental movement opened a can of worms for world leaders." It was Lurch's turn to speak up, and it startled two of the three *Star Seeds*, who had forgotten he was there. Astra was uncharacteristically focused on the topic being discussed, which also startled Joey and David.

"The entire African continent had been gutted, environmentally and socially. The Middle East was running on fumes – literally – and China was untouchable. It's almost impossible to control an atheist government, by the way. All that was left to mine in North America was in protected sites, like wildlife refuges, National Parks and Heritage Sites for the indigenous. Your leaders did their best working quickly to push laws through opening up all those protected sites, but their checks bounced anyway. Not even causing economic bubbles – forcing people to work two and three jobs just to survive – fixed the problem. Nothing, at that point, was enough to pull them out of the nosedive."

"The ironic thing is, the only thing the world powers did with all the advanced technology they got was use it to spy on and manipulate their own people," Joey said, starting to pace the floor. "For stupid shit, like votes and the latest fad food craze."

"So they came up with a scheme," Joey continued. "Implant a phobia of extraterrestrials through popular culture and street theater."

"Street theater?" Astra asked, still confused.

"Acting something out publicly so that one or more people witness it," Joey clarified. "Like Roswell, and *flying saucers*. They even used Project Mockingbird to implant science fiction stories in popular culture characterizing aliens in a way that equated them to communism. All the while denying any knowledge of the existence of intelligent life beyond this planet."

Astra realized Samara had hit the nail on the head when she said communism was a red herring. She also realized anyone recovering from being gaslighted by a spouse or lover was only halfway done. Until the human race recognized it had been gaslighted for thousands of years, there is no full recovery from its effects for anyone.

"But why?" David asked. "How would that cover their debt? Where would it get them?"

"It would get them to the place they are now," Lurch cut in before Joey could reply. "Ready to launch a false flag alien invasion, using advanced alien technology and military weaponry."

"Holy shit, when our own military comes to the rescue, the human race is going to turn against the extraterrestrials," Astra said, incredulous that she hadn't thought of the scheme herself. It was ripped right out of the US Department of Defense's Operation Northwoods playbook from the 1960s, and had *classic grifter* written all over it.

"And it will work, too," Joey said. "The people of Earth will turn against all extraterrestrials. Just like Pearl Harbor turned the American people against the people of Japan – any anyone of Japanese descent living in America – and Nine Eleven turned them against brown skinned people who carry a different bible."

"But why?" Astra asked, a distant, vague memory trying to get her attention. "Why go to so much bother if all they have to do is tell them to leave?"

"They want to kill two birds with one stone," Lurch replied. "Get rid of their debt while winning over the entire human population in the biggest protection scam ever run."

"The old *I'll keep you safe for a price* scam," David said, nodding in recognition.

"Sure, that part's obvious," Astra said, somewhat annoyed. "But what's the price?"

"Freedom," Lurch said. "The most precious commodity in the universe and absolutely essential for any emergent race with hopes of entering the intergalactic community as anything other than slaves. If the planned false flag event turns the people against extraterrestrials and any kind of hostile action is taken against a member of a single visiting race, it will most certainly result in the entire population being eradicated. No emergent race still engaging in hostile acts against others can be allowed to leave their home planet until they overcome it. Therefore it is policy to destroy the race rather than take any chances."

He paused for a moment and searched the eyes of the three he had been watching more lifetimes than he could count, and even he wondered if they were up to the task.

"And no one is coming to save you," he said. "The human race is on its own."

"Do the world's leaders understand this will be the consequence?" Astra said, incredulous.

"Of course they do," their *watcher* replied. "They don't care. They've earned their rewards and are assured survival in the event of an apocalypse."

The three *Star Seeds* gulped. By the time all traces of Joey's smile vanished, David had stopped grinning. And Astra's stomach was growling.

"Buy the ticket, take the ride," Joey said.

Nothing else needed to be said to know how important it was to take the upcoming meeting seriously. And to always listen to the wisdom of Hunter S. Thompson. That, and always pack a lunch when planning to go anywhere aboard a UFO. In the absence of a sack lunch, try to do your best to find a safe place to land where you can get something stuffed with pulled-pork. Without getting caught by the CIA.

"Wait," Astra said. "If the human race is on its own, what's the point of all the *watching* you freaks do?"

"How do you think your history gets recorded and stored where you can find it?" he replied.

# CHAPTER SEVENTEEN

"So, I've been wondering about something," Astra said, slightly sweet brown gravy dribbling down her chin adorably. "If the extraterrestrials are here for our rare earth metals, and the earth was created by those same extraterrestrials to be flat, how does that work? Because I'm confused. Why create this planet full of rare earth metals and intergalactically rare spices, plus all these humans to mine and harvest them all for you? Seems like an awful lot of trouble to go to. Not to mention unnecessarily convoluted. If you have the capacity to create this planet full of resources, why not just create the damned resources and ship them off to your trade routes?"

"Girl, how the fuck did we get from the impending annihilation of the human race to a flat earth?" Joey asked.

"The thought came to me when I was out in the desert and realized the reason there's no twilight like there is up north is because of the curvature of the earth," she replied.

In all the YouTube videos she'd seen insisting taking a level on an airplane would prove the earth is flat, Astra had not once seen that little factoid about twilight brought up. Having gotten it off her chest, she happily resumed devouring her third pork-filled sticky bun. He would have pursued the topic, but it appeared her squirrel had already run off with it, and chasing it down didn't seem worth the effort.

He also didn't seem to be enjoying watching his companions down their sticky-buns, despite the welcoming atmosphere of Boston's Chinatown. And it was making him grumpy. It would be a while before the time felt right to break it to his companions that emerging races are also not allowed to enter the intergalactic community until they overcome their addiction to slavery. Not just slavery involving members of the human community of races that differ from the self-proclaimed dominant one. And not just the enslavement of women and children, either.

Enslaving animals is also seen as barbaric in advanced races. After all, part of what qualifies them as an advanced race is knowledge that all souls spend time experiencing life in a non-human animal form at least once before advancing. It's pretty hard to eat pork after you've lived the life of a pig.

"I get all my news from the YouTube comments section," Astra replied, apparently having caught up with the squirrel. "One recent story that caught my attention involved two YouTubers arguing about the possibility versus impossibility of extraterrestrial life visiting Earth. I guess because it's covered by a giant dome certain logistical problems arise with visitors. And poor ET doesn't get to come eat candy and beg for change for the pay phone.

Or maybe the dome is supposed to keep out the space

dust. Who knows? It was hilarious watching them go back and forth calling each other delusional idiots. Haven't been able to stop thinking about a great side gig for David ever since. Wouldn't he be perfect for conning overweight people into suing the government for creating gravity? Of course, everyone knows who was really behind that. Which is why it's the Illuminati's fault obese people keep going over their weight limit and getting kicked off airlines. Therefore my idea would qualify as a *pointless scam.* Hence it being perfect for David."

After David and Astra finished indulging themselves with pulled pork sticky-buns, Joey finished his vegetable stir fry and the three of them took a relaxing walk through the Common. At least it would have been relaxing if their *watcher* hadn't creeped them out by lurking. The problem with a person spotting their *watcher* lurking is this: Once you've seen him, you can't unsee him. When the three *Star Seeds* walked up Joy Street so Joey could see where it had rained fat suits, Lurch amused himself by leaning against the Toc-h Lamp in front of their old apartment, his fedora tipped down over face.

"You are no Fred Astaire, Lurch." Astra said. The *watcher* was somewhat disappointed that his Gene Kelly impression was getting so rusty it was being confused with Fred Astaire. But his spirits picked up by the time they returned to his dinghy. Astra assumed since he couldn't enter the Disinfaux News headquarters, he was planning to hook up with some hot *watcher* for a little alien action while they were in their interview. She had it on good authority it's what *watchers* do when they're in New York. It had to be what was cheering him up.

"Swipe right, Lurch," she whispered to him as she took her place in the seat next to him. While she may have thought he had no idea what she was referring to, had she been paying attention she would have seen him wink. And giggle. The way only a *watcher* can giggle.

The problem with finding a parking space in New York City is – regardless what time of day – none of them were designed for the deluxe model space dinghy. Which leaves many operators of spaceships to their own devices when it comes to parking there. And therein lays the problem with finding parking in New York. Or more specifically, the half-mile stretch of air above New York.

It's not like condominiums, where you can actually own a piece of air. Not only is it first-come-first-serve, the regulations regarding cloaking are air-tight. Violate them and you're out. And if you've ever tried parallel parking a deluxe model space dinghy, you know how important visibility is. Therefore, the cloaking device needs to be disabled for that. And that can be problematic.

If a spaceship is spotted by a New Yorker, the operator of that craft is not given a second chance. His license to operate is suspended indefinitely. And his craft is impounded if he does not immediately vacate the area and head to New Jersey. In Jersey, he must submit to remedial parking and cloaking classes until he can demonstrate his ability to manage the complex task of parking in air space above the Big Apple. Without being seen by humans. Anyone who has driven a stick-shift in San Francisco can surely relate, since it is very similar to executing a hill-start manipulating the clutch and hand-brake simultaneously.

"Why are you parking?" Astra asked after losing herself studying her *watcher* deftly navigate the complex maneuver. "Don't we need to get out first?" Joey seemed to be the only one of the three who wasn't confused about how they were supposed to get down to Terra from a parking space a quarter of a mile straight up.

"It's all about intention," he said cryptically, answering her question for Lurch. It wasn't where the *watcher* would have started his answer, as it seemed to begin in the middle without any indication of what exactly they were supposed to *do* with their intention.

"Here's the thing about intention," Astra said. "I'm not entirely sure I trust its results. All my life I've intended to be tall and blond, with perky breasts. All I got for my intentions was this luscious ass. So you see: I'm a little leery of putting all my faith in intention. Especially when I'm a half mile up in the air and my intention is to land safely on the ground without getting flattened by a garbage truck."

"It has to do with how your intention resonates," Lurch explained. "The frequency at which it resonates determines how smoothly your ride to Terra will be. Focus on what it is you truly intend by going to the surface and giving this interview. You're already well aware it's with people we know to be causing harm to a large contingency of the population. At the lower frequencies, the idea of vindictiveness and personal attacks will seem attractive. But the higher your own frequencies resonate; you'll find your true purpose for going there. Focus on those frequencies. They will attract increasing amounts of the ambient energy vibrating at the same frequency. Combined with yours, a personal portal-for-one will transport you instantly."

"What, like some kind of cosmic *Slip 'N Slide*?" Astra said, skeptical.

"Yes, exactly like that. Only without the water and grass stains on your favorite bathing suit."

And so it was the three *Star Seeds* had their first lesson in taking the cosmic shuttle from their parking space to the Disinfaux News version of Disneyland. Only the birds don't fly upside down in New York like they do in Anaheim, California. And Alice in Wonderland wasn't there in a blue dress and white pinafore to greet them.

Luckily, their cosmic *Slip 'N Slide* delivered them to Fifth Avenue with such precision they only had to walk a short distance before reaching the Avenue of the Americas. And while there were a few narrow misses, none of them got any bird shit on them. Not even American bird shit. Nor did they encounter any CIA-sponsored *Men in Black*. Alice would have made a full report, but she was too far down the rabbit hole with the Mad Hatter by then. So was Astra Talitha. And she suspected both Lurch and the Mad Hatter may actually have had something to do with it.

They were greeted by an intern within seconds of setting foot in the lobby. He reminded Astra of the Young Republican she ran an *American flag lapel-pin* scam on at Harvard when she was still working Cambridge. Especially when he explained cheerfully they needed to empty their pockets and step through the scanner at the security station. Which seemed unnecessarily annoying to the three.

Thanks to Disinfaux News' diligent efforts, it was now mandatory for television studios to require security screening at all entrances. Of course, that involved the installation of expensive equipment and hiring of security personnel, which increased operational costs. And that, in turn, increased costs to their advertisers. Who passed the additional costs down to the consumer. Astra had often wondered why the Disinfaux News logo wasn't the Ouroboros; the snake eating its own tail. Only in this case the head of the snake was the disinformation network and the tail was the American people and their struggle to live in poverty with any kind of dignity.

The TSA reject took her mini-manicure kit with the cuticle scissors she loved. The blades were an eighth of an inch. "How exactly is an eighth of an inch blade a danger to anyone?" she asked, incredulous that something so tiny could possibly be seen as a threat to anyone except perhaps faeries, elves and Little People. Which as far as she knew didn't exist. In this dimension.

"In the right hands, this blade could be deadly," the security guard said with authority. Which apparently involved saying things with his hand on his holstered gun. "If you've ever watched an expert in Marshal Arts perform, you know they can turn anything into a weapon."

"Even if their Marshal Art is Roshambo?"

Sometimes Astra simply couldn't help herself. This was one of those times. She wondered if there were a lot of Marshal Artists expert in killing people with eighth-inch cuticle scissors fixated on committing terror attacks on news studios in New York. Or anywhere, for that matter. She was about to tell the guard that fear is for pussies when David removed his yarmulke and tossed it down on the conveyor belt with such force it made even the security guard jump.

"There," she said to the jumpy guard. "Now *that's* what I call a lethal weapon. Do you have any idea the kind of damage an annoyed Jew can cause in Manhattan when provoked?"

Not wanting to escalate the situation, the guard handed Astra's miniature manicure kit back to her with the cuticle scissors in their proper place. He then picked up the yarmulke and spent an exhausting amount of time examining it for explosives. Astra couldn't be sure, but it looked like he may have peed his pants during the process. Or perhaps his hands were prone to tremors, which had caused a mishap with his coffee earlier and she was just now noticing the lake that was gradually spreading across the front of his pants.

It reminded her she needed to use the restroom. All that Horchata on a space dinghy with no toilet can be problematic for the human bladder. Astra didn't hold out hope the graffiti in the Disinfaux News restrooms would be as cryptically enlightening as some she'd enjoyed. But more than anything else, Astra needed to freshen up. And she hoped they were early enough she could do just that before going in front of the camera. But within minutes of being escorted to the dressing rooms Lurch had arranged for them, the intern came back and told them the news crew was ready for them.

As she stepped from the green room, she noticed a familiar sight out of the corner of her eye. Three fat suits hung nonchalantly from the wardrobe rack between several different Barbie Doll dresses. She wondered what the women of Disinfaux News were wearing, if both their fat suits and their dresses were hanging in the dressing room. But as David and Joey met up with them in the hallway, the intern frowned.

"Oh darn. I meant to ask you to bring those fat suits," he said to Astra. "The anchors think they'll make good visual aids for the interview. Do you guys mind grabbing them?" Astra had no choice at that point but to conclude the women of Disinfaux News were going to be naked for their interview. What she didn't know was *why*. She looked down at her wrinkled khaki shirt stained with smeared cheesy-puff powder and slightly sweet brown gravy, and frowned.

"Am I going to be overdressed for this?"

But she wasn't. Nor were the ladies of Disinfaux News naked. And although they were dressed in the yawn-worthy cardboard-cutout standard which is tragically common to fashion tools like news anchorwomen, they were not wearing fat suits. And it was because of Astra Talitha. The last thing she expected was to find herself confronted by a group of angry women because she'd brought so much attention to fat suits they could no longer get away with wearing them. Without knowing she was doing it, Astra had outed the women of Disinfaux News for being posers whose spread of toxic disinformation had turned them all into anorexic skeletons.

And those bitches wanted payback.

For their panel of experts, the ladies had lined up a firing squad. They had managed to book a well-loved televangelist with a twist on the pro-life theme: He was rabidly anti-transmutation of alien entities. Next to him was Alex Jones, military contractor for Info Wars, a radio program dedicated to a continuous war on actual information. With a pathological love of manufacturing the modern conspiracy theorist's weapon of choice: things to blame at the top of their lungs on feminazis and minorities.

And next to the Great Bloviator was a representative from the Aleister Crowley Foundation, and last but not least was a *Man in Black* claiming to be from the US Patent Office. He looked like he was wearing flesh colored gloves to conceal the fact he had no hair on the back of his knuckles. But he wasn't fooling anyone. At least not anyone who knows an alien shape-shifter when they see one.

Astra knew there was going to be a panel of experts at the interview, but she was expecting experts like maybe some award winning journalist famous for bringing attention to the extraterrestrial involvement in cattle mutilations. Or maybe that doctor whose use of hypnotic regression has helped alien abductees recover repressed memories of their trauma, thus beginning a journey to healing. Experts like that would have no problem confirming the seriousness of what Astra and her team were up against.

Instead, the three *Star Seeds* were up against an extremely negative alien entity inhabiting a shiny man with shiny skin wearing a shiny suit who liked scamming people out of their shiny things, a dangerously obese Draco-Reptilian shape-shifter with an annoyingly raspy voice common to Reptilians, and a thoroughly confused LARPer who thought the interview was about the latest occult video game, *Aleister Crowley: Foundations*. The LARPer, a video game enthusiast, had made headlines by beating the game in six hours and sixty six minutes.

But none of them were as much of a problem as the CIA-backed *Man in Black*. Their weapons would have no problem getting through the security scanner in the lobby. Without causing any security guards to pee their pants.

Astra wasn't sure anyone in the studio was safe. She'd seen them shoot, and it was not pretty. She could only hope Alex Jones was there to demand aliens be required to put in time at the shooting range before handling *directed energy weapons* around humans.

"We were expecting you and your partner from the video, Miss Talitha," Stockholm Syndrome Sally said in explanation for there only being two guest chairs. Joey didn't mind standing. It gave him a better look at all the surfaces he could cover with a celebration of the Random he'd come prepared for. Even though he couldn't bring any spray paint into the building, it didn't mean he couldn't convert theatrical makeup into spray paint and load a squirt bottle with it.

Once Astra and David were seated, the grilling began. Neither David nor Joey were prepared for the evisceration the women of Disinfaux News were about to give the team. But Astra had a pretty good idea once she saw what she'd been set up for. Women can be as lethal on the battlefield as men, if not more so. And due to the all-male alpha-dog game they had needed to play just to get to where they were, their Stockholm Syndrome was to be understood. Or so Astra was trying to tell herself. Until the first shot was fired and it ripped into her gut. She wasn't the only one relieved it wasn't the *Man in Black* who fired it.

"Miss Talitha," Stockholm Syndrome Sally said.

"Call me Astra. Please."

"I don't know that you're in a position to ask anything here."

"Excuse me?"

"I'm sure you've heard about the public outcry there's

been surrounding your murder spree," Stockholm Syndrome Suzanne cut in. Astra would have given some thought to the habit Disinfaux News was in of hiring women whose names began with the letter *S* but she'd just been accused of mass murder so is to be forgiven for the oversight.

"Murder spree?" It was David's turn to jump in the path of the bullet fired at Astra. And she loved him for it, even if the bullet was metaphorical and she had no idea what was going on. Joey, on the other hand was scrutinizing the lighting scaffolding to see if he could fit a quote from SpongeBob SquarePants on it.

"Admit you've been murdering souls, you filthy Muslim!" the demon-possessed evangelical shouted. His face was a shade of red Astra had rarely seen outside a gynecologist's examination room. Which most evangelicals consider the same thing as Satan's breeding ground.

"Not until you admit you're a demonic alien entity who's taken this poor man's body hostage," Joey shouted, slapping his palm on the table in front of the perennially angry alien. No one had noticed the *Star Seed* cross the room as the demon was launching his deceptive attack on David. Because none of them knew that aside from a *scaffold name*, graffiti artists come equipped with speed, stealth and the leonine reflexes of a cat.

The young *Star Seed* then proceeded to jump up on the table in a single startling leap. Where he began squirting the demon with a mixture of pancake makeup, cherry red lipstick, witch hazel and mineral water. The mixture is well known among graffiti artists in several star systems to be the improvised recipe for *Tagger's Holy Water*.

"Cherry bomb! Out demon, you are not welcome here!" he shouted, continuing to squeeze the trigger of the squirt bottle in the demon's face. Astra could not have imagined being more proud of her compatriot. It takes talent to graffiti a news segment while it's being broadcast, and Joey Appolonia had that in spades.

"Cut! Cut!" a decidedly alpha male voice called out, obviously annoyed. Astra could only assume it was because he found the pressures of being alpha male too imposing. That could annoy anyone. "We can cut that out in editing, right?" he shouted to unnamed faces in the dark just beyond the reach of the studio lights. Turning back toward the anorexic ladies of Disinfaux News and their panel of undocumented yet inexplicably legal aliens, Alpha Dog ordered them to continue before attempting to tear a new one in Joey Appolonia.

Astra would have been concerned, but she had a hunch Joey had more experience in his little finger deflecting new ones being torn into him than most had in their entire bodies. And then some. Including all the baggage they carry around with them.

What she was more concerned about was the news that the interview was not live. It was being taped. Which meant their insurance policy wouldn't go into effect until it aired. And that meant the three would need to find a way out of the studio and back to Lurch's dinghy without being spotted by the CIA. It also meant they would need to play nice throughout the remainder of the interview, or risk it not being aired ever. Which would make their appearance there that morning the most pointless scam of all.

"I would like to thank our associate, Joey Appolonia,

for his demonstration of just one of the skills the staff at *Alien Investigations* brings to the table," Astra announced. Once again demonstrating the quick thinking a grifter as adept as Astra Talitha routinely brings into battle. And in this case, the news room. "Our ability to spot and identify alien entities is what puts us at the top of our field. And while there may be some concern about the handling of those alien entities we are able to detach from their poor suffering human hosts, I can assure you we are not killing souls. We'll leave that to the experts. Like you, Sally. We only offer them the option of transmuting into positive alien entities, or self-deportation, which I know you ladies are fans of."

"Look, you may be fooling these women here with this act," Alex Jones cut in before Stockholm Syndrome Sally could respond to Astra. "But it's obvious they're being willfully ignorant because of that pink hat agreement all you baby-killing feminazis make with each other. The point is: This isn't as innocent as putting fungus on the feet of grasshoppers before dropping them on Guatemala to wipe out their crops. Or dropping syphilis infected ticks on Russia. For obvious reasons. This is about humans being inhabited by aliens and the risk that poses to our freedom."

Astra was tempted to expand on the theme of freedom brought up by the Reptilian posing as an obese radio announcer. But the odds that the interview would be discarded were too great if she said too much about the alien agenda. Instead she smiled and addressed what the narcissistic alien had just said.

"Look, David Icke wasn't available to start *Alien Investigations* and figure out a way to remove alien entities *his* way, which everyone knows is the *only* right way. And despite the obvious limitations women have, my partner Samara and I were careful to bring two appropriately male experts on all things so foreign they're alien into the business. They've been careful to make sure no one forgets they are the Top Dogs, the Alpha of Alpha Males, the captains of non-capitulation in this industry. Believe me; they've kept us girls in our place. Mostly we make them coffee and sandwiches and polish their wood whenever they demand it. As it should be in any work environment where men have to put up with the presence of vaginas."

Alex Jones seemed skeptical, but Stockholm Syndrome Suzanne cut in with a question before he could launch an accusation that both Astra and Samara were energy vampires. She'd heard him accuse women of attaching themselves to men for the sole purpose of sucking the life out of them. And since his much-reported divorce, had elaborated on the details ad nauseam. His claims had reached a level of hyperbole unsurpassed in the conspiracy theorist community.

"What about the accusation that your agency is actually working with aliens, Miss Talitha?" Suzanne continued, surreptitiously making brief eye contact with the *Man in Black*. "We have it on good authority you're actually investigating a case involving an energy vampire looking for his ex-girlfriend. How can you defend subjecting a woman to the ravages of an energy vampire, not to mention any possible domestic abuse she may have escaped when she put distance between them?"

Astra was stunned. And not just because her client's confidentiality had obviously been breached. Hadn't she just been thinking about energy vampires? Scrutinizing every face in the room, she tried to locate the source of the intrusion into her thoughts, but realized she had a long way to go before she'd master the skill. Luckily, Joey Appolonia had nailed it eons ago.

The *Graffiti Warrior* opted for a less colorful approach with the alien subjecting them to remote neural monitoring. Having learned that all one needs to do is let an alien know it is not wanted, he began silently humming the words to the Blondie song, *Don't Go Away Mad (Just Go Away)* in his mind. When he got to the part where the lyrical alliteration repeats the command, both Alex Jones and the televangelist in red lipstick got up to leave. They had no choice. Interstellar law prevents them from staying where they are not wanted.

The *Man in Black* was startled, and the LARPer still had no idea what he was doing there.

"*Alien Investigations* is not just an equal opportunity employer," Astra said. "We serve anyone in need of help resolving issues of a foreign nature, including aliens. They're people too, you know."

It was at that point the demon in the televangelist showed his hand. Despite being almost to the exit and home-free, it has never been in the skill set of either negative alien entities or televangelists to hold their tongue.

"How *dare* you put us in the same category as humans!" he bellowed. Astra was relieved he'd removed his microphone, thus reducing the damage that can be done to the auditory nerve by a bellowing demon with a microphone. But before the cameras could fully readjust their focus, Alex Jones had thrown his arm over the televangelist's shoulder in a sign of brotherly solidarity. He then ushered him out the door as Astra contemplated naming a punk rock band *The Demon in the Televangelist.*

Which left just the confused LARPer and *Man in Black* to contend with. And confused Joey, since his command to leave worked on the other two aliens. Was it possible shape-shifting Reptilians in the CIA's *Men in Black* program had undergone some kind of alien-human hybridization and now fell under a different set of regulations? Were they like Dreamers in the United States, created and then brought here through no fault of their own? But unlike the Dreamers, not subject to any immigration policies whatsoever, even those stipulated by interstellar law?

And if there *had* been some kind of human-alien hybrid program involving the cooperation of the US government, when did it begin? On cue, the moment the thought occurred to Joey, the *Man in Black* held up a paper clip and smiled smugly. Joey was much happier when aliens were aliens and incapable of smiling. Watching what could very well be a product of *Operation Paperclip* was turning the young *Star Seed's* stomach. It was entirely possible the thought of the US bringing Nazi war criminals to this country so they could continue their barbaric experiments on humans had succeeded at what interdimensional travel hadn't: Making the *Star Seed* hurl chunks.

Creating tailor-made alien-human hybrids was a game-changer. Especially for Congress, which was *still* arguing about whether Mexican children brought here illegally have the right to stay once reaching adulthood. And they were *human.* What happens when the American public finds out acolytes of Doctors Mengele and Goebbels created an alien-human hybrid while Disinfaux News was distracting everyone with an argument about Mexican kids?

But it was David who once again saved the day with fat suits. He stood with such force his chair fell backward. Holding the fat suit he'd carried from Astra's dressing room up to the camera, he insisted the alpha-male director order a close-up.

"You see this?" he said. "This is why we're here. This is what's actually helping protect God Fearing Christian Americans™. If it wasn't for our discovery of a method for trapping negative alien entities, energy vampires would be the least of your problems."

"And for your information," Astra added, picking up on David's cue. "The energy vampire we represent was born and raised here. By decent, church-going Americans. Who sent him to band camp. As a result, he opened his heart and chose to walk with the Light. The ex-girlfriend he hopes to reconnect with was also an extraterrestrial born and raised here. That's why Samara and our consultant, El, are not here today. They are searching for our client's lost love."

The LARPer had begun to dab his eyes with the sleeves of his poet's blouse. Astra wondered if it was a characteristic of LARPers that they wear poet's blouses and cry over extraterrestrial love stories. She considered going into detail about what a climax reached in mutual ecstasy was capable of helping two people achieve, but decided against it when she realized the *Man in Black* was scowling at her and shaking his head menacingly.

"If I might add a shout out to a certain Lyran out there, I'd like her to know that her Emo vampire is looking for her. Also, our associate, El, is looking for all the lost *Star Seeds* who fell off the radar when someone used cloaking technology to prevent them from being found by anyone but the pharmaceutical industry. With the assistance of the psychiatric community. And medical community in general. I'm appealing to all of them to please sign yourselves out of whatever mental ward they've stuck you in and come to Sedona. There's a David Bowie concert in a secret location you need to attend. And after that we'll be discussing what to do next to help you connect you with your *Star Families* and help your *watchers* re-connect with you."

The LARPer had begun to sob. If Astra had brought a pint of chocolate ice cream and can of whipped topping, she would have given it to him at that very moment. He was the kind of guy women dream of; the kind of guy who would gladly join her for a night of watching *Transsexuals from Space* and binging on comfort food. Men like that were not only sexy as fuck, they weren't afraid of a woman putting on a little extra weight. Or a lot, depending on how much ice cream they put down together.

# CHAPTER EIGHTEEN

After the taping Astra asked the Stockholm Syndrome Twins when their interview would be broadcast. In her nicest voice. Her hope, of course, being the three *Star Seeds* might be able to kill time in the cafeteria until their insurance policy went into effect. But she was less than assured by their reply. It wouldn't air until it had been edited "for content." So the earliest it would be seen would be that evening.

Astra had to admit, she could see the obvious benefits of airing it later. Prime time was the optimum time to be breaking a story with explosive information about our government turning a blind eye to illegal aliens. Not a single viewer of Disinfaux News is willing to tolerate their representative being soft on immigration.

But of course the twins were too furious about Astra scooping them on the explosive news to do much more than storm out of the studio in perfectly synchronized *drama queen* fashion while they were answering her question. And it left the three *Star Seeds* alone to figure out how to survive reaching their rendezvous point with Lurch.

Alone with three fat suits.

Thus began the second major event in unexplained phenomena involving fat suits which failed to make it into the Boston Globe; not even the back of the Lifestyles section. Nor did it appear in the New York Times. Even the crossword puzzle failed to give the tiniest hint. And those more inclined to turn to the Word Jumble would be disappointed to find out the many things they weren't learning regarding the realm of all things so foreign they're alien. In which at this point even fat suits belonged.

Especially when the three stepped from their respective dressing rooms looking like stand-ins for the mixed-racial remake of the black remake of the white version of the Nutty Professor. But rather than try to squeeze a size 38 fat-suit body into a size *Double Zero Petite* Barbie Doll dress, Astra had another option. She and her companions were able to drape themselves in the tablecloths Joey found when scouting for beet juice in the cafeteria. He was hoping it might be more stable than cherry red lipstick. Of course, Astra had been wondering her entire adult life if there could possibly be anything more unstable than lipstick. Joey was only confirming her suspicions.

Joey was also not surprised to find the English Ivy framing the windows in the cafeteria was in fact artificial. This was definitely in keeping with what anyone with a shred of sanity would expect to find in the News Corp. Building. As usual, the quaintly picturesque scene created by the fake-news climbing ivy was yet another attempt by the disinformation industry to fool people by putting lipstick on a pig. Or in this case, beet juice. But it gave him an idea. After grabbing a stack of fresh tablecloths from the busing station, he yanked one of the fake ivy plants out of its pot and took it with him.

Looking more like stand-ins for the remake of a classic toga party with the ghost of John Belushi, the three stepped from their dressing rooms wrapped in togas. Tied at the waist with fake-news fake ivy, they topped their outfits with matching crowns of the same fake ivy. David's was especially festive with his Christmas-red yarmulke ringed with bright green ivy leaves. All three felt confident about their safe escape from the belly of the beast. They had only to make their way to the exit and out onto the Avenue of the Americas without any security cameras alerting the CIA to their actions. And as luck would have it, Joey's improvised *Tagger's Holy Water* took care of that.

Few people realize there really is no such thing as an insulated security system. If it contains the capacity to transmit a signal, feed from a closed circuit surveillance system can be viewed from anywhere by anyone with incentive to intercept that signal. No matter where it's being sent to or from. Which meant the moment the three *Star Seeds* stepped from their dressing rooms they would be identified by the CIA, and their comrades in alien arms would be waiting out on the Avenue with *directed energy weapons* set to *incinerate* as soon as they left the building.

Which is why Joey took the time to mix a fresh batch of *Tagger's Holy Water* in the cafeteria. On his way back to the dressing rooms he used it to write several poems in blank verse and one rhymed couplet on the lens of every security camera along the way. Never let it be said a *Graffiti Warrior* is anything less than a Renaissance Man.

The high silicone content of the fat suits they wore made the energy signatures of all three *Light Warriors* unrecognizable. As did the fat suits and cherry red lipstick they applied when putting the finishing touches on their makeup. If anything can be said for a news organization that relies primarily on suspension of disbelief for its market share, it's that there is plenty of theatrical makeup to go around.

Waving goodbye to their old friend the security guard, whose mother must have brought him some dry pants on his lunch break, the three sauntered out of the building nonchalantly. To the security guard, it was just another day. One that included three obese people in downtown Manhattan wearing togas and crowns of ivy.

But to the CIA in control of every surveillance camera in Midtown Manhattan, those red flags of Astra's that had begun to collect months earlier started popping up. And not unlike the trail of breadcrumbs left by a graffiti artist, or the *synthetic synchronicity* left by a *Random Warrior*, they led the intelligence conglomerate right to the *Star Seeds* before they got as far as Fifth Avenue.

As is the case with most Americans, Astra's curious lack of curiosity about the CIA had allowed her to underestimate them. Especially when it came to stepping off the Avenue of the Americas dressed as a pig in lipstick. While some may have chosen to discuss the issue at length, debating the many nuances involved, Astra had only one thing to say about the massive power freely given to the sprawling global intelligence conglomerate. Especially as it worked on behalf of the illegal extraterrestrial aliens stealing our jobs and raping our women.

"It is what it is."

As the laser fire began to singe the skirts of their togas, the three found brief cover behind the door of an Uber before its rider climbed in and the driver pulled away from the curb. The three were left taking on heavy fire with no cover. The Uber driver was relieved. The thought of three obese people in his mother's car was deeply unsettling. Laser fire once again cut chunks out of asphalt at their feet as they took on silent, deadly fire. No one in the sea of people passing by seemed to notice.

It did not look good for the team. Astra lost a lock of hair when a shot intersected with her attempt to reach for a chunk of asphalt. She thought perhaps she could channel a Palestinian child and throw it at something. Since like that child she was likely to die, it seemed as good a plan as any. She watched helplessly as laser shots came in rapid-fire and one of them grazed David's bicep.

But randomly, instead of seeing hopelessness, David saw a way out of the situation for all three of them. The glistening drops of deep red blood gave him an idea. Reaching for his red yarmulke, he stood up and began waving it as he slowly spun three hundred and sixty degrees while shouting at the top of his lungs.

"Vagina, vagina, vagina," he repeated randomly, hoping both sound and vision would work their Neuro-linguistic Programming magic in his hands as effectively as it had always done in the hands of the CIA.

Catching on to his intent, Astra and Joey sprang into action. With spray bottle in hand, Joey closed the gap between himself and the wall of the building closest to them. Without benefit of a scaffolding or stencil, Joey Appolonia made graffiti history that day. And saved the lives of all three *Star Seeds* as he began creating the most elaborate graffiti rendition of female genitalia in the history of breadcrumb sharing.

Seeing where her brothers-in-fat-suit-arms were going with the *Vagina Defense*, Astra briefly apologized to the transformational properties of the color violet for her impending transgression. But understandably, the *Warrior Messenger* needed to channel the power of red. Standing brazenly, her pudgy fat suit arms spread eagle, she wound them up three times just as she'd seen in the YouTube video. Envisioning a seamless merging of the Power of Red with the Power of the Vagina, she prepared to blast their opponents with the third wind-up.

Not unlike a major league ball player with a killer two-handed pitch, Astra Talitha thrust outward with both hands after the third wind-up. Her outward-facing palms let loose with a single word repeated three times.

"Transmute. Transmute. Transmute," she commanded.

And with that, Midtown Manhattan experienced an event that day which would be discussed in sex education classes for decades to come. But only in the public education system. In the mostly religious-based, private schools, there is no point in teaching sex education. And the reason for that is simple. Girls don't need to know anything at all about sex, and all boys are born knowing everything there is to know about it. Which is why the CIA and their Draco-Reptilian allies ran away when they realized they were up against the

*Vagina Defense.*

"Like I keep saying," Astra said. "Fear is for pussies."

Before the taxpayer-funded thugs could rethink their strategy and come up with a penile defense that hadn't been used to death since the beginning of time, the three sprinted toward their rendezvous point on Fifth Avenue. Only to find themselves intercepted halfway to their destination by two familiar faces.

El and Samara seemed to appear out of nowhere. It was disorienting to Astra, but not as disorienting as it was to the other pedestrians. It goes without saying a disoriented pig wearing lipstick and a toga can easily bring Manhattan to a halt if not handled delicately.

Thankfully, it wouldn't be that long before the team learned the ins and outs of interdimensional travel and its perks. One of them being the ability to walk through walls. They would even learn how to do it without projectile vomiting. Which in context would be considered a miracle in some galaxies.

"They nabbed your *watcher*," El said. "When he disabled his cloaking device backing into a parking space. They knew exactly where you'd be and when, it was only a matter of waiting for him to locate the only parking lot with available space."

"Where is he now?" Joey asked, his trigger finger getting itchy.

"They've got him on Floor Fifty One of the News Corp. Building."

"That's not possible," David asked. "That building only has forty five floors." If anyone would know how many floors are in that building, it was David Aeschlimann. After all, it hadn't been that long since he was removing a truckload of fat suits from it. But the studio he took them from was on an entirely different floor. And except for a very select group of humans and their extraterrestrial allies, the alien black site had been off the radar since Rupert Murdoch created it as his own personal playground. Never let it be said offering a man unlimited shiny things won't bring the very worst of humanity out in him.

"That's what they want you to think," Samara said grimly. "It's where they've been taking aliens accused of terrorism since nine eleven. In your wildest dreams you cannot imagine the kinds of torture they've come up with for them."

Unlike when Americans torture their human patsies and pretend it's because of Truth, Justice and the American Way™, there's no reason to pretend. They get to do it with impunity. Accountable to no one. For the sheer pleasure of it. When a human knows there's no international law stipulating what he can and cannot do with another sentient being, torture gets ugly fast. And stays that way. It's even worse when he thinks there's no intergalactic law.

Astra's heart sank. And despite both David and Joey being strong swimmers, theirs sank too. They blamed the Illuminati, who should have consulted them before inventing gravity. If it hadn't been for that devious move on the chessboard, they could have levitated to Floor Fifty One.

"You'd all be seen if you did that," El shouted, ducking from flying spew. While facilitating someone's first encounter with interdimensional travel can be an honor, there were certain things that made it less savory. Projectile vomiting was one of them. When they got their bearings, the

*Star Seeds* realized they'd been dragged to safe harbor through the outer wall of the building and ended up in a cabaret strip club. Astra was delighted to see the *Vagina Defense* was still in play.

"The only way to get into Floor Fifty One is the way we got into this club without having to show our identification to the bouncer."

Thus their first lesson in interdimensional travel began. And while it was an abbreviated version of the Interstellar University course, it was just as demanding. And the grade was based on surviving. Live to tell the tale, get an *A*. Fail, well that's what the *F* stands for. And at all times carry a vomit bag.

"Yes, but won't they still be able to see us when we walk through that final wall?" David asked, his pragmatism bolstered by Astra's. She nodded approvingly and made a mental note to kiss him as soon as she had the opportunity. It was clear to El the two worked synergistically, and once again she was reminded of the wisdom of the Council of Five for putting the two together.

"Not if Samara and I can maintain the *Cloaking Technique* long enough," she replied. "Hers isn't quite as strong as mine, since she's a hybrid. But she's had the best training there is. She's got this. I'm sure of it."

David and Samara made eye contact and smiled. For the first time, Astra noticed the energy resonating between them. The vivid image of lying on the kitchen floor in their Beacon Hill apartment flashed before her eyes. And with it, the discovery of an envelope stuck to the bottom of a frozen vegan entrée. Which would have been great to have just them. It had been so long since she'd eaten she was having a hard time remembering just when it was.

"That deed wasn't from a *pointless scam,* was it?" She asked. A school of images swam into view as her vision focused for the first time since her odyssey began. "And the Pinto? Conning it from that valet wasn't a *pointless scam* also?"

"None of my scams are," David replied.

"They're just random," Samara said, finishing his sentence.

"Samara is David's clone, Astra. She was created from his DNA when he was first abducted as a child," El explained. "And then hybridized to enhance certain characteristics."

"For many years he was prevented from recalling his visits," Samara continued. "They would bring him to the nursery ship to play with me. He read me books and sang me songs and taught me how to play air guitar."

Astra thought it sounded far too much like an interstellar Big Brother Program and was about to say so when Samara smiled.

"Yes, that's exactly what it was," she said. "He was my big brother."

Astra wondered if there were little Astra-alien hybridized clones up there waiting for her to come play Legos with them. The thought briefly led her back to that ridge in Virginia. It was the first tangible memory she had of that incident, and would have sucked her into its black hole if El hadn't come to the rescue. Still, her hand reflexively reached for her lower abdomen briefly as she wondered how anyone would know if their eggs had been harvested for cloning.

"All in due time, *Warrior Messenger*," she said. "Rescue *watcher* now. Trip down memory lane later."

And with that, three *Star Seeds*, an extraterrestrial, and one human-alien hybrid focused all their attention on mastering interdimensional travel as a means of passing through solid objects. Unsurprisingly, it was Joey who mastered it first of the three. Largely because he'd held onto the memory through epigenetics. He was also the only one of the three who didn't lose his cookies. Astra and David found the entire thing much more of a challenge. But before rush hour started and the workforce of Manhattan poured out onto the sidewalks to begin their commute home, the three were confident they could make it undetected into the secretive Floor Fifty One.

Except for the projectile vomiting, their plan went flawlessly. They were able to access the CIA black site unseen and begin implementing Phase Two of their plan: trapping the Reptilians guarding the site so they couldn't follow as they escaped. And that is where the plan unraveled. Full-blooded Reptilians are impervious to the *Vagina Defense*. They're not mammalian. The vagina has no power over them. Unlike human males, whose every motivation is the vag, reptiles lay eggs.

As Joey went to work spray painting the labia on walls and floor, the graffiti art inadvertently revealed their presence to the cold-blood emotionally infantile guards in the room. Too late to correct the mission's nose dive, he was about to dive for the next available dimension when the voice of Lurch tickled his auditory cortex.

"They cannot stay where they are not welcome," his voice said, reminding him of what he already knew but had forgotten in the fog of war. It was compounded by the fog of the vag. Even *Graffiti Warriors* are not impervious to its power. And when wars are started over the vag, the fog can be impenetrable.

As the combined cloaking strength of El and Samara wore thin, Joey retraced his steps and covered over the vag graffiti with four simple yet bold words: **NO TRESPASSING, STAY OUT!** The reason for this is simple. No defense has ever been found that surpasses the effectiveness of the *Vagina Defense* using only a single word. But Joey was doing the best he could. Four words would have to do.

As the Reptilian guards began to evacuate the room, the last of the cloaking strength was released by El and Samara while David untied Lurch from the rack. Having never actually seen a rack however, he could only assume that's what his *watcher* was tied to. As their little party of freedom fighters effortlessly passed up through the ceiling onto the roof, Astra tried not to open not-so-old wounds by asking Lurch about his ordeal. She failed miserably.

"Was it bad?" she said.

"Worse than bad," he replied, actually spitting. She was relieved his spit didn't show up in her auditory cortex along with his words. Cleanup could be messy. "They forced me to make human facial expressions. For hours. I honestly thought I was going to die."

"But you're immortal, dude," Joey said.

"Exactly," Lurch replied just before they all transported back to the space dinghy. Using nothing but their intention to get them there. Where there was no room for everyone to sit, even after Astra happily offered up her seat and made herself comfortable in David's lap. While he had always appreciated the merits of a large woman, the fat suit his beloved wore took that appreciation to a whole new level.

"Am I the only one who noticed when we were passing through those walls that the Second Dimension is, like, two-dimensional?" Joey said. Astra and David's eyes met with a look that said, "Why is he pretending he didn't already know that?"

It was followed by a look that said, "And why would he think we hadn't noticed the obvious?"

As red flags go, their failure to connect the obvious to what was yet to come was a sign of two dimensional thinking at best. In her defense, Astra was preoccupied with a question that had been on her mind since they escaped Floor Fifty One with Lurch.

"Which is more two-dimensional, flying through the ceiling, or our failure to discuss the fact that we all just flew through the ceiling? Because if we're going to fly, I want to know where the hell my wings are."

# CHAPTER NINETEEN

"We're not going back to Sedona right now, are we?"

She'd thought of several different ways to ask that question, but all she could hear was the unmistakable sound of dread in her own voice when Astra tried them out in her head. Of all the things a grifter with Astra's level of experience is prepared to tackle in life, addressing the Alliance of the Council of Five and the Galactic Federation was not one of them. Especially not as an essential component of the liaison for the human race.

More than anything, she just wanted to go back to her little storefront with her little *Star Seed* family and an alien-human hybrid or two. Maybe they could microwave some popcorn and wait for their interview with Disinfaux News to come on. And it was largely because she still wasn't entirely sure she and the others were up to the task of representing humanity, considering how blindsided they were by the Angry Women's Disinformation Network.

But their *watcher* didn't need to tell her she was right. Anyone as decisive as Astra is fully capable of figuring out the answer to her own rhetorical questions. Which is why she didn't bother asking their pilot just how he was going to navigate his way out of Earth's orbit without getting hit with shrapnel from the satellite China blasted with a nuke ten years earlier. Or how, for that matter, all the satellites and various space missions that had left the planet since then had managed to avoid getting shredded by shrapnel speeding at 73,000 miles per hour. Except for the one George Clooney and Sandra Bullock was in, of course. Which of course sent her squirrel madly searching for all mention of gravity in the *predictive programming* database.

Out of self-preservation, Astra opted to distract herself – and the squirrel – from thinking about where they were going and what they were doing. And how they would survive getting there in order to do it.

"So tell us how you two happened to be walking through that particular wall at that particular time," she said to El and Samara. The two latecomers to the party had seated themselves on the floor and were doing a form of Interstellar yoga she hadn't seen before. It reminded her of an old Steely Dan song about the logic of pretzels.

"I called out to them," Lurch said, which was a good thing, since El and Samara were deep into their yoga breathing. "Once connected to any star group or organization resonating at a higher frequency, all anyone has to do when they need assistance is ask for it by calling out and clearly stating their need. Samara was meditating on a hillside at her Workshop in Miracles and responded immediately with the classic alien-human bat signal indicating help was on the way."

Astra was curious about how this bat signal worked.

Were the bulbs expensive? Did it have a solar option? A remote? Did it have to be bolted down, or was it portable? What if the signal got crossed with a signal from the Orange Growers Association? Would they use toxic chemical sprays on the bat signal to eradicate any pests it might attract? Were bats included as a protected species in the Migratory Bird Act, even though they're mammals? As is often the case when Astra's attention is hijacked, squirrels got into the picture and began an attention span war with the bats.

"And El?" David asked, interrupting the squirrel versus bat showdown in Astra's attention span before it led to the squirrels nesting in the bat cave and chewing through the wiring.

"El was a little harder to reach," their *watcher* sighed. He was unaccustomed to the security measures used in casinos to prevent electronic interference with the Random, which always seemed to work to the advantage of the house. It was made that much harder by the fact it was at the Luxor.

"Her locating software took her to Las Vegas in search of the Emerald Tablet on a hunch. The cloaking there is the tightest in the galaxy. Hard to penetrate. Somebody knew exactly what they were doing when they built a gambling casino inside a pyramid. Hiding the Tablet there was genius, but not the kind of genius you'd ever want to base a weekly science program on for the kids to watch. Unless you wanted your kids to grow up knowing how to enslave an entire race of people. I had to send Samara there physically to retrieve her. They flagged a Space Uber and got here while you three were taping your interview."

"Locating software?" Astra said. "You mean like she has her own GPS?"

"Something like that," he replied with a nod, hoping she would see a squirrel and change the subject.

"Speaking of that interview," she said, unaware of the subtle effect Lurch's gentle subliminal message had on her. Largely because she thought she saw a squirrel sneak out of the bat cave and eye the dinghy's wiring suspiciously. "I've been wearing this gravy-stained khaki shirt for two days now and it's starting to smell bad. Actually, it's gone far past the point of just *starting* to produce stink. It's pretty much set up its own stinky government and gotten a Wikipedia page at this point. How acute is their sense of smell and/or fashion correctness where we're going?

Or will this be like those movies where before meeting with interstellar dignitaries the woman gets bathed in tears of joy wept by some cosmic Milarepa who just reached Satori in a cave somewhere? Then after being dried off by the flapping of hummingbird wings, she's dressed in a gown made of golden thread from the comments section on the New Message From God website. And then has her hair braided Princess Leia-style by Divine Orphans of the Stone Age, the New Age alternative to Queens of the Stone Age with a wholesome message."

El and Samara just ignored her. Lurch still hurt too much to make a facial expression, so just shook his head and sent a grunt to her auditory cortex. She startled him by grunting back. It was Joey who finally put Astra's mind at ease by explaining that in reality most extraterrestrials don't make it a habit of doing a lot of bathing. Water is too precious to waste on vanity where they come from. Regardless where that is. Unless of course it's the Planet Narcissus, which is entirely covered in water as smooth as glass.

"They also don't make a habit of wearing anything," he continued. "Obsession with clothing is a human invention, created by the petrochemical industry using time travel to go back and make sure body-shaming was included in all the religious texts worldwide."

"Don't you mean the textiles industry?" David said.

"Nope," Joey was confident in his knowledge. And equally confusing.

"How would it benefit the petrochemical industry to implant an obsession with clothing?" David asked, not willing to give up his pursuit of clarity. Which seemed paradoxical, considering his affinity for the random.

"Polyester is a cash cow for the petrochemical industry," Joey said, relieving David of his confusion. "Not to mention all the gas people burn driving to the mall to buy whatever new polyester fashion they've been programmed to buy. And then there's all the fuel used to ship the crude oil to the various countries that process it into polyester and its evil cousin, plastic. Why do you think the Alliance made sure to slip that line in the movie, *The Graduate*? Instead of getting the point, your entire race held a Tupperware party."

"What line?" David said, not sure how the conversation managed to derail.

"Plastics," Joey said, surprised the *Master of Random* hadn't picked up on that one. "You know, the party scene, where that friend of his dad asks him what line of work he wants to go into now that he's graduated from college? Dude, it's only the most famous one-word line in film history!" It would take time for David to fully understand the graffiti artist's affinity with brevity.

"Oh this is great," Astra moaned. "It's bad enough our performance under pressure is going to be put to the test. Like trying to keep the entire human population from being annihilated because of a few bad actors isn't intimidating enough. But now you're saying we have to do it naked. It's going to be just like all those dreams about showing up late for a test only to discover I've come to school naked, isn't it?"

Joey giggled. Divinely. "You said naked. Twice."

"Joey my friend," David grinned. "Don't ever grow up."

"The older I get, the more childish I become, dude."

"I had an uncle like that," David replied. "Had to wear diapers and everything."

Astra shook her head. She was still wearing a filthy khaki shirt and now knew far too much information about David's uncle. And plastic, for some reason.

It was El who finally woke from her blissful journey through the Yoga Star System and relieved Astra's fears. She explained that none of the dignitaries would be able to smell her. It's a little known fact that while aliens are capable of delivering odors directly to the olfactory nerve of any human, they themselves do not have a sense of smell. Which causes much debate on conspiracy theory websites about how extraterrestrials even *know* what smell they're delivering.

"Wait, so whenever someone thinks they're smelling their dead grandma's perfume, it's actually an alien manipulating their olfactory senses?" David asked, suddenly forgetting all about the smell of his uncle's diapers.

"Yes. Although there are occasions where a human

has a brain tumor or other complication with his electrical wiring that can have the same effect. Which leads us right back to discernment. Like how important it is for members of Congress to use discernment by ensuring everyone has decent medical care so they can get an MRI and find out why they're smelling their dead grandmother's perfume."

Lurch interrupted the smelly discussion by asking the *Star Seeds* if they wanted him to dock at the Federation station to disembark, which has a pretty steep parking fee.

"Or would you prefer I park further away in the free space and you transport yourselves?"

"I don't really care," Astra said. "As long as you don't let El and Samara drink all the Horchata while we're gone. The sugar in it is the only thing keeping me going at this point."

Transporting themselves to the visitor's dock of the Federation Station for Intergalactic Diplomacy went much more smoothly than transporting themselves to Fifth Avenue. Largely because there were far fewer people to worry about bumping into or being trampled by. In fact, there were no people. Only androids servicing visiting spacecraft and tending to machinery in need of repair. Astra was so busy steeling herself for the sight of a naked alien it didn't register at first that the androids were wearing denim coveralls. Much like she'd seen mechanics wear at auto shops she occasionally ran *monkey wrench* scams on.

"That's ironic," Joey said, giggling. The androids in coveralls did not giggle back, much to Joey's disappointment.

Astra and David did however, and had almost no time to do so when a naked alien draped in a sheet covering his naughty bits stepped through the wall and invited them to join him. If evangelicals had been there they would have screamed that he was a demon and performed an exorcism. Not because he was an alien, but because he only had a sheet covering his naughty bits. Which most extraterrestrials find amusing.

"Not to be rude, but we're new to this. Interdimensional travel still gives me vertigo. And we're fresh out of vomit bags," Astra said, boldly showing her strengths as a skilled negotiator right up front. "Is there a scenic route we can take to get to where we're going?"

The alien nodded and showed them where the door was. As they walked the labyrinthine corridors of the space station with *Modest Mouse in a toga*, he addressed Astra's confusion over his makeshift garment. And it was as Astra had suspected. They simply did not want to offend human sensibilities. When dealing with a race whose sensibilities have been shaped by an illogical superstitious-based sense of shame over something as ridiculous as nakedness, the polite thing to do is placate them. And then tweet snark about it as soon as the humans leave, to get it out of their system.

The serpentine corridors were lit exactly as the room had been in Astra's dream of the flying Pinto, which somehow delivered her to that meeting with the Council of Five. While there was no source any of the *Star Seeds* could see, no obvious lighting fixtures or panels behind which Cosmic fluorescent bulbs could be hiding, each dark corridor was instantly bathed in a soothing white light the moment their guide's foot crossed into its shadowy darkness. The further they walked into the heart of the station, the more Astra wondered why their hosts hadn't sent a shuttle. She was burning far too many calories for comfort. Would her booty get bumped from its position as *Galactic Booty Queen*?

At last their guide delivered them to a massive set of double doors. They appeared to be made of a finely polished wood none of them recognized. And they were framed in gold. David approved of the randomness. No one had to explain just why the doors swung open ominously as they approached. Opening doors was really no different from stepping through a wall. Only without the need for a vomit bag. Stepping into the massive, cathedral-like chamber, Astra instinctively looked up. Half expecting to see something rendered by a cosmic Michelangelo on the ceiling, she was startled to see there was no ceiling. Only stars. She would have been terrified if she hadn't been so enchanted.

"Welcome, Galactic Liaison for Earth Humans."

Astra was startled to see the Council Speaker was the same woman who did all the speaking in the dream she'd just been thinking about; the one with the Council of Five. It was a few moments before it finally sank in that it hadn't been a dream. Which meant she really was in a flying Pinto. As long as the only evidence of it was a video on the internet, she'd been content to believe it was an invention of digital manipulation. But Astra Talitha was finally coming face-to-face with the reality of her own experience. Her knees began to grow weak as the last of her calories gave out along with the need for the protective mechanism of denial.

When anyone goes as long without eating as she had, the biggest concern is losing stored fat. And in Astra's case, that fat was perfectly happy right where it was. Her luscious booty was not going to give any of it up without a fight.

"It isn't hunger you're feeling," she heard El's voice gently enter her thought-stream. "It's fear. It's lacking. You're afraid you don't have what it takes to do this, don't have the skills or the information you need. But you do. You've always known. You lack nothing. You got this, girl. Now scam the hell out of those bitches." Astra grinned. Turning to David and Joey, she held her hands out and took a hand from each of them in hers.

"We got this," she said, squeezing every ounce of love she had in her directly into them. The infinite loop of love created by that gesture of *Knowledge* elevated the entire room, including the sea of faces sitting in the gallery. The three of them giggled and turned to face the Alliance with confidence.

If anything truly game-changing could be said about that meeting, it was that the three *Star Seeds* discovered the vital importance of embracing the knowledge that they were, and always would be, connected by love. Infinite love.

"We all are," Samara's voice rang in, late to the cosmic conference call. But as usual, her timing was perfect. Her voice walked into the minds of the three as effortlessly as she had walked through that cement wall on Fifth Avenue.

"We understand you have called the missing *Star Seeds* to arms, and will be meeting with many of them this very night," the Council Speaker said. "You are to be congratulated on having achieved what we were unable to. You three have successfully *activated* many who were unreachable, and launched them into their a*wakening*."

Astra had always been told she was like a breath of

fresh air, but this was the first time she was compared to a strong cup of coffee. Allowing her thoughts to wander into the coffee aisle was never a good idea. Astra had been known to get lost for days in the coffee aisle trying to choose between Sumatra and Mexican Mountain Grown.

If anything could get her to retire her commuter coffee cup, it would be a ceramic mug with a squirrel on it. Samara picked up on that thought and passed a mental note to David that a coffee cup with a squirrel on it would make a great random present for Astra, but he should keep it a secret until she locates one. As usual, the message got lost in translation, leaving David to wonder why Samara suspected Astra of being a Secret Squirrel. And since when was it customary to exchange gifts when we celebrate the Random?

"We need you to take a message back to *God's Hidden Angels,* or what you are calling the *Star Seeds* for us: Educate yourselves about your *true* history. Some highly detrimental races, such as the Monarchian, Saudarian, and the Draco-Reptilian, don't align with any one federation. They're interstellar anarchists. Not unlike your Earth captains of industry, they will bend any rule, pay off any authority, take what they want and face no consequence.

The only defense against them is vigilance. And one cannot be vigilant about something one does not know exists. Other races have inhabited your planet for as long as it has existed. Most are so outside your paradigm that you cannot even recognize what you're looking at when you see them. Or hear them or feel them, for that matter. We call it paradigm blindness."

"You mean like the natives who couldn't see the clipper ships on the eastern shore of this continent when they first appeared because they didn't have a frame of reference?" David asked.

"Yes. Exactly like that. It took the village *Wise Man* to see those ships when all the others could only sense there was something there. This is very similar. Only it is imperative you find that *Wise Man* within yourselves. Part of the problem you humans are dealing with is having been led to believe you need a middleman between yourselves and the *Divine*, or what many of you call God, or Yahweh, or Allah. Or as we call it, *Knowledge*. This belief is in error. No one ever needs to reach outside themselves for guidance. We are all created with a perfectly calibrated inner compass that leads us to *Knowledge* organically.

"That sounds a lot like anarchy," David said, wondering what the point was of listening to anyone about anything. "Isn't sharing the same belief system what brings people together and defines a culture?"

The Council Speaker nodded.

"If the goal of your earth's organized religions was actually to bring people together with a common belief system, yes. Or bring them closer to the Divine. But that has not proven to be the case. Largely due to Monarchian influence, humans have been kept from looking inward and finding the common ground that's there to be found. Hence what you have now: the very definition of anarchy. Global spiritual anarchy has spread like a cancer throughout the entire human population. And the more volatile, the happier the colonists are. It lowers the resonant frequency of the entire planet, which attracts negative alien entities that attach to humans and do the work of keeping your race compliant for the colonists."

"But surely religious leaders can see this, right?" David said. "Aren't they teaching love, tolerance and inclusion to followers?" The Council Speaker shook her head.

"Your religious leaders like to call beliefs that could lead a person to *Knowledge* – especially those that differ from what *they* teach – *false religions* rather than risk losing any possible contributions to their collection plates. There are only three things that will sink a soul to the depths of spiritual despair and disconnect it from the Divine, as far as we're concerned: lack of endeavor to obtain *Knowledge*, non-attachment to *Infinite Love*, and attachment to *Corruption*. Yet you would be surprised at how many souls have been driven from *Infinite Love* by those same religious leaders.

Follow the shiny things. If it glitters like gold, it is not aligned with *Knowledge* and can only seduce you away from connecting with it. The same can be said for any man who collects, hoards, and walks the *Path of Shiny Things*. If a man calls himself a minister, preacher, priest, or prophet, yet owns a luxury automobile and his own jet airplane, the only thing he is ministering to is his own greed and ego. If you scratch the surface of his shiny skin, he will most certainly bleed Monarchian. They all do."

What the Council Speaker was saying reminded Astra of trying to find any consistent message about the extraterrestrial presence on Earth by browsing the internet. The result was little more than confusion and the chaos created by each person streaming a podcast, posting a YouTube video, or emailing a newsletter proclaiming that what the other guy was saying was *propaganda* designed to keep *the sheeple* asleep to the *truth.* But which truth?

To make matters worse, there were respected public figures out there claiming truth isn't truth. Astra had to assume the only reason they were respected was because they hadn't shape shifted in front of anyone with a camera. Yet.

"So the way around the problem is to find our own path, but what exactly is it?" Astra had always been confused by the cryptic words used by people trying to sound spiritually enlightened, and the word *path* was one of them.

"The path is the direction you choose for yourself on which you either walk with the Divine toward the *Knowledge of Infinite Love* – what we call *The Light* – or walk with ego, *The Dark.* I don't know how much more simple we can make this for you. It's not rocket surgery."

Joey giggled at the thought of performing surgery on a rocket. The sound filled the chamber with the unmistakable warming blanket of the *Divine Giggle.* Yet oddly, it gave Astra goosebumps.

"Listen to those goosebumps, Miss Astra. They're telling you something. Some call them *Goddybumps.* It's important to tune into the uniquely random way the Divine chooses to reach us with whatever message is tailored just for the individual. There is no one-size-fits-all way to enlightenment. The problem you humans have with that is twofold: Whenever the Divine speaks to us, that message must pass through our own personal filters. Those filters inform how we translate incoming messages. And our filters are formed by our own personal experiences in this life. Which is why there are so many contradictions in your

Bible."

"Yes! That's exactly what I've been saying!" Astra said, interrupting. "David, isn't that exactly what I've always said?" It really only ever takes a split second for Astra's squirrel to wake up and go on a game of keep-away with Astra's attention span. And the Council Speaker had said the one thing sure to make that happen: *personal filters.*

David rolled his eyes and hoped his beloved wouldn't launch into the same sermon she always did whenever they sat down to watch *Lost in Translation*. He also wondered if maybe Samara's mental note had meant to say *don't let Astra chase any squirrels.*

"And the other problem?" he said, not one to leave loose threads where squirrels might run off with them. Largely because he knew the risks.

"The other problem is you're too damned full of yourselves," she said. The distinct sound of exasperation in her voice as it vibrated in the auditory cortex of the collective Liaison made Astra snap back to attention.

"Granted, it's been fostered by those with an agenda you haven't been privileged to, but we've given you so many blatantly obvious clues about it we've lost our patience."

The three looked at each other and then the Alliance members seated silently in the gallery. Not a single thought was transmitted. The silence was deafening. They turned back to the Council Speaker, who continued to stare at them in silence. David wondered if maybe she'd lost her train of thought the way Astra was in the habit of doing. And with that, the silence was broken.

"There!" the Council Speaker shouted without moving her lips, causing the three to jump. "That right there,

Mister Aeschlimann. Your tendency to project. Your race needs to get a handle on the problem you have with your ego and projection. And not just when it comes to anthropomorphizing your deity of choice."

"Wait, we're talking about movies, right?" Astra wasn't trying to be obtuse; she was just easily distracted by anything resembling a squirrel when low on caffeine and calories. "Because they're all digital now, so we don't use projectors any more. Except for bat signals, I guess."

"You're close, *Warrior Messenger*. It is much like projecting a moving picture onto a screen. Rather than viewing and contemplating your own inner dialogue about yourselves, you project it onto other people, in essence objectifying them by turning them into movie screens. Then you tell them what they're thinking or doing or believing, and what they *should* be doing, or thinking, or believing."

Astra had no problem following the Speaker's train of thought, even though it caused her attention span to derail with the squirrel at the controls. She'd waded through Nabokov's dense prose while trying to run a *kegger scam* on Brett Kavanaugh when he was running an *ethics in law* scam at Harvard. While she was disappointed in Kavanaugh's lack of commitment to grifting – no doubt affected by his alcohol problem – she did appreciate Nabokov's attempt to alert the human race to exactly what the Council Speaker was talking about.

The central character was clearly projecting his own desires onto poor Lolita and then acting on it. Unfortunately, Astra learned firsthand that very few people got the point. Not unlike the central character in the novel, most simply projected the meaning that appealed to them onto the book:

All twelve-year-old girls want to be seduced by middle aged men. Especially fatherless twelve-year-old girls and those in the foster care system. Of any age.

As for Kavanaugh, she could only hope he would commit and one day run a truly worthy scam, like the one Clarence Thomas ran on the moral compass of America. There is nothing more worthy of respect for a grifter than seeing not one, but two fellow grifters make it onto the Supreme Court. Especially if those grifters are as accomplished at projecting sexual deviance onto young women as they both were.

"And this projection issue is a problem why?" David asked, not sure why the Council Speaker was making such an issue of a basic human psychological tendency. Astra made a mental note to pick up a copy of Lolita for him when they got back to Sedona.

"It's a problem because of this: Monarchians have used that *basic human psychological tendency* to begin convincing certain humans that they're so important to all of humanity they should be immortal."

"But we are, aren't we?" Astra said, not sure if she'd missed something when she was distracted momentarily by what she thought was a squirrel. "I mean, isn't that the one thing consistent in almost all of the world's religions, that we've got an immortal soul?" The Council Speaker nodded.

"Soul, yes," she replied. "Body, no. The colonists are no different from any corporation. They are always looking for ways to increase profit and reduce overhead. And providing labor for the interstellar trade routes has become too costly due to the physical needs of humans, who don't do well in captivity. So they developed a method of reproduction that cut back on costs and streamlined the care and feeding of humans by keeping them in homeostasis. But it had to be done from scratch. Abducting already grown humans and not returning them more than a few thousand times a year risked drawing too much attention to the extraterrestrial presence. So they started convincing your wealthy elite that they could achieve immortality by cloning themselves for spare parts."

"And people are actually buying into this?" Joey asked.

"They sure are. Never let it be said the wealthy elite are the brightest humanity has to offer. It's all that in-breeding. Why do you think Monarchians like working with them? They'll believe anything. Even that they will actually still have a soul after basically agreeing to provide livestock made from their own DNA. The reduction in resonant frequency basically turns them into fast food for the energy vampires, leaving an empty shell that is permanently inhabited by a Reptilian shape-shifter, who now has unlimited replacement parts." Astra realized her attention had wandered yet again when she found herself raising her hand like a kid in grade school.

"But wouldn't that basically turn the Reptilian into a *drama queen?*" she asked. "And more importantly, have they cloned squirrels yet? Because that would explain a lot." She really didn't think by that point the reason for her second question needed explaining. Even the members of the Alliance sitting in the Gallery were getting distracted by all the squirrels Astra had somehow managed to sneak on board.

Both David and Joey began to wonder if there was a

*Squirrel Defense* that might stand up in court for the criminally distracted. Or at the very least, hold up with the Alliance. Astra, however, had regained her focus. For the first time, she could see the monarchy in the *Monarchian Effect* and knew that it alone was enough reason to help the missing *Star Seeds* with their *awakening*.

By getting the wealthy elite to project onto the rest of the human race that we really want them to be around forever, the colonists had facilitated a way of ensuring the psychopathy gene gets off this rock. And the thought didn't just strike fear in Astra's heart. It struck fear into anyone who was made aware of the plan.

A faint murmur had begun in the gallery as the three were wrapping their heads around Astra's abrupt return from *Adventures in Squirrel Cloning*. It took all three *Star Seeds* to recognize dissent when they saw it. It looked nothing like dissent on their planet. Largely because no one was there to spray tear gas in their faces on the taxpayers' dime. As it turned out, some were growing impatient for the Liaison to state its case for the preservation of humanity on Earth. They thought the Council Speaker was stalling for time.

As well, her little foray off the topic into such things as asking the three to take information back with them to disseminate indicated she had already made up her mind how she would vote when the time came. It had been decided long ago that this meeting would be to present the case against allowing the human race to continue, and before making a decision allow the Liaison to counter with their argument in support of continuing human life on Earth.

And, as is often the case, there was information left

out. The impending Apocalypse, to be specific. Or what evangelicals refer to as *The Rapture,* most likely due to their devotion to the singer, Deborah Harry, and her new wave pop-band, Blondie. Because everyone knows how much evangelicals love new wave. Or is it just huge waves that wipe out civilization?

Hollywood, on the other hand, has always affectionately referred to it as *Armageddon.* Either way, it was already scheduled. No matter what the results of the discussion at this meeting, certain parties controlling the human race fully intended to carry out a plan they had laid the foundation for the moment time travel became accessible to Earth's ruling elite. It was mere child's play at that point to insert that little nugget of *Predictive Programming* into a religious text or two. The three *Star Seeds* didn't so much *hear* the words passing between those in the gallery and the Council Speaker. They *felt* the words cut into them like a kick in the gut with a steel-toed boot.

"*The Rapture?*" the three shouted in unison. Although none of the extraterrestrials had auditory nerves, they all recoiled in pain at the collective strength of the *Star Seeds'* voices. For once Astra was paying attention. She realized there's strength in numbers, and when those numbers come together collectively, anyone can be shouted-down. Even if that *anyone* doesn't have ears.

It took a while for the inaudible murmuring in the gallery to settle down and the Council Speaker to continue. During which time Astra wondered if it would be rude to ask if there would be coffee and cookies after their meeting. Or maybe sandwiches. While most people are made uncomfortable when the word *Armageddon* is thrown around by a bunch of extraterrestrials, it only stimulated Astra's appetite.

"You've reached the tipping point," the Council Speaker said. The three couldn't be sure, but it seemed like she said it with a sigh. "Your race has been both hybridized and spiritually castrated to the point that it's weakened you. Emotionally, spiritually, and genetically. Again, it is interstellar law that when a race has been polluted by *Intervention* to the point yours has, it's for the protection of the interstellar community that it be destroyed. Especially now that clones are being prepared to sell on the open market. We just can't let those genetics get out there."

"But I thought you *liked* us," David whined. Which made Joey giggle. Which in turn, made the entire gallery giggle. Only the Council Speaker remained stone-faced.

"It has nothing to do with Earthling sentimentality," she said sharply. "It has to do with racial purity. It must be maintained until you are enlightened enough to join the Cosmic community."

"Wait," Astra said with her usual clueless confusion. "You mean the white supremacists have been right all along with their *racial purity* fixation?"

"Yes and no," she replied. "Mostly no. Your white supremacists are a perfect example of what happens when a message from the Divine gets lost in translation. When filtered through their ego, it sounded to *them* like the Divine was telling them to maintain the purity of the Aryan race. Unfortunately, they failed to comprehend the message their own messiah gave them: *You are all one race, love one another as you would love me. There is no greater way to show your gratitude to the Father for giving you this life than to love all his children as you would love Him."*

"Whoa, slow your roll there, lady," David said, clearly skeptical of the claim that a messiah not once recognized by his own race as a messiah had brought anything to the human race but confusion about what to bring to his birthday party. "Now you're wandering into religion. Didn't you tell us religion is part of the problem?"

"Various cultural representatives of God have brought essential information to the human race about your Divine origins since the beginning of your time on Earth. There are many. Each and every one of them has been careful to instruct you to *not* make a religion out of them. But the best way to manipulate a race is to manipulate its perception of essential information about its Divine origins.

The *Akashic Records* clearly explain the interstellar concern over the manipulation of your Aryans' belief that wiping out first all the Jews, then all the dark-skinned people, then homosexuals, disabled people, outspoken women, and anyone they just don't like, would somehow return the Earth to some fictitious state of grace in an idyllic utopian garden. Magical thinking beyond the age of six or seven is a clear sign of extraterrestrial mind control."

Astra didn't know where to begin. *Akashik Records?* Was that what was transcribed on the Emerald Tablet? The part about the Aryans being drafted into some sick Cosmic MK-Ultra program was the only thing she had no trouble wrapping her head around. Nobody in their right mind would believe that *only* the whitest of white heterosexual men were the rightful rulers of this planet. And now she knew just *why* white supremacists weren't in their right mind. Extraterrestrial mind control. She also suspected she now knew just where the CIA got the idea.

"So basically, you're saying that anyone who believes one race is superior to another race is actually a *Manchurian Candidate*," she said. "And this Cosmic MK-Ultra program has somehow brought us to some kind of tipping point?"

"Yes," the Council Speaker nodded. "And not just one race or one type of person. No one race, gender, age, or socioeconomic classification of human being is superior or inferior to another. The implanted belief that there is a justification for subjugating another human being has been an illusion we had hoped you would see through and overcome."

David had always thought it ironic that the man who led his people out of Egypt, freeing them from the bondage of slavery was credited with having written an origin story stipulating women were created for the sole purpose of being men's servants. Isn't *servant* just a fancy title for slave with the illusion of benefits? The Speaker nodded her head and continued.

"Now you're catching on, Mister Aeschlimann. Monarchian influence can be seen as far back as your Old Testament. Further, even. And it continues today unabated. The moment you see a police officer plant a toy gun in the hand of an unarmed dark-skinned man he's just shot and killed, you can be certain it was Monarchian thought control pulling the trigger. Or the CIA. Same difference.

When your own legislature voted to make a plant illegal so they could get rich imprisoning people for possessing it, it was Monarchians writing that law. And then buying them a drink of a far more dangerous toxin to celebrate their legislative victory. When it's your own CIA transporting that plant product into your country you can be absolutely certain it's Monarchian paying for Air America's fuel and tree-top flying below the radar.

And when you walk into a Walmart or Victoria's Secret and buy products manufactured by those imprisoned slaves for almost no labor costs, it's Monarchian's handiwork that ensures you won't make the connection that supporting pure evil makes you a part of perpetuating it. Drinking at the well of corruption makes you a vessel of corruption whether you want to see it that way or not.

And it's not just the goods you buy. It's the fictitious narratives you buy into. One of the Monarchian's favorite ways to strip humanity of its empathy is to encourage humans to debase themselves by destroying another human being. Because the Monarchians implanted sexual shaming early on in human history, sexually degrading those who are smaller, weaker, less fortunate, or merely feeling indebted to those at a higher level of the hierarchy is one of their favorite pastimes.

Look at the headlines of any supermarket tabloid or internet news site and you'll see Monarchian handiwork in some salacious story about a Hollywood starlet or handsome young rising star doing shameless things. The only thing shameless about it is the general public idly standing by doing nothing but drool at the unfortunate young men and women taken hostage into the Monarchian system of control of everything – including your entertainment industry. That alone is reason enough for the Alliance to flip the switch and start all over. That kind of cultural control leads to catastrophic programming."

Astra began to suspect the Council Speaker was referring to those conspiracy theories about the Illuminati. After one too many YouTube videos about their alleged *Satanic* rituals, she had started affectionately referring to them as the *Illumigoatee*. And laughing skeptically at their Magic Bohemian Rhapsody Grove picnics in the middle of some acid rain forest in one of those highly secretive Secret Society locations only the billions of people on the internet know about. And anyone with season tickets to Disneyland.

For some reason they can't quite explain rationally, the conspiracy theorists always insist these people drink the blood of baby goats out of those Mason jars that can only be obtained at the Magic Kingdom. They also claim these *Illumigoatee* members acquire self-inflicted 33$^{rd}$ degree ego burns amassing their entire financial portfolio as some kind of bloodless blood sacrifice.

And just like her favorite Musketeer claimed in a scandal a decade earlier, those same conspiracy theorists insist the Mason jars must be free. Astra had long since given up trying to locate free Mason jars. Not even the thrift stores carried them.

She could never be sure if people were supposed to be afraid of the Magic Goat People, or feel sorry for them. They purportedly liked dressing in badly preserved goats' heads and robes bordering on fashion crimes for anyone with the kind of wealth to afford better designers. Which might make some feel sorry for them, but Astra never really cared about fashion, criminal or otherwise.

She did feel a sense of compassion for their lack of imagination, however. But only because they supposedly prance around in those tacky headdresses and robes flashing secret signs and their penises at each other. And anyone they can drug and drag there against their will, apparently. Especially Hollywood celebrities. Or wannabe celebrities. And goats. Astra assumed that was because you can take the farm boy out of the country, but you just can't take his goat away from him.

What seemed more plausible to Astra was that the *Illumigoatee* people were all underpaid Hollywood writers with overactive imaginations and too much time on their hands. Most likely they caught wind of conspiracy theorists' claims and decided to have a little fun with them. They were probably creating even bigger and badder stories to amuse themselves, passing the absurdity back and forth on the internet when some basement dweller with grease stains in his underwear intercepted one and thought it was real.

So to make it patently obvious it was all just tongue-in-cheek, those mischievous writers uploaded photos of roasted baby dolls – which they thought was hilariously funny because nobody in their right mind would actually believe it. Unfortunately, evangelicals on the internet believed every word of it. Hence all the videos on YouTube insisting the *Illumigoatee* forces everyone in the entertainment industry to have a sex change operation and eat babies in their Bohemian Grove Rhapsody blood rituals. Because the only thing that frightens an evangelical more than a transsexual is a transsexual who eats roasted baby dolls for fun. And then tries to use a public restroom.

Besides, Astra knew full well it doesn't take a secret society of goat-lovers to destroy a member of the entertainment industry. Just ask anyone in the pharmaceutical industry. All it takes is a well-paid drug dealer with a medical degree and a prescription pad. Add forty ounces of too much freedom and a Monarchian or two and you've got the perfect soul-shredding recipe. Just ask Amy Winehouse.

Only Joey noticed the Council Speaker look toward the Alliance in the gallery with exasperation as they all seemed to be nodding in agreement about something he knew nothing of. Largely because he had not been privileged to Astra's thoughts.

"One of your poets astutely pointed out that the medium is the message," the speaker said. "One has only to look at the medium channeling the messages being inserted into your popular culture to see the strings being pulled by the colonists. The problem your religious fundamentalists have is turning away from it and creating their own culture, which never solves anything. Especially when their entire belief system has been cut of the same cloth, care of the Monarchians."

Astra knew better than anyone that leaning into a thing was the only way to fully understand its purpose and the agenda behind it. While on the surface the agenda behind popular culture in 21$^{st}$ Century America may *seem* to be about corrupting hearts and minds through salaciousness, sensationalism and blatant polarization, her ambiance gave her the vision to see through the illusion. By first recognizing that it has the potential to do damage, and then leaning in even further, it's possible to actually see the strings of the marionette and trace them to the puppeteer working them. Only when she made a snap judgment about a thing and refused to fully examine it *for herself* did it sneak up later and bite her on her plumply padded posterior.

The key, as she saw it, was to be *in* this world but not *of* it. And to be in it meant being able to get along with others, even those who are of this world. Getting along with others is far easier to do when one is able to demonstrate a working knowledge of their metaphors.

"And that would be the *tipping point* of which you speak." Joey said to the Council Speaker, snapping Astra's attention back down from the tree she'd chased a squirrel into, and then built an entire mythology out of nothing but her imagination and obscure cultural references. "At the point where the general public is being influenced by members of the entertainment industry who are being tortured by the Monarchian agenda as a way of manipulating them. Have I got that right?"

Astra wondered if the women of Disinfaux News could be counted as members of the entertainment industry, but David poked her in the ribs with his elbow, which snapped her attention back to the actual conversation going on, with surprising success.

"Yes. And not just the agenda. At a certain point, your race will become so polluted with the genetics of not just Monarchian, but numerous races walking the *Dark Path,* that the risks of allowing you to continue to exist will far outweigh the benefits."

A debunked myth about a British military strategy referred to as *Prima Nocta* in some movie about William Wallace came to Astra as she flashed back briefly to another forest she'd recently visited. In the movie's fictitious storyline, breeding out the Scots by taking a man's bride before the consummation on their wedding night increased the likelihood any child born from that rape would have diluted Scot blood.

For the first time, Astra found herself wondering if that bit of fiction hadn't been inserted into the film as a heads up to the human race about what was being done to it while they were sitting in the dark eating popcorn and focusing on anything but what was really going on all around them.

"Your race is unique for a number of reasons. Your imagination, for one. Your complex emotional structure mystifies us. And your free will. It's the combination of complex emotions and imagination that allows you to put yourself in another's shoes, see the world from their eyes and create lasting characters in your remarkable fiction. And your free will gives you the determination to stand your ground and defend your right to creative expression. Why do you think the Monarchians have worked so hard to eliminate abstract thinking and the arts from your Common Core State Standards Initiative?

The colonists, like the Monarchian, Saudarian and Draco-Reptilian, seek only to eliminate what makes you divinely human so you'll do their bidding. It's the combination of your free will, imagination and remarkable depth of emotion that motivates you to push forward in the darkness, certain of the light just over the horizon. We have never encountered another race like you anywhere in the Universe. Your art is unlike anything that has ever existed. And it terrifies and enrages both the Monarchians and the Saudarians. The Draco-Reptilians don't really care, which is why they stick to targeting your political leaders. Neither would recognize an imagination if it came up and bit them on the ass.

And it's that depth of emotion that gives you the capacity to love with an intensity we've never seen before. It only takes three or more of you coming together in the name of love to elevate the resonant frequency of an area the size of a football field. Imagine using that field for hundreds – thousands even – to gather in the name of love instead of a contact sport that keeps players and spectators alike inured to the never ending need for violent physical conflict. That need would disappear. An entire state would elevate in resonant frequency beyond anything this planet has ever seen.

The truth is at this point, so much of your human culture has been saturated with the product of the Cosmic MK-Ultra program that all but a select few are helpless to it. There just aren't enough willing to gather with them in the name of *Divine Love* and wake the others from the spell they're under."

"Let me guess," Astra said. "The 144,000?"

"Not even they have been impervious to the programming, as evidenced by the lengths you've had to go to in order to reach those who failed to *activate*. And the reason for this is simple. By creating a world that is perpetually at war over resources and illusions like borders and racial or religious differences, a large portion of your race has been traumatized to the point of being dissociative.

The children of soldiers coming home with traumatic stress disorders can end up as traumatized as their soldier mothers and fathers. Collateral damage that's never addressed by your so-called *mental health* community, so nothing is ever done for them. And it's by design. The more dissociative an individual, the easier it is to program them through standard mind control techniques developed by your planet's intelligence industry – including the CIA – at the behest of the Monarchians. Dissociatives are more susceptible to suspension of disbelief and compartmentalizing.

And your pharmaceuticals make it so much easier for the agents of control. Drugs are essential to the programming necessary for mind control – including the psychotropics. How do you think the Monarchians get their hands on so many young performers to grind through their music and entertainment mill? They all grow up in American households, where parents are programmed to drug themselves with coffee and alcohol while lecturing their children on the evils of doing drugs.

And if those young performers should begin to come to their senses and speak openly about the Monarchian control they're under, there's always electroshock therapy. Those sadists have no problem wiping their minds clean and re-programming them. They may as well be synthetic sex-dolls, the way those poor souls are tormented. If not by the Monarchians, then by the humans programmed to belittle them."

Astra thought again of the YouTubers devoid of empathy, cruelly dismissing the victims of Monarchian programming. For the first time she found herself struggling to forgive them for their programming. Just because they were incapable of forgiving others for their programming didn't mean she had to be an asshole like them.

"No, those of you who are impervious to the programming are simply entrained through eons of lifetimes in various different heavens and hell-holes to be able to see through the bullshit, even if you don't realize that's what you're doing. It's not so much you're protected from it, as it's that your minds have been modified in such a way as to affect you differently."

"Okay, let's cut to the chase then," Joey said, always one to keep things moving forward. "Now that a huge chunk of this race has been hybridized and programmed by colonizing captains of commerce, you need to protect the Cosmic Collective from any of that psychopathy making it off this rock. We, on the other hand, are here to convince you there's an alternative. Have I got that right?" He looked to David on his left and Astra on his right for their nod of agreement.

"Feeling stuck in the middle with us, Joey?" Astra whispered, not sure he'd get the classic pop-culture reference. Until he whispered back that she would always be his joker. The clown to the left of him in a red yarmulke leaned in and scolded both of them with a mock frown.

"Yes, Mister Appolonia," the Council Speaker replied. "If there is anything we have not thought of to prevent your Armageddon, now is the time to enlighten us."

More than anything, Astra wanted a sandwich. A lunch break. A time-out to confer with her fellow liaisons. But here's the thing about three people who are really one unit: The power of their connection to *Knowledge* is magnified by the *Rule of Three*. Insights that occur to any single one of them can easily become insights occurring to all of them. Instantaneously. Which explains why the Liaison let out a giant triplicate gasp of recognition as one perfectly cohesive unit. And then slapped their forehead with the palm of their hand in the universal symbol for *Eureka! I've Got It!*

"Ladies and gentlemen of the jury," Astra said with a hyperbolic bow to first the members of the Alliance in the gallery, and then the Council Speaker. "The solution is simple. If, as you say, the intervention of these cosmic capitalists cannot continue if they are not wanted here, then we need to tell them that."

The startled ripple of murmurs that erupted told Astra this was not something they had thought of. Either that or they were considering pushing the button there and then. Much like all women of mental agility, strength and vision on her planet, Astra persisted.

"I propose we run a *sovereignty scam* on the US Congress, which shouldn't be all that hard considering what tools they are. We con them into passing a bill forbidding undocumented extraterrestrials from engaging in any form of commerce on Earth. The extraterrestrials must not stay where they are not wanted by the majority, right? So even though none of our leaders are willing to actually admit the alien presence is here, asking them to placate the masses by passing a tongue-in-cheek bill is a necessity for the well-being of their cash cow: Southern conservatives.

The Southern Strategy has been the single most effective political strategy in history. Why not use it to the advantage of the American people for once? We'll frame it as something that will help their grandmothers sleep more soundly at night without worrying about whether little green men are going to walk through the wall and see them naked.

And of course we'll lace it with a heavy dose of *What*

*About The Children.* We simply cannot have our children molested by extraterrestrial perverts. While I'm sure there are some perfectly nice aliens coming here, everybody knows most of them are criminals and rapists with a predilection for children. Which overshadows their love of taking naked pictures of Grandma and posting them on Instagram for the seagulls to leer over.

And to make it sound even more legit, we can tell them our man Joey Appolonia here can be our *Cultural Exchange Liaison* to whom all extraterrestrials must come with requests for special consideration, since he's the most familiar with all the races in the Universe."

Before all hell broke loose in the gallery Joey added what turned out to be the icing on the cake.

"Dudes, I can get some of my interdimensional contacts to walk through a few strategically selected bedroom walls and then post naked Grandma pics on Instagram to get the ball rolling. By the time we get to the House of Congress, Disinfaux News will have the public demanding action."

Not one to be left out of the conversation, David added his own contribution:

"The threat of Extraterrestrial Zionists walking through walls and performing unauthorized circumcisions on babies has never been greater, and I know some Rastafarians in Venice Beach who can arrange for some pretty convincing street theater involving badly behaved Jewish Little People that will scare extraterrestrial xenophobia into any doubtful congressman."

"Come to think of it," Astra added, "we shouldn't have any problem getting the white supremacists to protest in front of the House of Congress demanding they do something about racial impurity. And once we get both the House and the Senate to pass a *Declaration of Human Sovereignty*, it's a cake-walk to get it taken before the United Nations."

The gallery erupted into applause as every member jumped to his feet and the telepathic version of shouts of approval rang through the minds of the three *Star Seeds.* The Council Speaker, however, shook her head sternly and banged her gavel on the lectern. Which only the three Liaisons heard because they were the only ones with ears.

"You're forgetting something," she said. "You said it yourself, Astra: *What about the children?* There is still the problem of the genetics that have been infused into your race. Even if the extraterrestrial intervention is eliminated, you still have the spoils of war walking around with all that *Darkness* inside them. They will simply continue to invite more *Darkness* to continue coming here."

"So what's your point?" Astra said a bit too flippantly. "The human race has always done that. The only thing that has ever truly worked to temper the darkness we've always been born with is a whole lot of love, and managing our emotions. Which means increasing our emotional intelligence through instruction. Agents of control have used religion to keep us ignorant emotionally by creating an *All Good* vs *All Bad* polarity for thousands of years. So we replace that by going to the head of the US Department of Education and conning them into adopting emotional intelligence into their beloved Common Core as a curriculum item from kindergarten through high school."

"And exactly how to you propose you do that?" the

Council Speaker said, not bothering to hide her skepticism.

"By making them think that teaching children to manage the entire spectrum of human emotion will make them less likely to choose extremes in life. Like going into liberal arts in college. Or choosing certain sexual identities or gender identifications. Or abortions. Or thinking for themselves. We'll tell them we have it on good authority from the Alliance that the more emotionally balanced a person, the less likely they are to make flagrantly immoral lifestyle choices."

"But that's not necessarily true," the Council Speaker scowled. "I mean, some of it is, but not all of it. You've mixed it all together."

"Exactly. Fact and fiction work as a team, Mother Superior," Astra smiled sweetly. "It's called the *Confusion Technique.* Not only will the current US Secretary of Education love hearing what she wants to in it, the Texas State Board of Education will love printing it in their textbooks. And we all know how many states buy that shit to feed their kids. The goal here is to spread love and establish the teaching of emotional intelligence. Who cares how we do it, right? The authorities we need to convince don't have the vaguest idea what it is anyway."

"She's right," Joey said. "The only thing they've ever been able to wrap their little heads around is the *love-hate polarity*. Or as Astra put it, *Good-Bad.* All that shit in the middle is so complex it confuses them. Which is how Jacob bested that ET back in the day. He stood up to that Dire Wraith armed with a range of emotions the ET was defenseless against because it's only weapon was Hate, and it was calibrated specifically to destroy Love. Anyone who's studied the *Art of War* knows they cannot defend themselves in battle against an opponent they don't fully understand. The more we increase emotional intelligence across the planet, the less they will understand about us."

The Council Speaker smiled and nodded. Astra watched in admiration as the light surrounding her grew in intensity and encompassed the entire room. Without even hearing the words, she knew the Council Speaker was grateful they didn't have to carry out *The Rapture*. Removing only the 144,000 *Star Seeds* before annihilating the human population had weighed heavily on her soul. As consideration of genocide should for any being with a soul.

Astra realized that despite never having truly belonged to any one Earthly family, she'd had one watching out for her all along. And the Council Speaker was the perfect Cosmic Mother to fill the role of matriarch for her. The wise mother nodded in Astra's direction before sending a strongly worded message to her:

"Don't you dare send me a Mother's Day card, Astra Talitha. Why must you always be such a pain in the ass?"

Astra turned to her two companions and said the only thing that truly mattered.

"Group hug, gentlemen. Then sandwiches. There must be sandwiches. And coffee."

As the three-that-are-one turned to leave arm-in-arm, the Council Speaker's voice interrupted their reverie.

"Mister Appolonia, a word please." The three turned back, puzzled. After a moment in which something silent seemed to transpire between the Council Speaker and the *Graffiti Warrior*, he turned back to Astra and David and nodded a wordless, "It's all good," promising to meet back up with them at the dinghy. Once gone, the Council Speaker made it clear that it was up to him to set Astra straight on one important item.

"You know better than anyone how important it is that the three of you are on the same page with respect to just exactly who this deity actually is of which we speak when we mention *the Divine,*" she said, her clear blue eyes piercing him with precision.

"We are concerned she may not actually understand what she *knows,* which is to be expected. Her *activation* and a*wakening* have been abbreviated to just a few short weeks, rather than the standard slow process that takes years for most. Nevertheless, it is vitally important you set her straight. She recently posted a comment on YouTube, apparently in jest. She confronted some poor soul, demanding to know if they had any idea just what deity they were sending their thoughts and prayers to after a recent Monarchian-programmed mass shooting at a school. She said there was only one deity she could think of that required the sacrifice of children."

"How is that a bad thing?" Joey asked, trying hard not to giggle. "Isn't the whole plan to wake people up to the way the entire human race has been deceived?"

"Triggering a cognitive dissonance migraine in some poor soul who's been misled with deception is not going to wake anyone up, Mister Appolonia," she replied. "Bring her up to speed as quickly as you can, and come up with a plan for how you're going to work as a team to spread the message about the ancient deception that's forced the human race to live in the illusion that it's actually evolved beyond the Dark Ages. You and I both know it hasn't. It's still stuck in the same *love-hate* polarity it's been in for thousands of years. Make sure she examines the entire spectrum of the Divine, will you?"

"Yes ma'am," he said. "The Good, the Bad, and the Ugly."

"Glad you haven't forgotten your Sunday School lessons," she smiled.

"Just one question," he puzzled. "Which one of us represents which? I mean, I've known since day one all that *Warrior Messenger, Graffiti Warrior and Random Warrior* shit was only going to get us so far before one of them starts asking questions."

"You know very well you represent one of the two polarities," she replied patiently. "And considering you haven't spent this incarnation swindling people, I'm sure you've figured out which end. Am I right?"

"Yes Ma'am," he replied. "And may I say how much I appreciate the opportunity to represent the Good for a change. Just sayin'."

"Don't mention it. You've earned it. Especially after all you did to help get everyone underground before the Monarchians scorched the surface of Mars."

"Thank you," he blushed. "Means a lot to me, coming from you."

"And I'm sure you've guessed our David represents the other end of the spectrum," she continued. Joey nodded. "Which leaves Miss Talitha, the *Queen of Ambiance*. No one we have ever worked with has had a better grasp of the messy parts of Omniscience. She surfs the spaces in-between the Good and the Bad like she was the master of Mavericks on a stormy day. The messier and uglier the better. Hence her role as liaison representing the Ugly aspects of the Divine. The parts no one wants to look at or even admit exist. Especially your fundamentalists. Those poor tools."

Joey nodded, understanding completely the patience with which fundamentalists both needed and deserved to be handled. "They are indeed God's *special people*," he said.

So special that in all three Abrahamic religions: Islam, Judaism, and Christianity, the fundamentalists – or orthodox – blame females for the lustful thoughts and sexual misconduct of men. Because it's easier to blame the victim than it is to teach the perpetrator to control himself. All the while insisting females are the *weaker sex*. Even though they're considered in all three religions to have the superpower of self-control for both themselves and the entire male population. Hence the requirement that their superhero costumes be extremely modest so men don't lose control when they see them.

"Look at it this way," she said. "Consider the story of Job. You remember that one, don't you, Mister Appolonia?" Joey just nodded, knowing she was going to rehash the same old story again. But he was in for a surprise when she got to the plot twist.

"In the story of Job, God enters into a game of chance with the devil. Sits down and plays a game of Texas Hold 'em with the Morning Star. With nothing of any value to wager with but Job's undying faith in him. Which he gladly throws into the pot and goes all-in. And you want to tell me he's All Good?? On which end of the spectrum would you place him in *that* game of chance?

If the devil is sitting squarely on the Pure Evil end of the Good vs Bad polarity, and God has obviously vacated the Pure Good end, it's got to mean he's doing that ugly dance somewhere in the middle where all the colors mix together to make a mess out of the palette, wouldn't you agree?

That's where Astra comes in. She's spent her life mixing those colors. Spent it drinking at the water fountain of each and every culture this big bad ugly society of yours has to offer. She hasn't gotten stuck in any one genre like so many do. The Christians with their precious Christian rock. The hip-hop artists with their precious anger. The diehard classic rockers with their refusal to let go of the same old precious chords, look at the world around them with sober eyes, and ask themselves just what they've actually *done* with that preciousness over the decades.

Astra's ugliness comes from being able to relate to all of it. It isn't possible to get to the heart of the matter if the person you're doing that with is speaking in a metaphor you know nothing about. You can shout them down with your own metaphor again and again, and it's not going to do any good if you cannot first step into theirs and make it clear you don't just hear where they're coming from, you'll gladly hum the theme song with them as you escort them out of that one and into your own for a nice little tour of something they might appreciate.

Ask most evangelicals about Buddhism and they'll wrinkle their nose and tell you meditation opens the door to the devil. But what they fail to realize is Siddhartha couldn't reach Satori without doing that ugly dance on his way to battle with the devil. It's that Big Bad Ugly in-between the Good and the Bad that prepares us for the ultimate battle.

Am I saying meditation opens the door to the devil?

Hell no. I'm saying avoiding anything that might prepare us for a confrontation with the devil does. And more than anything else, focusing your attention on avoiding the devil altogether is the most effective way in the Universe of sending him an engraved invitation to come on in and feast on your very soul.

Remember the Law of Attraction the fundamentalists insist is nothing but a demonic device of New Age heretics, Joey? There is nothing demonic about the basic principle of the Law of Attraction. Ask any physicist. The more you focus on a thing, the more likely that thing will be attracted to you. So go ahead, focus all of your attention on not looking at the devil. Focus it on not thinking about sex. Or drugs. Or rock & roll.

The more you focus on what you don't want, the more what you don't want will be magnetically drawn to you. And meditation is one of the best ways to get around that little equation, because it will help you sort out all the knots that have been tied in the head and the heart of humanity. Those knots don't belong there. They weren't tied by the hand of God. They were tied by the hand of the interventionists who don't want you figuring any of this shit out. So they got men to stand at pulpits and recite lines they fed directly to their auditory cortex."

"I can just hear Astra now when it all finally sinks in," he grinned. "God isn't a noun. God's a verb, a state of being. Like a spaghetti western. If spaghetti western was a state of being and not itself a noun."

"The same principle goes for the entity Earth humans call Satan, Joey. Never forget that. And cultivating a state of being that makes a force manifest in the physical doesn't make it any less real to those being turned into collateral damage. You must always keep your ambition in check to ensure it doesn't veer into greed. Greed itself is the father of corruption. And corruption is the best way in the Universe to invite the devil to the table. Make no mistake about it; his days of poker playing are long behind him. Having mastered the art of the con, he's only playing with souls now."

Joey nodded thoughtfully and said nothing. Possibly because he couldn't get the theme song to a certain spaghetti western out of his head. Which led him to wonder if squirrels were contagious. But largely because he knew better than anyone the source of greed, and it sure as hell wasn't the devil. Unless the devil was the one who came in and made sure the human race never learned how to manage their desire. Because, as he learned from incarnating into an ancient tribe deep in the Amazon centuries earlier, *desire is the origin of bitterness.*

It's a matter of human existence that we cannot have everything we desire. It just isn't practical. Or as Astra would say, *pragmatic.* As an example, Joey had always looked at the soulless profiteers who own the entire fossil fuel industry. They've always had a burning desire to own the weather, and look how well that's turned out for the planet. Nothing practical about that shit whatsoever.

Joey had always suspected it was the devil that inspired organized religion to step in and tie the management of desire up in religious superstition. The result is the entire human race now being entirely confused about how to manage its own desire. Yet anyone who would point that out and question its effectiveness is automatically called out on YouTube by a fundamentalist and shouted down for not being woke. Again, not a practical approach to fixing the problem.

"You know I can see what you're thinking," the speaker said, breaking his train of thought. "We all can." Joey Appolonia blushed, a thing he rarely did. And it was adorable.

"And it's true. The human race has failed to collectively manage *desire*. Is it that hard to imagine that out of his mismanaged desire to be The Boss Of Everything, the Godlike Head of Humanity, man decided he was better than woman, more godlike and therefore given special powers she was not? Especially if there's a voice with an agenda of its own whispering in his ear, encouraging that lust for power. Where do you think the idea for *Headship* came from?

Once assimilated through cultural tradition, it wouldn't be long before mankind itself was accustomed to thinking of one type of human as being superior to another type. It's a slippery slope from there to slavery. Which is why the colonizers made sure to channel a message to go forth and multiply, so they'd have plenty of slaves to do their bidding."

"Hey, lady," Joey said. "Don't forget, I was there. I watched that shit worm its way into their genesis story and become gospel. I'm also well aware it's why you made sure humanity was given Homer Simpson to illustrate that not *every* man is suited to be the head of anything at all. Not even a family. And I hate to break it to you, but I don't think humanity got the point."

"Yes, I know," she said. "Which is why you and I both know how important it is at this point to step up our game. Humanity needs to understand there is a vast difference between that which is spiritual and that which is religious. The name of the game now, the only way to reverse the curse put on humankind, is through *spiritual growth.*"

"Yes, but to what end?" Joey asked, certain of the answer but still vague on the details.

"To untie those knots binding you collectively and free yourselves from the mistaken belief that existence is about anything *other* than love," she replied in her usual simple complexity. "Because love is all that truly matters. The more love is truly embraced and openly shared, the more it spreads through a community and elevates the collective resonant frequency.

Joey smiled. The Beatles had it right all along. *Love really is all you need.*

"And while it is entirely possible to grow spiritually from within the world view of just about any religion," she continued, "it isn't something that happens nearly enough. Largely because those religious leaders who manage their flocks have nothing to gain from it. They themselves have been infected with the greed virus. Therefore they scorn the idea of *spiritual growth* and portray it to their flock as something pagan, or worse: demonic. And then turn around and tell them God's love is conditional."

"Conditional?" Joey puzzled. "You lost me."

"Ever hear one of those evangelicals quote their beloved Jesus by saying '*Nobody comes to the father but through me?*'" she said. "You can't get more conditional than that. At least not in the way fundamentalists have cherry-picked it by taking it out of context and twisting its actual meaning. I assure you, it does not mean what all those evangelicals on YouTube insist it means. It's about Jesus, the embodiment of love; not the religion that built up around the person he was. No one fully realizes their own relationship with the Divine through any means but love. Unconditional love. But what evangelicals are spreading is what has worked its way into the human race over generations: a belief that even Jesus claimed God's love is conditional and the *ONLY* way to the Kingdom of Heaven is through not just *their* religion, but the fundamentalist version of that religion.

And that spirit-breaking conditional love has been projected onto parents, teachers, lovers, spouses, siblings, neighbors, and most tragic of all: their children. Becoming convinced that we cannot be loved unless we behave in a certain way, provide in a certain way, think in a certain way, or worship in a certain way, is the kind of demonic thinking you're likely to find in the Monarchian playbook. It serves only one purpose: control. In the same way fundamentalism does, I might add."

"Okay, so among the things you want me to keep an eye on with Astra is just how she portrays any given deity she happens to be talking about, and making sure she keeps her eye on the ball with respect to spiritual growth," Joey said, hoping to sum things up and get back to the space dinghy before all the Horchata was gone. "And love. Heavy emphasis on unconditional love."

"Yes," she replied before dismissing Joey and turning to leave. "We'll be listening in with our popcorn at the ready. But don't be surprised if we feel the need to interject a point or two if we think that squirrel you three have tried to keep secret has hijacked the topic and you need a little prompting to get back on track."

Joey chuckled as the speaker turned to leave. He watched her slender form move gracefully toward the doors, and despite himself his eyes drifted to her slim but muscular posterior. He forgot all about the Horchata and for a few brief moments thought only of how fine she looked for her age.

"One other thing, young Appolonia," she said, stopping at the massive doors and swinging that lovely posterior behind her as she turned to face him again. "Please tell her she is welcome to recite her comedy routines on stage in those seedy bars nobody goes to. Even if she's only doing it in her mind. When she speaks to the Alliance, she is to be mindful of her resonant frequencies. She must learn to be careful about not just her words, but her thoughts. There are spies everywhere. And word travels fast. Especially when it comes to the Monarchians and their beta slaves, the Illuminati.

Just because the Monarchians have scapegoated them for what they themselves have been doing to members of Earth's political and entertainment industries, it doesn't mean they aren't themselves a force to contend with. We all know how confused a population can get when one character on the stage is scapegoated by another. It can get so confusing the end result is the entire thing is dismissed as little more than pointless drama. But Astra Talitha has no excuse. She's woke. Make sure she stays that way.

And thank you. That stair master you recommended has done wonders for this ancient posterior. Now go have some Horchata before Astra drinks it all."

# CHAPTER TWENTY

It wasn't until she saw the mile-long string of *Star Seeds* marching their way into Sedona with nothing but starlight to guide them that Astra realized she may have underestimated the power of her *call to arms* earlier. 144,000 people take up more space than she realized at the time. If eighty percent of the original 800,000 *Star Seeds* sent here had not either perished at the hands of Monarchian-fueled greed and human corruption, or simply failed to *activate*, they would have needed a much bigger desert.

As it was, Astra couldn't help but wonder if the desert was too big. Too wide open, on all sides. Hadn't Lurch said they had all been identified by the CIA and watched closely for signs of *activation*? If that was the case, what was she thinking drawing them all out in the open like that? And what about all those the Alliance had identified as *activating* who were not part of the *Awakening*?

"I wonder how many of them were not sent here by

any of the *Star Families*, because identifying the interlopers is going to be a bitch," Joey said, echoing what Astra knew both he and David had been thinking right along with her. Astra wasn't sure, but it seemed to her she was beginning to get used to the *Hive Mind*. But isn't that always the case when human consciousness is going to the next level? It's always the visionaries and the explorers who pave the way for others. Or in this case, the grifters and graffiti artists.

"Especially if the Illumigoatee has been busy cloning them for the Monarchians," Astra said, reminding Joey he still had a job to do for the Council Speaker. "It's bad enough we'll be dealing with moles among our *Star Seed* brothers and sisters. Dealing with cloned *activated* moles is going to really put our skills to the test. Especially if they've got goat DNA."

"Never forget the power of the *Violet Flame* in transmutation," El said. "You've already seen it in action and know how effective it is." Astra considered mentioning that there were other colors equally useful in transmutation, but was pretty sure El already knew.

Lurch had decided to take the scenic route home once they reached Earth's atmosphere. And the crystal clear night couldn't have been more perfect for it. Especially when it came to viewing a brilliant beam of light none of them could see from the ground in Sedona, but was clearly visible from a few thousand feet. Never let it be said a *watcher* doesn't have a trick or two up his sleeve. And considering that beam of light was coming from Las Vegas, one doesn't have to think too hard to guess where he got them.

"What is that light over there?" Amara said. It didn't surprise him that she would be the first to spot it. "Did someone install a homing beacon for ET?"

"Something like that," David said, having already had the tour. "It's a beam of light shot straight into space from the tip of the Luxor."

"What idiot thought that one up?" Astra said, clearly surprised anyone would think it was a good idea to shoot a beam of light into space from the tip of a pyramid.

"Who do you think?" Joey said, joining his two teammates at the window for the view. "The entertainment industry. Metro-Goldwyn-fucking-Mayer, to be precise. Man I would love to get a crack at the mirrors channeling that light with my can of spray paint. Did you know Tupac was gunned down right outside the Luxor almost exactly three years after that light went up?"

Knowing what she did about how easy it is for alien entities to use highly channeled energy as a vehicle for entry into our world, Astra just shook her head. "Considering how much negative energy gambling itself attracts," she said, "isn't giving negative alien entities a homing beacon overkill?"

David just stood there giggling. He was the only one of the three who read Financial Times and knew the price MGM had paid for going into business with the kind of extraterrestrials who considered humans their own personal beasts of burden.

"I'm thinking it wasn't the lighting bills that put MGM in bankruptcy," he said. "Not even Criss Angel could Mindfreak them out of a nosedive like the one they took once they crawled into bed with the Monarchians."

"No wonder things have gotten so much worse on this planet since the nineties," Astra said, still clearly stunned that anyone would deliberately invite negative alien entities to come feast on human energy without getting a consensus of opinion on the idea. Or was that the point?

The space dinghy hovered over the highway snaking into Sedona as it occurred to the three that they may have won the battle, but there was still a raging war to deal with. Such is the world of the *Lightwarrior* in a modern-day spaghetti western.

"That reminds me: Did you bring that list of names you collected from our clients who came to us for negative alien entity removal?" David said. Astra had all but forgotten the list she'd kept for El. Reaching into one of the pockets of her cargo shorts, she pulled it out and handed it to her. El glanced briefly at it and looked up at Astra with fear in her eyes.

"We need to get back to the office right away," she said with an urgency that startled the three *Star Seeds*. "Emo is in grave danger." How the enigmatic extraterrestrial was able to determine that by merely looking at a list of names was one of those things Astra was learning would be revealed eventually. For now, they could only cut their scenic trip short and get back to *Alien Investigations*. And to their surprise, Lurch insisted he come down with them. But not so he could join them at the office.

"I took your advice and swiped right," he said to Astra. She couldn't be positive, but she was pretty sure he winked as he said it.

El suggested for all their safety they take the Cosmic Slip n' Slide down from the space dinghy to the alley behind the office. Astra and David were still having some trouble adjusting to it, but agreed Joey's infectious giggling on the way down helped a lot. The three agreed not to press El for an explanation why they were landing at the end of the alley where only a day ago they'd tried to get an Uber while playing duck and cover from alien laser fire. Instead they focused on her cat-like stealth and heightened awareness of surroundings.

"It's a *Dark Path* energy vampire," she said quietly, staying in the shadows close to the buildings as they worked their way up the alley. "Its spoor was all over that list. Which means it was in the office. And if it was in the office, then it picked up on my spoor. And my darling Emo's. One energy vampire might not be a problem, but the dark ones never travel alone. And that's the problem; they tend to travel in packs."

It was at that point the finely honed instincts of Astra Talitha began to tell her El just may be the Lyran of band camp fame. If by finely honed one means not dead or in a coma. She just wished David and Joey would stop giggling about it. There's nothing funny about being dead or in a coma. Besides, they could give their location away to a possible pack of not-so-bloodthirsty energy vampires.

"I'm not sure I understand just why you and Emo would be targeted by them," she said.

"No race as dedicated to the *Dark Path* as energy vampires is going to let its own kind get away with turning toward the *Light*," she said. "It weakens the overall strength of the collective. And sends the wrong message to others who might want to go there. They've been trying to hunt us down since band camp when they observed our astral stream leave for the heart of the galaxy. It's why I went into hiding. I knew Emo would be safe because they would see it all as my fault."

"Not much different from how Earth humans see women," Astra sighed. "Some things never change no matter what planet you're on."

Joey held out one arm indicating the universal sign for *Stop For Fuck's Sake* while holding his index finger up to his lips in the universal sign for *Shut The Fuck Up*. Flattening themselves against the building, Astra held her breath and listened for the sound of footsteps. Or anything that might indicate the stealthy approach of a pack of voracious energy vampires. She had to admit, they really hadn't thought through their whole *alley* approach. There was nowhere to take cover. The group was defenseless.

Just as that thought landed in her solar plexus and paralyzed her lungs, they heard a sharp crack, followed by another. And another. Again and again, rhythmically. And it was getting closer. Astra couldn't inhale. She couldn't exhale either. Her heart was beating too loudly. Thoughts resembling the way words sound when screamed by a terrified child were scrambling for position in her front temporal lobe. And she wished they weren't. She needed to think. But for the life of her she couldn't think of what she needed to think about.

*CRACK!*
*CRACK!*
*CRACK!*

She thought of the security guard at Disinfaux News and wished it was that easy to pee her pants. It might actually help. Turning to Samara on her right she was about to whisper something like "I want my mommy," when two figures followed the sound of the *CRACK* into a narrow sliver of light in the alley just ten feet from them. It was the dominatrix with her magic leather whip. And D.B. Cooper.

"Glad you could come to the party, pussies," the dom said. "But I'm afraid you're late. You missed all the fun. Bunch of vamps were here looking for you. Danny and I could tell they were up to no good when we saw them messing with this whiny little emo vamp who would not stop talking about band camp. So we showed them who owns this town."

It's a little known fact that energy vampires do not tolerate dominatrix energy. It's not so much an allergy as it is a problem with aggressive feminine energy. Some races just can't deal with it. Like the human race. Astra took a deep breath and thanked her bladder for hanging in there. While the others hung out in the alley decompressing, she made a mad dash for the office restroom, scouting for Emo as she ran up the hallway. She found him slumped against the door to the utility closet, curled in the fetal position. Weeping softly.

"She's out back, Emo!" she called out as she slammed the door and planted her lusciously grateful booty on the porcelain throne. "She's been looking for you."

Anyone who has never heard an emo energy vampire squeal with delight just doesn't know what they're missing. It sounded like a herd of emo vampires with happy feet was running down the hallway and out the back door. And even though she wasn't there to see him run into the arms of his lovely Lyran, she could feel the energy from where she sat. And it felt damn good.

Considering she hadn't been in the office for over a day, Astra thought she'd check her messages and maybe take a peek at the YouTube comments section to see what she'd missed. Never let it be said Astra Talitha was not impervious to a news addiction. Especially news as it's reported in the YouTube comments section. She honestly did not know why more people weren't talking about it. Switching the light on as she stepped into the office, it was impossible not to see the plant stand sitting in the middle of the room.

It was also impossible not to recognize it. It was the one from her dream that El and Samara were wrestling into the corner. She thought the wood looked familiar, but she couldn't place the stone. The closest it came to was green quarry slate. But not as marbled. And as smooth as a mountain lake on a windless day. Perfectly polished. The curious *Star Seed* plopped down on the floor beside it and ran her hand over the glass-like surface. It was warm and vibrated slightly. For some reason, Astra thought the frequency was familiar.

Because it was too heavy to safely lay on its side without risking damage to it or the floor, or both, she lay on her back and looked up at the underside of the stone. Perhaps there would be a manufacturer's label affixed to it or the wood frame. But what she saw was the last thing she expected. Symbols. Some kind of script. Was that Sumerian? Cuneiform? Why did it seem so familiar?

"Oh good, it's arrived," El said as she and Emo walked in. "They said they'd be delivering it sometime this afternoon. I hope you don't mind I told them where we hide the key."

"Hey, you're a redhead," Astra said, feigning surprise. It also didn't surprise her that the enigmatic alien was able to change her appearance with the shake of her head. Or that she'd told her contacts in Las Vegas where to find the key to the front door.

"Who wants to call Jerry and tell him his Emerald Tablet is here?" Astra said, wondering if he'd ever changed out of his bathrobe. "Samara got his contact info, so maybe she should do it."

Looking up at David's face looking down at her, she smiled as Joey joined in.

"Look, guys. More breadcrumbs."

"Ancient breadcrumbs," David said.

"That's how it's done," Joey said. "That's how it's always been done."

Astra was pretty sure Joey was there when it started being done. In fact, she was willing to wager he started it.

Samara brought cold quinoa salad and kombucha over from her shop while they waited for Jerry to arrive. While on the surface it didn't seem as high a priority as meeting up with the 144,000 out in the desert, they all needed to eat something. Waiting for him was no imposition if it meant refueling. And it gave them a chance to discuss the plan for the night ahead. Besides, there was something Astra had been wanting to ask Emo and El.

"You never did tell me what instruments you two played at band camp," she said, reluctantly swallowing *That-Which-She-Was-Learning-To-Swallow-a-Little-Less-Reluctantly.*

"You mean aside from each other?" Emo said, causing everyone in the room to blush except him and El. And Joey, of course. But that goes without saying.

"I played the Theremin. And it should be obvious what El played, considering she's expert at leading people where they need to go."

Considering what evangelicals were saying on YouTube about the mention of a flute player in the lyrics to Stairway to Heaven, Astra wasn't surprised El kept a lid on that little detail. Accusing women of witchcraft was making a comeback now that the White House was full of Monarchian-programmed Dominionists determined to drag the planet back into the Dark Ages it never actually left.

By the time the disheveled stoner had arrived, the division of tasks had been decided. Each would hold a workshop teaching the skill he or she was best at or most familiar with, and those who received the *Knowledge* would, in turn, pass on that *Knowledge* to the group behind them. Like a ripple, the tools of the *Light Warrior* would spread between them in an outward moving wave.

"The ripple of love created by that method could very well overpower any infiltrators in the crowd," El said. "They won't be hard to spot at that point. At which point Samara and I can use the *Violet Flame* to transmute them into *Lightworkers*."

While it was only a theory, the three *Lightwarriors* had every reason to believe it would work. They'd seen the effectiveness of transmutation.

And it came as no surprise to anyone that Jerry was himself a *Star Seed*. Especially when you consider most stoners have a gift for translating that which is so foreign it's alien. Which he was happily hyper-focusing his Sativa and caffeine-fueled attention on as they spoke. What started as whispered acknowledgement, quietly to himself, of one passage or another became a shouted exhortation as he transformed from a befuddled man of the stoner-age to a wizened teacher of *Greater Wisdom* before their eyes.

"Yes! It's all about the Light! Knowing the Light through *Love*. This is so cool. It says love is essential to elevating the collective resonant frequency. And get this: It connects ancient Greek mythology about Adonis to the Egyptian stele of Ba'al, and from there to more than one of the ancient Semitic religions. Specifically the Northwest Semitic language, where Ba'al was known as *lord*. Raise your hand if you learned any of this in school, kids. Did any of you know Adonis became known by that name, or that by the name Ba'al he was considered *King of the Gods?*"

Jerry the *Star Seed* had transformed before their eyes from a disheveled stoner to an erudite scholar of ancient mythology and religious history the world had been prevented from learning about, and Astra had a hunch he would be instrumental in changing that. She was about to say just that, when he gleefully continued. She saw no reason to stop him.

"Oh wow, it even explains the origin of the Fez! Did you know the early models were lined with a fine copper mesh and served as a Faraday screen to protect people from Annunaki thought control? And get this: it explains all those dreams I've been having about the Leviathan! Did you know the Canaanites and Phoenicians regarded him as the patron of sailors and sea merchants? It all goes back to ancient Egypt and leads to the Levant. Children, who can tell me where *democracy* is being spread and *defended* at this very moment?"

"Well that would certainly explain why we're seeing so many movie versions of comic book characters based on ancient mythology," Samara said. "It's the only way anyone is going to know what any of this is about! It would also explain the cartoon character, *Secret Squirrel*. Didn't his sidekick wear a Fez?"

"Is that why I've been thinking about Secret Squirrel so much lately?" David asked. Samara shot him a look while pressing her index finger to her lips that seemed to emphasize the *Secret* part of *Secret Squirrel*.

Luckily, Astra didn't notice the exchange. She had been reminded – once again – of the *Confusion Technique* and how effective it is in getting the masses to stop resisting the hypnotic trance it had been collectively subjected to. Yet despite seeing the warm golden glow coming from Jerry's entire being, she felt an uneasiness well up inside her, which Joey Appolonia was the first to spot.

"What is it, Goddess of Grifting?"

"Am I the only one who's worried that when word of all this gets out it's going to start a war between the New Agers, the Evangelicals, the Alchemists, the Jewish Mystics, the Atheists, and the Cosmologists?"

"Hey, if there's anything I've learned from covering signposts with breadcrumbs through several millennia of graffiti art, it's that all roads lead to Rome."

"Unless, of course, it is not Rome but some other city the traveler wishes to reach," David added, proving once and for all he actually learned something useful at the *Pointless Scammer Academy*.

"Exactly what the Tablet says!" Jerry said. "As long as your heart remains purified by *Love* as you're seeking the Light, it will reach out to you with directions when you need it. You just have to watch out for synthetic snakes, apparently. The Tablet distinctly warns against permitting anyone to engage in the manufacturing of demons. The universe has far too many demons already."

Astra wondered if that was a reference to the invention of the snake inserted into the Garden of Eden story. She also had the distinct feeling the issue of her ambiance being her own undoing was finally settled. Her lifelong habit of taking it all into consideration, including the squirrel randomly snatching her attention and dragging it to the top of the nearest tree, actually gave her a broader perspective on *seeking the Light*.

"Speaking of the *Light*, how is it you are able to find your way out there in the desert with such ease?" Astra said to El and Samara, who were organizing the planned activities with a confidence that mystified her.

"Don't ask me," Samara shrugged. "I just follow El's lead."

All eyes turned to El, who smiled enigmatically and explained.

"All this talk of hybrids, yet none of you picked up on the fact that I myself am one," she said. "Only not a hybrid of two or more different species. A hybrid of biological and synthetic. Basically, I'm an intergalactic version of your Earth GPS system. Too many Lyrans were being stoned to death, or taken into sexual slavery by Monarchian-inspired religious leaders when we came here to help members of *Star Families* with their *activation*. Out of an abundance of caution, the Alliance decided to create hybrids like me who would endure the abuses humans put each other through in all matters pertaining to sexual conduct. Especially the sexual conduct of your females.

"So you're programmed to know where your

assigned target's data is stored?" David asked, really not clear on why, if it was already known the past life information was stored in the heart of the galaxy, anyone would need GPS to find it.

"Yes. The heart of the galaxy is massive. A person could spend a lifetime wandering from one end to the other and still not find it. My programming has the exact location of every soul's data, and not just in this galaxy. In every galaxy in the universe. I may not be able to tell you much of anything about your past life, but I can pinpoint the location of your data for you. And it's come in handy on more than one occasion."

"How so?" Emo asked, leaning in for another whiff of his lover's spoor.

"You'd be surprised how many people get there and lose their way back."

Astra wasn't entirely sure just why El though it important to disclose that piece of information about herself, but she had a hunch it would come in handy at some point down the road. And she had no doubt it would be useful that very night finding a David Bowie concert in the desert. Locating someone who had already retrieved all their data and returned to share their wisdom had to be a piece of cake for her.

But for the Intergalactic Liaison, the concert and meet & greet was a thing they would have to miss. They had a job to do. And it involved getting to Capitol Hill. Somewhere in the back of her mind, what seemed to be a memory of long ago came to her of the three of them making the steep climb to a Shining City on a Hill and unfurling a flag while a single bell rang and a lone piper blew the notes to a song about

349

revolution written by a man named Johnny. Only this flag definitely wouldn't be a red flag. This time it would be the first flag of human sovereignty. On this planet, anyway.

And for the first time it truly sank in that Astra, David and Joey had done this all before. She glanced at the clock and was surprised to see it was past eleven. It seemed to her the group was stalling about getting out the door. She was about to say something when Joey pointed to the clock and grinned.

"Look, it's eleven eleven," he said. "God is telling us it's time to go."

"Hey, I still need to pay you what I promised," Emo said. Astra had completely forgotten about what *Alien Investigation's* first client had promised to deliver as payment for finding the lost love of his life. She was about to tell him he could pay her by holding down the fort while the three of them were gone. But he held up a leather sack resembling something from the gold rush days. Or a spaghetti western. As he bounced it up and down it made a melodic, metallic sound. Joey giggled.

"That could come in handy where we're headed," David said. "Considering how fond politicians are of bribery. Not to mention, their handlers. Especially when it involves rare Earth metals."

Astra graciously accepted the payment. But not before asking him for a favor. Emo would be keeping an eye out for Dark Path Energy Vampires when the gang was all out in the desert.

"You're all going to need to be on the lookout for negative entities of all kinds, both human an extraterrestrial," she said sternly. "Especially with the

144,000 at stake."

Which was why they would be starting that night's lessons with teaching them how to keep their own resonant frequencies elevated as a defense against the Dark Ones.

# CHAPTER TWENTY ONE

As the three walked down the steps of *Alien Investigations,*
they talked in that quiet, playfully familiar way *Star Seeds*
often do when they've been working together for more
lifetimes than any of them can remember. There were so
many things they needed to discuss on their way to the
nation's capital. None the least of which was just how they
would get there. The thought of driving to DC from Sedona
with the three of them crammed into a beat up old Pinto did
not exactly inspire any of them. Even if it had already
proven itself to be safer than any Pinto in the history of
disastrous automobile designs.

"At least the front passenger seat has plenty of
legroom," Astra pointed out, when Joey started making
noises that sounded like a whining graffiti artist. She was
just about to suggest they do Roshambo to see who got to
ride shotgun, when they noticed David was jingling a set of
keys in his hand. And the *cat-that-ate-the-canary grin* on his
face suggested he was up to something less than pointless.

"Let's forget the Pinto for now," he said. "I scored the

keys to the space dinghy when Lurch was distracted by a text message while he was on the Slip n' Slide."

"This. This is why I love you, David."

That first kiss was long overdue, but it was agreed upon by *watchers* in three star systems who made popcorn and tuned in, it was well worth the wait.

"Dude, this will give us plenty of time to figure out what we're going to do now that the apocalypse has been canceled," Joey said.

It was before realizing they weren't listening. And he would be entertaining himself for a good chunk of the trip. Which suited him just fine. He'd been giving it a lot of thought, and it seemed to him the business Astra had started was the perfect cover for the three of them to use while doing the work of helping humanity recover from the disastrous intervention by agents of control whose agenda nobody knew anything about but the entire human race had suffered from immeasurably.

The way Joey Appolonia saw it, there was more work to do than just running a scam on Congress. Sure, school kids were going to end up getting much-needed instruction on emotional intelligence. But what about the majority of the population that isn't school age? How were they going to be exposed to the concepts that would help the human race grow beyond the need to flip the switch and start all over?

Besides, most of them were walking around completely unaware of the extraterrestrial presence. And without knowing it, many of those people were actually helping advance the extraterrestrial agenda. How emotionally intelligent is *that*?

"There is one thing I've been wondering about our

current plan," he said, interrupting the longest kiss in the history of intergalactic broadcasting. "Have we got a backup plan in case the scam we presented to the Alliance doesn't work?"

"I actually came with one," David replied, pulling a thickly stuffed envelope out of his inside jacket pocket. "A little gift from our Las Vegas connections. Because all politicians are gamblers who like to think their luck is going to hold out, and because out-maneuvering them is often easier than scamming them."

"There's a difference?" Astra said, reaching for the envelope. "Still holding out on your partner, I see. Let's not make it a habit, okay David?"

Opening the envelope, she puzzled over what looked like a large number of deeds to an assortment of luxury estates in cities she'd never heard of. Shrugging her shoulders, she handed them to Joey, hoping he could make sense of them.

"Wait. I've heard of some of these cities," he said as he thumbed through them, just as puzzled. "But they're all just theoretical utopian dreams presented at Ted Talks. None of them have actually been built."

"None of them have been built *above* ground," David said with a grin. "To get to these cities, you have to go deep."

"Deep?" Astra said, still puzzled. "Please tell me we're not going to discuss the *Deep State* again. That shit gets old."

"Well, I guess you could call it a state," he said. "Deep underground. Where they plan to sit out the apocalypse in style, using those they bring with them for slave labor. And food."

"You mean agriculture, right?" she asked, assuming he meant slaves would be used as beasts of burden to tend the crops the elite would be consuming.

"No. I mean the meat the Monarchians have a taste for. They're especially fond of young meat. I guess it tastes just like pork. Why do you think they instigated the anti-vaccination movement? Vaccines spoil the taste of the meat. And that whole debacle with ICE ripping babies from their mothers' arms at the US border? Why do you think they did such a lousy job of putting any kind of tracking measures into place for those kids? Everyone knows they don't have a vaccination program in the villages those families escaped from. The Monarchians made sure of it."

Joey and Astra shuddered simultaneously as she vowed to never again touch a pork-filled sticky bun. As their understanding of just what David's backup plan consisted of sank in, those shudders were replaced with two divine grins of recognition.

"We're going to scam the hell out of those bitches, aren't we?" Joey grinned. And that grin lasted long enough for all three of them to ride the *Slip 'N Slide* up to the space dinghy. As is often the case, thinking through their plan produced an afterthought. Not unlike an aftertaste, only more bitter.

"We'll still be using the fear end of the polarity to motivate them, won't we?"

The three sat in silence. Each looked at the other as it engulfed them. Silence became a buffet in which versions of itself was the only thing there to select from. In an effort to escape the monotony of too much repetition-of-theme at the buffet, David glanced around the cabin of the dinghy, his eyes falling upon the three fat suits piled on and around Lurch's seat at his station. Wherein he let loose a giggle. But not just any giggle. A Divine Giggle.

"So we move to the other end of the spectrum and do it with *Love*," he said.

"Are you suggesting we go to Congress for a love fest?" Astra said. But Joey's eyes had followed David's to the pile of unoccupied fat suits, and deep into the heart of the Divine Giggle.

"No, my sister from some other mothers," he giggled. "He's saying we invite the negative entities that have occupied Congress to a love fest." David nodded his head in sync with the rhythm of the giggle, and Joey joined in. Astra glanced at the fat suits. Not unlike an incandescent bulb, her light of comprehension switched on in a eureka moment.

"We're going to lure those little demonic fear mongers out of their human hosts in Congress, aren't we?" she said. "Because the only thing they love more than a warm human body is a fat suit made of silicone!"

"And transmute them the way Samara showed us," David said, nodding enthusiastically. "Those who stubbornly refuse to change their fear-based ways of propagating hate can just self-deport."

The three of them sat nodding and grinning. Not unlike a *Slip 'N Slide*, the *love-hate* polarity was showing them that as usual, the only way out was to go through it, absorbing the energy of everything in-between the two. The thing about that is, once you've done the *Slip 'N Slide*, it's pretty hard to land back on the fear/hate end of the pole and want to stay there. Joey just kept grinning as Astra and

David once again landed on the love end and made no attempt to hide it. Love is, after all, the most pragmatic way to ride out this whole business of existence.

And that grin would have stayed right where it was all the way to DC, but Joey Appolonia still had a difficult task. It's not easy informing a person that they need to be more careful with what they say to others about their deity of choice, especially when it comes to questioning their assumptions about that deity's true identity and place of origin.

What Joey Appolonia didn't fully realize was Astra Talitha had always suspected there was something off about the deity she grew up learning about at the bosom of evangelical America. And except for the occasional lapse of judgment in the YouTube comments section, she tried to make it a practice to keep those suspicions to herself. After all, what was the use of starting a religious war? That kind of thing belonged in the hands of the professionals. They did such a masterful job with the Inquisition. And the Crusades.

Taking that sort of thing on by herself made no sense. It just wasn't pragmatic.

Even so, she had decided it couldn't hurt to occasionally revisit a thought she'd found herself wondering from time to time since she was a little girl. Just as long as she kept it to herself: Was it possible the Devil's greatest trick was not convincing the world he didn't exist, but convincing evangelicals – especially Dominionists – he was God?

The thought had always brought her to the love-hate polarity and the work done by agents of control to make sure it was fostered in the human race. Which of course would lead her to imagine a world without thought control.

A world where no one was told they belonged on one end of the spectrum or the other, but instead were free to learn and grow through what each one of us experiences of all of it – the good, the bad, and all that ugly messy stuff in-between.

For Astra, any other way than that to manage this existence did not seem to have turned out to be at all pragmatic. It was clear to her it's resulted in little more than moving the world away from love. And the further we get from love, the less connected we are to each other and the ultimate source of that love.

Of course, it wasn't much of a leap for both Astra and her squirrel to go from there to the issue of discerning which entity is whispering in one's ear at any given time: the one on the side of love, or the one on the side of hate? It was the pragmatist in her who seemed to be winning, as usual. As she embraced her *activation* more and more it occurred to her the best course of action might be to transcend the polarity altogether. Why not do everything in one's power to attract love, thus avoiding the issue of discernment altogether? Besides, who hasn't grown sick and tired of the discernment versus judgment polarity?

By elevating the frequency of one's electromagnetic field with love, Astra Talitha suspected it would make any person unappetizing to a hungry negative entity looking to feast on their soul. It only made sense, after all. Love itself is a power that transcends all limitations, therefore is infinite. Hate on the other hand is a force that must constantly be fed or it drops dead in its tracks. To be precise, it goes dormant and plays dead until someone comes along and feeds it. Which pretty much explains the difference between power and force.

Astra had spent a lifetime grappling with one force or another, and it never went well. It was time to embrace true power; one that was infinite and enduring. And it only made sense to her the best place to start was with the *Power of Love*.

She considered that the same entity which most likely had a hand in creating the human race was just as likely to have created the natural world as well. Including the fox and the forest from which it came. And the grasses that became the field of wheat through which that fox runs and digs a burrow for his family, connecting us all to that hand and its *Infinite Love* through the natural world.

Joey gazed happily at Astra cradled in David's arms. Having picked up on much of what she was thinking, he knew the Council of Five would be pleased. He watched her look at David and smile. And he giggled when, in just one of many eureka moments to come, she slapped her forehead with the palm of her hand.

"So *that's* the point of love."

For once, the squirrel wasn't the only one who knew what she was talking about.

# CHAPTER TWENTY TWO

The Tall Man leaned against the street lamp watching the three take the *Slip n' Slide* up to his space dinghy, and smiled with his eyes. It was going exactly as planned. It always was. He tipped his fedora in the general direction of his crew, then turned and headed toward the desert for a David Bowie concert, where a *watcher* he'd been chatting with online promised him a night to remember.

Once again, the people of Earth would sleep safe in the assumption there was someone watching out for them and there would be a tomorrow. With no knowledge that the three members of their Galactic Liaison were themselves under the watchful eye of an ancient alien whose sole job throughout eternity was to busy himself watching them. Because more than anyone in the history of the universe, they were the best equipped to deal with the things when shit gets real. And shit always gets real.

Even if they did cost him a fortune in Horchata.


The end.

"Nothing is more wonderful than the art of being free, but nothing is harder to learn how to use than freedom."

– Alexis de Tocqueville

# ABOUT THE AUTHOR

Adrienne Veronese grew up in the Pacific Northwest and attended the University of Oregon and Antioch University West in Seattle. She is the author of the Birch Bark Poems, the manuscript of poetry that was stolen by a Seattle-area con artist, thus beginning her decades-long fascination with con artists and the seemingly pointless things they sometimes do for no apparent reason that anyone with a conscience and sense of logic can quite understand. In an eerie coincidence, beat poet Gregory Corso also once had a manuscript of poetry stolen by a con artist. As chance would have it, Adrienne once threw a glass of beer in Gregory Corso's face for interrupting her during a poetry reading in Boston so he could announce to her audience that her poetry may suck, but from his point of view she's got a nice ass. Thus Corso's poetry being a footnote in some con artist's history, but Astra Talitha's ass living on forever.

www.ingramcontent.com/pod-product-compliance
Lightning Source LLC
Chambersburg PA
CBHW051943240626
47153CB00005B/1606